The Seducer

Laurie Palmer

PublishAmerica
Baltimore

First printing

All characters in this book are fictitious, and any resemblance to real persons,
living or dead, is coincidental.

At the specific preference of the author, PublishAmerica allowed this work
to remain exactly as the author intended, verbatim, without editorial input.

ISBN: 1-4241-8663-3
PUBLISHED BY PUBLISHAMERICA, LLLP
www.publishamerica.com
Baltimore

Printed in the United States of America

I dedicate this book to Willa DuBost, who spent countless hours editing this manuscript and encouraging me to keep going. Her love for writing inspired me to write *The Seducer*. I also want to thank my mother, Geraldine Johnson, who taught me how to persevere, my husband, Jim, who never gave up on me, and for my daughter, Elizabeth, who helped with the art work. Most of all, I thank my Lord and Savior, Jesus Christ, who gave me the ability and courage to write.

Part One

The Seduction

A Small Town in Vermont, Spring 1975

"Honor your father and your mother, so that you may live long in the land the LORD your God is giving you. (Exodus 20:12)

Chapter One

She ran into strange yet familiar woods. Darkness swallowed her. Sticks crunched, branches scratched, chilled air sucked in, blew out, pounded in her ears. She had to move faster; the thump, thump of footsteps grew louder. Laughter echoed through faint shadows. Massive trucks, stacked like a maze of dominoes, forced her to weave in and out, driving her deeper into blackness. The taunting cackle came closer. Was that his breath on her neck? Frigid fingers dug into her shoulder, terror crushed, pushed her down, down. The laughter screeched higher and higher, then drifted away to a steady buzz. She forced her heavy limbs to move and pressed the button on the alarm clock.

It took Carol a few moments to shake off the dream, the same one as last week and the week before. The nightmare lingered like an old wound. She always woke up afraid, but the fear had become less severe, like a pain you've had for a long time still hurts but you get used to it.

She would stay home from school, just say, "Mom I'm sick," and go back to sleep. School was no longer a safe place after what Josh did yesterday. He had pointed at her and laughed. She had been sitting alone in her usual corner of the cafeteria, gulping down a free hot lunch, when he yelled out her name. "Carol Wiederman, a weeeeirdman if you ever saw one!" Being made fun of was nothing new, but not by *Josh*. The last time they had played hide and seek, he had singled her out and acted like a boyfriend. They held hands, shared secrets, promised to meet again. Why had he kissed her? Was it all a big joke?

Her sister stumbled out of the upper bunk and pulled open drawers. "Jess, tell Mom I feel sick to my stomach. I'm not going to school today."

"Okay, whatever." Jess left the room, and Carol lay back in her bed. She closed her eyes and willed the nightmare away with pleasant images: waves crashing on the rocks, seashells embedded in wet sand, cool water circling her toes. The room faded away, her body floated into a place with no restraints, warm, peaceful, all hers. Boom! A voice of authority invaded her sanctuary, shattered her adventure.

"Carol, your sister said you're sick. You seemed fine last night. What's the matter?" Her mother sat on her bed and felt her forehead.

"My stomach hurts."

"Your head feels fine. This is the fifth time you've been sick this month. The doctor said there's nothing wrong with you. You'd better not be playing games with me." Her mom gave her the "I'm your mother" look.

"Good grief, Mom, can't you just believe me?" Carol slumped deeper into her bed and held her stomach. "You must really hate me if you think I'm lying to you."

"It's hard to believe you when you've done this so much."

Carol couldn't stand to have her mother look at her that way. She turned toward the wall and clenched her fists under the covers. "I don't care what you think. My stomach hurts, and I'm not going to school!"

"Wait a minute young lady. Your last report card was terrible. Your teachers are all saying you're not paying attention in class. You're a smart girl, Carol. Don't you care about your future?"

"What do you care about me anyway?" Carol sat up in her bed and glared at her Mom. "All you care about are your stupid boyfriends and getting it on with them! You don't care about me, so it doesn't matter what you say. I'm staying home. You can't make me go."

"How dare you speak to me that way? I'm your mother!" Her mother paced back and forth.

"I've taken care of you your entire life, fed you, clothed you, stayed up all night when you were sick. I never left you like your father did. Don't I have the right to find a man, to have some pleasure in my life? How dare you use that to get out of going to school. You'd better listen and listen good, young lady. This is my house, and you will do what I say! Now get yourself out of that bed and go to school right now!"

Her mother locked eyes with her, but Carol did not turn away. She held her focus, defiant and determined to not back down. Her mother turned away first, leaned against the wall, arms folded, gripping herself.

Carol waited a few minutes in the tense silence and then inched out of bed, making slow, light steps until reaching the doorway, her back to her mother. In a sudden, jerky motion, she turned on her heels and twisted her face into an expression of disgust and contempt. Half way down the hall, she shouted.

"I hate you! You're a slut. You don't care a bit about me! I'm going to do what I want and just see if you can stop me!" She ran into the bathroom, slammed the door, and locked it.

She sat on the burgundy toilet cover and held her breath. Footsteps tapped right outside the door. Would her mother blast through the barrier with her forceful voice and mighty arms? Would the old hair brush smack her behind? But nothing happened, the handle didn't move, no shouts exploded, no angry hands came to pull her out. She swallowed hard, gripped the sides of the toilet, and listened. Her heart thumped faster and louder than normal, but that was the only sound. What was her mom doing out there? Was she waiting for Carol to come out? Maybe she left to get a key to open the door. The minutes passed like hours. Finally, a bang on the door propelled her off the toilet seat.

"Carol, I'm going to be late for school. Get out of there!" It was just her sister.

"Just hold your horses. I'll be out in a minute."

The engine of their old station wagon came to life outside and tires snap, crackled and popped on the gravel driveway. Her mother was leaving. Soon, the engine revved into second and third gear, as the car sped down the road. She opened the door in relief, shaky but giddy at the huge victory. For the first time in Carol's life, her mother had backed down. She slid past her irritated sister, crawled back into bed and covered herself snuggly. *I'm going back to sleep. The house will be all mine today.*

The next time she awoke, warm sun drew lines across her blankets. She stretched, yawned, kicked of the suffocating covers, and made her way into the kitchen. The refrigerator hummed in the silent house. A perfect spring day framed the dining room window. Bees were busy attacking a lilac bush right outside, which also meant it would be a warm day. Her mom was at work, her sisters all in school, and she could do whatever she wanted.

The joy flittered away as she went into the bathroom and noticed her reflection in the mirror. A new splotch had erupted, added to the countless blemishes that covered her face. She pinched and squeezed at the intruder, but it wasn't ready to pop. Whenever anyone looked at her, they saw them. At school or in town, it did not matter. Nothing could hide them: not make-up, not band-aids, not even her hair. She might be pretty if it weren't for her pimples. No boy would ever like her when the red spots overpowered the blush-ivory tone of her skin. That's probably what Josh was laughing at. *Ugly, ugly, ugly!*

I hate you! I wish I could just rip you nasty bumps right off my face! She squeezed the new intruder again as hard as she could. All it did was get bigger and redder.

After eating a huge bowl of cereal, taking a long shower, and watching soap operas on TV, Carol changed into her bathing suit and sunbathed on the bright, green lawn. She rubbed baby oil on herself with the hope that it would make her sunburned. Maybe her red pimples would show up less on a red face. The warms rays relaxed and soothed like a sleeping potion, lulling her to sleep. Before long, the sunlight that started as comfort became a sizzling, baking, scorching oven. She rolled her sticky body off the lawn chair into the soft grass and escaped to the dark house. A glass of cold spring water brought relief from the tricky sun and a spell of dizziness. Carol pressed the glass against her forehead, sat down in the living room, and stared into the back yard. A breeze blew through an open window, and the smell of fresh cut grass mingled with the baby oil baked onto her skin. When summer vacation started, every day would be this lazy and easy-going.

Her drink almost fell from her hands as a loud knock pierced the silence. Who would visit at this time of the day, when no one was at home? Should she ignore it or find some clothes and answer the door? Crouching low to the floor, she made her way to the dining room and peeked out the side window. The most gorgeous guy she had ever seen stood outside looking at the screen door with confidence and smiling, as if he already knew she would soon let him in.

"Wow." Her heart thumped, the dizziness returned. Another sharp rap came from the door. What should she do? She was scared yet at the same time drawn to this handsome youth separated by just six inches of wood.

"Carol, I know you're in there. You don't know me, but I know you. Don't be afraid to open the door. I'm not going to hurt you. I'm your secret admirer."

Her heart was racing now. How did he know her name? How did he know she was home? She had never seen him around at school or in town. Deerfield had a population of only 20,000, and most of the people at her school had grown up together. If someone new came to town, everyone knew it. How could she have missed this *hunk*?

As if reading her thoughts, he said, "I'm new in town. You haven't met me yet, but I've been watching you from afar. Please Carol, open the door. I need to tell you something important."

What should she do?

10

She slid on the floor below the level of the windows to her bedroom. There, she covered her bathing suit with shorts and a tank top. Should she go to the door? Logic told her it would be foolish to talk to a strange man while home alone. Her mother would never approve. Yet, why did he know her name? What did he need to tell her? Bad people never came to Deerfield. Her landlord was just a few feet away in the house next to them. He had been mowing the lawn a few minutes before. She could scream if he tried to do something. Her body seemed to move on its own, out her bedroom, down the hall, to the front of the house, to the doorknob. An adrenaline rush pricked her armpits. She opened the door and stood face to face with the attractive stranger.

He had a perfect smile with pearl-white teeth and full lips. His dark brown eyes seemed to flash back an exciting secret. She opened her mouth, but said nothing.

"I knew you would come, Carol. Can I come in?"

"Um, I…I'm not sure—" He brushed passed her into the room. She turned around and noticed he had well-developed biceps and a tan accentuated by a freshly laundered, white t-shirt. He smelled clean like her mother's towels.

She continued to gape, glued to the entrance like someone frozen in time. His eyes sparkled and seemed to emit light. *Is it the sun shining on him or just my imagination?*

He took hold of her hand with gentleness and said, "Come, let's sit and talk." A tingle shot up from her fingertips through her entire body. He led her to the living room, and they sat down on the couch.

She wanted to speak, to ask his name, to quiz him on how he knew her, but he never gave her a chance.

"The moment I set eyes on you, Carol, I knew I wanted to meet you. You have beautiful eyes."

"Thank you. But—"

"And your hair…the perfect color. I prefer brunettes to blonds. Your auburn hair has so many different shades."

"How do you know—"

"You have the most perfect body. I watched you sunbathing. You're so sexy."

She blushed and tried to interject again. "What's your name?"

He gazed at her with his bright, strange eyes and reached out to stroke her hair. "I think you're the perfect girl for me, Carol." Before she could say another word, he was kissing her. His moustache tickled, and his breath tasted like spearmint gum. A new excitement swept over her, fighting with the knowledge that it was wrong to let him do this.

"Wait. I don't know you."

"Carol, look at me. Trust me."

Her willpower dissolved. He began to hold her tighter, kiss her harder, and the cautioning voice became louder. Suddenly, he pulled away, smiled at her again, and stood up.

"I have to go, my sweetness. But I'll be back. Don't forget what I've said. Here's a picture of me so you won't forget."

He handed her something, then moved away. His tall frame and the back of his head slipped through the front door and disappeared. Stunned, Carol hesitated a moment, then followed. No car was parked in the driveway, no footsteps could be heard on the road, no handsome stranger turned to wave good-bye. She grabbed the doorknob to steady her shaking hands. The hum of the refrigerator was the only noise in the house. If it were not for the photograph, a studio portrait that displayed all of his perfect features, she would not have believed he existed.

Chapter Two

Margaret leaned toward the bathroom door, reached out to touch the knob, but she couldn't do it; couldn't face the hate that came from her baby's face. No, it would be better to go away, get her thoughts together, think it through.

She drove by instinct, not paying attention to the road. Perhaps she should turn around and go back. It had been stupid to let that rebellious kid stay home from school. *I should have grabbed her out of that bed and marched her into the bathroom. Instead, I let her get away with it. What is wrong with me?*

Why did Carol make her feel so guilty? Her kids had never dared resist her authority before Richard left. Now her daughter treated her with complete disrespect. Carol had a way of bringing up all the undesirable and detestable aspects of her life, never letting her forget how horrible a mother she was for bringing home men. Sure, she had gone through several boyfriends since the divorce, but it hadn't been her choice to leave the marriage. Was she supposed to be a saint, raise six kids without complaint, alone, without a man?

A loud honk blasted behind her. The light had turned green. She accelerated, then realized it was too early to start work. Her eyes were puffy from crying, her face strained and tired without makeup. She pulled into the only strip mall in town and parked in the far corner of the lot.

Using the rearview mirror, she covered her face with foundation. Just a few strands of gray mixed with the reddish-brown of her hair. People who didn't know her guessed her age less than thirty-six years. Her slender body still caught the attention of men. But as soon as her six children entered the conversation, shock replaced interest. Most would gawk at her, their mouths open like a big bass, or they would turn away in embarrassment as if they had made an unforgivable mistake. Then they would come up with a quick excuse to get away. "Oh, I'd better get going. Have to get up early in the morning." The men who stayed were usually married. Did vows mean nothing to men?

Her boyfriends would have a hard time believing she had been a virgin on her wedding day. Only eighteen then and naïve, a good Catholic girl who made a commitment before God to love her husband for better or worse. Had there ever been any "better?" What she got was babies and a husband who cared more about the poor than his own children. Her most successful talent in life was getting pregnant. Nine months to the day of their wedding night, her first girl was born. Before the age of twenty-seven, five more girls followed, with a few miscarriages thrown in to keep her in a perpetual state of pregnancy. At least now the stretched skin on her stomach appeared somewhat normal.

Margaret put on the radio and finished with her mascara. Carol King was singing, "You just call on my name, I'll come running to see you again…you've got a friend." Would a day come when painful memories would subside and give her at least a moment's peace? She had sung those very words to her husband a few short years ago while they danced in the living room late at night. He had sung them back, then made love to her. Vacant, idle words and lies all of them. He was a master liar.

His crafty, calculating lying reached an epiphany right before he moved to Massachusetts. "Now that the house is sold, I think it's time to move back south," Richard said. He was home late and just coming to bed.

"Richard, what are you talking about? Why would I want to move back to the city? It's not a good place to raise kids."

"We've talked about this many times, Margaret. The people in the slums need someone to help them out of poverty. I can buy the old buildings for practically nothing and help the oppressed improve their neighborhood."

Margaret sat up in bed, awake. "Wait a minute, you are the one who talked about it. You've never asked what I thought."

They had argued until the morning hours. Richard was very persuasive. As always, she submitted to his plan.

"I'll take three of the children with me, move into one of the apartments, and get them settled in school. When the house closes, you can come down and move in with the rest of the kids," Richard said.

"I still don't understand why you want to split up the kids." Margaret clutched her pillow, wanting so much to sleep yet knowing it would not come for a long time.

"I told you. The older kids need to finish out school, whereas the younger ones will adjust better."

"Okay, but I'm not keeping Maurine. She's been a handful lately…stealing, getting into trouble, fighting. I'll only do it if you take her."

"Fine. I'm tired and have a ton of work to do tomorrow."

Richard rolled over and went to sleep without another word or even a touch, leaving her to agonized over the reality of his words.

A month later, Margaret called to let her husband know the house had closed and she was ready to move. He wasn't home and her daughter, Jessica, answered the phone.

"Where's Dad?"

"Oh, he's not here, Mom. He went to the store with Denise to get food."

"Denise? Who's that?"

"She's the lady who lives here with us."

The no good, lying, cheat was shacking up with a woman in Springfield, Massachusetts.

Remembering that day always made her want to scream. It was as if a lightning bolt had charged through the phone and zapped the life out of her. Fourteen years of marriage over in a split second, with a few simple, revealing words from her daughter.

It was all Richard's fault. Since then, their oldest daughter was in drug rehab, and now Carol was rebelling. Well, he wasn't going to ruin her life anymore. She'd find a way to make it work. Carol would just have to understand that things were different. She still loved her, but Carol needed to learn that she had her own life, too.

A car drove by, and she looked at her watch. *I'm going to be late for work.*

Margaret started the car.

Chapter Three

Carol searched the shoulders of the road through a rain-streaked window. The bus made its way up a steep, winding hill lined with newly leafed Maples. She rubbed the black leather of her purse and pictured the photo of *him* hidden in a zippered compartment. All week, she had sought her mysterious admirer, checked out every boy at school, in the grocery store, in town, and inside every passing car. He was not there; he had disappeared, vanished like the sun, replaced with chilly, drizzly clouds.

No one knew about their encounter. It belonged to her alone; her mother or sisters could not steal it away. Their kiss lingered on her lips, still fresh with the taste of spearmint, a sacred secret to relive and dream about day and night. If only she could attach a name to his perfect face. How about a princely name like Charlton or Damien or Parker with a number three after his last name? Better yet, a rugged name like The Fonz or Rocky? No, none of them worked. His name had to be different than any name she had ever heard.

The bus pulled into a new housing development of large, two-story Victorians. Carol hoped the Barrett's had ice cream sandwiches. Every day after school, she babysat their eleven-year-old daughter, Tina. The "spoiled, rich girl" irritated her with "I'm bored" statements every five minutes, but her house was the best. It was a mansion compared to the little, three-bedroom cottage she shared with her five sisters and her mom.

The highlight of Carol's day was raiding the well-stocked refrigerator and wandering through the house pretending it was her own. It was huge with three whole bathrooms, two stories, and a full basement. Her favorite was the guest bathroom which was always clean and had fragrant soaps in a crystal dish. Some smelled like lilac, some like honeysuckle, and her favorite like green apple. She could sit in the formal living room and pretend to entertain the rich and the famous or lie on the bed in the untouched guest room with a polished cherry bedstead and dresser. Sometimes she would rest on Tina's canopy bed with its pink bedspread and matching curtains, but it was often a mess. Instead, Tina usually found her curled up in window seat in the family room which overlooked the back yard landscaped with a pond and small waterfall.

Carol snatched an ice-cream sandwich and made her way toward the family room. Just as she rounded the corner, a tall man walked down the hall. Startled, she drew back and dropped her prize on the floor.

"Did I scare you?" The man made for the kitchen and paper towels.

"Yes. Who are you?"

"You must be the babysitter. I'm Todd, Tina's older brother." He put the dirty paper towel in his left hand and stretched his right to her.

"I'm Carol. Nice to meet you." She took his hand, noticing his fingers were long and pale.

Todd finished cleaning the mess, then stood by the sink. He adjusted his glasses and tucked a lock of light-brown, shoulder-length hair behind his ear.

"Thanks for cleaning the mess for me. Um, how come I never met you before?"

"I attend the University of Vermont. I'm home for spring break."

"Oh." Carol noticed him looking at her. She wondered if he were staring at her pimples.

"So, are you a high school student?"

"Not yet. I'll be a freshman next year at Deerfield High."

"Oh, you look older than that. I thought you were at least sixteen."

Carol hoped she wasn't blushing. She looked down and picked at her fingers. Did he really think she was older?

"Here, let me get you some more ice cream. I think I'll have one, too." Todd took out two ice cream sandwiches and led her into the family room.

Todd stayed and talked to Carol the entire afternoon, even after Tina came home. He did not appeal to her the way Josh did at school. He did not come close to her secret admirer either, but he was a man and seemed to like her. He was smart, too. He used words Carol had never heard before. He told her he was majoring in political science and wanted to be a teacher. He had "done extensive research into the Arab-Israeli conflict" and considered himself "an ideological nonconformist in a complacent, capitalistic society."

As Todd used an Almanac to show her where all the Middle Eastern countries were located, Carol thought about *him*. His body was so strong and muscular. Todd's was like one straight line. Finally, Todd closed the book.

"Carol, do you want to go bowling with me Friday?"

"Um, I don't know. I'd have to ask my mom." Should she even think about Todd or wait for her mystery man?

"I understand. How about you tell me tomorrow when you come over."

On the drive home, Carol relived her two hours with Todd. No boy had ever given her so much attention. It couldn't hurt to go out with him once. But would her mom have a fit when she found out he was twenty years old? Carol was almost fourteen and not even in high school. Then she remembered her mom went out dancing and drinking with her friends every Friday. The answer was simple: just have Todd come over after her mom left.

So, Carol went out with Todd that Friday. He picked her up in a yellow bug and opened the door for her. She felt awkward at first, afraid some of the kids from school would see them together. But he took her to a restaurant in Brattleboro, a ten mile drive to the south, where no one knew them. He treated her like an adult, not a kid, talking to her about college and government and "fanatic conservatives." After dinner, they went bowling. She only scored 68 to his 120, but it was fun. On the way home, he stopped at Dunkin Donuts and she ate two of her favorite kinds: chocolate and cream-filled. Then, at her house, he held her hand and said, "I had a great time tonight, Carol." His hands were sweaty, and she was glad he didn't kiss her.

Carol was relieved to find her mom not home yet. She had just started going out with a noisy, greasy-handed mechanic named Mac who had several children of his own. He liked to play Hank Williams records, and whenever Carol heard, "*You're cheating heart*," it made her want to punch someone. It was sickening the way he touched her mother when they were together. It was even more disgusting the way he smiled at her and winked when she wore a bathing suit. One day, Mac was on the couch "making out" with her mother. When her mom left the room, he staggered up to Carol and said, "You're going to be a real heart breaker with a body like that." His beer and cigarette breath reeked as came close to her face and squeezed her arm. Carol had turned away and escaped to her room, a mixture of revulsion and excitement stirring her thoughts into a messy, rotten stew. The creep would probably be spending the night tonight, and Carol wanted to be out cold when he came home with her mother. It took a while before sleep came, as Mac's ugly face, stinky breath, and drunken laugh loomed behind her closed eyes. She threw him out of the picture and put *him* in instead, pretending he had taken her on a date instead of Todd.

***

Margaret arrived home around midnight. Mac needed to work in the morning, so he went to his place. Jessica was still up watching television.

"Hi, Jess. Everything go okay tonight?" Margaret shut off the TV and sat on the couch next to her daughter.

"Hey, I was watching that."

"Jess, it's bedtime. So, you're sisters didn't give you any trouble did they?"

"No. We watched TV and ate popcorn. All except Carol, that is." Jess stretched and grinned.

"What do you mean? What did Carol do?'

"Oh, nothing much. Just go out on a date with some guy."

"What!" As Jessica shared her story, Margaret could feel her blood pressure rising. She stormed into Carol's room and pulled her out of her bed.

"Carol, wake up right now. Who is this Todd guy you were with tonight? How dare you leave home with a strange boy without telling me!"

Carol shook herself from Margaret's grip. "You weren't home anyway, so what does it matter? You were out with that Mac guy who's married. At least Todd isn't married."

"I've had enough of your disrespect, Carol. What I do has nothing to do with your disobedience. Todd is too old for you. I don't want you to see him again. And you're grounded!"

Carol's smooth, childish face turned into the features of an ugly, angry witch. The skin around her jaws and eyes contorted and her teeth clenched as tight as her two fists. "And just what are you going to do to stop me? Kick me out? Send me to my Dad's? Spank me? Tie me up so I can't leave?"

"That's enough!' Margaret took a deep breath. She knew she needed to take decisive action, but regret and confusion clouded logic like thick fog. Her daughter continued to glare at her with an "I dare you" look. She suddenly felt weak and unable to speak. Maybe she *was* a horrible mother and a terrible role model. How could she stop Carol from behaving wrongly when she was having an affair with a married man?

Margaret turned away. "Carol, if you know what's good for you, you'll do what I say. I'm going to bed."

Margaret went into her room and fell on her bed exhausted. She had failed again. Maybe Carol would do better living with Richard. No, that was a stupid idea. His girlfriend wasn't going to get her fangs into her child. If only God were really out there, maybe he would help, but he had abandoned and betrayed her.

If he existed, he was too cruel to trust, let alone answer her prayers. All her life, she had been a good Catholic and said her prayers every night. What good did it get her? She had lived through Richard's failed business, unemployment, constant lack of money, and bankruptcy for what? To raise their kids alone and find comfort in a married man? Life made no sense to her anymore.

She hugged her pillow and thought about Carol, her strawberry baby. The family had spent that warm, June day at several strawberry festivals, and later that evening, she went into labor. Her third girl was born at 4:44 AM, weighing over nine pounds and perfect, her head the most symmetrical of all her babies. They named her Carol, which means "joyous song."

Carol was a joyous song. She had a vivid imagination, loved to make up stories, and sang all the time. She asked more "why" questions than the other girls. If the answer was unsatisfactory, she would sit and concentrate, her little hand pressed against her chin, then declare her own logical explanation. "The sky is blue because blue is the color of the ocean, and when you look out at the ocean, the colors run together." Carol's favorite place was the beach. She loved to walk down the shore and collect seashells and get lost. Margaret had several frantic memories of her daughter wandering off at the beach.

Carol's favorite song was "Those Were the Days My Friend," and she practiced it day and night until she was certain her voice matched the artist on the radio. Her sisters teased her mercilessly, but Carol recorder her voice anyway, confident of future fame. Just like she would someday be the first woman president. Carol was the most serious of her girls, a crusader against favoritism, injustice and dirt. She became very angry with Maurine for having a favorite sister, wrote a letter to the editor about the Vietnam War, listened at the door to make sure her youngest sister washed her hands after going to the bathroom, became so tired of the mess in the house she cleaned it herself for a week.

Since the divorce, Carol had become quieter, spending time alone in her room, playing her flute for hours. Margaret was not allowed to touch her, kiss her, or hug her. She especially avoided Margaret when men came over, making it very clear that no one would ever replace her father.

Where was the baby who couldn't get enough hugs and kisses? Where was the little girl who made "I love you" cards and left them on her pillow? The daydreamer who made up stories at bedtime rather than the other way around? The smiling preschooler who taught to her baby dolls to read? The schoolgirl who laid out all her new clothes in anticipation of the first day of school, who built forts out of blankets in the summer, climbed trees to read books, made a birthday cake for their cat, swung and sang for hours in their back yard even in the middle of a snowstorm? How had her daughter turned into the hateful teenager sleeping in the room next to her?

Margaret felt too tired to even brush her teeth. She crawled under the covers and washed her pillow with tears.

Chapter Four

Todd came over almost every day during Spring break. Because Carol didn't need to baby sit Tina while he was home, he would drive up in his yellow, 60's bug after school and take her to his house. Todd's parents hardly spoke to either of them. They never even ate together as a family. It was obvious they did not approve of her, so she spent as little time in their presence as possible.

On Saturday, Todd took her to Rutland for the day. They walked through several shops, and he bought her a silver necklace from a quaint jewelry store. He then took her out to lunch at Friendly's where they shared a banana split for dessert. Going out to eat and shopping at anything other than a large department store was rare in her home. Her mother made just enough for them to live day to day. No one had ever done so much for her, and she felt special, pretty, and even forgot to think about her ugly pimples for a while. Sometimes Todd's vocabulary made it difficult to understand the conversation, especially when he discussed politics or history, but he never called her stupid.

Carol spent two whole weeks experiencing all kinds of new things. She would stay with Todd until bedtime, and he even helped her with her homework. Her Mom would be waiting up to yell at her, but nothing ever came of their fights. She still did whatever she wanted.

Todd introduced one of the new things while they were parked alone in his car. He showed her a plastic bag of something that looked like dried grass and said, "Statistics show that marijuana is less harmful to your lungs than cigarettes. It's also less addicting. The tobacco companies lobby against marijuana because they don't want competition."

"Is it like cigarettes? I've tried cigarettes and they're gross. They almost made me throw up."

Todd took out a strange contraption from his bag in the back seat. "No. You don't even have to smoke it like a cigarette. Let me show you."

Todd put the dried weed in a receptacle at the bottom of a plastic pipe. He filled the tube with water, and it made her think of a bubble blower. He packed the weed with his finger, then lit it. The smoke smelled different than cigarettes, a sweeter smell, more like burning leaves.

Todd put the pipe to his lips and inhaled. Little bubbles formed in the water. "See, Carol, the water keeps the smoke from burning your lungs as much. Try it." He handed her the bong.

"Are you sure I won't get addicted to this stuff? My mom said smoking pot leads to taking harder drugs."

"That's not true at all. She doesn't know what she's talking about. I've never tried anything else. Like I said, smoking cigarettes is a whole lot worse than this."

Carol turned and saw Todd's grayish blue eyes through his glasses—bright, excited, yet a little nervous, a man who knew what he was doing yet at the same time a little boy who wanted to share his secret treasure. He'd been so nice to her all week, and he was the smartest guy she had ever met, an honor student at the University of Vermont. He must know what he's doing, and she did not want to disappoint him. "Okay, I guess it won't hurt."

She placed her lips at the top of the pipe and breathed in. The smoke went down her throat, but it didn't make her cough. She took another puff. Something changed immediately.

All her tension ebbed away as if someone had poked a hole in her and bled it all out. Actions and speech played in slow motion, and every problem or worry left with the smoke that escaped through the open window. Todd's face, the gauges on the dash, the pine tree outside the car window, all became larger and more detailed. Wow! There were so many lines etched on her hands, so many fine strands of cotton weaved into her shirt, thousands of pieces of hair on her arms. Time stood still. It didn't matter if her mom yelled at her, it didn't matter if her sisters made fun of Todd, it didn't matter that her teachers were disappointed with her grades. Who cared what tomorrow might bring? All that mattered was the warm, comforting sensation that enveloped her body and enhanced the pleasure of here and now.

On the last night of his vacation, she was alone with Todd in the basement at his house. Tina had gone to bed, and they were sitting together on the floor. Todd took her arm and started gently touching her from her shoulder to her fingertips. This made her uncomfortable, but she did not want to hurt his feelings. He did the same thing to her other arm, then started exploring her eyes, her nose, then her lips with his fingers. Soon, his mouth was on hers. Like the jerk of a light switch, she felt a jab in the pit of her stomach and pulled away. In contrast to her secret admirer, Todd's breath smelled like phlegm. "I'm not ready for this."

"Sorry, Carol. I'll take it slower." She let him put his arm around her and hold her close.

Todd's first love letter came the week he started classes again. After reading it, Carol panicked. Sure, it was great to have him pay attention to her, but "I will love you forever and always," that was too much. Friendship, yes; love, no. She pulled *his* photo out from under her pillow and closed her eyes, remembering how handsome *he* was, how *he* made her legs weak, how *his* mouth tasted like spearmint. *Why didn't you come back like you said you would? It's you I want.* She decided to call Todd that evening and break it off.

Carol stammered through five minutes of awkward politeness before she mustered the strength to say it. "Todd, I'm really sorry. I don't want to go out with you. I'm too young."

Silence returned her announcement. Carol thought she heard Todd crying.

"Todd, are you there? I'm really sorry. I hope you're okay."

"Sure, I'll be fine. Thanks a lot." He hung up the phone.

Carol felt relieved until Todd called her back the next day.

"I went to a gun store today."

"A gun store? Why?"

"I bought a gun."

"Why would you buy a gun?"

"Because I no longer want to live."

"Todd! You can't be serious! You'd be crazy to do such a thing!"

"I love you, Carol. I can't live without you. I'd rather be dead."

"No, don't say that!"

"I can't help it. You're the only good thing to happen in my life and now you don't want me. I'm no good."

"No, Todd, you're a great guy. I'm just so young, and this is all new to me. I still want to see you. I just want to take it slower."

"You mean it, Carol? I can take it slower."

"Sure, I mean it."

Carol spent the next half hour convincing Todd that his life was valuable, and she would take him back to prove it.

Chapter Five

Running again, over sticks and rocks, brushing against gigantic trunks, almost falling. Don't look behind, push on, ignore the sharp pain, breath in more air. A clearing appeared ahead. If she could reach it, perhaps there would be a road or a house. She made it to the edge of the field, then stopped cold. The clearing ended at the lip of a steep ravine. Turning around would bring her back to death, but so would stepping over the cliff before her. She turned her head and listened, covering her mouth to silence her heavy panting. Wind wove through the tops of the tall pines in an eerie wail, but the sound of undergrowth crunching under heavy boots and the huff and puff of labored breathing, they had stopped. She uncovered her mouth and sat on a rock. Abruptly, two red eyes appeared above her, and at her chest level, the silver of a knife reflected the moonlight, flashing bright amidst the darkness. The knife plunged. Her mouth opened to shriek, but nothing came out. I have to fight, get away. She commanded her legs to kick, her fists to punch; they remained ineffective appendages, flopping around like a rag doll. The knife sunk deeper, the blood oozed out. No! It's a nightmare. Wake up! Change it, make it stop! It was useless. Over and over, the silver blazed just before it was thrust into her soft flesh. And he laughed.

She struggled to control of the vision of her own death, too afraid to wake up, too afraid to stay asleep. She was certain those two eyes were still in the room with her, hovering just above her head. Paralyzed by terror, she could not move or cry out. It felt like someone had placed one of those x-ray blankets on top of her. *Mom! Help me, Mom!* She shouted in her mind, but her mouth wouldn't work. If only her mom would come through the door. She recalled the Lord's Prayer from her days of catechism. "Our Father, who art in heaven, hallowed be thy name." She forced out an audible whisper, sensing that the "thing" in the room was angry with her prayer. It only made her more determined. "Let your kingdom come, let your will be done, on earth as it is in heaven." The vision of the two eyes burned in fury. "Give us today our daily bread, and forgive us our trespasses as we forgive those who trespass against us." She tried to picture what Jesus looked like in books, but he did not have a clear face. Instead, she thought of the bright light that always surrounded his head. "And lead us not into temptation, but deliver us from the evil one." The ominous presence did not leave, but the prayer somehow kept her safe from it. It stayed with her all night long, and all night long, she reiterated the prayer so it would not overcome her.

***

Margaret ran through a store searching frantically for her little girl. "Have you seen my baby? She's only two. Please, help me find her!" She asked one person after another with no response. The cashier stared through her, punching in amounts on the cash register and placing groceries in bags. Another women kept examining heads of lettuce even after she shouted in her face. One after another, the people continue their activities like senseless robots, ignoring her pleas. She ran to a pay phone and called the operator, but the phone rang busy in her ear. She darted outside the store, stood in front of a car, but it almost drove over her. Back into the store again, she panicked, shouting to deaf ears. "Someone please help me!" Sprinting as fast as she could, she raced through the parking lot and down the street. Suddenly, a tall man dressed in black ran into her and grabbed her arm. All she could see was a formless face and two glaring, red balls.

She screamed and awoke from the terror. Mac breathed heavily next to her. The child in her dream was Carol, and she wanted to go into the next room and make sure her daughter was okay. Fear kept her riveted to her pillow. Her daughter would reject her because she knew Mac was in bed with her. Carol would tell her to get away, remind her of her repulsive behavior, glare at her in revulsion. Her situation with Mac polluted her as a mother, made her unworthy of her daughter's trust and affection. Why had she allowed this man into her life? He was married, and the only thing she enjoyed about him was the physical intimacy that temporarily filled the emptiness that gnawed her insides every day. Yet, despair and loneliness returned in the morning when Mac complained about his hangover, his need for a cigarette, and went home to his wife and kids. *Oh God, if you are real at all, please keep my Carol*

26

safe. Please bring her back to me. Forgive me for all the wrong choices I've made. Please don't let her pay for my mistakes.

Her body shook as pain and shame splintered her heart until she could no longer restrain the tears. Next to her, Mac snored.

***

After what seemed like years, faint shadows overcame the heavy blackness in Carol's room, and the night of terror ebbed away with the daylight. Carol forced her cramped body to move out of bed, down the hall to the bathroom. When she returned, the picture of her mystery man lay on the floor beside her bed.

I don't want anyone to see this. She quickly hid it under her pillow and covered it with blankets.

Chapter Six

Todd listened to his *Santana* album and unwrapped a set of blue index cards. He placed them with the white and yellow ones separated by dividers in a new holder, moving to the music as he worked. Several boxes of cards were stacked with the numerous books that filled every space on his side of the dorm. He loved his selective collection, which included thorough notes of both college texts and his own books. An entire section was dedicated to the Middle East. Someday he would use his research to educate the world about the unjust treatment of the Palestinian people.

He took the dividers and labeled them: "Education, Appearance, and Personality." He danced in his chair and smiled, remembering Carol's youthful face and well-proportioned body. For the first time in his life, Todd had something all his, someone to love him, someone to make him feel good about himself. Not like his old crush from high school. He invested hours in that girl, helping her with homework so she could keep her grade point average high enough to please her parents. While she studied her textbooks, he memorized her features: her naturally highlighted, blonde hair, petite nose, tiny mouth and ears, her slender waist, her ample breasts. Oh, she smelled so good, like perfumed fruit. It made him think of a blueberry pie, and he wanted to eat her up. So many hours he wasted fantasizing about their future together, how he would take her in his arms and kiss her passionately, how he would tell her he loved her and ask her to marry him. In their senior year, he gathered enough courage to ask her out. She laughed at him and said, "I can't go out with you, Todd. You're *ugly*!" The word "ugly" echoed in his mind even still. His mother had described him the same way to their neighbors when he was eight years old. "Todd was the ugliest baby you've ever seen!"

Carol didn't say he was ugly when he asked her out. Instead, she thanked him for a wonderful night after their first date. She let him hold her hand, listened to his dreams, and said more than once how smart he was. The only reason she wanted to break up with him was because he moved too fast. He would be careful not to rush. She was a lot younger than he was. But that made it even better because she believed whatever he told her. Carol was an unrefined block of marble that he could mold and polish to be the perfect woman for him, just like Eliza in Bernard Shaw's *Pygmalion*. She looked to him and trusted him for everything.

The first thing I'm going to do is fix her completion. Her acne was her only flaw, that and her breasts were a bit small. There was a device in one of his magazines that guaranteed it would increase breast size. Perhaps it would work. Certain silky undergarments would also enhance her bust line. He had already purchased a book on sex to prepare her. They would wait until her fourteenth birthday for the first time, but he could begin teaching her some things as soon as possible.

He took a blue card and wrote down these goals. Then, from the education section, he listed several items: teach her to speak correctly, help her complete her school work and improve her grades, give her lessons over the summer. He jotted down certain books that would help her.

Under the personality section, he listed some of her perturbing habits such as picking at her pimples and biting the skin near her fingernails. It annoyed him the way she giggled like a silly schoolgirl at every little comment he made and when she coughed without covering her mouth. Teaching manners was essential, especially if his parents were going to accept her. Education was also crucial so they could engage in intellectual conversations.

After he finished with the index cards, Todd took out a yellow note pad and began a letter. *Dear Carol. I miss you so much I can hardly stand it. I can't wait until I see you next weekend. You are the ideal girl for me. I bought a book for you I think you'll enjoy. It's called Pygmalion, but you may have seen the movie, My Fair Lady. We can read it together. I have another surprise I can't wait to show you....*

***

Carol placed Todd's latest letter in her special box under her bed. He would be home for the summer on Friday, and she couldn't wait. She needed to finish the last chapter in *Pygmalion* so they could discuss it together. He had written to her about it in one of his letters. There was an ancient myth about Pygmalion and how he sculpted a perfect woman, then prayed to Venus to make her come alive. Venus answered his prayer. She came to life, he named her Galatia, and they lived happily ever after. Todd said she was his Galatia.

Carol stood up and smiled at her reflection in the mirror. A new girl smiled back. Todd had given her some of his prescription cream and antibiotics for acne, and most of her pimples disappeared during the last month. He paid for a perm and hair cut, and her limp, brown hair now flowed in soft curls to her shoulders. Her green eyes stood out thanks to eyeliner and mascara. Her lips glistened with dark pink lip-gloss. Her cheeks blushed. All she needed was a flowing, white gown with matching gloves and she could pass as a duchess, just like Eliza. *Except I can't talk right.*

"How do you do?" Carol enunciated her words and curtseyed. "I'm Princess Rowena from Romania."

She took the hand of her imaginary prince. "Certainly, I would love to dance with you, Prince Damien." She waltzed around the room, eyes closed. Suddenly, she stopped and plopped onto the bed. The prince in her daydream was not Todd, but the mystery man whose picture lay hidden under her pillow.

She took *his* picture out and stared for a minute, then shoved it quickly back to its hiding place. "I'm sorry Todd. I really do love you."

The door crashed open and her sister plowed in. "Who are you talking to?"

Carol turned to her sister and snarled. "Jess, haven't I told you a hundred times to knock first? I'm not talking to anyone."

"Yeah, right. Probably talking to your Toddy baby. Oh Todd, I love you Todd, you're so smart, Todd—"

"Jess, will you shut up!" Carol threw a pillow and it hit her sister right in the face.

"You think you're so hot, don't you? Well, I think it's totally gross that you're going out with such an older guy. I'm sixteen, and I wouldn't go out with a guy like that. Of course, I already have a boyfriend close to my age." Jess put her hand on her hip and stuck up her nose.

"You may be sixteen, but I'm bigger than you. I can beat you up. You'd better take it back, Jess." Carol charged for her sister, but she slammed the door and bolted away. Carol pursued her, but she almost rammed into her mom.

"Dinner's ready. Both of you quit your fighting and sit down." Margaret turned quickly around and headed for the dining room. Carol noticed she didn't even look at her.

Later that night, Carol finished *Pygmalion*. It didn't make sense. Eliza was supposed to marry the professor, not Freddy. She wondered who Todd was supposed to be. Was he supposed to be Professor Higgins, the one who transformed Eliza from a flower girl to a refined lady? He couldn't be like Freddy. He was stupid. But Professor Higgins was also mean and old. Todd wasn't mean and old. Maybe she was reading too much into it.

Still, it bothered her a little that Todd wanted to change her. What did he not like about her? Did he see her as a poor, uneducated waif? Did he think she was dumb? She took his letters out and read them again. He said over and over that he thought she was pretty, that he loved her, but he never said she was smart. *Well, I'll prove to him that I am.*

She walked past her family who were all watching television, found a dictionary in the bookcase, brought it back to her room, snuggled under the covers, and started reading. "Aardvark, aback, abacus…" She fell asleep before finishing the first page.

Chapter Seven

Carol threaded a pair of teal earrings through her pierced ear, then stood back to admire the results. Not bad. All through Junior High, she had been taller than most of the boys and girls. Her early development made her feel out of place with her peers, but now it gave her an advantage because Todd was over six feet tall. With the make-up, she hoped to pass as a college student.

She wore one of her two nice outfits: an aqua and green pheasant dress with wide, lacy sleeves. She wanted to look nice for Todd today because it was their first date since he came home for the summer. Her mom had bought her the dress at the beginning of eighth grade. They almost didn't buy it because of the length, but her mom had finally succumbed to her whining. It showed off her already tan, slim legs.

She heard the distinct sound of Todd's Volkswagen, grabbed her purse, and ran to reach the door before he did to avoid a scene with her mother.

"Carol, I told you to clean the bathroom before going out today." He mom was in the kitchen washing the breakfast dishes.

"I cleaned it yesterday." Carol didn't want to talk to her mother again. She had already argued with her that morning about spending the day with Todd.

"Will you be home for dinner?"

"I don't think so." Carol turned and faced her mother. Margaret was leaning against the sink, watching her with sad, baggy eyes. She wore her old, fuzzy, pink bathrobe, the same one from when Carol was a baby. Many mornings Carol had snuggled on the couch with her mom and stroked the soft fluffiness of the pink flannel. Now the robe appeared ragged and worn, just like her mother. The thought of touching that ratty bathrobe repulsed her. She turned to leave, to get far away from her mom's gloomy face.

"Wait a minute."

Carol looked back, reading for an attack. *Okay, give it to me, Mom. Lecture away.*

"I love you, Carol."

She froze, surprised at her mother's words. A strange heat pressed against her cheeks, leaving her confused and embarrassed. She wanted to say she loved her mom, but the words would not come. The heat surfaced with hot tears, even though Carol willed them away. Her mom must not see her cry. "Todd's waiting. I've got to go…"

Todd greeted her with a big grin and an approving glance that spread from her head to her toes. "You look great, babe. I like the dress." He put his hand on her knee. "How about a kiss?"

A kiss first thing in the morning seemed icky to Carol. She had just gotten use to kissing him at night. But he would be hurt and disappointed without one, so she gave him a quick peck on the lips.

"I was hoping for a bit more. Especially after exciting me with that dress." Todd squeezed her leg.

"We have all day."

"That's true. And I have a great day planned. I'm diving [driving] down to Massachusetts so we can go to a big mall."

"Really! I haven't been to the mall since the last time my Dad took me over a year ago. Todd, I can't believe how nice you are to me."

"I'm going to buy you some clothes for summer. Do you need a bathing suit?"

"Well, my mom talked about getting me one for my birthday. I've been using my sister's hand-me-down."

"I don't want my girl wearing an old bathing suit. We can start with that."

"I can't remember the last time I got to pick my own bathing suit." The sun shone bright and warm in a brilliant, blue sky, an omen of more wonderful times to come. Balmy, fragrant air blew through the window and lifted her hair. It smelled fresh and clean like clothes that had been dried outside. Only two more weeks of school, then a long summer vacation. She would turn fourteen soon. With Todd, all kinds of cool things could happen. He always seemed to have money.

Todd's fast driving only added to her anticipation.

***

Carol rummaged through her bags reviewing all her treasures while they waited for their food at an A&W drive-in somewhere between Springfield, Massachusetts and the Vermont border. Deerfield had an A&W, too. Every few months, her mom would splurge and take them out. Carol loved the bacon cheeseburgers and root beer floats.

They had purchased her fist bikini, a sundress, a pair of shorts, a couple of shirts, and new fancy underwear Todd picked out. The only time she ever received so many clothes at once was when her rich uncle sent a huge box of clothes her cousins no longer needed. Most of the clothes were her size, providing several new outfits. She remembered parading a matching, pink pant and shirt set with kitten faces that even came with pink shoes. Her sisters had been so jealous. She wore it until the pants showed her ankles.

"I still have one more gift for you. Remember, I told you about it in my letter?" Todd reached for her hand.

"That's right. When do I get it?" Carol stuffed the items back into the bags and threw them in the back seat.

"Later, tonight."

"Why do I have to wait until tonight?"

"You'll see." The waitress came with a tray of food and hooked it onto the driver's window. Carol grabbed a bag of fries and stuffed some into her mouth.

"Todd, where do you get all your money from anyway?"

Todd swallowed a bite of his hamburger before answering. "Well, I get an allowance from my parents. I also worked for my Poly-Sci. professor. I'm good at saving my money."

"And you spent all this money on me? Todd, I feel bad."

"You're worth it, Babe." He squeezed her hand.

"Where are we going after lunch?"

"You'll see. That's also a surprise."

Todd drove back to the outskirts of Deerfield. The outskirts meant out in the country because between towns were large, undeveloped areas of land or dairy farms or houses with acreage. Todd drove down an unfamiliar dirt road and stopped at a run-down, single-wide mobile home. "Where are we?" Carol asked.

"It's a friend of mine. I need to pick something up."

Carol started to open the door. Todd held up his hand. "You don't need to come in. I don't want to stay. I'll be right back." He was out of the car before she could say another word.

Why didn't he want her to come in? Was he ashamed of her? Todd hadn't mentioned anything about his friends or introduced her to anyone. He probably didn't want them to know he was dating someone so young. Carol frowned and picked at her fingers. A grungy, shaggy dog came up to the car, wagged its tail, and growled. She was glad to have the metal of the car protecting her. The lawn looked like it had never been mowed, and junk littered the driveway and edges of the trailer: abandoned car parts, tires, an old refrigerator, a rusty milk box, a broken bicycle. On the side of the house stood one lonely lilac bush, the only colorful item on the landscape. It seemed to cry out, "Get me out of here. I don't belong in this place." She didn't belong there either.

Todd returned a few minutes later with a paper bag. He took out a plastic sack of hashish and hid it in a special compartment under the dash. "Oh, now I understand why you didn't want me to come in. Your friend is a dealer."

"You're actually smart sometimes, Carol." Todd started the car and spun the wheels like he was running from a robbery.

Todd's words stung. Was he just joking, or did he think she was stupid? She wanted to ask him, but then it might spoil their afternoon. The day had been perfect so far. *I'm sure he was just joking.*

"So, I take it we're going to get high this afternoon." Carol giggled "That's not my surprise, is it?"

"No. You just won't give up on that, will you?"

Boy, is he touchy or what? Maybe she was being too pushy. Maybe he was nervous because he just bought an illegal substance. Maybe it was just her imagination. She looked out the window, thought about her new clothes, and pictured herself in the sundress, blue with yellow daisies, form fitted to show off her chest and small waist.

Todd drove further into the country, then down a dirt road that turned into an overgrown path with huge mud holes. Trees surrounded them so they were invisible, unless another car came down the path. Todd took out his bong, and they smoked. Carol felt relaxed and sleepy. Todd got into the back and pulled out a wrapped box from underneath the seat. "Now, here's your surprise, sweetheart."

Carol tore the pink-flowered wrapping from the box and threw it on the floor. Inside was a large picture book called *The Joy of Sex.* This was her surprise? Her head felt like it did sometimes when she got up too fast. How could she tell Todd she didn't want it? She could feel his probing stare, but kept her head down. She knew her cheeks were red. Her mother had given her a book on where babies came from when she was twelve, and it covered all the basics. But it didn't have pictures of naked couples, and she still didn't know exactly what a man looked like without clothes.

Todd took the book from her and opened it up. Sure enough, glossy, colored photos of naked men and women covered every page. If she hadn't been high, she would have run away. "Carol, it's a perfectly natural thing to have intercourse. You don't need to be ashamed. It's a basic need, just like eating or drinking."

"I know, but it seems dirty to me. I don't know why, but it does."

Todd took her hand. "Carol, I want you to look at these pictures. You need to get over that feeling. There is nothing wrong or dirty about it."

"I can't. Maybe if you let me do it on my own, it could do it. But it's too embarrassing to look at them with you."

"Here, why don't you smoke some more pot. It may loosen you up." Todd handed her the bong.

Carol obeyed. Soon, she was drifting in and out of reality. Todd showed her the pictures, and now they seemed funny. She giggled. Before the end of the evening, she saw his body, and he saw hers.

Later that night, Carol rushed past her family to her bedroom. She wanted to change her clothes and wash them before they noticed the smell of smoke on her. She sprayed herself with perfume, put on clean pajamas, and stuffed her dress underneath a pile of laundry in her hamper. She was just about to take her hamper to the basement when her mom knocked on the door.

"Carol, are you okay? You didn't even stop to say hello."

Carol glanced around her room to make sure she had not left out anything suspicious. She put down the hamper, threw the bag of new clothes in her closet, picked up the hamper again, and opened the door. "Sorry, mom. I spilled soda all over my dress, and it felt like I'd wet my pants. I'm going to do a laundry."

"At this time of night?" Her mom sniffed the air. "What's that smell?"

"My new perfume. Todd bought it for me. Don't you like it?"

"It's a bit strong." Her mother gave her the "something's up" look. "Carol, have you been smoking?"

"No, Mom." Carol pretended to drop her clothes so she didn't have to look at her. "We went bowling, and it was smoky in there."

"I hope so. You know how stupid it would be to start smoking."

"Mom, don't you trust me? Don't you think I'm smarter than that? Now, I need to wash my dress before the stain sets." Carol passed by her mom before she had a chance to reply.

"Carol, I want you to be here for dinner tomorrow. You can eat dinner with your family on Sunday. And you still have homework and school Monday."

"Okay, Mom. I'll be home for dinner tomorrow if it makes you happy." She was relieved to walk down into the cool basement alone and stuff her smelly clothes in the washer. She took a good whiff of the detergent before poring it into the water. It cleansed her nostrils and made her feel better. What Todd told her must be true, but she still felt dirty and exposed. No one had seen her naked since she was ten years old.

***

Carol stood by the road in front of her school waiting for Todd. He said he'd pick her up after school, that they had something important to do. She pulled the hood of her windbreaker over her head as it rained. A chilly breeze blew right through the thin cotton, and she paced to stay warm. The sunny, warm weather of the weekend had turned cloudy and cold with a drop of thirty degrees since Saturday. That is New England weather for you—totally unpredictable.

It seemed like forever before his familiar car drove up. "I'm freezing," she said, rubbing her hands. It wasn't much warmer inside his car. The heater didn't work very well.

"I'm sorry I'm late. My Dad decided to give me the 'have you found a job yet' lecture. But the good news is he gave me a contact for the summer. A friend of his needs someone to do typing, filing and light bookkeeping while his secretary is on maternity leave. I can type fast, and I'm good with math. I just don't want to have to answer the phones."

"Well, I wouldn't say that if you want the job." Carol unzipped her backpack and pulled out an apple left over from lunch.

"Hey, don't you think I know that?" Todd had never raised his voice to her before.

"I'm sorry, Todd. I'm sure you'll get the job. Maybe they won't even have you answer the phones."

They drove in silence a few minutes before Carol had the courage to speak again. Todd kept sniffling and rubbing his nose. He did that a lot because of his allergies. She nibbled on her apple. Her chewing seemed so loud in the quiet car. "Where are we going?" she finally asked.

"I told you the other day."

"When? I can't remember."

37

"The other night when we, umm, you know, we were looking at the book."

"I was pretty stoned. Guess I forgot."

"We're going to Planned Parenthood. Do you remember now?"

"Planned Parenthood?" Carol concentrated. She vaguely recalled something about it. "I didn't think you wanted to do that right away."

Todd gave her an irritated look and pressed hard on the accelerator. She jerked backwards a little. "Carol, don't you remember we discussed contraceptives. If we're going to start on your birthday, we need to get you ready now."

Carol looked down at the apple core clutched in her hand. She had laughed when he told her they would start having sex on her 14th birthday, thinking he wasn't serious. She thought about asking if they could turn around, but he was in such a bad mood.

"I told you how important it is that you don't get pregnant. The earth is already overpopulated. There are thousands of children who are starving to death right now because their parents don't have access to birth control. I think it's ridiculous to have children when we can't even feed the ones that already exist. We can't take any chances. It would totally ruin our lives if you got pregnant. And abortions are expensive."

Abortion! The word made her shiver. Her mom would never want her to have an abortion. The whole idea of having a baby made her want to vomit. She wasn't too happy about the way Todd was treating her, but how could she argue with him? It was better not to take chances.

"Todd, you're right. I'm glad you're thinking. I'm sorry I forgot."

They arrived in Brattleboro and headed downtown. He pulled into an old Victorian house and drove into a large parking lot in the rear. The door to the clinic was in the back. A small sign read *Planned Parenthood Federation of America* in dark blue letters. It was pretty tricky the way they made it look just like any other house from the front. She guessed they didn't want to make it too obvious. Many people, including her mother, didn't like Planned Parenthood because they performed abortions.

Todd got out and started for the building. When she didn't follow him immediately, he came back, opened the door, and said, "Let's go."

"I'm coming. I need to get rid of my apple core."

"They'll have a wastebasket in there."

"Should I bring a book to read?"

"Carol! I don't give a rip what you do. Let's go!"

Todd grabbed her hand, and she shuffled after him into the clinic. Inside, it looked like a doctor's office. There was a receptionist's desk with a long counter. New green, shag carpeting filled the large reception area and several metal chairs with blue bottoms were arranged around coffee tables laden with magazines and literature. The walls were a bright yellow and covered with posters of women and men hugging each other, of families holding the hand of a happy child, and a giggling infant with the words, "It's Better to be Chosen," above its head. There was a picture that displayed a woman at various stages in pregnancy labeled, "The Development of the Fetus." Several patients, mostly young women, were waiting. A girl huddled in a corner, clutching her boyfriend and looking frightened. She couldn't have been much older than her. Carol could tell she was pregnant because her stomach already stuck out. She shuddered at the thought of the girl getting an abortion. Her mother had told her abortion was killing a baby.

"Carol, pay attention. You need to fill out this paperwork." Todd shoved a clipboard into her hands.

"Oh, it's no big deal." The receptionist smiled. "You don't need to be nervous. Everything is kept completely confidential here."

"I'm fine," Carol lied, not wanting the receptionist to think she was only thirteen. "I'll bring this back in a minute."

The questionnaire was short and asked for very little information about her family. Most of the questions were about her sexual activity, when she had her last period, whether she experienced certain symptoms, and if she thought she was pregnant. At the bottom of the last page, a paragraph told her that, even as a minor, she had a right to contraceptives, and they would not contact her parents. It also told her they would do a physical exam, blood work, and a pregnancy test before dispensing contraceptives. She was relieved her mom would not know and signed the consent form.

"It'll be a few minutes," the receptionist said as Carol returned the clipboard.

Carol read a pamphlet about the various methods of birth control. It seemed the pill was the easiest and most effective one to use. Todd was engrossed in a magazine he brought with him. The pamphlet also explained that abortion was practically painless and took only a few minutes. It was not at all dangerous. Still, she was glad she didn't have to do that. She glanced at the corner to see if the pregnant girl was still there, but she had been called to see the doctor. The boyfriend waited with his elbows on his knees, staring at the wall.

Carol started reading the book she brought, *The Catcher in The Rye* by J.D. Salinger. Todd had given it to her. The main character of the book, Holden, reminded her of herself. The adults in his life just didn't understand how he felt. They were always judging him and telling him he wasn't good enough or old enough to make his own decisions. They couldn't see that on the inside, he really cared about people. Her mom felt the same way about her. She could just see the horror on her Mom's face if she saw her now.

She was just getting into the book when a nurse came out and called her name.

Carol stood up and looked at Todd. "I'll be waiting for you out here," he said. "Don't worry. It won't hurt." He patted her hand.

"My name is Nancy." The nurse led her through a door and down a hall with several more doors. She stopped in front of a scale at the end of the hall. "We need to take your weight and height."

Carol took off her shoes and stood on the scale. "One-twenty-five." Then she stood against the wall. "You're five feet eight inches. It must be nice to be so tall." Nancy was about five three and probably weighed twice as much as Carol. Still, she was cheerful enough.

"Now let's find you a room." Nancy led her down another hall with several doors. She opened the third one and motioned her inside. The room contained a sink, blood pressure machine, and the typical paraphernalia. The only thing different from her regular doctor's room was the examining table had two stirrups at the end of the table. *What are those for?*

"These contraptions are to hold your legs when the doctor examines you." Nancy touched the stirrups, as if reading her mind. "Don't worry, dear. Only female doctors do the examinations here. Now, get up on the table so I can take your blood pressure."

"What is the Doctor going to do?" Carol asked. Nancy wrapped her arm with the blood pressure cup and began to squeeze, not answering until she finished.

"The doctor will check you out to make sure there's nothing wrong with you. She'll do what's called a pap smear to screen for uterine cancer." Nancy opened a cupboard and pulled out a plastic cup with a lid. "Before the exam, you need to urinate into this cup. There is a pen in the bathroom. Put your first and last name on the top."

"Okay." Carol took the cup. Nancy opened another cupboard and took out a hospital gown.

"When you get back, I want you to take off all your clothes and put this on. Do you understand?"

"Yeah, sure. Where's the bathroom?"

After Carol took care of the cup of urine and put on the gown, she waited on the table, her legs dangling, for what seemed like an hour. She bit off two layers of skin around her thumbs and counted the little white dots on the ceiling tiles, all the time wondering exactly what the doctor would do to her. She hated the idea of meeting someone for the first time exposed except for a thin layer of cotton. At least she wasn't having her period.

After counting two-hundred-thirty dots, she heard a muffled scream. Goose-pumps formed on her skin, and she shivered. Was it that girl getting an abortion? The pamphlet said it wasn't supposed to hurt. She heard another scream. Suddenly, Carol wanted to get dressed and leave, but Todd would be furious with her if she did. *That poor girl. And she didn't even have her mom with her.*

A skinny, middle-aged woman finally emerged and announced, "I'm doctor Collins," and extended her hand. Though she wore a white lab coat, Carol noted the gauzy dress, bare legs, and leather sandals. Her attire was like the hippies who lived in the communes scattered around Vermont.

Doctor Collins was nice enough, but Carol still felt dirty and invaded by the exam. It was bad enough that Todd had seen her naked, but at least he hadn't touched her *there* yet. When it was over, the doctor left the room for a few minutes so she could get dressed. The doctor returned with a round, plastic case and a bag full of something.

"These are your birth control pills, Carol." Dr. Collins pulled a cylinder of pills out of the bag. "Your exam shows that you have not been sexually active yet and are not pregnant. You're smarter than most girls your age."

"Thank you."

"If you're careful to take your pills every day, you should never have to worry about an unwanted pregnancy. But you *must* not forget to take them, or they won't be effective." Dr. Collins went on to explain how she would start her period when the blue pills ran out. "Take the white pills for five days, then start a new pack. Any last questions?"

"No, I don't think so."

"Good. Here's a prescription you can use when these run out." She shook Carol's hand again and left.

Todd stood up when Carol returned to the waiting room. "Everything okay?" He smiled and put his arm around her.

"Yeah, I'm all set. Let's go." Carol was happy to get out of that place and back in the open air. She never wanted to go there again.

Chapter Eight

Running through the woods again, away from her attacker. To the edge of the cliff, she slipped over and down and landed on an examining table—naked. Had to find her clothes, protect herself. Two sinister, red eyes glowed above her, an ominous snicker echoed in the empty room. She reached for something, anything to cover herself, but clutched only air. Her feet were being pulled into the stirrups. No! Get away! *She thrashed and kicked.* I've got to wake up! *He kept laughing and pulling. She saw herself break free and roll off the table, then end up back in the same place. Her legs made it to the floor, moving away; then, smack, again on the cold slab looking into the burning eyes of evil.* Wake up, wake up!

Sun filtered through the shade, and she could hear her sisters talking and moving about in the house. It was the first day of summer vacation. That thought restored some of the energy sapped by the nightmare. It would be hot enough to wear her new bathing suite today. The smell of pancakes drifted into the room. She was hungry.

"Is there any batter left?" she asked her little sister Liz who sat at the dining room table eating a pancake loaded with butter and maple syrup.

"I don't know. Ask Jess." Liz kept eating.

Liz was the only person still in the house. She wore her favorite orange and yellow poncho, and it made Carol warm just looking at her. The rest of her sisters were outside in the back yard. She walked into the kitchen and found a bowl with a small amount of batter at the bottom. She added more mix and poured it on the griddle, forming one, large circle.

After breakfast, Carol took a quick shower, donned her bathing suit, and joined her sisters outside. She found a lawn chair, sat down next to Jessica and watched her younger sisters play. Their mom needed to buy Liz some new clothes. Her brown bellbottoms rode well above her ankles showing four inches of growth in the last year, all added to her long, skinny legs. Liz was setting up her household inside a tent made of blankets draped over a clothesline and secured to four chairs with clothespins. One corner contained utensils, food, and drink. The rest of her "house" held her blanket, pillow, and baby dolls. Carol thought Liz, at 12, was rather old for dolls, but that didn't stop her from attending to her imaginary "home" and "family."

Marie, age 10, and Jean, age 8, were playing on the swing set. Jean sang, "Thumbelina, Thumbelina, tiny little thing, Thumbelina dance, Thumbelina sing" while pumping up and down on the swing, her long, blond pony tail bobbing behind her. Carol's parents were certain Jean was going to be a boy, and she obediently took on the role, becoming the tomboy of the family, at least in appearance. The oversized, blue, checked shirt and dungarees contradicted the softness of her blond locks and her melodic voice.

Marie practiced her flips on the bar. It was a miracle that her glasses stayed on. Marie had fine, dark hair and an athletic body that never quit moving. Her mom said it was God's sense of humor that her most active child would wear glasses. Marie had broken more than a pair since she started wearing them at four. "Hey, did you see me do a double?" she shouted, turning to each of her sisters for a response.

"Good job!" Carol gave her sister a wave of approval. Marie spun around a couple more times to show off her new accomplishment.

Jessica smelled like baby oil and already had a little pink on her shoulders. Her hair took on a lighter hue in the sun, revealing blond highlights. She wished her hair was as light. Jessica was scanning a glamour magazine, marking the pages with new hairstyles. She had practiced a few of them on her family with fair results. Certainly, her talents were a step above their mother's. Her idea of a haircut was to put a bowl on their heads and cut around the edges.

"So, Carol, where's Todd today? You've spent almost every day with him since he came home from college."

"He started a job." Carol rubbed baby oil on herself, then viewed the open meadow behind their house. Deciduous woods marked the outer property line of five acres of field where the grass already measured at least a foot high. Patches of white daisies stood out against the green. To the right, the neighbor's cleared lot expanded at a gentle slope to the top of a great sliding hill. To the left, a row of white birch trees fenced the other neighbor's house. Carol had spent many hours in their yard climbing the huge maple trees, picking apples, running through the field, and exploring the woods. Her Mom told her they had been fortunate to find their little house, which stood behind their landlord's newer, larger home. Most of the families with their income had to live in subsidized housing, which had a reputation as the "ghetto" of the town.

"Hey, Jess, do you remember when we went on our hike through the woods last summer? Remember how we ended up in this cow field?"

"Yeah" Jess chuckled. "We got scared when this cow started coming up to us. You dropped your lunch when you ran. But it worked great, cause the cow stopped to sniff it."

"That was fun. We wondered if we'd ever find our way back."

"Well, I'm the one that found the way back. You've always been bad with directions. If we'd listened to you, we'd still be lost."

"Shut up." Carol threw the bottle of baby oil at Jess, but it missed her. Jess threw a towel back at her, and they horsed around for a while.

"Hey, Carol, do you want to go on a hike today? It's so nice out."

She thought for a minute. "I don't know. I feel kind of lazy right now and want to work on my tan."

"Say, did Todd buy you that bathing suit?"

"Yeah, do you like it?"

"I do, but I doubt Mom will."

"Well, she'll get used to it."

Carol relaxed and soaked up the warm rays. A few moments later she felt a soft touch on her shoulder.

"Carol, want to come see the place I made?" It was Liz.

Carol yawned and stretched. "In a minute."

"I brought out some chocolate chip cookies Jessica made yesterday."

Now that sounded good. Carol slid out of the chair and strolled over to Liz's little shelter. Her dolls were sitting in little chairs next to a miniature table ready for a tea-party. Liz had even placed a cup of daisies and violets on the table. "This is nice." She sat down on the grass floor. "Where are the cookies?"

Later that day, after lunch, some of the neighbor kids came by for a visit. Josh was one of them, and he brought a friend visiting from Maryland, a huge guy who reminded her of Hoss from the Ponderosa. They weren't allowed to have boys over when their mom wasn't home, but the younger girls knew better than to tattle.

The whole gang of kids played blind man's bluff. When Josh was *it*, he went right to Carol. She did her best not to give herself away, but he knew it was her, even though he pretended not to. He spent a long time touching her face. "You know who I am," she said, shoving him to the ground.

Carol couldn't help but notice how tan Josh already was, and how he seemed to have grown taller. She had been taller than him at the beginning of school, but now he was at least an inch higher than her. His voice had also changed, and he had a few dark hairs on his chin. Her eyes met his for a second, but she turned away. *I shouldn't be thinking about him.*

"Hey, Josh, did you know Carol has a boyfriend." Jessica stood between her and the boys, her hands on her hips.

Josh looked at her. Was he frowning or did she just imagine it? "No, I didn't know that. So, who's the guy?"

"Oh, you don't know him. He's older."

"Is he in high school? My sister probably knows him."

"I doubt it." Carol grabbed a bouncing ball and started to kick it around the grass. She wished Jessica hadn't told Josh about Todd.

"Carol's boyfriend's in college." Jessica just couldn't keep her mouth shut. If they had been alone, she would have slugged her one.

"Oh really?" Josh said. "College? Isn't he a bit old for you, Carol? I can't believe your mom would let you go out with someone that old."

"Oh, just shut up. What do you know anyway?" Carol turned away from them and walked down to the swing set. She noticed her sister was flirting with Josh's friend.

A few moments later, she felt a cold shock. Josh had the water hose and was squirting her.

"Aaaah! You're going to get it now!" Carol ran into the house and locked the door. She collected her weapons: water pistol, balloons, and pitchers. She filled them with water, snuck into the basement and went outside through the cellar door. Jess didn't see her coming, and she blasted her with a water balloon. "That's for having the biggest mouth in the world!"

Before the water fight was over, everyone was soaked. But Carol didn't care. The temperature had climbed to the high eighties, and it was refreshing to dry off in the sun.

After the boys left, she and Jess decided to surprise their mom by making dinner. Margaret had taken out hamburgers and hot dogs, so they went to their landlord, Walter, and asked if he could help them start a charcoal fire in the stone fireplace in the backyard. They cleaned off the picnic table and brought out a card table for supplies. Liz made a salad, and Marie and Jean set the table with the red-checkered tablecloth they always used with picnics. Carol and Jessica made the hamburgers and hotdogs, and cut up watermelon. The smell of meat cooking on a charcoal fire made Carol's stomach rumble.

Carol went inside to slice some cheese for the burgers. She heard the phone ring. It was Todd.

"Hey, babe, did you have a good day?"

"Yeah, I did. Did you?"

"It was okay. I do have to answer the phones. I don't like it, but it pays."

"Jess and me are making dinner for my mom. We're having a cookout with hamburgers and hotdogs. Do you want to come over?"

"Oh. I thought we could do something together."

"I'm sorry. If you come over, maybe we can go somewhere after dinner."

"I'd probably ruin the evening for your mom. I think it would be better to see you after dinner. Why don't you give me a call when you're done."

"Okay. I'll call you later, then."

"Wait a minute. Did you remember to take your pill?"

"Oops. I forgot."

"Carol, how many times do I have to tell you how important it is to take your pill every day? I can't believe you forgot again. This is the second time."

"I'm really sorry, Todd. I'll go take it right now."

"Good. As soon as we hang up the phone, okay? Call me later. Bye."

"Bye."

Carol ran to her room, took the pills out of her purse, pushed one out of the foil backing, and ran back to the kitchen for a glass of water. She gulped it down just as her mom pulled into the driveway.

***

The barbeque went well. Carol's mom seemed happier than she had in months. Carol ate and ate until she could hardly move, then found a little more room for watermelon. She took a piece and swung on the swing set with Liz. They had a contest to see who could spit their seeds the farthest. Soon, Marie, Jean, and even Jess joined the contest. Before long, they were spitting seeds at each other, but not in anger. It was just plain fun.

When dusk arrived, Carol's mom brought out marshmallows, graham crackers, and chocolate so they could make s'mores. She sat down next to Carol.

"Carol, I have a surprise for you. I'm taking the day off on your birthday. We can spend it at Lake Sunapee. How does that sound to you?"

"Oh Mom, that sound's great!" She loved Lake Sunapee, swimming after baking in the sun, then getting hot again, then swimming again.

"I have another surprise. Your Dad called me at work today. He wants you and your sisters to come down for the weekend before your birthday. He wants to take you to the amusement park in Holyoke."

"Are you kidding! Really!" Carol was so excited she flipped her stick with the marshmallow and it landed next to her sister, Jean. She couldn't believe her good luck. It would be the best birthday ever—first a day at the amusement park, then another day at the lake.

"Mom, I'm so happy!" she hugged her, then pulled back like she'd made a mistake.

"Hey, let's all sleep outside tonight." Liz stood up and went to her mom. "What do you say, Mom. Can we?"

"I don't see why not. It's not supposed to rain. And you don't have school tomorrow."

Like a stampede, Carol and her sisters put down their sticks and rushed into the house to find their air mattresses and sleeping bags. It would be warm enough to sleep without a tent. "I can sleep in my little house," Liz said.

Just as Carol found her sleeping bag in the closet, she heard the phone ring. Then she remembered she forgot to call Todd.

"Carol, it's for you." She heard Jess yell from the kitchen. She dropped her bag and sprinted to the phone.

"Todd, I'm so sorry I forgot to call you back. It's just my mom brought out the marshmallows and…"

"Hey, it's okay. I'll come over now. Meet me out front."

"All right. Wait, I have something to tell you. I get to go to Holyoke and ride on the roller coaster the weekend before my birthday. Then, on my birthday, mom is taking us to Lake Sunapee. Can you believe it?"

"What? You're going to be gone for two days? What about me? What about all our plans for your birthday?"

It felt like someone had just popped her prize balloon. She had totally forgotten about their plans.

"Maybe you can come with me. I can ask."

"We'll talk about it when I get there. I'll see you in a few minutes." He hung up.

Later that night, as Carol zipped up her sleeping bag and gazed at the star-filled sky, sadness stole the pleasure of the day. She had her first fight with

Todd, and was glad her sisters were all asleep so they wouldn't hear her crying. His angry words swam around in her head like hungry piranhas. "How could you be so selfish, Carol? I spent hours and lots of money planning your birthday. Can't you get out of it?...I guess you don't really love me like you say you do." Of course she loved him! She tried to talk him into coming with her family, but he said he wanted to be alone with her, that he'd go to the lake if it were just the two of them. Why couldn't he just learn to hang around with her family? Maybe then her mom would learn to like him. But no, Todd was stubborn. She felt like he was making her choose. By the end of the night, she had calmed him down by promising to go out with him after they had cake and ice cream.

Still, she wondered about their relationship. It seemed all Todd, Todd, Todd. When did he care about what she wanted? She loved him, really she did. But sometimes he could be so unreasonable.

"Carol." She thought she heard someone say her name. "Carol." She heard it again. Careful not to wake her sisters, she slipped out of her bag and tiptoed toward the front. A figure appeared out of the darkness, startling her.

"Carol. Don't be afraid. It's me, Todd." He pulled her to him in a bear hug. "I had to come by and apologize for my behavior."

"Gee, Todd, you scared me!" Carol whispered. "How did you get here? I didn't hear your car."

"I parked down the road and walked. Carol, I love you. I'm so sorry."

"It's okay, Todd. I love you, too."

Before long, they were kissing. He did care about her, enough to come back and make it right. Later, Todd agreed to join them for dinner on her birthday. They were making progress. When Carol returned to her sleeping bag, the stars looked so beautiful. She'd never seen so many. This time, she fell asleep thinking about Todd.

Chapter Nine

Todd threw himself on the bed and hugged his pillow, smug in his cleverness. The situation had become unstable earlier, but he turned it around. Everything was fine with Carol now. They would still have their special night together, just as he planned. Sure, he'd have to endure her crazy family and put up with her ultra-conservative mom for a few hours, but it would be worth it. So long as he had Carol to himself later.

It could actually be a good thing to spend time with Carol's mother. Perhaps she would learn to trust him more. He would be extra nice to her, flatter her, amaze her with his intellectual abilities. He would find some time to talk to her and give a speech about how he knew Carol was younger, how he would be careful not to push her. He'd have to make sure to keep his hands off Carol while her mom was around. He could do it.

Todd pulled out his notebook from under the bed and listed ideas on how he could impress Carol's mom. Nothing was going to keep them from their night of magic. He'd been patient to wait these months. His mind wandered back to Carol.

He turned back a few pages in the notebook and re-read his notes about Carol's birthday. He crossed out some of the activities and reorganized them to fit the new schedule. The cabin would be available after three, so he could go there early and arrange everything: champagne and hors d'oeuvres, a little marijuana, his stereo. She would wear the new sundress he bought her and the black panties and bra. The under wire in the bra would lift up her breasts and make them stick out. He could picture himself taking off her dress and seeing her with them on. It would be perfect.

Todd dropped the notebook on the floor and crawled under the covers. He closed his eyes and let the fantasy continue: Carol's baby face and green eyes, the soft curve of her cheek. He ran his finger down her neck, then down...

***

"Let's go on the roller coaster again!" Liz motioned to Carol and Jess to get in line. Carol's father, Richard, had dropped them off at 1:00 and wouldn't be back until 11:00 PM when the park closed. They had spent the entire day going on one ride after another, since they had a pass that allowed them to go on all the rides as much as they wanted.

"Okay, but I still want to go on the Tilt-A-Wheel and the Scrambler again," Carol told her sisters.

"And I want to go on the Ferris Wheel and the Octopus," said Jess.

"And the Bumper Cars, too" Liz added. "I've got to get you back for last time."

"Hey, look at those boys smile at us. I think they're following us." Jess whispered to Carol. "What hunks."

"That's cuz they're Puerto Ricans. You like their dark skin." Carol jabbed Jessica. Both girls had noticed guys looking at them all day. Jessica wore a lime-green halter top and cut-offs that cut high. Carol had put on her new sundress.

"All you two think about are boys, boys, boys." Liz shook her head. She wore a pair of hand-me-down, yellow shorts that were too big for her and a red t-shirt.

"You just wait a couple of years." Jessica poked her in the arm.

"Wait, they're coming over here," said Liz. "Now look what you've done."

Jessica ran her fingers through her hair and straightened out her shirt, then pretended to not notice the boys.

"Well, hello." Two dark, young men came up to them. They wore shorts and t-shirts that showed off their muscles. They also had big, silver crosses around their necks and leather bracelets around their wrists. "You want to ride with us?"

"Thanks, but our Dad's going to be here soon." Liz folded her arms and eyed them suspiciously.

The men ignored Liz and kept looking at Jess and Carol. Jess gave them an encouraging smile, while Carol glanced at Liz. The taller one smiled and said, "We saw you chicks on the Ferris Wheel. You kind of stuck out, if ya know what I mean?"

"Thanks, but my sister's right. We need to go meet our Dad," said Carol, turning toward Liz.

"It was awfully nice for you to offer." Jess giggled and batted her eyes.

The men lingered for a moment, then shrugged. "Well, let us know if you change your mind. We could have a lot of fun, if ya know what I mean," said the shorter one, winking at Jess.

Carol sighed, relieved, as they walked away. "Jess, you know better than to flirt with those guys. You have no idea what kind of guys they are. Thanks, Liz, for being so level headed."

"Someone's got to protect you crazy teenagers. Especially *her*." She gave her sister an expression of disgust.

"Hey, look, it's our turn next." Jessica nudged Liz.

The three of them squeezed into the seat together. Carol's heart beat with anxiety as they climbed up, up, the steep hill. She always panicked on the first incline. When they reached the top, the car plunged down and picked up speed. Her stomach fluttered, excitement overtook fear, and she lifted her hands and screamed. By the next hill, she didn't want it to ever stop.

Next, they rode the Bumper Cars. Just like she promised, Liz smashed her good in the rear. She tried to catch up to her and get her back, but ended up hitting an old man instead and spun around backwards. He laughed, then smacked her back. When she finally moved again, she couldn't reach Liz, but plowed right into Jessica from the side. Jessica didn't even see her coming. Her shocked expression was hilarious, and Carol couldn't stop laughing. Until Liz smacked her again. "You little Brat." She struggled to turn her car around, but the power stopped.

"We're doing this again." Carol pulled Liz back in line. "I'm going to get you if it takes all night."

It took all night. Carol, Jess, and Liz spent the rest of their time on the Bumper Cars, and Carol never did get Liz back. "Hey, its 10:45," said Jess. "We'd better head for the entrance."

Later that night in bed, Carol imagined herself going round and round on the Ferris Wheel, her hair flowing in the warm, night breeze. She tried to picture Todd with her, but instead her mystery man materialized in the seat. She deliberately changed it to Todd, remembering their last kiss. Maybe they could go to the amusement park together later in the summer.

The next day was a bit of a let down. When Carol got up to go to the bathroom in morning, two cockroaches were in the sink. She hoped that they hadn't been crawling on her during the night. Her Dad woke them up early. It was a two-hour drive back to Deerfield. Of course, her Dad was up at five every morning that she could remember.

When she finished her shower, her Dad was waiting in the little dining nook. "Happy Birthday, Carol." He gave her a quick hug and kiss on the cheek. His thick, black beard tickled her.

"Thanks Dad." Carol looked around. "Where's Marie and Jean?"

"They went with Denise to the store."

"Oh. What's for breakfast? Something smells yummy."

"Denise made French toast. She left some in the oven."

"Yum." Carol walked over to the oven and helped herself. She didn't care for her Dad's girlfriend, but Denise did make great French toast. It was sweet and had plenty of cinnamon.

"So, Carol, I was thinking. How would you like to stay with us a few weeks this summer?" Her Dad was sitting at the table with his cup of coffee, probably the second or third of the day.

"What?" She wondered why her Dad was asking this. No one had stayed with him more than a weekend since her mom came and took her sisters away. "Are you talking about just me, or me and some of the other kids?"

"Just you, unless one of your sisters wants to join you." He tapped his fingers on the table.

Carol looked at her plate and cut her bread into small pieces. She didn't know what to say. Was her Dad trying to be nice, or was this a scheme of her mother's to get her away from Todd? "Why do you suddenly want me to stay with you?" she said, concentrating on her food, not wanting him to see her hesitation.

"Well, you're growing up so quickly. I just thought it'd be nice to spend some time together." She watched her dad rise out of his chair, go over to his desk and take something down from the shelf. "Here. It's your birthday present."

Carol looked up at him as he handed her the gift. He had a strange expression, like both guilt and concern. She dropped her eyes and unwrapped the gift. Inside a shoe box were two card games called Rook and Phase 10, and one of those Rubik cubes no one could figure out. Her friend brought one to school one day, and not one person solved the puzzle. "Thanks Dad," she said, giving him a hug.

"So, what do you think about spending some time with your old man? You could help Denise with her Head Start program. Maybe earn some extra spending money tearing apart old buildings."

"Sounds like great fun, Dad," Carol said. She had no desire to spend time with Denise or tear down buildings. Last summer, she came for a weekend, and they spent the entire time with crowbars and hammers breaking up old, rotted sheet rock and loosening bricks in her Dad's five story slum buildings. He bought them to fix them up and help the poor people find housing, but the city condemned them and demanded they be torn down. Her Dad told them to be careful to save the bricks because they were worth money. No, working in smelly, dusty, hot, old slums was not her idea of a fun summer vacation.

Her Dad was playing with her Rubik cube while he waited for Carol's answer.

"Whose idea was it for me to spend some time here? Yours or Mom's?"

"Well, both."

"What do you mean?"

"Well…"His cough gave him away. He was nervous, and her Mom had probably told him about Todd. She may as well get it over with.

"Did Mom tell you I had a boyfriend? Is that why you want me to come?"

"Yes she did. But that's not why I want you to visit us. It'll be nice to spend some time with you." Her Dad was lying.

"Okay, Dad, tell me straight. Did Mom call you and ask you to take me in this summer to get me away from Todd?"

"No. It didn't happen like that. I called about your birthday, and she told me about him. That's true. But I'm the one that offered to take you for a few weeks."

"Oh, so you are trying to get me away from him." Carol took her plate to the sink and started to scrub it with vigor.

"Not exactly, Carol. But I have to agree with your mother. This kid is a lot older than you. I think you should take it more slowly, that's all."

"Well, like you should talk. You're not exactly the best role model." She regretted these words as soon as they were out. She stole a glance to see his expression. He didn't say anything, but kept working on the cube.

"I'm sorry Dad. That was uncalled for."

"It sure was, young lady. Let's just stick to you." His voice had risen an octave, and Carol shuddered to think what might happen next. Her dad had a nasty temper. Though he'd never done it to Carol, he had whipped Maurine with a belt more than once.

"Dad, I'm really sorry. Could you let me think about it for a while? Can I let you know later?" She'd already made up her mind not to visit, but she figured now wasn't the best time to tell him.

"Fine, Carol. Let me know when you decide." He pushed out his chair and threw her cube onto the table. "You'd better start packing. We need to get out of here soon." He opened the door, walked outside, and slammed the door behind him.

Relieved, Carol retrieved her cube and turned it over. She couldn't believe it. All the colored squares were perfectly lined up. He had solved the puzzle while arguing with her.

Chapter Ten

A perfect day for a birthday! Carol couldn't have asked for better weather. The early afternoon sun soaked into her skin, adding to her tan. Today, she smelled like coconut instead of baby oil and was glad. It made her think of a tropical island in the Caribbean, so inviting, especially the clear water and white sand. She lifted the elastic band of her bathing suit to check her color. Not as brown as the picture on the Coppertone bottle, but getting darker. In a few minutes, she would be hot enough to go for another swim.

She closed her eyes and listened to the sounds: giggles, happy squeals, swishing sand, splashing water. She loved the noise of people on the beach. Having her birthday in the summer made her feel special because her family always had fun. Her eighth birthday had been her favorite. They spent a week at Hampton Beach, New Hampshire in a cabin. Her Mom and Dad got along then. She had her cake, ice cream and presents in the cabin and received the big, punching ball she wanted and new sunglasses. She lost the sunglasses in the sand the first day, but it didn't matter. They strolled the boardwalk and rode the rides at the amusement park.

The next morning, Maurine woke her up at 5:00 AM to see the low tide. They snuck out of the house while everyone else slept and explored a deserted shoreline that only the evening before had been crowded with tourists. She watched the sun rise and slip above that evasive line that stretched into nothingness, a gigantic fiery ball reflected on the water, breaking apart as it turned into powerful waves that crashed into land, angry with the resistance the sand and rocks made in their journey. She sat on one of these defiant rocks, watched the tide turn, and dared the waves to reach out their commanding tentacles and draw her into the swirling surf. With a mixture of fear and anticipation, she predicted how close each foaming finger would come to her toes. Eventually, the superior sea won the battle. She retreated to search for treasures before the throng returned and found many whole snail and clamshells and an unbroken starfish. The scent of the salt air, the squawks of seagulls fighting over scraps, the never ending motion of the tireless sea—it was heaven. A dream came alive in her young heart that day to live in a cottage by the sea. She would have to share this dream with Todd.

Her Mom tapped her on the arm and brought her out of her reverie. "What are you daydreaming about?" She sat on a lawn chair next to her, reading a book.

"Remember the trip to Hampton Beach on my eighth birthday? I love the ocean."

"I know you do. We had a great time there. I don't think I can remember a time when you were as happy as you were that year." Her mother paused a moment, looking out onto the lake. Then she chuckled.

"You also loved to get lost at the beach. You were always the one who'd wander off."

"Remember when you guys forgot me?" Carol sat up. "We were going to the beach, and you left me behind. I was so scared."

"I'm sorry about that, Hon. Your Dad was in a foul mood that morning and kept rushing me. We realized we left you behind only five minutes down the road."

"It seemed like hours to me."

"I'm sure it did. You were only four."

"Mom, Carol, come in the water!" Marie ran up to them, sand stuck to her legs, water dripping off her hair.

"Marie, stop getting me wet." Carol shooed her away. "Go stand by Mom."

"Come on, Carol. We're at the beach to swim. Jessica's out on the dock talking to some boy."

"Give me five more minutes. I want to be nice and hot before I go in."

"I'll go in with you, Marie," her Mom said, rising from her chair. She wore a one piece bathing suit with red and white flowers that covered part of her thighs. You could see a few stretch marks, but her Mom didn't look nearly as heavy as most women her age.

Carol watched her mother and Marie head for the water, then looked further out to the dock. Jessica sat hugging her legs, talking to a teenager with sandy hair. *I think I'll go check this out.* She waded slowly into the water, allowing herself to adjust to the cold. The hardest part was when it reached her belly button. When the water made it over her stomach, she dove in and swam further out on lake. She practiced her forward flips and backward flips, enjoying the dizzy feeling and the thrill of knowing she was in deep water. Then she headed for the dock to dive off the diving board.

Carol talked to Jessica and the boy for a few minutes, but they ignored her. She practiced her diving, concentrating on jumping as high off the board as possible and keeping her legs together. "Not bad," said the boy with Jessica. I guess she was good enough to get his attention.

Carol talked to Jessica and the boy for a while, finding out his name was Brad. Then she realized she was hungry. "Race you to the shore," she challenged Jess.

"I'll beat you," said Jess.

"I'll beat you both," said Brad.

"Okay, we'll see." The three of them dove off the dock and raced to the shore. Jessica came in first, Brad second, and she was last. Jessica had always been the best swimmer in the family.

When they arrived at their spot, Brad said he'd see them after lunch and left to find his family. Everyone else had already eaten. Carol grabbed two ham and cheese sandwiches, potato chips, watermelon, and can of orange soda. She sat next to her mom, who was the only one with a lawn chair.

"Do you want to borrow my chair while I help Marie and Jean with their sandcastle?"

"Sure. Thanks, Mom." Her Mom was being so nice to her today.

"It's not fair that you get the lawn chair. I'm the oldest here." Jess complained. "I'm getting sand in my sandwich and a hornet is trying to get into my soda."

"I can't help it if you were born in December." Carol bit into one of her sandwiches, happy that the sand didn't make it to her chair. A wasp did find her soda, however.

"It would be perfect out here if it weren't for the wasps."

"You should have seen this huge one in the dressing room. Poor Jean held onto Mom's leg and wailed. You could probably hear her outside." Jessica said this while another wasp flew around her head.

"Let's just eat quickly and get back to swimming," said Carol, cramming her sandwich into her mouth.

"Yeah. I want to spend more time with Brad"

Carol finished one sandwich and her chips, then put the watermelon and the second sandwich back. Then she and Jess threw their soda cans in the trash so the wasps would leave them alone.

When they left for home around 4:00 PM, Carol could tell her shoulders were sun burnt. She was glad her mom gave her the front seat because it was her birthday. She didn't have to put up with her sisters. Marie was upset because she wanted to finish her sand castle, and Jean sobbed and whined about her sunburn. Jessica bored Liz with details about her encounter with Brad and how they exchanged phone numbers.

"Mom, I told Todd we would be home by 5:00. Are we going to make it?"

"We should be okay. I have to make one stop at the grocery store, but it should only take us 45 minutes to get back to town."

"I hope so. I don't want him to be sitting around waiting for us. He's kind of nervous about it."

"Oh, why's that?" Her mom combed her fingers through her curly hair.

"Well, he's never really talked to you much. He doesn't think you like him."

"It's not a matter of not liking him, Carol. I don't even know the man. He hasn't made much effort to get to know me."

"I'm sorry, Mom. You're always gone when he shows up." Carol scratched her shoulder and it started to throb.

Margaret started to say something, then closed her mouth. After a minute, she said, "Let's not spoil your birthday over this. I will do my best to get to know Todd. I just hope you realize that it's not easy for me to see my little girl with someone his age."

Carol wanted to argue with her mom, to tell her that she was old enough to be with Todd, to tell her he was a lot better than the guys she brought home, but she also didn't want to ruin the day. "Todd is very respectful, Mom. You'll learn to like him." Carol yawned.

"I think I'll take a nap now, if you don't mind."

"Go ahead."

***

They arrived home after 5:00, but Todd wasn't there yet. Carol used the "it's my birthday" excuse to use the bathroom first. She showered and put on the new undergarments and sundress Todd had given her. She finished with earrings and make-up in her bedroom. She stood back and examined her reflection in the mirror. Her sun-darkened face glowed, and she knew she looked great. She listened for Todd's voice in the living room, but didn't hear him.

Her suspicions were confirmed when she walked out to the dining room. "Mom, have you heard from Todd? Did he call?"

59

"No, dear, I haven't." Her mom had changed into dungaree shorts and a sleeveless, white blouse that accentuated her tan. She was making a salad to go along with the chicken that had been cooking all day in the crock-pot. Potatoes were boiling on the stove. Jessica was shucking corn. They were having her favorite meal: chicken, mashed potatoes, and corn on the cob.

"Where's my cake?" she said, looking on the counter.

"It's in the frig so it won't melt." Her mom stopped cutting vegetables and stood in front of the refrigerator. "But you're not going to see it until after dinner."

"Oh, come on, Mom. Just let me peak."

"No. You can help your sisters set the table if you want. Or just go watch TV."

"Is it chocolate with chocolate frosting?"

"What do you think?"

Carol gave up and went into the living room to look for her pile of presents. Liz was just brining them out of Margaret's room and setting them on the coffee table. One of the gifts was a big box with a bright blue ribbon on top. She went over to touch them.

"Carol, get away from here," said Liz. "You have to wait until later to guess what they are."

"Gosh, what can I do then?" She went outside to wait for Todd. She paced back and forth, watching each car that drove down the street. *Why is he late?*

"Carol, dinner's ready!" Jean shouted through the window. She ran inside, hungry.

"Mom, did Todd call? Should we wait for him before eating?"

"No, he didn't call." Margaret placed a steaming, roasted chicken on the table.

"I suppose we can save him some food," said Carol, sitting at the head of the table, the place of honor for the birthday girl.

Noisy, excited voices, clanking of plates and dishes being passed around filled the room, followed by relative quiet as seven females enjoyed their ample meal. Carol had a leg and part of a thigh, two helpings of mashed potatoes with gravy, two cobs of corn, and some salad. By the end of the meal, there was not enough chicken left to even make soup. Then she realized Todd still hadn't arrived.

"Mom, do you think I should call and find out why Todd's so late?"

"It's up to you." Her mom was in the kitchen preparing the birthday cake. "Do you want to wait for him before starting your cake?"

"Maybe a few minutes. I'm full."

"I want cake now," said Marie.

"Me, too," Jean echoed.

"It's Carol's birthday. You girls can wait a few minutes. Why don't you go out and play."

"But Mom—"

"Don't 'but Mom' me. Now get."

"Wait, I think I hear Todd's car pulling up." Carol went to the window. "Yeah, it's him all right." Carol's stomach suddenly hurt as she went to the door to meet Todd.

"Hi, Carol." Todd gave her a nervous smile and a quick look over.

"Hi, come on in." She turned to see her mom standing behind her.

"Please to meet you, Todd." Margaret extended her hand.

"It's a pleasure to meet you, Mrs. Weiderman." Todd took her hand and shook it, meeting her eyes for a moment, then he looked beyond her to the rest of the family. "I'm sorry I'm so late. It looks like I missed dinner."

"That's okay," Carol interjected, giving Todd a private look that said, *you'd better explain yourself later.*

"You're just in time for cake," said Margaret. "Why don't you sit down, and I'll bring it out. Jess, go get a folding chair from the basement."

Carol had Todd sit next to her at the table. Jessica left to find a folding chair and called Jean and Marie in from outside. Liz just examined Todd, saying nothing. Carol knew Liz felt uncomfortable around him.

"How old are you again?" Todd asked Liz. He reached under the table and touched Carol's knee.

"Twelve. How old are you again, Todd?" Liz knew how old Todd was, and Carol frowned at her.

"I'm twenty."

"Birthday cake's ready." Mom carried the cake to the table. Fourteen candles covered most of the eight inch, round, chocolate cake. "Everyone come sing happy birthday to Carol."

The atmosphere remained a bit tense as the family ate. Carol did her best to enjoy her cake with two heaping scoops of vanilla ice cream. Mom asked Todd about his family, how many siblings he had, etcetera. Then she asked him about college. He explained how he was majoring in Political Science and some day hoped to be a university professor. Then he shared how he had done extensive research on many subjects.

"I'm also a feminist," Todd said, eating his last bite of cake.

"Oh. My ex-husband Richard also claims to be a feminist. I can't say that I support the movement." Mom started to clear the table.

"I'm surprised you'd say that, being a single mother and all. The ERA would guarantee that employers pay you an equal wage. It should help you raise your family."

"What's the ERA?" Carol asked.

"It stands for the Equal Rights Amendment." Todd gave her a look that said *I can't believe you don't know this.* "It was first introduced into congress in 1923, right after women gained the right to vote, but wasn't approved by the U.S. Senate for state acceptance until March 1972. Thirty states have already ratified the proposed amendment. We need three-fourths of the states to ratify before it becomes an amendment. I'm sure we'll see this anytime now."

"Richard worked with the Liberty Union Party to push passage in Vermont. But I don't think it will help women and families. Instead, it's breaking them apart."

"How can you say that?" Todd sat up straight and looped his hair behind his ear. "Don't you think you deserve equal pay for equal work?"

"That part I agree with." Mom picked cake crumbs off the table onto a napkin. "What I don't agree with is that a woman should be treated like a man and expected to work outside the home to support herself and her children. Kids need their moms at home."

"But you're a single mom out in the workforce. You need to be treated as equally as a man."

"If my husband wasn't so concerned about changing the world, I would still be at home raising my children like I always planned to. Because my husband treats me like a man, he hasn't paid one dime of child support. And he left me to fool around with one of your feminists who have taken on all the negative aspects of manhood and think they can cohabit with anyone they feel like, even if it breaks up families. No, I'm sorry Todd, but I still have old fashioned values." Her mom finished picking up the table with more energy than normal. Todd squeezed her knee extra hard.

"Ouch!" Carol pushed his hand away. Neither Todd nor her mom heard her, but kept on arguing.

"Mrs. Weiderman, I don't think you understand the full magnitude of what you are saying. You are mixing up your husband's actions with the truth of the amendment. Giving women the opportunities they've never had before, giving them access to a man's world, will only strengthen women and their families. They won't be stuck in the traditional role of wife and mother, where they are exploited."

"I wasn't exploited until my husband became a feminist. Besides, I enjoyed being a wife and mother more than I enjoy working full-time and still having to be a full-time mother on top of it."

"Todd, don't you think we should get going. It's getting late." Carol stood up and touched Todd on the shoulder.

"Mrs. Weiderman, have you even read the amendment? Do you know what it says?"

"I've read it a few years ago when Richard was still here. I remember enough."

"Mom, when are we going to give Carol her presents?" Liz interrupted. Carol could have kissed her.

"That's right." Mom sighed with relief and followed Liz into the living room to bring back the presents.

The next few minutes went much better. Carol received a cute lavender top from Jessica, a bead set from Liz, pink earrings from Marie, and barrettes from Jean. Then her mom brought the huge box. She tore the bright, balloon-covered paper and opened the box. She pulled out several wads of newspaper before finding a black case at the bottom.

"Oh my Gosh! It's a flute! A new flute! Mom, I can't believe you bought me my own flute!"

Carol opened the black case and gently picked up each shiny, flawless, silver piece. She put the flute together and played it. The sound was greatly superior to her old, rented one.

"Thank you so much, Mom." Carol went to her mom and gave her a big hug. "I still can't believe you did this. Where did you find the money?"

"Oh, I have my ways." Her mother smiled, kissing her on the cheek. "Why don't you get out your music and play us a tune?"

"Carol, we really need to get going." Todd stood up, looked at his watch and pushed his chair under the table. "The movie starts at seven."

"What time is it now?" Carol wanted to stay and show Todd how well she could play.

"It's 6:45. We'll barely make it."

"I'm sorry, Mom. We need to go." Carol put her new flute back in its case and grabbed her purse and a sweater.

"When will you be home?"

Carol turned to Todd for an answer.

"If you don't mind, Mrs. Weiderman, I'd like to take Carol to the outdoor movies and the last feature doesn't end until 1:00. We may not be home until after 2:00."

Carol hoped her mom didn't pick up on the inconsistency. The outdoor movies didn't start until dusk, which was after 9:00.

"I guess." Her mom had turned away and went to the kitchen sink.

"Well, it was nice meeting you. Thank you for the cake." Todd took Carol's hand and headed for the door.

"You, too." He mom didn't even turn around.

Carol unlatched her hand and ran over and hugged her mom's back. "Bye Mom. Thanks again for a great birthday."

"Bye Dear." Her mom gave her a quick glance. Carol thought she saw tears in her eyes. She rushed to Todd and they left.

***

Margaret turned from the sink, walked to the window and watched her daughter get into Todd's car. After hesitating a minute, she followed them outside, but the car had already pulled into the road. She should have stopped them.

I can't stand that man! He was in many ways a carbon copy of Richard—so full of himself, smarter than anyone else. His opinion was God's. The little geek had no idea what life was all about. He looked down from his ivory tower and told her what she needed to do to raise her family. She'd like to see him try for a day. *Oh dear God, that's what he's doing with my Carol—he's raising her to be what he wants!*

She suddenly had an urge to smoke a cigarette and thought about checking to see if Mac had left any around. She hadn't smoked in eight years. Why had she let that creep take off with her little girl? The day had gone so well. Carol had even let her kiss her cheek. She didn't want to spoil her birthday, and she had held her tongue many times just to make the day special for her. But now she knew she had made a terrible mistake to let her daughter be anywhere near him. She slumped down onto the doorstep as her stomach churned, burping up the taste of cake and stomach acid.

Why had she let that pimply faced kid get away with a bold-face lie? They weren't going to a movie at 7:00. He just wanted to get out of there. What was he really up to? Two o'clock in the morning? Why did she not insist on an earlier time?

Margaret clenched her fists. Todd was up to no-good. She knew this deep in her soul. He was a monster out to consume her baby. She pictured herself getting into her car, going out to find them, and bringing Carol home. This is what she needed to do; she knew it. But she just sat there on the steps doing nothing. Death had swirled its way into their home, captured her daughter in its trap, and now wrapped itself around her broken heart, paralyzing her in its grip. She was a fly caught it its web. She put her face in her hands and let the sorrow pour like hot darts onto her legs.

"Mom, what's the matter?" Liz sat down beside her and put her arm around her.

"Nothing, I'll be all right."

"It's Todd, isn't it? You don't like him, do you?"

"No. I don't."

"Neither do I. Why don't you go after them?" Liz stood up and folded her arms.

Margaret turned to her daughter. "Do you really think I should?"

"Yes. And I'll go with you."

"You are wise beyond your years, Liz. Okay, let's go."

Margaret rushed inside, told Jessica what she was doing, then dashed to her car. Liz was already waiting. They screeched onto the road and drove into town. They checked the movie theater, but, as Margaret suspected, no yellow VW was parked in the lot. Then they headed to the only outdoor movie in the area, ten miles south. Todd had lied about that, too. They did another drive through the town and past Todd's house, but they never found them.

***

"Man, I'm glad that's over." Todd placed his hand on Carol's soft thigh and started to caress it. He was so excited that this moment had finally arrived that he could hardly stop himself from taking her right then.

Carol pushed his hand away. "Todd, why did you have to argue with my mom like that? I thought you'd never quit. If Liz hadn't interrupted, you two would have gone on all night."

Todd put his hand on the steering wheel and held back his anger. "We were just having a lively intellectual conversation, Carol. I debate like that all the time with adults. I was just treating her as an equal. I can't help it if her ideas are so archaic. I'm just helping her realize that she has been brainwashed by the right-winged fascists who desire to keep her in bondage. Do you think women should be treated as second-class citizens?"

"Well, no, but—"

"That's what the ERA is all about. Helping her obtain equality. I was just helping her see that." Todd drove around a curve a little fast, screeching the tires.

"Todd, slow down. You're scaring me."

Todd swore in his head. Mrs. Weiderman was ruining their evening. He wanted to tell Carol what he really thought of her—a blind, foolish woman who had probably driven her husband away with her outdated ideas. She was a fossil who had not supported her husband in his enlightenment. No wonder he left her. But he wanted this night to be perfect, so he took a deep breath and chose his words carefully.

"I'm sorry, Carol. I don't want to spoil our night together. Can we change the subject?"

"I just want to say, I know my mom has old fashioned ideas, but she really is a nice person. She saved her money—and she doesn't make a lot of money—just so she could buy me a flute. I don't like my mom a lot of the time, but I still love her."

Todd glanced at Carol and saw that her emerald eyes were large and moist. Her look worried him, but at the same time he was more turned on than ever. He had to shut his mouth or he'd lose her. Man, she looked so sexy in that tight-fitting sundress. Her face, arms, and legs were nice and tan. Everything was ready at the cabin.

"Okay, Carol. I won't talk about your mom anymore tonight. By the way, have I told you yet that you look beautiful?"

Carol blushed and stared at her lap. After a moment of silence, she said, "Todd, why were you so late tonight? You missed dinner."

Boy, she really is uptight. "I'm sorry about that. I was so busy preparing for our evening together that I lost track of time."

"Where are we going, anyway? To the outdoor movies?"

"No. You'll see. It's a surprise."

"Oh, okay." Carol looked away from him, out her window. He wasn't sure if she was over being upset or not.

"Are you going to forgive me? I really do want to make this the best birthday ever."

"Sure, I forgive you." He could see she actually was crying now. "But I just want you to get along with my family, especially my mom."

This was turning out to be a lot more work than he thought. He couldn't understand why Carol was so upset, but he had to calm her down. He reached his hand over and stroked her hair and dried her tears with his fingers. "I'll try harder next time to avoid controversial topics with your mom. Okay?"

"Okay." Carol swallowed.

"Come here." Todd pulled her head onto his lap. "I love you, Carol. It'll all work out."

He held her and rubbed her shoulders gently as they drove the rest of the way to the cabin. Her mascara had streaked around her eyes, but she could fix it when they arrived.

Todd squeezed her as he pulled into the long, dirt driveway that led to the lone cabin in the woods. "Here we are!"

"Where are we?" Carol broke from his grip and looked around. "Whose house is this?"

"Ours for the night. I rented it."

"You mean, we're here alone?"

"That's right. Just you and me, Babe." Todd went to Carol's door and opened it for her. She hesitated, obviously scared. He'd have to loosen her up.

"Don't be afraid, Carol. We love each other, don't we?"

"Yes, Todd. I'm all right." She followed behind him into the cabin.

Todd had decorated the one-room hunting cabin as best he could. He covered the small Formica table with a white linen tablecloth and napkins, two white candles, two champagne glasses, and a bottle of champagne. The counter of the small kitchenette held plenty of snack food: smoked salmon, a cheese ball, English crackers, and a chocolate cheese cake. On the queen-sized bed covered with a white, dotted bedspread, he had placed a dozen red roses, a box wrapped in silver paper, and a large card.

"Todd, everything looks so romantic." Carol went over to the bed, picked up the roses, and put them to her nose. Then she gave him a hug.

"Why don't you go to the bathroom and fix your make-up while I put on some music."

"Okay." Carol grabbed her purse and went into the small bathroom.

"Yes!" Todd rubbed his hands together. He put a Led Zeppelin record on his stereo, unwrapped the champagne bottle, and twisted the corkscrew into the top. The cork came out with a loud "pop" and fizz. He quickly poured the champagne into the glasses. Then he lit the candles.

"I've never had champagne before," said Carol, walking out of the bathroom. "What does it taste like?"

"It's bubbly and makes your tongue tingle. Try it." He handed her a glass.

She took a tiny sip, then made a face. "It's not as easy to drink as soda."

"You'll get used to it. Are you hungry? Do you want to try some smoked salmon?"

"What else do you have?" Carol went to the kitchen counter to see. "Ooh, a chocolate cheesecake. Let's have that."

"Sure." Todd took some plates out of the cupboard and cut them each a piece of cake. They sat at the small table, ate their dessert, and drank champagne. Todd took Carol's hands in his and caressed her fingers.

"Carol, this is the happiest day of my life, being here with you."

"You really mean that?" Carol giggled. The alcohol was working.

"I'm dead serious." He looked into her eyes. "I want you to know you are the first girl I've ever done this with."

Carol blushed and lowered her eyes. She pulled her hand away and poured herself more champagne. Todd could see that she still was tense.

"Let's dance," said Todd. "They're playing Stairway to Heaven."

Todd took Carol into his arms, held her close, and moved to the music. She stumbled and stepped on his feet a few times, which was good because he knew she was intoxicated. He began to kiss her neck and glide his fingers up and down her back. He was having a hard time controlling himself. She started to giggle and wouldn't stop. He took her into his arms and carried her to the bed.

She responded to his touch as they made out, but as soon as he started to unzip her dress, she stiffened again.

"I need to go to the bathroom." She pulled away.

"Why don't you open your present first?" He handed her the silver package.

"Oh, sure." She unwrapped the square box and took out a silky, silver negligee. She stared at it for a few moments, rubbing the material with her fingers.

"Thank you, Todd."

"Why don't you go put it on. But leave your underwear on. I want to take that off myself."

While Carol was in the bathroom, Todd took out his stash of marijuana and prepared to smoke it. When Carol stepped out of the bathroom, she looked much older than her age. She was breathtaking, a knock out. Todd wanted to run over and grab her, but instead he watched her take slow steps toward him. He knew she was still nervous, and he wanted to get her good and stoned.

"Here, Carol, take a puff of this. It'll relax you."

"Will it have a weird effect because I've been drinking?"

"No. It'll work even better."

Todd gave Carol plenty of time to feel the effect of the drug. When she started dancing around the room in slow motion, her arms raised, singing "Bye bye Miss American Pie, drove my Chevy to the levy, but the levy was dry," Todd knew it was time. He embraced her and she fell into him.

Everything went perfect after that. She melted into his arms. Then, when they both were unclothed, he remembered something.

"Carol, did you remember to take your pill?"

"What?" she giggled.

"Your birth control pill. Did you take it this morning?"

"Yes, Toddy, I took my little, tiny pill."

Nothing held him back then. Now he could prove he was a man. He unleashed all his pent-up passion, his years of rejection, on this gorgeous, young girl who gave herself to him. It was all he imagined it to be and couldn't wait to do it again.

When it was over, he noticed Carol had tears in her eyes.

"What's the matter? Did I hurt you?" He held her to his chest.

"No. I don't know."

"Didn't it feel good?"

"Sure. It's just…never mind. I'll be okay." She got out of the bed, put on her clothes and looked at the clock radio. "I'd better get home. It's 1:00."

"Okay." He put on his clothes and saw that she had already gone out to the car. He couldn't understand why she was so upset. Maybe it was because it was her first. Next time he would slow it down. It would get better. He'd learn how to make her happy. In spite of her reaction, he still reveled in the success of the night.

***

Carol let the warm spray pound her body. She relived her night with Todd. At the time it felt right, but now she could not understand why she kept crying. Her mom had been waiting up when she came home. Her mom knew—she could tell. She just looked at her with a strange expression of sadness. Carol had walked past her without saying anything and went to bed. She had wanted to shower that night, but she didn't want to make her mom even more suspicious. She woke up feeling so dirty. She could smell him on her.

She remembered listening to her mom with her boyfriends and how disgusted it had made her feel. Yet at the same time, a new desire stirred in her, and it made her shudder to think of herself like that. What had she become? She didn't want to be like her mom. She despised the way she slept with people like Mac.

It had happened so fast. Todd turned into this groping, frantic animal. It didn't hurt until the end, and only a little, but it seemed beastly anyway. And now she wanted to scrub it off, take it all away, be clean again. She knew her mom had waited until she had married her dad to do it. Would people be able to tell she had done it? When she went to high school, would they know? Would Josh be able to tell?

She lathered the soup and cleaned herself again. Then she slid down into the tub, hugged her legs, and sobbed while the water splattered on her head and dripped over her. Her tears, her childhood, her innocence joined the water droplets and grime washed down the drain.

Part Two

Caught in the Fowler's Snare

One and One Half Years Later

He who dwells in the shelter of the Most High will rest in the shadow of the Almighty. I will say of the Lord, 'He is my refuge and my fortress, my God in whom I trust.' Surely he will save you from the fowler's snare.

Chapter Eleven

"Yes! I'm finally finished—for the forth time!" Carol said, turning from the typewriter with a heavy sigh. She had finished typing the forth version of her essay on George Orwell's *1984*, incorporating all of Todd's corrections and suggestions, and she was proud of the outcome. Surely Todd wouldn't find anything wrong with it this time. Now she could finished her Algebra homework and study for her Biology test.

"Here, Todd. I'm done. And after reading this book, I've decided to stop watching television." She stood up and handed her essay to Todd who was busy reading on his bed. They were studying in his room like they did every weekday.

"You're going to stop watching TV?" Todd looked up from his book. "That's an admirable idea. I'll join you. Not that I watch much now anyway."

"Thanks, Todd. It will be easier to do if we both do it together."

Todd smiled and took the essay. He read it with his correction pencil handy. Carol felt hopeful when he made it through the first page without a mark. But soon she saw him writing little notes in the margin. How could she re-type the essay and still have time to complete all her other homework? She had worked so hard to make sure everything was correct. She picked at her thumbs and waited, holding back the tears as he made more marks.

"Not bad, Carol." Todd handed the paper back. "Just a few spelling and punctuation errors. Your conclusion is pretty good, but I would change the last sentence so that it doesn't end weakly. I wrote a suggestion at the bottom of the page."

Carol took the paper back to the desk and re-read her conclusion. *should be italicized*

In the end, Big Brother's constant torture and degradation succeed in convincing Winston that one plus one equals five, war is peace, wrong is right, and hate is love. With the betrayal of his lover, Julia, doublespeak is now a permanent pattern in his psyche, truth squelched by constant violence and depravation. Orwell ends his book with the bleak conclusion that evil inevitably wins, that it will be useless to fight Big Brother in this futuristic, one-world-government society. Is this our future? Has television become so ingrained in our lives and technology so advanced that power-hungry dictators could soon take over the entire world? Something within us cries against this lack of hope. Certainly, there will be those who will refuse to tolerate such evil, who will rise above with altruism to stand against despotism, people such as Frederick Douglas who taught himself to read and overcame the horrors of slavery even while being whipped daily. Perhaps that is the purpose of Orwell's ending: to put outrage in our hearts so that we will refuse to tolerate such a future. If this is the case, he has succeeded with this reader.

As Carol thought about her conclusion, she remembered something.

"Todd, there was a girl in class today, Kelly, who read a verse from the Bible that was really interesting. She said Jesus predicted that some day we would be under the control of a one-world leader called the Anti-Christ who would use technology to subject the whole world to his control. She read a verse that said in the end times people would replace truth with lies, just like Big Brother in *1984*."

Todd put his book down and sat up in the bed. "What did your teacher do when this girl read from the Bible? Did she let her keep reading? That girl should *not* be reading a Bible in a public school."

Carol knew she had crossed a line with Todd. He was against anything to do with Christianity.

"Well, yes. She told Kelly that reading the Bible was not allowed in school, and then ignored her when she tried to make more comments. But what she said was interesting. You know I don't believe in the God of the Bible, but I still wonder if Jesus could have had some insight that was beyond his years. He could have been a great man, just like Gandhi."

Todd took off his glasses, sniffled and rubbed his nose. Then he stood up and paced as he spoke. "Carol, you need to be careful around girls like Kelly. They take words from the Bible out of context to confuse you, to convert you. It makes me angry that she even brought that Bible to school."

"Todd, Kelly's a nice girl. I didn't even know she was a Christian until today. I think Mrs. Crandall was a bit harsh with her."

Carol knew she should have not contradicted Todd. He came over to her chair, kneeled on the floor, squeezed her shoulder, and made her look at him.

"Carol, do you have any idea what these fanatic Christians teach? They think people like me and you will go to hell unless we believe the same way they do. Trust me, Kelly thinks you're nothing but a piece of dirt. People like her don't want an earthly leader because God is their dictator. Their God wants everyone to be his perfect, little robots. Do you think our love for each other is wrong?"

"Of course not!" Carol turned her eyes from his penetrating stare. His gray eyes were large without his glasses and only inches from her face. "You know I love you, Todd. You know I'm not about to become a Christian, that I don't believe in God. I just thought it was interesting, that's all." Carol lowered her eyes. "But you're right. I know you're right. I'm sure she read it out of context."

"Of course she did." Todd touched her face. "You know I love you, Carol, that you're the most important thing in my life. Let's not argue." He started to kiss her, but she turned away.

"I love you, too, Todd. But I've got Algebra homework and a big Biology test to study for. And I got to re-type some of my essay still. If I don't get going, I'll be up all night."

"Sure, babe. I understand. Get your work done so we have some time for you know what later." Todd returned to the bed.

"Like I really have time for that!" Carol said to herself out loud.

"Did you say something, Carol?"

Carol struggled to think of words that sounded like what she said. She was afraid of what Todd might do if he knew what she really thought. "Yeah, I said, 'I'll try to hurry and make time for that.'"

"Okay, Babe. Now get busy."

Relieved, Carol grabbed a sheet of paper and rolled it into the typewriter. What was wrong with her? She didn't mean to say such a thing. It wasn't Todd's fault she had so much homework. But how could she think about such a thing with so much to do? Maybe if she could type one page without making a mistake. No such luck. After typing the first paragraph, an entire sentence was missing. She pulled out the paper, crumpled it into a ball, and threw it hard into the wastebasket.

***

She was in a classroom, rummaging through her books and papers, looking for it, but it wasn't there. There was something very important

75

missing, but what was it? She flipped through the pages of books, threw out all her papers on the ground, frantically searching. Where is it? I've got to find it. *Taunting and laughter echoed in the background. Someone said,* You're going to flunk, you're going to flunk. *Carol ran down the hall and out of the building. She had to go back to Todd's and find her essay.*

She awoke in panic. As she made out the dark shadows of the furniture in her room, reality relieved the fears of a bad dream. Her essay was stowed safely in her binder, but she had forgotten the French quiz first period. How could find time to study for it now? How could she be so stupid to forget it when it was written plainly in her planner? Maybe if Todd had left her alone last night, she would have seen it.

She threw back the covers and tiptoed around the room, gathering her clothes, careful not to wake Mrs. Randall, the old lady she stayed with. Mrs. Randall had suffered a stroke and had to use a walker to get around her old home. She was afraid to be alone at night, so Carol slept in her guest bedroom. The arrangements were great because Carol didn't have to sleep at home and hardly ever saw her mother. She would ride with Todd after school every day. He was student teaching in the History Department at Deerfield High. They had to be careful to hide their relationship so that Todd would not get in trouble. She would wait in the library until all the buses left so her peers didn't see her leave. Todd told his superiors Carol worked for his parents.

Carol opened her bedroom door slowly and glided down the hall with careful steps. In the small kitchen nook, Mrs. Randall had placed a box of Raisin Bran, a bowl, and a spoon on the table the night before for Carol's breakfast. Once she found out that Carol liked Raisin Bran, it was there for her every morning.

Carol took some milk from the refrigerator and ate her cereal in the dark, silent house. Mrs. Randall had an old fashioned clock on her mantel in the living room, and the soft tick tock made Carol crave the warmth of her bed and more sleep.

It was 5:45 AM when she left the house, burdened with her backpack full of dirty laundry and all her heavy books. The freezing air of January seeped through her unzipped coat and prickled the inside of her nose. She sprinted across the street to her family's newly purchased house, an old, two story Victorian that appeared quaint on the outside but was falling apart on the inside. Her mother had finally saved enough to afford her own home, and they had moved in at the end of last summer before Carol started her sophomore year.

What her mom didn't realize is how much work it would take to get the house livable. Since then, Margaret had started half a dozen remodeling projects, like the front steps that still needed a new railing. They took the rotted railing down, but never replaced it. Carol was careful as she made her way up the four steps that led to the entrance.

A stray, black cat they had taken in met her at the front door, meowed, and rubbed her legs. When she unlocked and opened the door, the cat streaked by so fast Carol hardly saw him. The first thing she did was turn up the heat. A loud clunk sounded from the basement as the old, oil furnace came alive. Though warmer than outside, it was probably only 50 degrees in the house. Thankful that she made it before any of her sisters were up, Carol rushed up the creaky stairs into the bathroom. She turned on the makeshift shower that was added to a stand-alone tub and let it run for a while to warm the cold air. She shivered while undressing in the chilly, extra-large bathroom. It was the price she paid for having the bathroom first.

After showering, combing her hair, and brushing her teeth, Carol gave the bathroom to Jessica who had been pounding on the door and waiting in the hall for five minutes. Her mom was still in bed when she whisked out of the house and ran to the bus. Jessica had friends who drove her to school, so she had an extra half hour every morning to get ready. A cold wind whipped through her wet hair, so Carol put on her hood and zipped her coat. As she did, she spied a girl named Abby who also had wet hair. Abby wanted to look cool for the boys, so she kept her head uncovered and coat unbuttoned, even when the temperature dipped below zero. Already, Carol could see ice forming on Abby's curly bangs. *I'm so much more mature than her* she thought, smiling at Abby and saying, "Good Morning."

Carol did her best to study her conjugation of verbs for the French quiz while the bus bounced on the snow-covered roads and students shouted and jostled in their seats. "Vendre, to sell; je vends, je vendis, je vendrai, je vendrais…" As the bus neared the high school, Carol rushed through the verbs, retaining little. She hadn't received anything less than a "B" all year in her classes, but this time she might fail.

Carol hoped Mrs. Meeks would wait until the end of class for the quiz, but as soon as attendance was taken, she told them to prepare. As Mrs. Meeks gave them the words in English to conjugate, Carol could feel her heart pound so loudly that she was sure the girl next to her could hear it. Perspiration stung under her arms, her stomach churned, and her mind went blank. She did her best to write something on the paper, but an "F" was inevitable.

Carol remembered little of the lesson. Instead, she scolded herself for forgetting to study and calculated how an "F" could affect her perfect grade. When the class ended, she remained glued to her seat. When the rest of the students were gone, she made her way toward her French teacher.

"Mrs. Meeks, I failed the quiz today. I know I did. How will this affect my grade?" Then, to Carol's total surprise, she started to cry.

"Why don't you sit down." Mrs. Meeks motioned to a chair by her desk. "Carol, you are one of my best students. One failed quiz won't hurt your grade that much."

"But I have straight "A's" so far, and I want to keep it that way. I'm sorry, Mrs. Meeks about the crying. I feel so embarrassed." With that statement, the tears rolled even harder down her cheeks.

Mrs. Meeks handed her a tissue. "Carol, it's okay to cry sometimes. Don't be so hard on yourself." She paused until Carol blew her nose and calmed down.

"Carol, do you do anything for fun? You should be having the time of your life at your age."

"What do you mean by fun? I like to read and learn."

"But do you participate in any extra curricular activities or clubs? Any sports?"

Carol gave Mrs. Meeks a blank look. "No, I don't have time for any of those. I have a full load of classes."

"You mean, you don't even have a study hall?"

"No." Carol looked at her watch. She didn't want to be late for her Algebra class. "Because of my excellent grades last year, my counselor let me out of study hall."

"Well, I know you need to get to your next class." Mrs. Meeks stood up. "Why don't you come in after school and we'll talk about making up that quiz."

"Really?" Carol gathered her backpack and purse. "Thank you so much, Mrs. Meeks."

"One more thing." Mrs. Meeks touched Carol's shoulder as she turned to leave. "I want you to take some time and have fun. Okay?"

"Okay. Thanks again." She hurried from the room to her next class.

She met with Mrs. Meeks after school, and Carol was able to look over her notes and take the quiz again. Then she showed Carol a picture of her husband

and baby girl. She had always like Mrs. Meeks because she was young, pretty, and had a cheerful attitude. Now perhaps they could become friends.

***

Amada Meeks gazed down at her sleeping two-year-old, stroked her blond curls, and thanked God for such a beautiful, healthy child. Then she tiptoed in the dark to her bedroom and slipped into bed, careful not to wake her husband. She read the time on the alarm clock: 12:05 AM. Sometimes she would wake up and just check on her little Julia for no apparent reason. Watching her sleep gave her a feeling a well-being and contentment. She could make out the features of her husband's masculine face as he snored lightly on his side. She and Steve had been married three years last August, and she loved him more every month. *Thank you God for all the good things you have given me.* As she snuggled with her husband, who instinctively took her hand, she thought about one of her students who had cried in her classroom that day. This was the second year Carol had been her student, yet she really knew very little about her. She had always been an outstanding student, never gave her any trouble, and seemed older and more serious than the rest of her students. She seldom giggled with the other girls and never flirted with the boys. Instead, many of her classmates copied her notes, asked her questions, and used her as a tutor. Watching her break down stirred something in her heart for the young girl. There was something wrong in Carol's life. She sensed it in her spirit.

Amanda Meeks turned away from her husband and whispered a prayer for Carol Weiderman. *Dear Lord, I don't know what is going on, but please show Carol you love her. Protect her from evil. Help me to reach her, give me wisdom on how to lead her to you…*

Chapter Twelve

Carol threw her dirty clothes into her laundry basket and rushed out the bedroom door. "Whoa!" She halted, almost falling. Her mom stood in the hall wearing a long t-shirt, her hair a mess from sleeping all night. "You scared me, Mom. Why are you up so early?"

"I haven't had a chance to talk to you all week. The only time I get to see you is if I get up this early."

"I'm sorry, Mom. What do you want? I'm going to be late for school if I don't get going." Carol looked toward the stairs.

"I'd like you home for dinner tonight. I have something I need to talk to you about."

"Oh." Carol turned her eyes toward her mom. "What's up? Have I done something wrong?"

"No. It has nothing to do with you. I'd rather not talk about it now. Please just be home for dinner, okay?"

Her mom had an uneasy expression. "Is everything all right? Is someone sick?"

"Everyone's fine, Carol. Don't worry about it. We'll talk tonight."

"Okay. I'll come for dinner. What time do you want me home?"

"Six-thirty would be nice."

"I'll see you at 6:30." Carol gave her mom one last questioning look, then trotted down the stairs.

On the long ride to school, Carol tried to guess what her mom wanted to talk to her about. She had been home so infrequently she didn't even know how her sisters were doing. Jean had the flu a few weeks ago, but was fine now. Liz was doing well in Junior High, and Marie had made a new friend down the road and seemed happy. Maybe Jessica was in trouble. Jessica had a steady boyfriend who was a true deadbeat. He lived in the government housing, and Carol doubted he would graduate from high school. *I hope that jerk didn't get her pregnant.*

No, that can't be it. If Jessica were pregnant, she'd know about it before her mom. Maybe it had something to do with her dad. Or maybe it had something to do with her mom's new boyfriend. She had only met him once, but now that she thought about it, his motorcycle had been parked in their driveway often during the last few weeks. Wasn't he married, too? She thought so. Why did her mom always picked the married guys?

"Are you asleep?" Her seatmate nudged her arm. "We're here, and I need to get out."

"Sorry. I was just thinking."

"Well, think while you walk." Carol stood up and let her out. It would be difficult to concentrate on her studies today while she wondered what her mom would say that night.

***

Margaret placed another layer of noodles on top of the mozzarella and tomato sauce. Hopefully, her home-made lasagna would put Carol in a better mood and help ease the shock of the news she had to share.

"Mom, do we have any tomatoes for the salad?" Liz was looking in the refrigerator. "I can't seem to find any in the vegetable drawer."

"I think Marie unpacked the groceries. Look on the other shelves."

"Oh, here they are." Liz took the cellophane-wrapped carton of tomatoes to a Formica table at the end of the kitchen.

Margaret paused and observed the run-down room. Though it contained lot of square footage, it only had a little counter space on either side of the sink. Two newly, white-washed cabinets lined the wall next to the small window above the sink with a matching number of bottom cabinets. A stove and refrigerator stood together against the opposite wall. The stove pipe used the same opening as the original wood-burning stove, and brown stains marked peeling, yellow-flowered wallpaper around it. Milk crates lined the rest of the wall, storing items that could not fit into the cupboards. The black and white linoleum dated from the 1950's and exposed patches of the wood planks where it had worn through. Margaret had plans to remodel the kitchen, but someone else would have to do it now.

It won't do any good to think about it. Margaret covered the top layer of the lasagna with cheese and eased it into the oven. One of the hinges on the oven door was loose. She opened the refrigerator, took out a bottle of beer, and sat down in the living room to wait for Carol, rehearsing words in her mind. She would tell her gently, show her she had no choice in the situation. Carol had to understand the severity. It could all work out for the best. Certainly, it would be an opportunity to get her away from that conniving, conceited Todd.

The black stray meandered to the couch next to her and started scratching on the arm.

"Shoo! Get out of here! Kids, why is that cat in the here? I told you a million times I don't want him in the house!"

The cat sauntered away, not at all intimidated by her scolding. *Just what I need. Another thing to worry about.*

"Marie, I want you to grab that cat and get it out of here now!" Marie was the only child in the living room, watching television with her Barbie doll. She immediately dropped her doll and went after the cat.

About a half an hour later, Margaret heard Todd's car pull up and Carol walk into the kitchen. Margaret waited in the living room, not wanting to appear too anxious.

"What smells so good?" Carol went over to the oven to take a peak.

"Be careful. Don't open the door or it will fall on you," Liz warned. "Mom made lasagna."

"Lasagna? Yum." Carol opened a cupboard and took out a bag of chips. "Hey, Liz, what is Mom going to talk to me about anyway?"

"I don't know. Why don't you ask her yourself?"

"Well, you don't have to be such a snob about it."

Margaret kept the conversation pleasant and general throughout dinner, asking Carol about school and Todd. The older girls already knew what she was going to say, the two younger sensed something was up, and they glanced at her from time to time. Carol focused on the lasagna and chocolate cake, which gave Margaret hope her strategy was working. When Carol was finished, there was silence as five girls sat and waited for her to begin.

"I don't know if you are aware of it, but your father refuses to pay his court-ordered child support. Because of this, I've had trouble keeping up with the bills."

"No, I didn't realize that, Mom." Carol licked frosting off her fingers. "How long has this been going on?"

"Since your father left, I'm afraid. He's never paid one dime of child support. But I didn't think he'd rather go to jail than pay it." Margaret took a deep breath. She didn't want to lose her self-control before explaining the rest.

"Dad's in jail? When did that happen?"

"He was in jail only a day," Liz interrupted. "That was last week."

Margaret looked at her younger girls, Marie and Jean. Marie played with her hair nervously and Jean was sucking her thumb. Their eyes were wide with concern. She didn't want to alarm them. "Marie, Jean, I think *Happy Days* is on. Why don't you girls go watch TV."

"Okay, Mom," said Marie. "Let's go, Jean." Jean broke away and ran to her mother.

"I don't like Daddy in jail, Mommy. Why's Daddy in jail?"

"He's not in jail any more, Jean. He's going to be fine." She gave Jean a hug. "Now go watch your show."

After the younger girls were gone, Margaret continued. "Like I was saying, I counted on the child support to help pay the mortgage. Without it, I don't think we can keep the house."

"But you just bought it." Carol pushed her plate away and bit her thumb. "Are you behind in payments?"

"Yes, I'm afraid so." Margaret started collecting plates around the table. "We'll have to move."

"Move! Where are you going to move?"

"To Westminster. Jim is renting a house, and he's agreed to let us live with him."

"What!" Carol rose from the table. "Isn't Jim married? What about his wife and kids?"

"Jim's been separated from his wife for six months now. His kids are all grown up. Carol, will you please stop and listen to me. The house is big and has a good-sized basement."

"I just can't believe you, Mom. It was bad enough when you brought them home, but now you're going to shack up with this married man? Well, you all can go, but you can bet your life I'm not moving!"

Margaret clutched the seat of her chair as anger boiled like a pressure cooker ready to explode. "Carol, you are only fifteen and still a minor. I don't believe you have much choice."

"That's what you think! I've got it all arrange to graduate a year early at Deerfield High, and I'm not going to let you and your stupid love affair mess it up."

"I'm sure we can work out a similar situation with the new school. With your grades, there shouldn't be a problem."

Carol stood eye to eye with her mother. "Listen to me *carefully*. I will not move to Westminster with you, *period*. Whatever I have to do, I will do, but I will not leave Deerfield!"

"Calm down. I'm sure we can work something out."

Carol took her coat from the hook by the door and put in on. Then she started to leave. "Forget it, mom. Like I said, I'm staying here. There is nothing more to discuss."

Margaret sprung from her chair and grabbed Carol's arm. "Wait just a minute, young lady. This discussion is not over."

"Don't touch me! Don't you ever touch me again!" Carol pulled her arm away and shoved her mother hard. Margaret fell into a chair first, then onto the floor. Carol gave her a hateful look, then stomped to the front door.

Margaret pulled herself up and followed. "Carol, stop! Get back here!" She reached out and took hold of Carol's hair. "You stop this instant!"

"Ouch!" Carol swiveled around and squeezed her mother's arm until she let go. Then she shoved her again. "I *said*, don't you touch me! Do you want me to call the police and tell them you're abusing me?"

Margaret floundered, dumbfounded by Carol's harsh words. Before she could recover, Carol was gone. She grabbed her car keys from the kitchen counter and started to follow. As she turned to leave, Jean latched onto her leg, sobbing. "Mommy, Mommy, what's the matter? Is Carol really going to call the police?"

"Jean, it's okay." Margaret slumped to the floor and pulled her young daughter on her lap. She gave Jean a bear hug as her chest heaved.

"Mom, you're hurting me." Jean pushed out her mother's arms.

"I'm sorry, Jean. I seem to be good at that."

"Mom, it's not your fault. It's Carol." Liz sat beside her mom and put Jean on her lap. Marie and Jessica also sat down next to their mom, but did not say anything.

Margaret put her head down. It had all backfired on her again. Carol despised her as a mother, and nothing she could do or say would change her mind. She rubbed the spot where Carol had bruised her wrist and recalled the night of Carol's fourteenth birthday when she and Liz had tried to find Carol and Todd. She had driven around searching for her, but it was too late. She had waited too long. She had failed. She lost her that night. Going after her now would do no good. Todd had replaced her. Carol belonged to *him*.

***

Carol hiked as fast as she could down the hill, her feet crunching on the icy snow, glancing behind for her mother's car. She couldn't, she wouldn't, let her mom stand in the way of her plans. If she tried to get the police to bring her home, she would tell them how terrible a mother she was. She practically lived on her own anyway. She ate breakfast at Mrs. Randall's and dinner at Todd's. The only thing she got from her mother was the free hot lunch at school. Nothing much would change if her family moved to Westminster without her. She would just have to find another place to take a shower and do laundry. Mrs. Randall only had a bathtub, but she had a washer and dryer in her basement. She could shower at Todd's house.

Why didn't her mom understand how important school was to her? Couldn't she see she wanted to go to college and make something of herself? Couldn't she see how much Todd had helped her grow up and become intellectual? No, she didn't see because she was too preoccupied with her own life. Well, she could have her life, and Carol would have hers. Hers and Todd's.

White puffs of condensation from her labored breaths stood out in the dark, and Carol realized it was a cold, winter night. She zipped her coat and tied her hood snuggly around her face, but she had left without her gloves and could feel her fingers becoming numb. She had also left her boots, and her sneakers were already soaked from trudging in the snow. She felt inside the pocket of her parka and found some change. Good, now she could call Todd from a pay phone downtown.

She deposited the dime in the payphone and let it ring. Mrs. Barrett answered.

"Can I speak to Todd?"

"Is this Carol?"

"Yes."

"Hold on a minute."

The tears were falling by the time Todd reached the phone. "Todd, I'm downtown. I ran away. I'm cold. Could you come get me?"

"Sure, babe. What happened?"

"I don't want to talk about it now. Just come quick."

"I'll be right there."

It seemed like hours before Todd's familiar yellow bug pulled up. Her hands and feet were frozen. She paced to stay warm and scanned the street for her mom's station wagon, but it never came by. When she finally tumbled into Todd's car, she couldn't stop shaking.

Todd held her close and rubbed his hands on her back to warm her. "It's all right, Carol. I'm here now." But Carol still felt like something was very wrong. There was a sense of fear and dread that she could not explain. Why had her mother not come looking for her?

Chapter Thirteen

Carol shut off the alarm and stuck her head under her pillow. The words "Monday, Monday, can't trust that day," sang in her head and described her feelings precisely. How did it become Monday again already?

She dragged herself out of bed and peeked through the frosted window. A street light displayed flurries falling on at least foot of snow that had accumulated overnight. Deerfield, Vermont seemed to forget Spring came in March. Winter still had its cold grip on the frozen town, and Carol had to go out in it.

She ate her raisin bran as usual, put on her parka and boots, and made her way down the front steps and to the street. A quiet swish from falling flakes was the only noise, and the chilly, moist air made her to think of snow covered with maple syrup for some reason. Actually, real maple syrup and homemade pancakes sounded delicious. She was sick of raisin bran.

Carol could not help but admire the way the fresh whiteness made the street that, only the day before, was rutted with dirty ice and potholes appear fresh and new. It would make a perfect Currier and Ives Christmas card. She hated to ruin it with her footprints, which made deep holes in the lawn as she trudged toward the house. Her family had moved out weeks ago, and the house stood cold, dark, and empty. She always felt a little afraid going there by herself. What if some vagrants broke in or a felon was using it for a hide-out?

She looked around the house and the front porch before walking to the door. As she began to unlock it, she noticed something was wrong with the shades and curtains by the entry window. It was as if they had been cut. She tensed with fear and wondered whether to open the door. The snow continued to fall with a soft hush, and the frigid air penetrated her coat. All she wore underneath was pajamas. She turned the key and slowly pushed the door. A black form flew out. Carol jumped back, slipped, and fell onto the icy wood. She glanced all around, but whatever it was had disappeared. *It's just the cat*, she realized. *Oh no! The cat had been left in all weekend!*

As she made her way into the house, she saw that the cat had made his litter box right by the door. The stray must have sneaked in when she had been there Friday morning. When it realized it was stuck, it had tried to get out of the house and had shredded all the curtains and shades in the process. As Carol put on the lights in each room, she found that it had not left one window untouched. The house, empty except for dust, amplified each of her steps, and she felt like an intruder, herself. She found a few more piles of waste and even some places where the cat had dug into the wood floors enough to make it splinter. *Great, now I'll have to clean up this mess later.*

After school, Todd drove her to the house to help her repair as much damage as possible.

"Boy, that cat sure did a job on this place." Todd was in the living room examining the drapes that had fallen off the rods after the cat had jumped on them. "You'd of thought a mountain lion had been left in here."

"He must have gone completely crazy." Carol was busy picking up a pile of litter in the corner. "Man, this is gross. How could that cat poop so much when it didn't even eat anything?"

"Maybe it found a stray mouse."

"If that's the case, we'll probably find a mouse head." Carol used her gloved hands to scoop the last piece into the garbage bag. "Todd, could you pass me that ammonia? I need to scrub this spot."

"Sure. You know, I don't think there's anything we can do about these curtains. You'd better call your Mom and let her know what happened."

"Great. I haven't talked to her for weeks. Now I have to call and tell her I left a stray cat in and it made a huge mess. She's desperate to sell this house so she doesn't have to file bankruptcy."

"She'll know it's not your fault."

"I hope so. Otherwise, I might have to start taking showers at your house."

About an hour later, Carol and Todd had swept up the last pieces of plastic and cloth and scrubbed the final soiled spot. "Well, I think we've done all we can do for now. Let's get out of here."

"Wait. There's one nice thing about this empty house." Todd came up behind Carol and put his arms around her. "Why don't we go check out the bedroom upstairs?"

"Todd, there's no furniture in the house."

"Who says we need furniture."

"Well, I'm not in the mood the do that right now. I just inhaled cat poop and disinfectant for the last hour. I just want to get out of here."

"Oh, come on Carol." Todd started to kiss her neck.

Carol pulled away. "Not now. I haven't even started my homework, and you know how long it takes me to do my Algebra. I have another test tomorrow."

Todd pouted. "I thought you liked it."

"I do. But I have too much on my mind right now."

"Fine. Let's get out of here." Todd pulled away abruptly and picked up cleaning items.

Later that afternoon, Carol took a deep breath and dialed the phone in Todd's room. She didn't want to call her mother at all, but she needed to get rid of the guilt.

"Hello," a male voice answered the phone. Carol swallowed hard. She hadn't expected Jim to answer.

"Hi, could I speak to Margaret?"

"May I ask who's calling?"

"Her daughter, Carol."

"Oh, hi Carol. How are you?" The last thing Carol wanted to do was small talk with her mother's boyfriend.

"I'm fine. I need to tell Mom something."

"Okay, hold on." Carol's hand shook while she waited. Her sisters were making noise in the background.

"Hi, Carol. Is everything okay?"

"Um, sure Mom. I'm fine."

"Good. I haven't heard from you in a while."

"I've been busy with school." Carol heard a scream on the other end of the phone. Marie was wailing to her mom about something Jean did.

"Carol, hold on a second." Her mom yelled, "Jean, go to your room and wait there until I'm off the phone."

"Sorry, Carol. Jean and Marie are fighting. Maybe I should call you back."

"Wait, Mom, it'll only take a minute. I've got some news for you."

"Oh. What's up?"

"You know that black stray that kept hanging around the house? Well, somehow it got stuck in the house all weekend. It tore your curtains to shreds."

"What? It did what?"

89

"The stray, black cat got stuck in the house and ruined all the curtains and shades. I went over today and picked up the mess."

"Great! This is just great! How did that darn cat get in there anyway?"

"I'm sorry, Mom. I may have let it in by mistake."

"Thanks a lot, Carol. Now what am I suppose to do? I've got to sell that house soon or I'll lose everything. Lord, what's next?" Carol could still hear the two girls yelling.

"Mom, I'm sorry. Really I am. At least I picked up the mess, including all the poop."

"Well, I don't know where the money's going to come from to fix this. You don't have any money do you?"

"Mom, you know how thick my load is at school. When do I have time to work?" Another piercing scream came through the phone.

"I can't deal with this right now, Carol. These girls are driving me crazy. I'll call you back later."

"Okay, Mom."

"Bye."

"Bye." Carol slammed the phone down. "She thinks it's all my fault and wants me to pay for the damage! I can't believe it. I don't think she even heard me say that I cleaned up the mess."

"Are you sure, Carol? What did she say?" Todd was at his desk taking notes on a book he was reading.

"She asked me if I had any money cause she said she didn't have anything left to fix it. She said she had to sell the house right away and that this could ruin her chances."

"I'm sure she's just stressed out. I can't believe she'll really try to make you pay for all the damages. Just let her calm down."

"It's easy for you to say, Todd. She's not your mother."

"Hey, I'm just trying to help."

"I'm sorry! I'm just all stressed out about this. I didn't mean to take it out on you."

"Sure. You'd better get started on your homework. It's getting late."

"Oh, that's right! I have that Algebra test tomorrow."

It was after 11:00 when Carol made it to her room. She was exhausted, but couldn't sleep. She tried reading *Steppenwolf* by Hermann Hesse, but it only depressed her. Henry had just made the choice to end his life and was walking through the streets in the rain, agonizing over his decision. "Sooner or later the moment would come to take out my razor and cut my throat (page 96)." She could identify with him. Life was just one dreadful mistake after another, and no matter how hard she tried, someone was always unhappy with her.

She took out her bong and some marijuana, and smoked to relax. She opened her window to air out the room and let the cold swirl around her. Then she stuck her head out of the window into the freezing night until her teeth chattered. Instead of feeling better, it made her even more lost and lonely. Her mom hated her. She didn't even ask Carol how school was going. She didn't care at all about her 4.0. All she did was worry about herself. She didn't even have to call her mom and tell her what happened. She didn't have to go and clean up the mess. But did her mom even notice it?

Todd's family despised her as well. Todd's parents treated her like another piece of furniture. About all they said to her every day was a polite, "hello" and "good-bye." Even Tina ignored her now that she had a new baby sitter.

Did anyone really care about her? Todd said he loved her, but he never was satisfied. He was always telling her she needed to read this, study that, and not eat too much. Her breasts were too little. If she were as beautiful as he said, why did he keep looking at his porno magazines?

She thought about crawling out the window and curling up in the snow. How long it would take for her to freeze to death? If she just fell asleep, would it hurt? How long it would take for them to find her body? Mrs. Randall would see that Carol hadn't eaten her cereal, come into the room, and when she looked out the window and saw her, would probably die of a heart attack. Then it would be days before someone came and found both of them dead.

"You're being stupid," Carol told herself. *Of course Todd loves you. Besides, you don't want to hurt Mrs. Randall.* She shut the window and sat down at an old, accordion desk in her room. Inside several cubby holes, Mrs. Randall kept pictures and postcards of her trips with her late husband. Carol thumbed through them. The old, black-and white pictures gave her a strange feeling of nostalgia, even though she was not old enough to remember the days portrayed. She stopped at one where Mrs. Randall and her husband posed at a beach in Florida. They were both so young and good looking. She would never have guessed Mrs. Randall once looked pretty. Then she read a love letter sent by her husband over fifty years ago. He kept telling her how much he loved and missed her. Carol felt like she was invading Mrs. Randall's privacy and stuffed everything back in its proper place.

She pulled out a box from underneath the bed and took out the wallet-sized photo of her secret admirer from almost two years before. She often wondered if it had been a dream, but the picture was proof something happened that day. It had to have come from somewhere. His perfect smile seemed to mock her. Was it just a joke some guy had played on her? Did he come from a neighboring town, have his fun, then go back to his friends and tell them how gullible she had been?

You're a fake and a fraud. You lied to me! She threw his picture back into the shoe box, shut off the light, crawled under the covers and began to daydream. She was at her graduation ceremony speaking to a huge crowd, the Valedictorian of her class with a perfect 4.0. As she finished her outstanding speech, teachers, parents, and fellow-students clapped, then stood and applauded more. The principal stood next to her and announced that she had touched his heart more than any other Valedictorian.

After leaving the podium, she took off her robe to reveal a tight-fitting white-dress that accentuated her suddenly enlarged bosom and tanned, slender legs. Her hair flowed down her shoulders in wispy curls, and her teeth shone as bright as her dress as she smiled to all her admirers. All the good-looking jocks herded around her like hungry wolves, asking her if she would go out with them. She walked into them and pushed them aside. They were beneath her now.

Someday she would show them all what she could do, that Carol Weiderman was smart and beautiful and great.

Chapter Fourteen

Italicize

$15x^2 + 45x-10$…5(3x+9x-2)…(3x-5)(x+2)…no, that won't work. She thought and thought about the Algebra problem, but couldn't quite figure it out. She factored the numbers with different combinations, but each method was wrong. Only five goes into 15 and 45 and ten. What's missing? Find it quickly. Time's ticking away.

How did she end up outside the school? She dashed through the front door and down the hall, anxious to get back to the classroom, but where was it? Down one hall, then another, only to reach a dead end. Once more outside the school. This time woods all around and no building. I've got to get back to school, but where is it? Go toward the lighter area. When she reached the opening, it ended in a steep ravine. I've been here before, but when? A sharp wind blew from the valley at the far bottom of the cliff. She couldn't go back. Someone had followed her. Goose-pumps formed on her arms and legs as the wind whipped.

He's here, and he's going to kill me. I've got to get away! She couldn't move, legs and arms heavy as lead. He came closer; his warm breath on her neck. Still, her body was frozen, eyes riveted to the rocky embankment that would be her peril. Violent hands pushed her and she fell, and fell, and fell.

Carol never hit the bottom of the cliff. Instead, she seemed to fall into her bed, dizzy and disoriented and paralyzed. She took deep breaths and made sure her arms could move before opening her eyes, reassuring herself like a small child that it was just a dream. It had been years since she had that nightmare, not since she had met Todd. Why was it back now? *Probably because you have your Algebra final today.* Still, the sensation of that push off the precipice lingered, as rotten and putrid as her morning breath.

The time was only 4:00 AM, but the horror of the dream kept her awake. She could make out shadows from the furniture around the room, and envisioned the evil presence from her dream lingering in the corner, waiting to jump at her with a knife. She put on the lamp beside her bed. In the light, the accordion desk and chairs, the corner lamp, the curtains, stood quiet and still, nothing out of place. *It's all in your imagination. It's just a silly worry dream.*

Her book bag was next to her bed, so she dragged it onto her lap and took out her Algebra text. She had planned to give herself an extra half-hour to study one last time anyway, so she stayed underneath her warm covers and reviewed the eight pages of notes, formulas, and sample problems for the final. She remembered all the methods to solve for two variables, including factoring and the quadratic formula. She reviewed graphing equations on the x and y axis and the rules for absolute value. But some of the words problems were still confusing. How do they figure out the equations? She memorized the types of problems and the subsequent equations. As long as the instructor used similar questions, it would be all right.

By the time school started, the quadratic formula swam around in her head repeating itself like an irritating parrot: x equals negative b plus or minus the square root of b squared-4ac over 2a. As soon as her Algebra teacher, old Mr. Johnson, passed out the test, she wrote the formula on top of the page, as well as all the other rules she had memorized. She plunged into the problems, completing each calculation twice and checking the answers by placing them in the equations, only guessing on two questions, including one unfamiliar word problem. When the bell rang, Carol set down her pencil, satisfied and certain her Sophomore year would end with a 4.0.

Because it was finals week, Carol had no more classes. She had to wait half an hour for Todd, so she walked to Mrs. Crandall's room to pick up her final paper, *The Stereotyped American Woman*. It had taken hours poring through periodicals and cutting out pictures for the report on women's role in advertising, and she wanted to see the affirming "A" Mrs. Crandall would give her.

Mrs. Crandall was at her desk grading papers. She stopped and looked up at Carol.

"I can guess what you are here for." She found a stack on her desk and pulled out a thick paper protected by a clear report cover. The cover page of the report displayed a picture of a housewife cleaning her floor. Mrs. Crandall held the report for a moment, and opened her mouth to speak. Then she closed her mouth, handed the paper to Carol, glanced at her for a brief second, then turned away to re-pinned her long salt and pepper hair.

Carol flipped to the last page of the report. A "B-" written in red ink sent a shock through her like a bullet. She stared at the page, re-reading it, willing herself to remain calm, certain Mrs. Crandall had made a mistake. Finally, she took a deep breath and croaked, "Why did I only get a B-?"

"Did you read my comment on the bottom?" Mrs. Crandall said, averting her eyes to her pile of papers.

"No." Carol read the last page. "Paper is well-written, but is biased. Need to use a variety of sources for a research paper to be valid."

"But I had more than the required number of sources. I used several different periodicals."

"Yes, but they were all similar sources with the same perspective. You reached a conclusion before you began the research, then only used sources that would support your conclusion."

"I don't understand." Carol frowned, her hands shaking.

"Carol, did it ever occur to you that some women believe taking care of their family is as much a career as being a doctor or a lawyer?"

"What are you talking about? The only reason women feel that way is because they haven't been given the opportunity to do anything else."

Mrs. Crandall put down her red pen and took off her glasses. "Carol, do you know what I did before I became a teacher?"

"No."

"I stayed home and raised three wonderful children. I could have taught while they were growing up, but I wanted to be the best mother I could possibly be. I have a master's degree in English Literature and Education, but taking time to raise my children was the most fulfilling career I have ever chosen."

Carol stared at Mrs. Crandall, not sure what to say. Finally she said, "At least you had a choice. What about the women who never have a chance to do anything else? And why are women portrayed as sex symbols and housewives most of the time on TV and in magazines?"

"Carol, I agree that advertisers tend to use sex appeal to sell products. I don't object to you showing that fact. But you also need to give validity to the role of motherhood instead of condemning women who find fulfillment in this role. There are two sides to every story. You only portrayed one side of the story in your report."

"I don't think you're being fair. Women already know about the roles of wife and mother. They need to understand that there is more to life than that."

"I'm sorry you don't understand, but my grade is final." Mrs. Crandall picked up her red pen and returned to grading. The conversation was over.

Carol stood for a minute, then asked, "What is my final grade in the class? How much did this report hurt my 'A'?"

Mrs. Crandall took her grade book out of her desk drawer and found Carol's name. "Your final grade is a 93%."

Carol signed with relief. "Thank you, Mrs. Crandall." Carol put her report into her book bag and left.

She sat down in the library, took out the report and read it. There were very few red marks or comments in the body of the paper, except the final death sentence. It still didn't make sense that Mrs. Crandall had marked it down. The evidence was so clear that women were shown as sex symbols and housewives more than anything else by the media. Todd had reviewed the report and told her it should receive an excellent grade. She tilted her head down, ran her fingers through her hair, and squeezed stands in her fists. It wasn't fair after all the work she put into the paper. *Mrs. Crandall has probably been brainwashed by her chauvinistic husband,* Carol concluded. *She just took out her views on me. I really deserved an "A." I'll ask Todd if there is some way I can make a complaint about her.*

While Carol thought about taking her paper to the principal's office, two girls in her grade came and sat at the table next to her. They were apparently very happy because they could not stop giggling.

"My Dad told us last night that we get to go to California in July! We're going to go to Disney Land and Knots Berry Farm." The first girl squealed to her friend.

"Man, that sounds so cool. I'm jealous." The second girl jabbed her on the shoulder.

"But Mary, don't you get to stay at your cabin by on the lake again? You get to go water skiing. I've never been water skiing."

"You're right. I love spending our summers at the lake. I'm going to end up with a fantastic tan."

"Well, Southern California is full of sun. We'll see who gets the best tan." The girl gave her friend a challenging smile.

"When are you going? Maybe you can spend some time with us on the lake and learn to water ski."

"Oh, that would be great. Then my summer would be totally perfect."

"*Totally perfect,*" Carol whispered to herself. Those girls sounded so immature, and their incessant silliness was irritating. Still, Disney Land and water skiing would be fun. She hoped to take a class at the University of Vermont with Todd, but other than that, she had no plans for summer vacation. Instead, she had to look for a job.

The girls were laughing again. Annoyed, Carol decided to wait outside for Todd in the warm sun. She gathered her belongings and said good-bye to high school until September. One more year at this place, then she would be graduated, hopefully as valedictorian.

Carol sat down on the curb in front of the school and tried to read *The Feminine Mystique*, but the bright sun made her sleepy. She slept maybe five hours the night before, and the first thing she'd do when they reached Todd's house was curl up in the family room and take a nap. It would feel so good to not have to study for a test or do homework. She closed her eyes and pictured herself at the beach soaking up the sun, listening to the ocean sing its enchanting song. The last time she was at the beach was on her fourteenth birthday when they spent the day at Lake Sunapee. That was the day everything in her life changed.

As soon as Todd pulled up to the curb, Carol jumped into the car before anyone could see them. Thankfully, Todd was finished with his student teaching, so next year they wouldn't have this problem.

"I have good news," Todd said as she buckled her seatbelt. "I received a letter from The University of Vermont, and they'll allow you to take the same United States Government Class I'm taking. That means you can stay with me in Burlington."

"Wow! That's great." Carol clapped her hands. "I can't believe it. I'll be like a real college student."

"One of the youngest college students. If you do well in the class, they'll give you credit."

"With your help, I'm sure I'll do fine." She leaned over and gave him a kiss on the cheek. "Wait, the only problem is, how am I going to pay for it?"

"It's already done. My parents don't know it, but I used the rest of my college money for your class. Because it's summer, they have single dorm rooms available. You can just stay with me, and no one will know the difference."

"I still can't believe it. I'm going to live in a dorm and take a college class when I'm only sixteen." Carol paused and thought of a problem. "Do your parents know I'm going with you this summer?"

"I haven't said anything about you. They know I'm going, but they don't know what you're doing. I'm not going to say anything unless they bring it up."

"I hope they don't ask me what I'm doing this summer. If they do, do you want me to lie?"

"No. Just tell them you'll be visiting me in Burlington. They have to get used to the idea of us living together anyway."

"What am I going to tell my mom?" Carol picked at a pimple on her chin. "She asked me the other night whether I would be staying with them this summer."

"Margaret will learn to accept it, just like she's learned to accept that you are staying in Deerfield. You haven't live with your family for almost four months anyway." Todd pulled into the concrete driveway of their large home. His parents were still at work and his sister in school, so they could relax together for a while.

Carol forgot her backpack and closed the door to the car in a daze. She was entering the halls of academia, on the same level as adults. She felt like she had just stepped into a new arena, welcomed into an exclusive club. Who needed Disney Land or water skiing? She was on her way to success and achievement, a modern woman out to conquer a man's world. So much had changed in the last two years. In a few days, she would be sixteen. The silly, fourteen year old girl was gone forever, replaced by an intelligent, intellectual young woman. She ran over and gave Todd a bear hug. "I'm so happy I could just *scream.*"

Chapter Fifteen

"Mom, the phone's for you. It's Carol." Liz yelled down the basement stairs.

"Just a minute." Margaret added soap to a load of laundry and started the washer. Then she walked slowly up the stairs, afraid to pick up the phone. Whenever Carol called lately, it seemed the news was bad. What was she up to now? She had really hoped Carol would spend the summer with them so they could re-establish their relationship. She was still so young, and should be with her family—and away from that conniving Todd.

"Hello."

"Hi, Mom. How are you?"

"I'm fine. How did your finals go? How about the Algebra? I know you were worried about that."

"I got an A- on the Algebra final. It was easier than I thought. I should have straight "A's" again this year.

"That's great, Carol. I always knew you were a smart girl."

"Mom, I want to tell you something."

"Oh." Margaret sat down in the dining nook. The fluttering in the pit of her stomach told her she was not going to like what was coming next.

"I get to take a college class this summer at the UVM. Isn't that great?"

"A college class? How did you manage that?"

"Todd helped me apply a few months ago. Because I'm doing so well in high school, they're letting me take a U.S. Government class. If I do well, I can get college credit."

"Wow. That's impressive, Carol. But where are you going to stay?" Margaret rose from her chair and rummaged through the piles of papers and belongings on the table: bills, school papers, candy wrappers, a discarded apple core.

"On campus. Where else?"

"On campus!" Margaret took a deep breath. "Carol, where are you getting the money for this? Is Todd's family helping you out?"

"Yes, as a matter of fact, they did."

"So, are they paying for your room and board, too?"

"Well, sort of…"

"Carol, what is Todd doing this summer?"

"He's taking the class with me."

Margaret slumped back into the chair. He was up to no good again.

"Oh, and where is Todd staying?"

"In a dorm."

"Carol, are you and Todd going to live together while you're taking this class?"

"Well, yeah. We are."

"So you're not going to spend any time with your family this summer?" Margaret could not sit still now. She paced. Jean had sneaked into the room to listen to the conversation, and she almost ran her over. Three more figures hovered in the hallway.

"I'll come by to visit. Maybe we can take a drive to the lake or something."

"Carol, how can the University of Vermont allow you two to live together? And how could Todd's parents allow this?"

"Mom, wait. Todd's parents don't exactly know that detail yet."

"Oh, really? And when do you plan to tell them?"

"We'll tell them when we need to."

"I can't believe the UVM would let you guys do that."

"Mom, things are different now. Living together is not the big sin it once was."

"For goodness sakes, Carol, you aren't even sixteen yet! There's got to be a law against this!"

"Mom, stop! Stop or I'll hang up and never come to see you this summer!"

Margaret took a deep breath and ceased her pacing. "Okay. But please just listen to me a minute. I don't mind you taking a college course. I think that's great. But please, let's find another place for you to stay. How much does a dorm room cost anyway? Maybe I can find some extra money."

"It's nice of you to offer, but we've already arranged everything. Mom, Todd and I practically live together already."

"But Carol, you'll be alone up there. It's not the same, believe me."

"Mom, how can you tell me it's not okay to live with Todd when you've living with Jim?"

She always knew how to throw the last punch. Margaret slammed her fist on the counter, took another deep breath, and said, "That was mean and low, Carol. I'm a lot older than you. You're still a child."

"That's where you're wrong, mother. I'm not a child anymore. You've got to accept that."

"Wait a minute, who's the child and who's the parent here? I'm your mother, and I deserve your respect."

"I do respect you, mom. But you need to respect me. I've shown that I can live on my own for four months now. I have my own life, and you need to accept it."

"Fine, just fine, then." Margaret swallowed hard. "Are you coming home for your birthday, Carol? Can I at least wish you a happy birthday before you leave?"

"Sure. I'm not leaving until June 29th. Just let me know when."

"Okay. I'll let you know."

"Well, I need to get off the phone. It's long distance you know."

"Oh, I suppose it is."

"Bye mom."

"Bye." Margaret slammed down the phone, then turned to see four worried faces staring at her.

"Carol's not coming home this summer, is she," Liz said.

"No, she's taking a class at UVM with Todd."

"Mom, I'm sorry," said Jessica.

"So am I," said Liz. "I wish I could tell them a thing or two."

"Mommy, why doesn't Carol like us?" Jean pouted.

"Yeah, she never comes and sees us. She doesn't act like our sister anymore," Marie said.

"It's that stupid boyfriend of hers, not you guys." Jessica patted Marie's head.

"Girls, if you don't mind, I need to go and lie down for a while. Jessica, can you watch over things for me?"

"Tom's coming to pick me up any minute."

"I'll keep an eye on the girls." Liz put her hand on her mother's shoulder. "You can go lie down."

"Thanks, Liz. I can always count on you."

"Marie, Jean, why don't we make a cake for Jim." Liz led her sisters into the kitchen.

Margaret made her way down the hall to the master bedroom and closed the door. She sat down on the new bed Jim had bought them when they moved into the house. It had a feminine, white-painted frame, and Jim had allowed her to decorate the room with a quilted bedspread and lacey, white curtains. It was the nicest bedroom she had ever had, the newest house she had ever lived in. The appliances all worked, and they even had a dishwasher. Still, staring out the window without seeing, she did not know how to go on. She could not cry. She could not scream. She could not move. The hurt was like a cut that had bled so much there was no blood left. All that remained was an empty shell that would shrivel up and die.

She had waited too long with Carol. She should have put her foot down in the very beginning and stopped Todd from taking her child. Should she try to interfere now, call the University of Vermont and tell them her daughter planned to stay with that statutory rapist? But what if they found out Carol didn't live at home anyway? So far, the school had not caught on to the fact that Carol did not live at home. She could be opening a can of worms.

She could call the Barretts and let them know what their son was doing. Yet, they also must know Carol didn't live at home and spent most of her time with Todd. They had allowed Todd to do what he was doing right under their noses. They paid for Carol's class, so they must suspect they will be together. They probably didn't care what he does. She had never even met them. She knew who they were through her colleagues at the Community College where she worked. Mr. Barrett was an engineer, and Mrs. Barrett was a psychologist. They had moved from Connecticut a few years before to get away from the city. They had plenty of money. They'd probably snub their noses at her.

She'd just have to give it up, like everything else in her life. Just like the idea of marrying the first man who truly loved her, the man she now shared her bed with every night. Jim treated her so much better than Richard, adored her from their first date, and enjoyed spending all his free time with her. He even had a way with the kids. He'd play games with them and gave Jean and Marie piggyback rides whenever he was home. Jim said he wanted to marry her, but his wife refused to sign the divorce papers.

It's just not fair! Margaret grabbed a book from the nightstand and hurled it to the floor. A small pamphlet fell out of it, and she glanced down at the title.

It said, "Did you know you are loved?" Then she looked at the book on the floor. It was Jim's old Bible. *Oh, no, I'm sorry, Jim.* She picked up the book and the pamphlet and set them on her lap, making sure the Bible had not been damaged. She knew Jim had attended church faithfully until he started dating her. His church dis-fellowshipped him when she moved in with him.

She set the Bible back on the stand carefully, then looked more closely at the booklet. It had a colorful picture of sunshine breaking through dark clouds. Curious, she read the first page. *"For God so loved the world that he gave his only begotten son so that whoever believe in him shall not perish but have eternal life."* John 3:16. She recalled the pictures of Jesus from the catechism books of her childhood: him reaching out to the children, teaching the people, healing the sick, hands and feet bleeding, nailed to a cross. She loved Him then, as a child. It was all a lie. Jesus didn't love her. If He did, why had so many bad things happened to her?

No, Jesus couldn't love her. According to the Catholic Church, she was a total failure. They would never take her back now. Both she and Jim were tainted, soiled, rejects. The only good thing they had was their love for each other.

She had the urge to tear up the incriminating leaflet and burn it in the fireplace, but it didn't belong to her. She snapped the little book shut and returned it to its original place in the Bible, then curled up into a ball and thought about Jim. He would be home around midnight, and she would hold him in her arms and love him. Maybe Carol was lost, maybe God couldn't love her, but Jim loved her. That would have to be enough.

Chapter Sixteen

Carol stood at the top of the Old Mill at the University of Vermont and let the cool breeze blow through her hair. She had never been in such a tall building or experienced such a view. All the windows in the circular tower were open, and had a view of the campus, the lake, and Burlington in the distance.

"Wow, I can see everything from here. Lake Champlain is huge. I can't believe I'm staying in such a beautiful place. It's like being on vacation."

Todd took her hand. "I'm glad you like it. This was my home for four years."

"Look at that steeple with a clock on it. Does it chime every hour?"

"Yes. In a few minutes, you'll hear it for yourself." Todd paused and stared at the brick church with a white steeple and a clock tower. Carol saw that it was 9:45. The sun would soon set on the hills and lake to the west. Todd had rushed her to the top of the Old Mill before dusk so she could see the spectacular sight.

"Did you know that there are 300 buildings on this campus? As you can see, most of them are brick and are neoclassical architecture with pillars, archways, and steep, conical roofs. See that building over there." Todd pointed to a four story structure not far from them with a coned roof and arched doorway in similar style to the one they were in. "That's Billings Student Center. Notice the rounded end of the building with windows all around, like this tower but much bigger. You can sit there and study. Next to it is Cook Commons where the cafeteria is located. The food's not the greatest, but there's plenty of it."

"What about that building? It's one of the few that is not made of brick." Carol pointed west toward the lake.

"That's Southwick Hall where we have all our musical performances. It's definitely modern architecture. Look at the end. That part of the building was just added and is shaped like a piano."

"You're right. It is. Wow, I feel like one of the elite being in this place. I bet everything here cost a lot of money to build."

"Well, the UVM has been around for a while. Since 1791 as a matter of fact. And I bet you don't know what UVM stands for."

"For the University of Vermont, of course."

"You're wrong." Todd grinned. "It stands for Universitas Virdis Montis, University of The Green Mountains."

"You're kidding. I always thought it meant University of Vermont."

"Well, it is called that now. But its original name was Universitas Virdis Montis and that's what the letters U.V.M. stand for."

"Wait a minute. Doesn't Vermont mean Virdis Montis or green mountains? So, technically Universitas Verdis Montis translates as the University of Vermont, so I'm correct." Carol nudged his arm.

"Well, I guess you're right." Todd turned away. "Hey, look, the sun is setting on the lake." Reds and oranges painted wispy clouds and gentle waves with its fire. The golden ball turned darker and larger as it sunk into the hills. A soft wind seemed to announce the magic moment with a rustling of leaves in a stoic maple below them.

"Oh, it's gorgeous. I've never seen anything like it."

"It sure is." Todd hugged Carol close and gave her a squeeze. Then he gazed down at her, lifted her chin gently toward him and touched his lips to hers. Soon, they were kissing in the fading light. It was the most romantic moment they had ever shared.

"I think I'm going to like it here," Carol whispered as Todd embraced her.

"I know you will. Hey, let's go find our room and get settled."

"Let me have one last look." Carol lingered over the panorama and watched the last rays of red light splash on the windows of the majestic, brick buildings that lined the area called The Green. She imagined what happened inside. She envisioned professors taking notes from dusty textbooks, students attentively listening to their instructors lecture, research scientists scribbling complicated formulas on chalk boards, students having heated debates in the common areas. It was as if she had stepped into a new world, an elevated world where intellect, education, and money called out from every corner.

The wind picked up and blew in colder now through window. It broke the tranquil spell of twilight. Night brought with it hesitation. What if she didn't belong here? She was nothing but a poor teenager from the dinky, little town of Deerfield who said stupid words like "over exaggerate" and "ax" instead of "ask." Would her professor know she was only sixteen? Would people look at her and see who she really was and wonder why she was there?

As they exited down the long flight of stairs, Carol held Todd's hand like a child. What would tomorrow be like in her first college class? Would she say something stupid? What would she do if the professor asked her questions? She didn't want them to know her age. She felt like running home, but that was three hours away. No, she had to go forward into this new arena, the world of academia.

When they stepped outside, another gust from the lake bristled against her bare skin, sending a shiver down her spine. Goose bumps formed on her arms. She leaned closer to Todd for warmth. He rubbed her arms and held her while they strolled toward the parking lot.

The campus was now dark and still on the quiet, Sunday, summer night. The temperature was much cooler than at home. As she leaned into Todd, Carol heard footsteps.

She squeezed Todd's hand and spoke in a hushed tone. "Did you hear anything behind us? I'm too afraid to look."

"No." Todd stopped and turned around. He scanned the horizon and listened for a moment. "There's nothing there. It's probably just the wind from the lake rustling the leaves or something."

"It sounded like someone walking."

"Maybe it echoed from somewhere else. Carol, don't worry. I'm right here." Todd put his arm around her and led her on. After a moment, Carol heard noise behind her, and it felt like she was being watched. She remembered her nightmares and the dread she had that long night years ago in her bedroom when an evil presence kept her up until daybreak. What if its clammy fingers grabbed her and pull her into a dark void?

A loud clang rang out from the church steeple, and Carol jumped.

"Carol, are you okay? It's just the clock tower letting us know it's 10:00."

The bell rang nine more times, and with each one, Carol winced.

"I don't know what's wrong. I just have this feeling of doom that came out of nowhere. I mean, only a few moments ago, I was full of happiness."

"You're probably just insecure because this is your first time away from home. It's perfectly natural to be afraid of something new."

"Maybe you're right. I am kind of nervous about starting class tomorrow. I'm probably the youngest person in the class."

"You'll do just fine, Carol. Don't worry. You'll probably do better than most of the students."

"Do you really think so?"

"I know it." He gave her a reassuring squeeze. "Look, our car is just up ahead. We'll get inside and head straight for the dorm. There's plenty of parking in the summer because hardly anyone is here."

When they reached the car, Todd unlocked her door and opened it for her. Then he got in on his side.

Carol placed her hand on Todd's shoulder. "Todd, thanks for being so understanding. I'm so glad you're here to share this with me. It'd be really scary without you."

"I wouldn't want to be anywhere else, babe." He gave her a quick kiss and started the car.

***

Carol sat on the steps to her dorm and enjoyed the warm sun on her shoulders. She was reading her U.S. Government textbook while Todd attended a psychology class. He had to take two more classes to finish his teaching degree. Because they were sharing books for the U.S. Government class, Carol had to read and study when Todd wasn't using them.

Carol liked her class and was amazed at what she was learning. She never realized that the President of the United States was elected by the Electoral College instead of popular vote. At first she didn't understand how or why the founding fathers came up with the system, but the more she read, the more she comprehended their motives and wisdom. She also never understood that her country was a Representative Republic, not a Democracy. The United States stood for a union of democratic states that came together to form a republic. The constitution guaranteed that each state would have equal representation with two senators regardless of size and state representatives based on the population of the state. The Electoral College worked the same way. Each state had two electoral votes for their senators and electoral votes for each of their representatives. Giving power to each state through the congress kept the president from forming too much control. It was a balanced system with the executive, legislative, and judicial braches performing checks and balances.

Carol finished taking notes on the chapter for the Electoral College, set her papers down, and stretched her legs to catch the sun. The mid-morning air smelled of a rose bush nearby, the lake, and water droplets steaming on hot pavement as sprinklers nourished the many plants and flowers on campus. A mixture of birds calling, bees buzzing, and people talking swirled around her, but it was pleasant. The campus was not as busy in the summer as the fall, and she could see small patches of students on the lawns and outside buildings conversing quietly. It would be nice to find a blanket, a nice shade tree, and a good book to read. She had just started *East of Eden* by John Steinbeck and wondered if the main character, Adam, would ever return to visit his evil brother.

Carol was just picking up her books when she heard someone approach on the walkway downhill from the dorm. Wondering if Todd was finished with class, she glanced down the path. A tall, sandy-haired man was sauntering toward her, his steps self-assured, his head lifted up. He wore a white, button-up shirt, open at the collar, grinned with straight, white teeth, and the sun reflecting against the blond in his hair and the white made him stand out like a sparkling diamond. Something about him seemed very familiar, and as he approached, Carol almost dropped her belongings. It was *him*! Her mystery man from two years ago, the same one who gave her his picture. He had the same smile, the same flashing brown eyes.

Carol forced herself to breathe, knowing if she did not, the dizziness would overtake her. Did he recognize her? He was staring right at her as he came closer. Should she make the first move or turn around and run inside? Heat flashed through her, pricking her with beads of perspiration. Her mouth was parched. She swallowed, and her lips clamped together. Just like her first encounter, she stood paralyzed, unable to speak. He came within ten feet of her, halted, lifted his hand and motioned for her to come to him. Then she heard her name.

"Carol!" Her eyes locked with his. She wondered if he were speaking to her telepathically because his dazzling smile never changed.

"Carol!" Todd tapped her on the shoulder. Startled, she jerked around and hit him in the face.

"Ouch!"

"Todd, I'm so sorry. Are you okay?"

Todd rubbed his chin. "I'll be fine. What's the matter with you? You look like you've seen a ghost."

"Oh. You just scared me, that's all. I didn't see you coming."

"No, you were staring straight ahead at something and ignored me until I tapped you on the shoulder. The expression on your face was, well…a mixture of fear and pleasure. What were you looking at anyway?"

Carol had turned around and was searching the landscape for her mysterious man. He was nowhere to be found. He had disappeared again.

"Carol, did you even hear what I said? What are you looking for?"

"I thought I recognized someone I used to know. But I don't see him anymore."

"Oh really? And who is this guy you thought you recognized."

"Someone from my old neighborhood."

"From Deerfield High?"

"No. I knew him before I met you." Carol sighed and shifted her books in her arms, careful to avoid Todd's questioning eyes. She would have to give up on finding him now.

"Carol, is this some old boyfriend you never told me about?" Todd grabbed her arm and started leading her up the stairs.

"No, nothing like that. He was just an acquaintance. He spent a summer vacation with one of my childhood friends."

Todd was silent until they made it to the third floor, down the hall, and into the dorm room. A desk stood on each side of the room by the windows, along with two separate bureaus and closets. The two twin beds had been placed together in the middle to form one. Carol broke free of Todd's grip and put her notebook and text on her desk. Todd threw his backpack on the bed and followed her.

"Okay, Carol, I want to know all about this guy you thought you recognized today. I thought we had no secrets from each other."

"Todd, I had forgotten about him until now. It was a long time ago. Just a stupid school-girl crush."

"From the expression on your face, it looked like you still have a crush on him."

"Don't be ridiculous. I doubt it was even him. He didn't stop to say anything to me, so you have absolutely nothing to worry about."

He touched her shoulder, then turned away and looked out the window. He took off his glasses, rubbed them on his shirt, and put them back on, still focusing on the horizon. Carol grabbed a cup from the bookcase above her desk.

"I'm thirsty. I'm going to get a drink of water. Do you want some?"

"No." He took a tall glass and a bottle of vodka from the top of his dresser and poured a couple of inches in the bottom. He found orange juice in the refrigerator and filled the glass. He put the glass to his lips as Carol quietly snatched her purse and slunk out the door.

In the safety of the bathroom, she unzipped her purse, reached into a secret spot under the lining, and pulled out *his* picture. She rubbed her fingers around the edges of it. It was real and it was the same man she saw on the walkway.

She wanted to run outside and search for him, but Todd would be suspicious if she didn't come back with a glass of water in a few minutes. No, she would have to wait.

"Darn it!" she said out loud. "What am I going to do now?" She would have to wait until Todd's next Psychology class. Should she wait on the steps or go walking around the campus? Surely, he would be back to find her. She stared at his picture, and her heart raced at the thought of seeing him again. He was so handsome, so muscular, so perfect. If only he had come back two years ago, perhaps she would be spending the summer with him.

Carol heard the bathroom door creak open. She put the photo back into the zippered compartment, turned on the faucet, and filled her glass with water. She took a deep breath and headed back to the room.

***

Carol and Todd spent the next few hours in the room. She knew Todd was in a foul mood and avoided him. He drank his vodka and orange juice and read his porno magazines on the bed. She hated it when he read those magazines. It made her feel inadequate, especially when he bought the kind with pictures of girls with large breasts. He tried a couple of times to get her to lie on the bed and read them with him, but she pretended work on an essay on the advantages of the Electoral College over the popular vote.

Instead of reading, she daydreamed. Her mystery man shared a picnic with her on the shores of Lake Champlain. He told her how beautiful she was and fed her grapes. He ran his hand through her hair and traced her cheek with his fingers, making his way to her lips. Then he drew her face to his and touched her lips to his own.

"I'm sick of sitting in this room." Todd tossed his magazine and sat up. "Let's go to town."

Carol yawned. "I'm kind of sleepy. Are you sure you want to go now? Can I take a nap first?"

"No. I'm hungry. Let's go."

Carol stretched and put on her sandals. "Well, I guess I'm hungry, too."

She had a hard time keeping up with Todd as he marched out of the room, down the three flights of stairs, to the parking lot. She wished he would let her drive, as he had a couple of drinks already. He didn't bother to open her door for her this time. She slipped into her seat and did not even have a chance to put on her seatbelt before he was speeding out of the lot.

After they ate at their favorite hamburger place, Todd drove them to the same part of town he bought the porno magazines. It was the only part of the city where iron bars covered the store fronts at night. They passed several taverns and convenience stores, then stopped at a run-down movie theater. The sign outside did not even advertise the movie.

"What's playing?" Carol asked, reluctant to follow Todd into the theater.

"You'll see."

When they stepped inside the dirty room, Carol realized what kind of movie they were going to see. An unshaven man at the counter gave her a look-over and a lustful grin. She noticed she was the only female in the place. A middle aged man passed by them with his head down and bought a ticket.

"Todd," Carol whispered. "I don't want to do this."

"Oh, it'll be fine. You need to learn to live a little."

"No, I mean it. I don't want to go in there."

"Well, then you can just walk home." Todd folded his arms and stared at her with an expression she had never seen before. It scared her. She knew he meant it.

"Fine," she said after a few seconds. She focused on an empty cigarette pack on the floor while Todd bought the tickets, keeping her eyes down as they went in.

When they got in the car to go home, Carol tried to erase the pictures from her mind. Revulsion and shame fought with an unwanted excitement. It made what she and Todd did together some animalistic act, and she wanted to cry. How could those actors do that with each other without any feeling? She wanted to take a shower and clean the dirt off from that place. Who knows what all those guys were doing while they watched the movie? She felt grimy, disgusting, guilty, and degraded.

She started to tell Todd, but he grabbed at her. He had only one thing on his mind now. As soon as they were back in their room, he went after her with ferocity. She tried to pull back and say "no," but Todd was not about to relent.

***

Carol stared at her book and read the same sentence over and over. She had waited by the stairs to her dorm every day that entire week, but never saw *him*. Today, she spent an hour roaming the campus hoping to find him. Was he real at all, or had she dreamed him up? But she hadn't even been thinking about him when it happened. He appeared out of nowhere. It didn't make any sense.

Todd was at his desk taking notes for a psychology test. Ever since the day she saw her mystery man, Todd has been sullen and possessive. Earlier that morning when they were in the US History class, Todd had snubbed her when she told him about her "A" on their first test. She never expected such a high grade and thought he would be proud of her.

"I can't understand why Professor Wills gave you such a high score on that essay," he told her later in their room when he looked over her test. "It must be because you agreed with him about the Electoral College. I had so much more substantiation and facts in mine."

Carol turned to the back page of Todd's test booklet. The professor commented, "You did not stick to the question. I was not looking for a debate, but an unbiased explanation of the pros and cons of the Electoral College."

"Well, it says here that he didn't want you to debate the issue."

Todd grabbed the test from her hand. "I know what it says. If you read my answer, you'll see he's full of it."

"I'm sorry, Todd. I'm sure you're right."

"Some professors just want little robot students who regurgitate what they lecture in class." Todd got up and poured himself a drink. "Let's just drop it."

Conversation had been sparse since then. She did not know how to handle Todd's moods or his jealousy. He had always encouraged her to do her best, and now he was angry when she did. Why couldn't he just be happy for her success?

She noticed Todd put down his pen and pull out his porno magazine. Their love life had also taken a turn for the worst. Todd had become very demanding and kept asking her to do weird things, things she would never think of doing on her own. She tried her best to be open-minded, but it seemed wrong. He also asked her to use a device that was supposed to increase her breast size. He had his gentle moments, and he said that relationships were both give and take. He told her he would do anything she wanted to do, but what she wanted was moments like the first night at the top of the tower. She tried to explain that she wanted romance, but complained they had very little money for it. It was true. Todd's parents refused to give them any extra money when they found out Todd had paid her tuition. They were not eating at the school cafeteria, and they did all their cooking on a one-burner hot plate. They ate lots of hot dogs and sandwiches.

Tonight, they would have a treat: boiled chicken with potatoes and carrots. The smell of chicken stewed in bay leaves and parsley cheered her a little.

"Todd, after dinner, can we go for a walk by the lake and maybe have dessert at that little restaurant on the way?"

Todd put down his magazine and faced her. "Well, maybe. I'll have to check and see how much money I have left."

"If we can't afford dessert, it still would be nice to walk by the lake."

"Okay, but I want you to look at this." He handed her the magazine. "I want to try this tonight."

Carol glanced at the picture and turned away. She wanted to throw the magazine back at Todd and refuse.

Todd knelt by her chair. "You don't look too excited. What's wrong?"

Carol let the magazine fall to the floor. "It looks so unsanitary. And I think it would hurt."

"We can both clean up real good before. I'll be very gentle."

"Todd, what's wrong with just doing it the natural way? This doesn't seem natural to me."

"Okay, if you don't want to do it later, we don't have to." He paused. "Carol, I'm sorry I was so grumpy earlier today. It wasn't your fault Professor Wills is an inane, close-minded, pompous fool. We can go for the walk, and I'll try my best to be romantic. I love you."

Carol looked at Todd and some of the old excitement came back. She really did love him. He was trying. He probably sensed her preoccupation with seeing her mystery man. In her mind, she had cheated on Todd, and she felt bad about it. She had been so stupid to go looking for him when there was a man who loved her right in front of her.

"I love you, too." She wrapped her arms around his neck.

"Hey." Todd pulled away. "I forgot to show you." He pulled a plastic bag out of his backpack. "We already have dessert for tonight. Kevin sold these to me today."

"What are they?"

"Magic brownies. We can have them after our walk."

***

She was desperate to find a bathroom. Down the long corridor she ran, opening door after door, asking the occupants if they had a bathroom inside. "No," they answered or they glared at her. Her bladder screamed for relief. I'm going to wet my pants! Finally, she found a bathroom, but people crowded the room. She waded through old ladies and little children, unable to wait her

113

turn. She made it to the front of the line just as a man came out of one of the stalls. He grinned at her and laughed as he passed by. It was the same man who worked at the x-rated movie theater. She opened the stall door, and filth covered the toilet. She looked in the next stall and found the same. She opened door after door, but each toilet was soiled. At the end of the long row of stalls, there was a toilet out in the open. The crowd stared at her, but she had no choice but to use it.

She awoke to an intense sensation to urinate. Beside her, Todd slept deeply. The alarm clock read 2:00. She had to go to the restroom that instant. She put on a pair of shorts and a shirt, grabbed her keys, and rushed out the door. The hall was dark with only pale night lights to mark the way. She switched on the bathroom light, and the brightness hurt her eyes. Adjusting to the florescent bulbs, she was relieved to find the bathroom free of people and the toilets clean.

After she urinated, it still felt like she still had to go. A sharp, stinging sensation shot up into her abdomen, and stomach acid surged into her mouth. As she turned to flush, she noticed the water in the bowl was red. *Oh, dear God, what's wrong with me?* Terrified, Carol stumbled back to the room, holding her stomach.

"Todd, wake up." She shook him. "Something's wrong with me. I'm bleeding."

Todd rolled over. "What?"

"I'm sick. I think I should go to the hospital."

Todd leaned on his elbow. "What are you talking about?"

"I feel like I have to go to the bathroom even when I just went. And blood came out."

"Okay, don't panic." Todd sat on the side of the bed.

Carol wiggled around the room, bent over and clutching the painful area. "Todd, I've got to go to the bathroom again. I'll be right back." She ran out.

When she made it to the toilet, nothing came out but blood. Tears poured down her face, and she doubled over as sharp pains came in waves. She was afraid to leave the toilet. How could she make it to the hospital when she felt like going every second?

"Oh, mommy, mommy. I want my mommy," she said out loud, sobbing in pain and terror. "I want to go home."

Chapter Seventeen

From her cubicle office, Margaret dialed the number again, and it rang on and on. No answer. She had tried to reach this student the previous week, but the phone was either busy or no-one answered. If he didn't talk to her soon, he would not have time to reschedule the class that had been canceled for fall quarter. She knew the young man had a wife and small child and desired to finish his associate's degree from the Community College of Vermont in the fall so he could better provide for his family. As she placed the receiver back on the phone, she decided to stop by his apartment on the way home from work. Deerfield was a small town, and Margaret knew where he lived.

The receptionist walked over to her cubicle. "There's a call for you."

"Do you know who it is?"

"It's your daughter Carol."

"Okay, thanks Shelly."

Margaret took a deep breath and watched the call bottom blink for a moment. Carol hadn't talked to her since her birthday, hadn't even called once to let her know how college was going. She most likely wanted or needed something from her. *I might as well get it over with.* Margaret let out her breath, punched the button, and picked up the receiver.

"Hello, this is Margaret Weideman, can I help you?"

"Mom, it's me."

"Carol, are you all right? You sound upset."

"I'm at the UVM medical clinic. I'm really sick."

"What's wrong?" Margaret put her hand to her throat.

"They say I have a bladder infection. Mom, it hurts real bad. I bleed when I go to the bathroom. I can hardly stay still. I couldn't sleep at all last night."

Margaret could hear the desperation in Carol's voice. "I'm so sorry, baby. Do you want me to come up there?"

"Um...I don't know." Carol paused for a second. "Mom, the doctor needs to talk to you. I don't have any money or insurance information."

"Is Todd with you?"

"Yeah, but his parents didn't give him any extra money. Could you talk to the doctor?"

"Sure, Hon." After a few moments of silence, a man's voice came on the phone.

"Is this Mrs. Weideman?"

"Yes."

"Are you Carol Weideman's mother?"

"Yes, I am."

"Your daughter has an acute bladder infection, but she's under age. I need your approval before I can treat her."

"Oh, certainly. You have my approval."

"We'll allow the verbal approval for the moment, but we will have to send you paperwork to sign. We will also need your insurance information. Do you have insurance?"

"Yes, I do. I can get that." Margaret reached for her purse while she cradled the phone between her shoulder and head. She pulled out her wallet and found her insurance card.

"Mrs. Weideman, how far away from here are you?"

"Three hours drive."

"Well, if you can't stop by, we could mail the forms."

"I don't know. I can come up there if my daughter wants me to."

"That's your decision." Something in the tone of the doctor's voice bothered her. Did he think she was a negligent mother?

"Doctor, how is my daughter doing?"

"She'll be fine once she starts taking antibiotics. We gave her some medication to help with the pain."

"Will she need a follow-up appointment? Should I get her into my family doctor?"

"We can check her urine again in a week to make sure the infection is gone. It's up to you if you want to have her seen by your doctor. Bladder infections are common for girls who are sexually active."

Margaret set her wallet down on the desk hard. She did not like the Doctor's tone at all. Was he trying to find out if she realized her daughter was having sex? Was it an accusation that she was allowing her daughter to be in a dangerous situation?

"Can I talk to my daughter again?"

"After you give the receptionist the needed information. Hold on just a minute."

"Wait, doctor…" It was too late. He was gone.

Margaret gave the receptionist all the required information, then asked, "Can I talk to the doctor again?"

"Well, he's with another patient. We have a busy schedule here and only one doctor."

"How about a nurse?"

"I can have her call you back."

"Never mind. I want to speak to my daughter again."

"Hold on just a minute."

Margaret tapped her pen restlessly against the desk while listening to dead air for several minutes. As soon as she was finished talking on phone, she would tell her boss she had a family emergency and needed to leave. It was 2:12 PM. If she hurried, she could be back by 9:00 or 10:00. Liz was home and could make dinner for the younger kids.

"Mrs. Weideman? This is Todd."

"Todd? Where's Carol. I want to talk to her."

"She's with the nurse right now. She's going to be okay."

"She sounded pretty upset when I talked to her. I'm coming up there."

"Wait…Mrs. Weideman, Carol's fine. You don't need to drive all the way up here."

"I want to! She's my daughter!"

"Well, by the time you get here, Carol will be in class."

"I don't care. I can wait for her. How can she concentrate in class if she feels that bad?"

"The pain medication is starting to work. She's a lot better already."

"I want to talk to her, Todd."

"Well, this is a long distance phone call, and she's still with the nurse."

"Either I talk to Carol right now or I'm coming up there."

"Okay. Wait just a minute."

On hold again, Margaret stood up and paced in her cubicle. Her colleagues were glancing at her with curiosity. She had the urge to hang up and get into her car that minute. That controlling Todd was just trying to keep her from her daughter. He never wanted Carol near her family because then he couldn't control her every move. Maybe she would come home this time. But that would mess up her class and hurt her record. Maybe she could come home on the weekend and recuperate.

"Mom, it's Carol."

"Oh, sweetheart, how are you feeling?"

"I feel better."

"Are you sure? You sounded shaky just a few minutes ago."

"The pain medicine is beginning to work. I'll be okay."

"Hon, I can be there in three hours. Just tell me where the clinic's located."

"Mom, no, you don't need to come up here. I'm doing a lot better, really."

"But I want to. I want to be there for you."

"Mom, it's okay. It's too far for you to come. The doctor said bladder infections are not that serious. It's just that it's the first time it's happened to me so I was scared."

"Please, Carol, tell me where the clinic is. I want to see you."

"No. I'm fine. Todd's taking care of me."

"But Carol."

"No, Mom. I have to go now. Thanks for your offer. Goodbye."

She hung up before Margaret had a chance to say another word. Margaret put the receiver down slowly. She did not even have the number to the clinic to call back. She rushed to the bathroom before the entire office saw the tears streaming down her face. Every time she made an attempt to love her child, something was there to keep her from her. It wasn't right, it just wasn't right. Carol did not belong to Todd, yet he held her in his grip like a spider in a web. The first time she talked to Carol, it was plain she wanted her mother. Todd did something to convince Carol to change her mind. If she went to her now, Carol would probably tell her to go away. The doctor at that office must think she's a horrible mother. Maybe she should drive up there just to show the doctor she wasn't an abusive parent. At least Carol would know she really does care about her.

"Margaret, are you in there?" Shelly knocked on the door. "That young man you've been trying to get in touch with is on the phone."

"Okay, just a minute." She had to take this call.

By the time Margaret had finished with her phone call, it was already 2:45. Her boss came in right after that and talked to her until 3:15. He walked out before she had a chance to ask him if she could leave. She stood to follow him, then slumped back into her chair. What was the use? Carol didn't want her, and even if she did, Todd would find some way to intervene. She opened the folder left on her desk and started working.

***

"Todd, can you believe it? My first college class and I got an *A*." Carol and Todd were walking back to their dorm. Carol was re-reading the comments on her final paper. She hugged the paper to her chest and skipped down the pathway.

It was a hot, muggy day in early August. An even layer of clouds blocked the sun and held in the heat like a greenhouse. Todd's navy-blue tee shirt was already wet and sticky. He could not understand why Carol wanted to skip. Big deal, she got an A on her first college class. He was used to getting A's in all his classes. The only reason she did so well was because he had helped her.

"Carol, slow down. It's too hot!" Carol stopped and turned to him. She had such a big smile on her face, like a child who had just be given a Christmas present. He shouldn't spoil her mood, but he would have to. They had adult problems to deal with.

"Thanks, babe." Todd forced himself to smile.

"Todd, is something wrong? You don't seem very happy. You did all right in the classes didn't you?"

"Of course I did. I'll show you when we get to the room. Professor Wills gave me an A+ on my final paper. And I aced the Psychology class."

"Oh, Todd, that's great!" Carol took his hand and gave it a squeeze. "I owe this A to you. I would never have done so well without your help."

They walked without speaking for a few minutes. Todd had so much on his mind. He did not know where to start or how to tell her.

Carol broke the silence. "So, if you did well in both your classes, why do you seem so gloomy?"

"Well, I was going to wait until we got to the room." Todd rolled up his paper, stuck it in his back pocket, and wiped his sweaty hands on his jeans. "There's a bench over there. Let's sit down and talk."

"Sure." Carol's green eyes met his. Today, she looked more like a child than a woman. It was his responsibility to take care of her. The weight of it pressed on him like the heavy moisture in the air. He looked away.

When they reached the bench, Todd sat down and took off his glasses. Sweat from his forehead had dirtied the lenses, and he used his tee shirt to wipe them off.

119

"I might as well tell you straight, Carol. We're practically broke and have no place to live."

"What?" Carol turned to him. He did not want to look at her. "What are you talking about?"

"I told you my parents were upset with me for paying for your tuition, remember? Well, not only did they say I wasn't getting any more money, they told me I had to find a place to live."

"You mean you can't, we can't, stay at your house?"

"That's what I mean."

"Todd, why didn't you tell me this before?" Carol swiped her forehead with her arm and picked at her fingers, like she always did when she was upset. She would bite the skin by her thumb nail and pull it off. He hated when she did this. He grabbed her hand.

"Carol, stop chewing your thumbs."

"Leave me alone." She pulled her hand away and put her thumb to her mouth. "What are we going to do, Todd? We have to pack and leave UVM today. I can't stay with the old lady anymore. She found someone to take my place. And I doubt my mom would let us live together at her place."

"We're not going to live with your mother!"

"Then just where *are* we going to live?" Her eyes became more yellow when she was angry.

"I don't know." Todd put his elbows on his knees and placed his head in his hands. "Let me think a minute."

"Well, let's start with money. How much do you have left?"

"About $500."

"That's not broke. I thought we had like ten dollars left."

"Five hundred dollars is nothing when you have to support yourself." Carol could be such a child at times. She had no idea what responsibility entailed.

"Look, Carol. I need to find a job and a place for us to live. Five hundred dollars will only last a few weeks, especially if we have to stay in a hotel. We have to pay for food, gas, lodging, everything."

"I know. But at least we have something."

Todd did not answer. Carol stared straight ahead, her hands on her lap, fingers busy scratching on the sore spot of skin on her thumb. He recalled the cold stare his father gave him when he handed him his last check. "Todd, this is the last support check you will receive from your mother and me. You will be finished with college, and it's time for you to make it on your own. Use it wisely."

He had sat in his father's study like a wayward student before the principal. Bookcases lined the cherry-paneled room, and an antique grandfather clock passed down from his grandparents drilled a steady "tick, tick" from the corner. The massive cherry-wood desk that separated them gave his dad an air of wealth and power. His mother stood next to her husband, her stern expression a silent agreement with his announcement.

"Dad, Mom, I'm really sorry that I didn't ask you about Carol."

"We've already been through this," said his mom, her voice flat and controlled. "You betrayed our trust, and this is the consequence."

"You'll have to find your own place to live when you get home from college," said his Dad as he put his checkbook back in his desk drawer. The check was lying on the desk, waiting for Todd to pick it up. He knew that once he did, it would be over.

"Can't we have a few days when we get out to find something first?"

"No!" His mother's shrill voice rang in his ear. "We do not condone your behavior, and we will not allow you and your under-aged girlfriend to live in our house."

His parents glared at him in unison, two drill sergeants daring him to defy their authority. The "tick, tick" of the clock droned on, the only noise in the room. If they had shouted at him or if his mother had cried, it would have been easier. The resolve of disgust in their eyes was as effective as a judge's gavel banging a guilty verdict on a criminal. Fighting them would be useless.

Todd had taken the check and escaped their frigid, unforgiving eyes. He had walked away, but the judgment of those eyes remained. "You are not welcomed here anymore," they said. "Don't even dare to penetrate our fortress. You will fail."

Todd stood up. They had to move out of the dorm room today. "We'd better get packing."

"Okay." Carol followed behind him, head low. Todd kicked at every rock, stone, or litter that had the audacity to enter his path. Life wasn't fair. His parent's did not understand his love for Carol. No matter how hard she tried, she would never meet their standards. She would always be the uneducated, poor babysitter who went after their son for his money. The only way he could go home was to give her up, and he could not do that. She was his life, and to be cut off from her would be death. He could not imagine being without her now. Life before her had been a desolate, dry desert of loneliness. He had no friends, and the only girls he had were in his dreams. The first day he met her, hope stirred within. She sat with him, listened to his dreams, and even smiled. When she smiled, he realized she was beautiful. Like a rose bud in the first stages of blossom, half-girl, half-woman, Carol was waiting to be groomed, watered, and plucked. Since that day, he had tilled the soil, planted the seeds, and let his garden grow into a delicious, succulent, blooming masterpiece. He could taste of her fruit any time he wished, and nothing would keep him from his garden.

No, they would find a way somehow to make it. They had each other, and that would be enough. No one—not his parents, not her mother, not money or circumstances would keep them apart. She was his forever.

Todd turned around and clutched Carol in a desperate hug. "Don't worry, Babe. It's going to be all right. As long as we stay together, we'll make it."

Part Three

Fresh Air Through an Open Window

Six Months Later

I planted the seed, Apollos watered it, but God made it grow. (I Corinthians 3:6)

Chapter Eighteen

Carol read the information Mrs. Meeks passed out about the trip to France for the forth time. As a third year student, she was eligible to spend two weeks in France and live with a French family. Students would visit Paris for a few days, then head south to Lyon to meet their families and go to school with a French girl or boy their same age. If only she could afford to go on the trip. Two-thirds of her classmates were going, and they talked about it every French class. Some of them were already writing to the students in France selected for them. But Todd was just a desk clerk and barely made enough to pay the rent on their apartment. He had been unable to find a teaching job at any of the local schools. There was no money for her to go.

Memories of last summer lingered like the odor in the wastebasket under the sink. She would take out the garbage, wipe the container clean, only to have it return dirty and stinky again the next week. Thoughts of the heat, the humidity, the stench, the dirt, the fear, the uncertainty, the fights. After finishing their classes at the University of Vermont, she and Todd had scrambled to find a place to live and jobs to pay for an apartment. Carol would never forget spending two weeks in a room above the old Deerfield movie theater. They slept in a dirty cubicle with a hundred year old mattress and about the same aged linoleum floors, and a shared a bathroom down the hall with all the local transients. The shower stank of mildew and whatever other seething stuff grew on the floor and in the soiled drain. She wore thongs whenever she went in there so she did not have to touch anything. As for the toilet, she preferred to use the restrooms at restaurants or even the rest stop on the freeway.

Carol scratched and shivered as she thought about the hundreds of tiny red marks that had covered her arms and legs. They had resorted to sleeping on the floor on a double sized air mattress to escape the fleas. "I can't take this anymore!" she yelled late one night. "We're out of calamine lotion, and I can't stop itching!"

"Carol, quiet down. We don't want that scary old man knocking on our door again."

"But I can't sleep, Todd! I have bites everywhere!"

"So do I, but you don't hear me complaining." Todd rolled over on the air mattress, and his weight tilted it in his direction.

"I can't help it." Carol smashed her body into the mattress to keep from sliding. "How long are we going to have to stay here?"

"I told you, we can't afford anything else."

"I think I'd rather live in a tent than this."

"I'm sorry, but I told you it would be tough until I found a job."

Carol sat up and rubbed her arms. "Well, I can't take this much longer. Maybe I should just go back to my Mom's until you get a job."

"What?" Todd turned toward her. "You're not serious. We agreed to stick together no matter how hard it got. You can't abandon me now. Where will I go? I have only about $100 left. And your Mom would never let me stay there."

"Well, I don't know. Maybe you should just talk to your parents and see if they will change their minds. Anything's better than this."

Todd swore and sat up. "I can't believe you'd have the gall to ask me that. Hey, I chose you over them, and now you're complaining? You'd better think about what you're saying to me."

"I'm sorry, but I only said it because we are running out of money and living in a flee bag hotel with a bunch of street people for neighbors."

"Do you think I like it any better than you? Do you think I'm purposely turning down jobs? I've been out every day, up and down town, driving all around, looking for a job. I don't see you out there working either. It's not like I'm the only one without money."

"Todd, you're being mean. If that's the way you feel about me, I'm going home!" Carol got off the floor and grabbed her pants from on top of her suitcase.

"Oh no you're not! You can't just leave me here after all I've done for you." Todd took her arm and pushed her back to the floor.

"You keep your hands off me!"

Someone thumped on the wall. "Hey, you guys shut up!"

"Okay, we're going to get kicked out if you don't settle down. Now stop right now!" Todd squeezed her arm hard enough to make her scream, then covered her mouth to stifle it. Afraid to move, she sat on the plastic mattress doing her best to hold back the tears. Todd had never hurt her like that before. Should she make a run for it or stay? If she waited for Todd to fall asleep, she could sneak out, find a pay phone, and call her mother. But then she would have to admit she'd made a mistake with Todd. Could she face the disgrace? Then again, could she stand living like this another night? No, she could not. Todd had not even apologized. She would wait and make her move.

It was so quiet she could hear the buzz of the neon light outside the window. She turned to see if Todd had fallen asleep. Then he spoke.

"Carol, are you okay? I'm sorry I grabbed your arm."

She willed herself to say nothing, to remain a rigid statue that would not allow him to break through her cold determination. But then he touched her.

"I'm really sorry."

The tears came fast and furious. "You hurt me, Todd. I bet I have a huge bruise. My arm already hurt with all the bug bites on it. You shouldn't have done that. I don't want to be here anymore."

"You're right, I shouldn't have. I just don't want to lose you." Todd paused. "I know you don't want to be here. Neither do I. But we're on our own now, and we have to depend on each other. We can't go back to our parents. They don't understand our relationship. They don't understand how much we love each other." Todd put his arms around her. The statue shattered.

"Just be patient, Carol. It won't be much longer. I have a second interview at the Howard Johnson's tomorrow. If I get the job, we can probably stay there at a reduced rate. Now lie down and get some sleep."

Carol cried for a few more minutes, then lay down. She stared at the ceiling and bit her tongue to keep from scratching. She never did sleep that night. The next day, Howard Johnson Hotel offered Todd a job, and they were able to move out. Later that week, Carol started working in the café attached to the hotel, and they saved money on food as well. What a wonderful day it had been when they moved into this apartment. The landlady seemed like an angel then. She did not even ask for first and last down, and they only had a $50 damage deposit. The six hundred square feet of space felt like a mansion after that suffocating room.

"See, Carol, it all worked out. We managed on our own," Todd had told her. That had been the best night of a horrible summer. If only she could forget the rest.

Carol sighed, tossed the pamphlet on the old, green couch, and walked into the compact kitchen to start dinner. She had taken out hamburger that morning before school, and it had unthawed in the sink, leaving blood stains on the white porcelain. She threw the messy meat into a large pot and set it on a burner. As she turned on the stove, flames came to life with a whoosh, leaving a faint odor of natural gas. She stepped back. Whenever she used the gas stove, she thought about the author of *The Bell Jar*, Sylvia Plath, who committed suicide with a gas oven.

A half hour later, her homemade spaghetti sauce with onions, carrots, celery, and green pepper, simmered on the stove, erasing the gas smell, filling the one-bedroom apartment with an enticing aroma. She had become quite a cook since moving in with Todd, and she knew how to feed them well on a limited budget. The sauce would last through the end of the week.

Carol just started her Algebra homework when the phone rang.

"Hello?"

"Hi Carol, it's Mom. How are you doing?"

"I'm okay. Todd should be home soon for dinner. Everything okay with you?" Margaret did not call very often, so Carol wondered what was going on.

"Everything's fine, Dear. I just wanted to talk to you about something."

"Oh, what?" Carol stirred the sauce on the stove.

"Remember that trip to France you were talking about at Christmas? Well, Jim and I have been talking about it, and if you want to go, I think we can pull it off."

Carol stopped stirring the sauce and stood speechless for a few seconds. "What did you say?"

"Do you want to go to France?"

"Yes, oh yes I do! Mom, are you serious? Do you really mean it? Are you sure you can afford it?"

"Yes, Carol, we can. Jim and I have a little extra tucked away."

"Oh my, oh my, I can't believe it! Do you really mean it?" Carol jumped up and down, then remembered she was in the upstairs apartment. Her landlady lived below, and often complained about the noise.

"Yes, we mean it. Why don't you come by this weekend and we can discuss the details. Mrs. Meeks said you needed a down payment by next week, so bring all the paperwork, and we'll fill it out."

"Okay, sure, Mom. I still can't believe you're doing this. I get to go to France! Wow! I never thought I'd have a chance to do such a thing. Thanks, Mom, thanks so much."

"We love you, Carol. You deserve such an opportunity, especially the way you've worked so hard at school."

Carol took a deep breath and swallowed hard. "Oh, Mom, I don't know what to say. Thank you so much. Thank Jim for me, will you?"

"Of course, Dear. Well, this is long distance, so I'd better go. Why don't you stop by Friday night."

"That'll work. Todd works late on Fridays, so I'll have nothing else to do."

"Great, we'll see you then."

"Okay, Mom. Thanks again….and…I love you."

"I love you, too."

That was the first time Carol had told her mother she loved her in years. She stumbled back into the living room and sat down on the couch, wiping the tears that had dripped all the way to the top of her cranberry, turtle-necked sweater. She had neglected her family since moving in with Todd, only coming around for birthdays and Christmas. Yet they had not disowned her. They stilled loved her, and now her mom and Jim had found a way to scrape together $1,000 to pay for a trip she had only dreamed about minutes before.

She picked up the discarded pamphlet and outlined the pictures of Paris and the Eiffel Tower with her fingers. In a few months, she would be boarding a plane that would take her to the picture. She kissed the shiny paper and hugged it to her chest. Then she danced around the room. "Paris, sweet Paris, you call to me from across the sea. Soon you shall be mine, my sweet Paris. J'amour Paris."

***

Carol peeked through a slant in the metal blind as she heard the door to Todd's VW bug slam. She had been counting the minutes until he arrived home. The table was already set, complete with green salad, a bottle of white wine, and French bread purchased from the store down the street. She had changed into a jean mini-skirt and pink blouse and curled her hair. When Todd could be heard on the last step, she opened the door to greet him. "Todd." She gave him a big hug before he was over the threshold.

"Wait a minute, Carol. You're making me drop my stuff." Todd had a folder of papers and his lunch box in his hands. His coat had a dusting of snow, and his glasses were fogged over. He pushed past her and let the papers and lunch box drop on the Formica table in their small dining nook, almost tipping over one of the wine glasses. Carol doubted he even saw the table settings.

"What a day! I've never seen such whiny, simple-minded imbeciles in my life. 'My room smells like smoke, the sheets made us itch, I need extra shampoo, the room's too hot, the room's too cold, the pool's too cold, our neighbor's are making too much noise.'" Todd pulled off his snow-laden boots and threw them in the entry, then squirmed out of his heavy coat and tossed it on a chair. "On and on and on they complain with never a thank you. Then my boss gives me this contract to look over in my spare time! He's paying me peanuts but wants me to be his lawyer! It's because he's such a tight wad that all his customers complain. But I'm the one who has to take it!"

Carol opened her mouth to say something, then closed it. Todd did not even notice that she had dressed up for him. She wanted to say something, but didn't want to ruin the evening. She retreated to the kitchen, drained spaghetti noodles, and set the warm items on the small table.

Todd was sitting in the living room, unlacing his brown tie, loosening the collar on his brown shirt, taking off his brown shoes. "Man, I've got to find a better job. I don't know how much longer I can stand it. My schedule is all screwed up, working day shift during the week and swing shift on the weekend. My days off are in the middle of the week while you're at school. I hate it! And I hate this stupid uniform!"

"Todd, are you hungry? Dinner's ready."

Todd stopped and finally noticed the table. He sniffed the air. "Hey, it smells great in here. Looks like we're having spaghetti. And you set the table with wine glasses. Did I forget something? Is there some special occasion I missed?"

"No. I have something I want to tell you. But let's start eating first."

Todd took a seat at the table, poured himself a full glass of wine, and gulped down half the glass. "This is just what a man needs at the end of a lousy day. A glass of wine and a beautiful girl waiting for him."

Carol smiled and dished out the food. Now she was glad she made the extra effort to celebrate.

The room was quiet for several minutes as Todd vacuumed a plate full of spaghetti, salad and French bread. Carol picked at her food and waited for him to ask her about her surprise. As the minutes droned on like years, she could wait no longer.

"Todd, I thought you'd want to know what we're celebrating."

"Sure, Hon, what's up?" Todd cut himself another piece of bread.

"My Mom called today with wonderful news."

"Your Mom?" Todd put down his bread and looked at her. "What did she want? Don't tell me she's planning to marry that Jim guy."

"No, silly, the news has nothing to do with her. It has to do with me."

"Oh." She had his undivided attention now.

"Yes. Remember that trip to France I talked to you about? The one that most of my class is taking in the spring? Well, you're not going to believe it, but my Mom offered to pay for me to go."

"What?" Todd's gray eyes met hers.

"I'm going to France! Can you believe it, Todd? I'm going to Paris, then to Lyon to stay with a French family. It's like a dream come true."

"Your Mom is paying for the trip? How can she afford it?" Todd turned away and twisted spaghetti noodles with his fork.

"I don't know. I think Jim helped her."

"That's great." Todd did not even look up from his plate. Where was the smile she expected? Wasn't he happy for her? Instead of sharing her joy, Todd stuffed his face and avoided her glance.

"Todd, aren't you happy for me?'

"Sure, Carol. I'm happy for you."

"Then why do you look so gloomy?"

Todd set down his fork, put his hair behind his ears, and refilled his glass with wine before answering. "It'll be great for you, Carol, but did you ever consider what I'm going to do while you're gone?"

"I'll only be gone a couple of weeks, Todd. You'll do fine without me. Are you sure that's all?"

Todd got up from the table and took his wine into the living room. "I don't know why I'm not happy for you, Carol. I guess I sound selfish. Maybe it's because I couldn't pay for it myself. I mean, we're a household now, and I should be able to help pay for your trip."

Carol sat down beside Todd and took his hand. "Todd, you shouldn't feel bad at all. You've been out of college less than a year. It takes time to find a good job and save money."

"I hate my job."

"I know. You'll find a better job soon. Don't be so hard on yourself."

"And I wish I could go with you. There'll be other guys on the trip, and guys in France will hit on you. I wish I could be there to protect you from them."

"Oh, for goodness sakes, Todd." Carol pulled away and went back to clear the table. "It always comes back to the same thing. You always worry that I'm going to take off with some other guy. I'm sick of your jealousy. You think every guy is looking at me, and it really makes me mad because you don't trust my love for you."

Todd rose from the couch swearing. "You just don't get it, Carol! It's not you I'm worried about! You have no idea what kind of creeps are out there, ready to prey on pretty, young, naive girls like you."

Carol turned and glared at him. "And since when I am a naïve girl? I think you've taught me just about everything there is to know about guys and sex."

"That's it, Carol. Now you've gone too far." Todd kicked a chair, grabbed his coat, and headed for the door. "I'll talk to you when you can be civil."

"Wait, Todd, I'm sorry. Where are you going?"

"Out for a while, until you cool off."

"Please, Todd, wait. Let's talk this out." Carol reached for his arm, but he pulled away.

"Carol, I will not allow you to treat me with disrespect. Think about that while I'm gone." With those words, Todd turned, opened the door, and left. Carol pushed his work papers on the floor, threw his lunch box into the living room, ran to the bedroom and slammed the door.

***

Carol picked up a folder of papers on the seat next to her and pulled on the door handle, hesitating. She was parked next to her Mom's old, blue Rambler station wagon in the paved driveway of the house Margaret rented with Jim. It was the newest home her family had ever lived in, an under ten year old split level with cedar siding painted white with green trim. The house had a fenced yard in back, and woods surrounded the rest of the acre of land it stood on.

She had never tried to be nice to Jim before, and today she worried that she would come across as an unappreciative, spoiled child. Whether she liked him or not, he had helped her Mom with the money, and she wanted to make a good impression. She even wore the navy slacks, rayon, button-up, white blouse, and navy loafers Jim and Margaret had given her at Christmas. She was glad the driveway had been shoveled because she forgot to put on her boots.

She sighed and stepped out of the car. Before she had a chance to knock, Jean was in the doorway to greet her.

"Carol!" Jean gave her a big hug. She seemed taller than at Christmas and actually wore a pink shirt with her dungarees. Jean was growing up.

"Hi Jean." Carol smelled something cooking as soon as she entered the house. "What's that wonderful smell?"

"Mom's been cooking roast beef in the crock pot all day."

Carol followed Jean up the entry steps into the dining room/kitchen area. Jim, Marie, and Liz were sitting at the table playing Parcheesi. Margaret came out of the kitchen, took off her oven mitts, and embraced Carol, kissing her lightly on the cheek. "We're so glad to see you, Dear."

Carol didn't flinch at the kiss and returned the hug. She noticed Margaret had let her hair grow out, and the soft, shoulder-length curls made her look younger. She wore an apron that said, "World's Best Cook," a Christmas present from Jim.

"Hi Mom. I smell more than roast beef. Are you making one of your yummy apple pies?"

"What gave you that idea?" Jim's baritone voice filled the room. He rose from his chair to greet her. "It wouldn't be the pot holders in her hands that gave her away would it?" He gave Carol a bear hug. Marie and Liz followed behind, wrapping their arms around her together.

"Nice to have you home," said Liz.

"Me too," said Marie.

"Thanks, Sisses. Nice to be here." Carol smiled. Liz had become quite a young lady. She wore a knitted, white sweater and jeans that showed her maturing figure. Gone were her gawky, skinny legs, and her dark hair and skin tone against the white gave her a striking appearance. The best part was that Liz was not even aware of her beauty. Marie was not far behind Liz in height. She had gained at least two inches over the summer and had reached a height of 5'6" already, just an inch away from Liz's 5'7." At twelve, Marie was still a girl, a muscular, athletic girl who could outrun many boys her age. She played soccer in the fall, basketball in the winter, and baseball in the spring.

"Is Jessica going to be here tonight?" Carol set down her folder and took a seat at the long table.

"She's working. Tom lost another job, so she's been working extra hours at the A&P."

"Oh, that's too bad. I'm glad Todd at least has a job."

"I need some help setting the table," her mother called from the kitchen.

"Let's set the game on the coffee table, girls. We can finish it after dinner." Jim picked up the game board.

"I'll get the dishes," said Carol.

"I'll help you." Liz followed her into the kitchen.

"Mom, is that an artichoke you're cooking?" Carol opened the lid in the double boiler. "It is. I haven't had an artichoke in years."

"I thought you might like that," said Margaret, pouring gravy into a bowl.

Once or twice a year, her mom would buy an artichoke, and they would dip the leaves in butter and eat the edible portion at the end of the leaves. When they reached the heart, each would get a small bite of the delicious delicacy.

"Man, I'm starving all of a sudden."

"Well, let's get this dinner on the table, then."

Carol loaded her plate with roast beef, mashed potatoes, gravy, salad, and artichoke. "This is great, Mom."

"Thanks."

"And the best thing is that I didn't have to make it."

Jim chuckled and smiled at Carol. "Now that's when true appreciation comes. When we know how much work it takes ourselves."

It didn't take long for her family to consume the food before them. Carol thought she could eat no more, until her mom put the apple pie on the table, still warm and radiating an aroma of apples and cinnamon.

"Did you leave some room for pie and ice cream?" Margaret asked.

"I always have room for your apple pie." Jim reached for Margaret's hand and squeezed it. Her Mom gave him a big smile. Carol had to fight the old feelings of anger whenever she watched her mother be affectionate with men. She had to admit that Jim treated her mom better than her other boyfriends, maybe even better than her father had.

After dessert, everyone cleared the table, even Jim. He also helped with the dishes, and the cleaning was finished in no time.

"Well, now that the work is done, let's talk about that trip." Jim lead Margaret by the hand, and they all sat down again at the table, including Liz, Marie and Jean.

"Mom, should I get the books we checked out from the library?" asked Jean.

"Sure, go ahead."

Jean ran downstairs and returned with a stack of picture books about France, including an Atlas.

Carol retrieved her folder and put it in front of her mother. "Here's the paperwork I need filled out. I put in all the information I could, but I don't know about health insurance. Am I still covered by your insurance?"

"Of course you are," said Margaret. "You're still under eighteen. The insurance company doesn't know that you don't live here."

"Well, that's good." Carol turned away and reached for one of the library books. She glanced at the colorful pictures of vineyards and midieval architecture while Margaret and Jim read through the papers and filled in the blanks. Margaret took her checkbook out of her purse and wrote a check.

"Everything looks good, Carol. You can give this to Mrs. Meeks on Monday, and you should be good to go." Her mom put the check and the forms back in the folder and handed it to her.

"You guys, thanks so much." She got up from her chair and gave her mom and Jim a hug. "I still can't believe you did this for me."

"Carol, I noticed you have a hole in your sock. Do you need some clothes for the trip?"

"Oh, you guys have done too much already. I'll be okay."

"When was the last time you bought any new clothes?"

"You and Jim gave me this nice outfit for Christmas. I'm fine."

"Well, we didn't buy you any underwear." Her mom gave her a funny look. "When was the last time Todd bought you some new underwear?"

"We don't have much money, Mom. I haven't worked since summer because my workload at school is so great, and we only have one car. Things have been tight."

"Then let's plan a shopping spree before your trip."

"Oh, Mom, are you sure you can afford it?"

"Don't you worry about it, Carol. We want this to be the best two weeks of your life. We want to do this for you, and we don't want you thinking twice about taking it from us."

Carol locked eyes with Jim, and a tangle of emotions churned within. She didn't want to like him, but his kindness made it difficult. For the first time, she realized he was not just another one of her mom's faceless boyfriends, men who came and went, who she chose to ignore and forget. Jim's eyes were as blue as a clear winter day after a snowstorm, when the air was new and clean. He wasn't the most handsome man in the world—he dressed like an old Vermonter with his red and green checkered shirt, and the gray streaks in his hair showed his age—and he was always chewing on a toothpick or something else. But his eyes had a special quality. A warm sensation spread to Carol's chest, and she had to lower her eyes because she was afraid if she didn't, he would be able to see straight into her soul.

"What do you say we all play a round of Uno." Jim turned his focus to Jean.

"Uno. Yeah, let's play Uno." Jean ran from the table to the game closet.

Carol played Uno with her family. Later she spent time poring over the library books with her mom, Liz, and Jim. She learned that Liz loved her high school psychology class and had excellent grades. Liz shared Carol's aspirations to obtain scholarships and complete a college degree.

"Liz, maybe you could come spend a weekend with me some time. I could help you with your homework if you like, and we could look at colleges together."

"Thanks for the offer, Carol, but I'd like it even better if you spent a weekend here. Then I could show you the book I've been working on. I have my own room now, so there's plenty of space for you to sleep."

Carol knew Liz did not feel comfortable around Todd. She wondered if Todd would let her spend a Friday night and Saturday with her family. He worked both Friday and Saturday night anyway.

"I didn't know you were writing a book? What's it about?"

"It's about a Jewish girl during WWII. A Nazi officer who hates what he's doing falls in love with her and helps her and other Jewish prisoners escape."

"What a great idea? Where did you come up with that?"

"I thought about it after I read *The Story of Ann Frank* again. It's probably not written as well as you would write it, but it's my first book."

"I bet you're doing a great job. I'd love to read it."

"I'd let you read it now, but my best friend, Lisa, has it."

"Well, I'll just have to come back soon, then. Let me talk to Todd about spending the weekend. In the mean time, let me know if you have trouble with any of your homework. I've probably already done what you're doing in your classes."

Carol also noticed that Jean and Marie were quite fond of Jim. When it was bedtime, Jim let Jean ride his back to bed. "Will you read me a bedtime story?" Jean asked.

"How about you read me a bedtime story? Have you finished *Charlie and the Chocolate Factory* yet?"

Jean giggled as she held on to Jim's shirt. "No. I've been waiting to finish it with you. Last time, you made me read an extra five pages because you wanted to find out what happened to the greedy girl who blew up like a giant blueberry."

"I can help read if you get tired, Jean," said Marie, following Jim and Jean into the bedroom. "*Charlie and the Chocolate Factory* is one of my favorite books. I've read it twice."

Carol's dad had given them piggyback rides to bed a few times when they were very young, but she did not remember him ever reading them a story. He was too busy.

Carol had such a great time that she forgot to look at the clock. When the phone rang, she realized it must be quite late.

"Carol, it's Todd on the phone," said Liz.

"I guessed it would be him." Carol sighed and took the phone.

"Where are you?" Todd yelled. "I've been home for an hour. It's almost midnight."

"You're kidding. I had no idea it had gotten that late. I'm sorry."

"Well, I was worried you got into an accident or something. You could have called."

"I said I was sorry, Todd. I'll leave right now."

"You'd better."

"Okay, I'll see you in a few minutes." She hung up the phone.

Carol rushed to find her folder, her coat, and her shoes. "Hey, drive carefully out there," said Jim, touching her shoulder. "It's awfully icy this time of night. If you want, I can drive you home."

"Oh, no, Todd needs his car in the morning."

"Are you sure, Carol? You can spend the night here if you want."

"Thanks, Mom, but I'll be fine. I'll drive slow."

"All right, if you're determined."

"I'll say a prayer for you," said Jim. Carol gave him a funny look. No one had ever offered to pray for her before, and she didn't know what to say.

"Well, thanks for the wonderful evening. I'll talk to you later." She gave hugs all around, then headed down the steps.

The cold air hit her with its arctic blast, and as she saw Mom and Jim watching her from the warm, lighted home, she wished she were still inside. She shivered from the cold and the thought of dealing with Todd's wrath. Best get it over with before it became worse. She started the car and her tires made a crunchy noise as they moved on the frozen street where the melted snow had turned into ice. It would be a slow drive back to the outskirts of Deerfield, some ten miles away. She didn't believe in God, but it was somehow comforting to know that Jim was praying for her.

***

Carol followed her French teacher's white Volvo up Elm Street Hill. It was Friday afternoon, Todd was working swing shift at the hotel, and Mrs. Meek asked her if she would like to come to dinner and discuss the trip to France. She had never visited her home before, had never met her husband or her daughter, Julia, though she had seen their pictures on her desk. The picture depicted the perfect family: her husband tall and handsome, their daughter a smiling baby doll, and Mrs. Meeks, petite with lovely eyes and a contented smile. Carol wanted them to regard her as an adult, not a teenager, and her heart rate increase as they pulled into the Meeks' driveway.

Her teacher's home was a modern rambler built behind a recently remodeled, nineteenth century Victorian. The yellow and white house sat on the edge of an expansive parcel of land that included a cleared field, a fenced horse pasture, and rounded hills beyond. It reminded Carol of the little cottage she lived in after her father left. A medium-sized Collie greeted Mrs. Meeks as she opened her car door, its tail wagging with joy. Carol now wondered if she and her husband came from a rich family, making her even more nervous. Her only exposure to wealthy people—the Barretts—had not been favorable.

Carol stepped out of the car slowly, waiting for direction from Mrs. Meeks on what to do next. She froze as the Collie wagged its way toward her and sniffed at her legs. He had muddy paws and mud matted on his long hair. The word mud went along with March in Vermont. Melted snow equaled mud puddles.

"Jeanie, come here!" Amanda Meeks called her dog. "You leave Carol alone. Don't worry. She won't bite you. She's just checking you out." When Jeanie did not retreat, Mrs. Meeks took her by the collar and led her to the fenced back yard.

"Come on Jeanie. You need to learn to be polite to our guests. You naughty girl, what have you been into? You're a muddy mess. And we just gave you a bath on Sunday."

Carol followed with quiet, careful steps.

Mrs. Meeks closed the gate on the unhappy Jeanie, who whined to be let out. Carol was thankful that the dog would not be in the house with them.

"My husband brought Jeanie home last summer as a gift for Julia. She's a great dog, just a bit rambunctious. She still acts like a puppy."

"I've never had a dog," said Carol. "I was bit as a young child, and I've never learned to feel comfortable around them. Jeanie seems friendly, though."

"It's okay. Dogs can be overwhelming at times. I never had one until I married Steve. I had to learn to accept them." She paused, then led Carol to the front door. "Let's get out of the cold and into the house." They day had started sunny, but clouds were moving over the hills to the west.

Carol loved Mrs. Meeks home the minute she stepped into it. If she and Todd could afford a house, she would want one just like it. The large, oak-floored entry had a wooden bench where you could sit and take off your shoes. It opened up into a huge living room, also with oak floors, a cathedral ceiling, and floor-to-ceiling windows that overlooked the open field and wooded hills beyond. Dark clouds were gathering in the distance, but the sun still shone on some of the trees, giving the hills a light green tint from newly budding limbs. A blue leather couch and matching Lazy Boy faced the view, and Carol imagined sitting and watching the landscape for hours. A bird house stood just outside the window, and a chickadee flew in, jabbed some birdseed, and flew out.

"Why don't you have a seat? I'm going to change out of this skirt, then I'll fix us something warm to drink. Would you like coffee, tea, or cocoa?"

"I'll have tea, thank you. Do you need any help?"

"No, just sit down and relax. I'll be right back."

Carol sat down on the couch and sank into its soft cushions, stretching her feet onto the Oriental rug finished in a subtle flower motif of various blues. Matching framed paintings of New England landscapes covered one wall, and the other contained a large wood stove bordered by grey tiles with photographs of the family on either side of the stovepipe. The living room flowed into a dining area and kitchen, giving the home an expansive feel. The dining room windows, adorned with green and white lacy curtains, formed a nook and overlooked the same area as the living room. Birdhouse wallpaper bordered the dining area and modern kitchen, which was furnished with light oak cabinets and an island. A square, wood table with white-painted chairs and wood seats added to the Vermont country decor. On the single wall in the dining room hung a large, embroidered tapestry that read, "God Bless Our Home."

Carol leaned back on the couch and her eyelids became heavy. She was almost asleep when Mrs. Meeks returned. She had changed out of her plumb suit into bell-bottomed, un-hemmed dungarees and a pastel blue sweater.

"Here's our tea," Mrs. Meeks set two porcelain tea-cups and saucers with painted sapphire flowers edged in gold on the oak coffee table. "I'm going to add some wood to the fire and warm this place up."

"Mrs. Meeks—"

"Carol, you can call me Amanda. We're not in school, and we've know each other long enough."

"Okay. Mrs…I mean Amanda, is your favorite color blue?"

"Yes." She laughed. "I guess my furnishings gave it way." She poked a smoldering log and threw some kindling into the wood stove. A moment later, the fire came alive with warm orange and red flames.

"I love the way you have your home decorated. It's so homey and comfy."

"Why, thank you Carol. So, what's your favorite color?"

"I don't know. I like them all. I could never pick a favorite. As a child, I didn't want to hurt the feelings of all the other colors by picking a favorite, so I liked them all. Except black."

"Black is the absence of color or light." Amanda threw in a couple of small logs, closed the door to the wood stove, took her tea cup, and sat on the Lazy Boy. "So, let's enjoy a few moments of tranquility before my husband, Steve, arrives home with Julia."

Carol sipped her tea and inhaled the sweet-smelling steam. "What kind of tea is this?"

"It's chamomile. It's an herbal tea. Do you like it?"

"Yes. It feels nice and warm. I'll have to buy some next time I go to the grocery store."

Mrs. Meeks knew that Carol lived with Todd, not at home. Carol confessed it one day when Todd was unable to pick her up from school. She had seen Carol standing out in the cold and given her a ride to the hotel. Carol was glad she kept it their secret and not told anyone else at the school.

"I'm so glad you're going to France. You're going to love it. We'll spend four days in Paris, then ten days with your French family. You'll see Notre Dam, Versailles, La Tower Eiffel, and eat the best food on earth. Their *fromage* is heavenly."

"I can't wait, Mrs…, Amanda. It's going to take me a while to get used to calling you Amanda."

"You've been calling me Mrs. Meeks for almost three years, so be patient with yourself." Amada took a sip of tea, then set her cup on the coffee table.

Carol, you're not like my other students. You're already living the life of an adult. I want you to know that I see you differently, and though I'd rather not let the other students know this, I feel I can treat you like a friend more than a student."

Carol looked at Amanda, so pretty and sincere. She didn't have any friends except Todd, and smiled at the thought of having an adult relationship. "Thank you, I'd like that."

"As a friend, I hope you don't mind me saying this, but I'm hoping you will learn not to take life so seriously and have some fun on this trip."

"I want to, I really do. But I still feel bad that Todd can't come with me. He's never been to Europe. His parents have, but they didn't take him with them."

"Carol." Amanda touched her shoulder. "You're a very caring, sensitive woman, always thinking of others more than yourself. But you've been given a gift here that only comes once in a lifetime. Todd will have his own opportunities, and there will be times he won't be able to share with you. God created us all as unique people, and if everything was doled out exactly the same to everyone, it wouldn't have as much impact as experiences that are handpicked for each individual and their needs. I believe with all my heart that God has handpicked this trip for you, to give you a chance to learn, laugh, grow, and experience something only for you. Do you understand what I'm saying?"

Carol stared at her hands and picked at the skin on her thumb. Was Mrs. Meeks telling her it was okay to be selfish sometimes? Was it okay to enjoy herself and not worry about Todd? Mrs. Meeks, Amanda, was going by herself without her husband. They seemed happy.

Carol looked up. "How does your husband feel about you going on a trip without him?"

"He's excited for me. He knows how much I enjoy my students and visiting France. He came with me one year, and it exhausted him. He likes to go at a slower pace."

"So, you guys don't always do everything together?"

"We do most things together, but we also have our own interests. Part of loving one another is helping your spouse to become all that God created him to be. Steve is an engineer and sometimes spends hours working on a design that I can't understand for the life of me. But he can't speak French. We share our interests with each other, but we also know that we're different people with different talents. Besides, when we do something separately, it gives us something to talk about when we're together." Amanda smiled.

"It's not like that with Todd and me. We share everything. He reads all my papers, and he helps me with everything I do."

"Does he do anything you aren't involved in?"

Carol felt her cheeks become hot as she thought about the pornography. She couldn't tell Amanda about that.

"Well, Todd does extensive research on the Middle East, so I guess he does some things without me."

"How about you? Is there anything you do that's all for you?"

Carol picked another piece of skin off her thumb. What *did* she do that was only for her?

"Well, some day I hope to write a book, but right now, there's not enough time for it. With school and taking care of the apartment, it's hard."

"How about reading? Do you have any spare time for reading?"

"Oh, I read all the time. Todd has this list of books I've been reading since I started high school."

"What kind of books?"

"All kinds. Classics mostly, and feminist books."

"Do you like science fiction or fantasy at all?"

"Sure. I like all kinds of books."

"Wait here. I have something you might enjoy." Amanda went over to a bookcase and pulled out a set of books called *The Chronicles of Narnia* by C.S. Lewis. "These were my favorite books when I was your age. They may look like kids books, but there's a lot of deeper material hidden inside. I think you'll like them."

Carol looked at the cover of one of the books called *The Lion, The Witch, and The Wardrobe*: two children riding on a lion. They did look like children's books, but she knew Mrs. Meeks thought of her as an adult. She wasn't sure whether she would show them to Todd. He might think she was reading below her level.

"Thanks." Carol set the books beside her purse on the couch.

"Oh." Amanda set down her tea cup. "I forgot to take out my photo albums of France. I wanted to show you pictures of where we're going."

"Great."

Carol sat next to Amanda while she told her all about Paris and Lyon. Her albums included a little diary of each day's events. When they came to the picture of her group at a restaurant sharing a five course meal, Amanda announced, "I think I'd better start dinner. I'm hungry, how about you?"

"After looking at that picture of French pastries, you bet."

"Have you ever had fondue?"

"No."

"Well, you're in for a great treat. I have beef and chicken."

Carol followed Amanda into the kitchen. Amanda took out a little, black kettle and set it on the counter. "This is a fondue pot. I put in this delicious sauce, and we dip our meat into it."

"Sound likes fun. What can I do to help?"

Amanda opened the refrigerator and pulled out lettuce, tomatoes, cucumbers, and peppers. "If you want, you can work on the salad."

A few minutes later, Carol heard Jeanie barking.

"Steve and Julia must be home." Amanda washed her hands, dried them, and went to the door to open it for her husband. A tall, handsome man with blond hair wearing a navy suit walked through the door holding an adorable little girl in his arms.

"Hi honey." He smiled.

"Mommy!" Julia, stretched her hands toward Amanda.

"How are my two favorite people in the whole world?" Amanda took Julia, then kissed her husband.

"It's good to be home."

"Steve, I want you to meet my favorite student." Amanda turned around and motioned for Carol to come. "This is Carol."

"Nice to meet you." Carol shook his hand. He had a firm, dry grip.

"Amanda's told me about you. Only good things, of course." Steve chuckled.

"I sure hope so." Carol met Steve's hazel eyes. She liked him already.

"And this is our daughter, Julia. Julia, can you say 'hi' to Carol?"

Julia squeaked a little "hi," then buried her face in her mother's shoulder.

"Hi, Julia. I like your pretty pink dress. Is pink your favorite color?"

Julia sneaked a look at Carol and nodded.

"You are such a pretty little girl." This time Julia gave her a big smile and squirmed out of Amanda's arms. She ran down the hall to her room, returning with a well-loved stuffed cat and fuzzy, pink blanket.

"This is Mewer."

Carol kneeled down and pet Mewer on the head. "What a nice cat you have there."

***

Carol had a great time with Amanda, Steve, and little Julia. She ate fondue for the first time, poking her small pieces of beef and chicken with a skewer and dipping it in a tangy sauce. Amanda served the fondue with roasted potatoes and salad. For dessert, they had strawberries dipped in a chocolate sauce. After dinner, they played Scrabble. Steve won, but she made second place. *I can't believe I did better than my teacher.*

Ten o'clock came too soon. She had to rush to make it back home and fix Todd his dinner before he returned from work. Todd was excited about some meeting with Yassar Arafat and the United Nations, so he was not in a bad mood, and they did not fight. He was very affectionate. Still, as she closed her eyes, she recalled her evening with Steve and Amanda: their comfortable house, their darling daughter, the way they looked at each other and laughed, the way they made her feel welcomed and accepted, the way they could discuss issues like politics, God, and family, and even if they disagreed with her, she still felt like they had listened. Carol knew they were Christians, and she'd always thought Christians were pushy and judgmental. But Steve and Amanda were not like that at all. They were her friends.

That's what was missing with her and Todd: they needed good friends. She was sure that once Todd met them, he would like them, too. Carol fell sleep imagining the four of them having dinner together at the Meeks' wonderful home.

***

She had to find it or fail the class. What happened to her paper? How could she go home and get it, yet make it back to class?

She was back in her apartment, throwing papers off the counter, frantic to find it. She rushed to her bedroom and looked through the dresser drawers, rummaged through her book bag for the fifth time. She was in her car, looking under the seats. She was back in class now. The teacher asked everyone to pass in their papers. It was not there.

"I have to go to the bathroom," she said, standing up. It felt like she would have an accident if she did not find a bathroom. Down the hall she ran, opening door after door. Where did the bathroom go? She found it, but it was littered and filthy. She was back at her house now and saw herself walk to the bathroom and begin to sit on the toilet, then she would end up in her bed again. Every time she made it to the toilet, she found herself back in the bedroom. She was going to burst from the pain. I have to wake up. I have a bladder infection.

When she could touch her bed and know she was no longer dreaming, she ran to the bathroom for relief. The relief did not come; the pain only worsened after her bladder was empty. She went to the kitchen, took a glass from the cupboard, filled it with water, and gulped down the entire glass of water. It would be a long night and a long weekend without a doctor to prescribe her antibiotics.

Chapter Nineteen

Margaret pulled onto the freeway. She was taking Carol to Hanover Medical Center, near Dartmouth, the best medical clinic in the area. She had arranged for a specialist to see Carol to help her with recurring bladder infections. If she had not made the phone call to Carol on a Sunday night, she may not have known Carol was so sick. When Margaret had taken her to her gynecologist on Monday, Carol had been miserable from enduring the pain all weekend.

"You're awfully quiet. Are you feeling sick again?"

"No, I'm fine, Mom. Just a little nervous."

"I know what you mean. I've had bladder problems myself. The infections are wicked, but the tests they run aren't bad at all, if I remember correctly."

"I don't know about that." Carol turned toward the window. "When I went to this one doctor in Deerfield, the test he did was terrible. I hope they don't do the same thing today."

"What doctor is that?" Margaret put on her windshield wipers as snow mixed with rain began to splat on the glass. "I can't believe it's almost cold enough to snow in April. I guess that's the price we pay for living in Vermont."

Carol rubbed her hands together as if to confirm her mother's declaration. "The doctor I went to is Karl Johnson. He's the only urologist in Deerfield."

"I've never heard of him, which is strange. You'd think Dr. Haley would recommend him if he were closer?"

"He's a jerk." Carol folded her arms.

"Why do you say that?"

"He thinks I'm a slut, probably believes I'd be doing the world a favor if I just died."

Margaret turned to her daughter, her mouth agape. "Carol, those are pretty strong accusations. What did he say to make you feel like this?"

"It's because of what he did to me." Carol kept her gaze away from Margaret, focused on the wet window. Margaret swallowed as her heart raced and her stomach lurched. She told herself, *remain calm, don't scare her away.*

"What did he do, darling." Margaret touched Carol's arm and spoke with a soft, soothing voice.

"Oh, Mom, it was awful the way he treated me. The first strange thing was that his nurse asked me to undress and put on a hospital gown. When he came into the room, I asked him if he needed a urine sample. He said, 'No, I always extract the sample straight from the urethra to prevent contamination.' I wondered how he was going to do that, but didn't ask. Then he told me to get on the examining table. He checked my breathing with a stethoscope, then began to push on my abdomen. Of course, it made me feel like I was going to have an accident. After he did that, he asked me how many bladder infections I'd had and what symptoms went with them. Then asked me when I started becoming sexually active and how often I had sex. I told him, and he told me that was why I was getting so many bladder infections. He said if I just behaved myself and stopped acting like a hussy, I wouldn't have to worry about it. Then, then came the worst part…

"What did he do to you?" Margaret's soft tone was gone. Her blood pressure was rising with each word.

"Oh, Mom, it was so awful. He, he used some kind of tube thing to take a sample straight from my urethra. And he wasn't even gentle about it. He kept complaining about the young generation and their promiscuity while he did it. It hurt so much, especially because I still had symptoms. Then, after he pulled out the tube, I couldn't hold it in, and I made a mess on the table. I wanted to die right there. I felt like the lowest of the lowest, a no-good slut. He just said, 'Get dressed. My nurse will clean up the mess.' Then left without even looking at me."

"I could kill that man for what he did to you."

"I wanted to walk out of there without seeing him again, but I didn't. Instead, after I dressed, he came back in the room with a prescription and a piece of paper. He told me if I couldn't abstain from sex to follow the items on the list. He asked me if I had thought about what I'd do if I got pregnant. He said if I were his daughter, he'd give me a good whipping. Then the appointment was over. To make matters worse, when I started to walk out of his office in a daze, the receptionist ran after me and demanded I pay for the appointment, even though I had insurance. I gave her twenty dollars just so I could get out of there." Carol's face matched the rain-streaked glass.

Margaret reached in the glove compartment, pulled out a box of tissue, and handed it to Carol. "Oh, Hon, I'm so sorry. I can't believe a doctor would be so cruel and unprofessional. How long ago was it? Why didn't you tell me?"

"It happened last summer, just before school started again. I was too ashamed to tell you. I didn't even tell Todd about it."

"Honey, you shouldn't be ashamed. That doctor is the one who should be ashamed. He should be sued, have his license taken away for such horrible treatment. He hasn't heard the last of this, I can tell you that. When we get home, I'm going to let him know a thing or two."

"Mom, No!" Carol's expression became that of a frightened animal. "Please don't! If you do, others in the town will find out about it, and I don't want them knowing about me."

"But, Carol, that man is a beast. He should be punished for what he did to you." Margaret gripped the wheel and took a deep breath. "There's got to be some way we can make him pay for what he did."

"Please, Mom, you've got to promise me you won't say anything. That's the reason I didn't tell anyone about it until now. Todd could get into trouble if too many people knew we were living together. The school doesn't even know you moved or that I'm not living with you any more."

"They don't?"

"No, if they did, it could ruin my graduation. Because you don't live within the school district."

"You're right. I can't believe I didn't think about this before." Margaret paused. The entire situation was so wrong. Carol should be living at home with her. She tended to forget that Carol was still only sixteen and a minor. Why had she allowed her to see Todd in the first place? She should have never let it progress so far.

"Carol, please forgive me. I haven't been the best mother. I haven't been there for you."

Carol turned toward her. "Mom, don't be so hard on yourself. I'm the one who made the decision to leave."

"Still, it's my responsibility to make sure you're taken care of. I should know more about what's going on in your life. I haven't been strong for you. I've been too preoccupied."

"You couldn't have stopped me and Todd from living together, if that's what you're thinking. I want to live with Todd. I don't want you to think letting us be together was a bad decision, because it wasn't."

Margaret started to say more, then stopped herself. She did not want to start an argument. As much as she hated to do nothing about Dr. Johnson, she did not want to lose her daughter again.

"Okay, Carol. I won't tell anyone about it."

"Not even Jim."

"But Jim won't say anything."

"Not even Jim, Mom. Promise."

"Okay." They rode the rest of the way in silence. Margaret rehearsed several sentences in her mind, things she wanted to say to Carol, words of love and comfort and encouragement, but she was afraid it would be misunderstood. How could she express herself without revealing her true feelings about Todd and their situation? Carol needed to escape Todd, that much she knew. It made her sick to think of little Carol having sex with him at only fourteen years old. Only God knew what he did to her in private. In truth, it was Todd's fault that Carol was having bladder problems. But Carol could not see any of this yet. She had to handle her with delicate hands, build back their relationship. Carol sharing what had happened to her was a first step in that direction.

Margaret pulled into the clinic parking lot and parked the car. She turned to Carol and hugged her close.

"Carol, I just want you to know how sorry I am that that man treated you so horribly. Thank you for trusting me with it. Don't let his judgment of you stick. You are not a slut or promiscuous or a horrible person."

Carol buried her head in her mother's chest and let the tears flow.

"I love you, Carol. Don't you ever forget that. Let's put the past behind us and start fresh. I want you to feel free to come to me with anything. I want you to know I'm here for you, no matter what you do. Even if you killed someone, I'd still love you."

Carol let out a soft laugh. "Oh, Mom, I don't think you have to worry about that. I'm not planning to kill anyone anytime soon. I would have killed that doctor already if I was going to resort to murder."

Margaret chuckled and squeezed her daughter one more time before letting go. Carol dried her eyes, and they walked together into the clinic, Margaret's arm around her daughter. It felt good to hold her child after so long. She remembered something Jim had told her last week about a verse in the Bible. He said sometimes God used bad situations and turned them around for good.

Maybe Carol's trouble with her bladder was being used to bring them closer together.

***

"Hi honey, I'm home." Carol closed the door behind her. Todd was sitting on the couch reading, his brown coat and tie thrown next to him.

"Hi, Babe. How did it go with the doctor today?"

Carol took off her coat, flung her back pack on a chair, and sat down beside Todd.

"It went pretty good. At least there's a chance that I can get relief from these darn infections."

"Oh, how?" Todd put down his book and put his arm around her. "But first, you haven't given me a kiss yet."

Carol panted a quick kiss on his lips, then continued. "Dr. Kirkland was very nice. She was a woman doctor, so I felt like she understood me better. She told me there's an operation where they stretch the urethra. I'm scheduled to go into the hospital after graduation in June."

"An operation? That sounds serious. How long will you be in the hospital?"

"Don't worry, she said it's was a pretty simple operation. I'll only be there one night."

"Still, you'll have to go to Hanover for the operation. I hope I can get time off from work to go with you."

"Well, if you can't, I'm sure my Mom can help."

Todd gave her a strange look. "I should be able to make it. So, did the doctor give you any more information about the operation? I want to know exactly what they plan to do to you."

"She gave me a stack of papers. They're in my backpack. Can I get them later? I'm dead tired."

"I'll get them. And while I'm up, do you want some pizza? I brought a pizza home. I figured you probably didn't feel like cooking tonight."

"That would be great. Thanks, Todd. It was very thoughtful of you to think about dinner."

"No problem." Todd rose from the couch, went into the kitchen, opened a pizza box, set a couple of pieces on a plate, filled a glass with water, then set it all on the coffee table for Carol. Next, he opened her backpack and pulled out a stack of papers and a book.

"Hey, Carol, what's this book you're reading, *The Lion, The Witch, and the Wardrobe*? It looks like a kid's book.

Rats. She forgot that was in there. She was afraid to tell Todd the truth, so she lied. "Oh, that book. It's a reading assignment from my English teacher."

Todd brought the book and the stack of papers to the couch and continued to flip through the book. "This looks like something a junior high student would read. I can't believe a high school teacher would assign such an easy book."

"She said there was deeper meaning to it than just the story."

"Oh, like what?"

"I don't know. We just started it."

"I've never seen or read this book, but for some reason, the author C.S. Lewis looks familiar. Has he written any adult literature?"

"I don't know. Todd, let's look at the papers the doctor gave me, okay?"

"Sure, okay." Todd set the book down. "I'm just curious about why your English teacher would have you read children's fantasy."

Carol pulled one paper from the stack and handed it to Todd as she spoke. "Todd, you need to read this paper. To lower the chances of getting bladder infections, we both need to be more careful not to spread bacteria when we are intimate."

"Come on, Carol. I take a shower every day. I can't be that dirty."

"Just read it, okay? I hate to say it, but I never had a problem with my bladder before we started having sex. Dr. Kirkland said some women have short urethras, which means bacteria can get into the bladder more easily. The main ways I can get the infections is from not wiping myself well enough after using the bathroom or from sex. If we both clean ourselves first and follow the rest of the items on the list, it will reduce the chances of infection."

"Man, this takes all the spontaneity out of it."

"I'm sorry I have this problem, Todd, but it's not like I did it on purpose. And from now on, I refuse to have sex the other way, if you know what I mean."

"Well, I sure hope the operation you're getting fixes the problem. It puts a cramp on my style." Todd set the paper down.

"Me, too. Anyway, I'm set to have the operation on June 20th. Until then, the doctor gave me an ongoing prescription. She told me to take an antibiotic every time we have intercourse."

"Wait, I just remembered something. Your Dad sent a letter. He said something about wanting us to visit around June 20th." Todd went into the dining room, found the letter, and brought it back to Carol.

Carol took the letter. "How come you opened the letter without me?"

"It's addressed to both of us. Remember I've been writing to him. I really like your Dad. He's such a visionary."

Carol read the letter, then set it down. "What's this stuff about refunding lists? He wants to use our address and as many other addresses as possible?"

"I'm sure your Dad told you about his grand scam to take back money from the greedy capitalists and use it to help the poor. It's a perfect plan! First, he saves labels from major manufacturers so he never buys the product to begin with. Then he uses the labels and sends them in for free refunds. The more addresses he uses, the more refunds he can send in for, taking more money away from the capitalist pigs. It's like Robin Hood, but so much safer. They'll never catch on to what he's doing."

"Of course I remember, Todd. We've been saving labels for him for months now. But he's never asked to use our address and other addresses before. We're more involved when we do that."

"Oh, for goodness sakes, Carol. Don't you trust your Dad at all? Don't you think what he's doing is a worthy cause?"

Todd was facing her now, giving her that look that said, "Don't be stupid." She didn't want to fight with him, even though she had misgivings about becoming too involved with her Dad's schemes. She turned away from Todd's stare, folded the letter, and headed toward the dining room. "Of course I support my Dad. You misunderstood me. We've never done this part before, that's all. Anyway, let's talk about when we can go visit him. Let me look at a June calendar."

Carol took the calendar off the wall and returned to the living room. "Let's see. My graduation ceremony is on June 14th. If you can get the time off from work, we can visit my Dad before I go in for the operation on the 20th."

"That's a good idea because you'll need to start looking for a job as soon as possible. The only problem will be getting enough time off for both the trip and your surgery. I'll check with my boss next week so he'll have plenty of time to plan for it."

"I'm really glad that I don't have to have the operation before my trip to France. Which reminds me, I'm going to baby sit for Amanda Friday night. You'll be working anyway, and I'm going to need spending money for the trip."

"Carol, I told you that I can give you some spending money for the trip. I hope you don't make it sound like I'm not helping you with money at all." Todd pouted.

"Amanda knows your helping. But I also want to help Mom and Jim with buying clothes for me. They're already paying for the rest of the trip."

"I guess. I just wish I could find a teaching job. Do you think you'll get home before I do?"

"I think so. Hey, my pizza's getting cold." Carol picked up the piece on the plate and took a big bite of sausage, pepperoni, onion, green pepper, and black olives in a thick, cheesy crust. "Yum, this is good pizza. Where did you get it?"

"They opened a new pizza place in Deerfield. Remember that restaurant that used to be in the silver, streamline trailer on the hill on the way to town? It went out of business, and is now an Italian restaurant called Papa's." Todd went into the kitchen to get another piece of pizza.

"That's right. I saw their sign on the way home the other day. I'm glad there's decent food there now. That other place, Rosie's, was a dive."

"I also brought us a frozen, Pepperidge Farm cake for dessert."

"Ooh, what kind?" Carol jumped up to look in the refrigerator.

"Chocolate of course."

"Todd, you're a real price, did you know that?" Carol gave him a hug.

Todd returned the hug with a spicy, saucy kiss. As Carol finished her dinner, she was relieved and happy that she had avoided arguing with Todd. She was learning how to handle his moods.

***

Margaret lumbered up the stairs into the kitchen. Jim was cooking ground beef on the stove.

"Oh, Jim, you're making dinner for me. You're the best." Margaret gave him a hug and a kiss. He was wearing the checkered, blue flannel shirt that matched his eyes.

"Anything for my special lady."

"What are you making?" Margaret looked on the counter. "Let me guess. Hamburger stroganoff."

"You're not only beautiful, but a genius, too." Jim hugged Margaret to him while he chopped the cooking meat with a metal spoon.

"Where are the girls?"

"Liz took them to the library. They should be back soon."

"Good. It will give us a chance to talk." Margaret took an onion, fresh mushrooms, and a garlic clove from the refrigerator and started to peel the onion. The strong smell invaded her nostrils and irritated her eyes.

"This is one strong onion."

"Try peeling it under running water. It won't smell so bad."

"Do you think it will keep the smell of onion and garlic off my fingers?"

"It'll help."

Margaret followed Jim's suggestion and peeled the onion under the water. She did the same for the garlic glove.

"I stopped by Deerfield High to talk to Amanda Meeks. She's such a wonderful woman. Did you know that she has befriended Carol? She's really taken her under her wing, and I'm so glad she's going to be there for her while their in France."

"I've only met her once, but I liked what I saw." Jim added the cut onions, garlic and mushrooms to the beef and stirred.

"Carol's going to baby sit her daughter for spending money, which means they'll be spending more time together. If any one can help get Carol away from that awful Todd, Amanda Meeks is the one to do it. I learned something else about her today, too."

"What's that?"

"She's a Christian, like you. She goes to this new church in Charlestown." Margaret took out some beef stock from the cupboard.

"Oh," said Jim. "What's the name of the church?"

"New Life Church."

"Do you know what kind of church?"

"She said it's non-denominational. Is that Good?"

"Maybe. It depends on what they believe."

"Well, I wouldn't know. But she did invite us."

"Oh, really." Jim added the beef stock and spices and turned down the stove. "So, does she know about our living arrangement?"

"Yes, I told her. And what she said surprised me so much, especially after the way your old church treated you."

"Let's sit down while this simmers." Jim took Margaret's hand and led her into the dining room. "So, what did she say?"

"She said it was not her place to judge what you and I were doing together. That was between us and God."

"Really, she said that?"

"Yes, and she also said that no one in her church would reject us for it either. She said not to let it stop us from receiving what God had for us."

Margaret paused and looked at Jim, who was staring straight ahead and lost in his own thoughts. She knew Jim missed attending church, that it hurt him deeply the way his friends of many years rejected him when he broke up with his wife. Margaret turned the diamond ring on her left hand around and around. Jim had given her the engagement ring at Christmas, but they had not yet set a date because the divorce papers were still not final. She knew that Jim wanted to legitimize their relationship, and she longed to be his lawful wife. Yet, she was not ready to embrace his faith. Scars of rejection from the Catholic Church when she divorced Richard still ran deep. Jim told her that because Richard had cheated on her, she had Biblical release of their relationship. Still, she also knew the Bible did not accept the concept of two people living together who were unmarried, and Jim's ex-wife had not cheated on him. Would she be considered an adulteress because she slept with Jim when he was still married?

"Margaret, would you consider trying Amanda's church with me? If you don't like it, we don't have to go back."

"I don't know Jim." Margaret turned to face him, and his deep blue eyes locked with hers. How could she resist the pleading in those tender eyes of his? She sensed in his eyes and expression that he had loneliness and longing for something she could not give him. She knew it had something to do with his belief in God, but could not understand why he still loved God after all the pain he had experienced. She had asked Jim that once, and he told her just because others had rejected him, God never had. Jesus still loved him. He believed it, too, because she would catch him praying sometimes. It was like he had a part of himself she could not reach or touch, and sometimes it made her angry. Then at other times, she wanted to believe it with him. But how could God love someone like her?

Somehow she knew that to refuse the gentle, kind man who had brought hope into her desolate life would hurt him even more.

"Okay, I'll try it. But no pressure. If anyone tries to convert me, I'm getting up and leaving, understood?"

"Understood." Jim reached over and took her hand. "Thank you, Margaret."

Margaret smiled. "How could I say 'no' to those puppy dog eyes of yours?"

The sound of car doors slamming and girls giggling announced the arrival of the children.

"I'd better put on some pasta," said Margaret, rising from the chair. She squeezed Jim's hand one more time before releasing it to return to the kitchen.

***

"I finished *The Lion, the Witch, and the Wardrobe*," said Carol. She had driven home with Amanda Meeks after school on a Friday afternoon. Amanda and Steve were going out for the evening, and Carol was watching Julia. She was helping Amanda fold laundry while Julia played with a play house that was a duplicate of her grandparent's Victorian home, a Christmas present from Grandfather Meeks.

"If you don't mind, I'd like to lend the series to my sisters. They might enjoy them more than I did."

"You didn't like the book?"

"It was okay." Carol hung a little lavender dress with white lace in Julia's closet. She didn't want to hurt her friend's feelings about the books, and wondered how to tell her without sounding too harsh.

"Was it too childish for you?" Amanda asked.

"Mommy, Alice is making chocolate chip cookies." Julia pulled on Amanda's arm. Julia's miniature doll was in the kitchen by a tiny wood-stove.

"That's great, Dear. Let us know when she's done making them."

"Well, it was written for children, but I kind of found it nice to just relax and read something easy for a change. No, that wasn't it. I was looking for the deeper meaning, and I found it pretty simple."

"I see." Amanda put a pile of underwear in Julia's white dresser. "Sometimes it's the simplicity of a truth that is deep."

Carol paused and let Amanda's words sink in. What did Amanda mean? She wanted to ask, but didn't want to sound stupid.

"Well, it seemed to me that the entire story was a fairy tale version of Jesus' death on the cross. I took enough catechism as a child to remember the story."

"That's right. Aslan represents Christ's sacrifice for us." Amanda sorted pink, white, blue, and purple socks.

"And I didn't understand the ending. Why would the kids become kings and queens? It's unrealistic to think that children could rule a world without fighting. It was definitely all fairy tales. And I didn't understand how the children could go back through the wardrobe after they had grown into men and women and become kids again after being adults. Once you're an adult, you can't become a child again."

"Carol, come see my cookies. Do you want one?"

"Sure Julia." Carol kneeled on the floor with Julia and pretended to eat one of her cookies. "Yummy, can I have another one?"

"Here." Julia gave her a pretend cookie. "Mommy, I'm hungry. I want to eat."

"In a little bit, Julia. Let Carol and me finish with the laundry. Why don't you show Carol how well you can do your new puzzle?" Amanda took a wood puzzle of Noah's ark and several animals in pairs from the shelf. Julia took the puzzle and began to take it apart.

"Well, I don't agree with you about adults not being able to become children again. Jesus said in the Bible that we should all be like little children because children have absolute faith in their Father. And as far as the children ruling as kings and queens, the Bible also says that we will rule and reign with Christ when he returns."

"I don't want to be disrespectful, Amanda, but I don't believe the Bible like you do. You've got to remember, as far as I'm concerned, the Bible is also just a fairy tale." Carol looked out the window, decorated with rainbow colored curtains that matched Julia's rainbow bedspread, and picked at her fingers. She was torn between hurting Amanda's feelings and expressing her dislike of Amanda pushing her Christian views.

"So, do you believe Jesus existed?" asked Amanda.

"Yes, historically, we know he did. He was a great man, and I like some of the principles he displayed, especially about peace and loving your enemies. But he was just a man. I think people made him into a God just like the Greeks and Romans made ordinary men into Gods to explain why good and evil occurs in the world."

"Have you read the Bible, Carol?"

"No. But I learned the stories as a child in the Catholic church."

"I suggest you read it for yourself some time and find out just what Jesus said about himself."

"I don't know. I can't believe in a God that allows the evil that's in the world. I'm sorry, Amanda, but I'd rather not talk about this anymore."

"Sure, Carol. I didn't mean to pressure you or anything. But I would like to say one more thing Try to remember being a child and how simple and joyful life was then. When we go on our trip to France, I want you to experience the freedom of becoming like a little child."

"Mommy, I'm really hungry." Julia whined. "When's Daddy coming home?"

"Soon, dear. Let's go out and watch for him, and I'll start dinner."

***

"Carol, read me another story, please." Julia tumbled down from her bed to the bookshelf and pulled out a large picture book. Carol rushed to keep her from dropping it.

"Julia, it's past your bedtime, and we've already read four books."

"But I'm not tired yet. Pleeeease." Julia looked darling in a light green jumper with built-in slippers, braided blond hair, blushed baby cheeks, and wide eyes, sparkling like crystal marbles.

"Okay, but just one more."

Julia opened the large, expensive book, edged in gold with thick paper. After glancing, Carol realized it was a Bible story book. *Great. Just what I need to read*

"Read this one. It's my favorite." On the page was a picture of Jesus with children of different races and ages surrounding him. He held a little girl much like Julia in his lap. The caption read, "Let the little children come to me, for theirs is the kingdom of heaven. Luke 18:16."

Carol read the story quickly, then set the heavy book on the floor. "Okay, little princess, I read one last story. Now into bed with you."

"Oh, just one more. Pleeease."

"No, it's time for bed right now. Your Mom and Dad won't be happy with me if their little girl wakes up grumpy in the morning because she didn't get enough sleep. Now let's go brush your teeth and use the bathroom."

After taking an extra long time brushing her teeth and using the toilet, Julia was tucked snugly in her bed, her tickle blanket and stuffed kitty in her arms.

"Good night, Julia."

"Wait, we forgot to say prayers. Mommy and Daddy always say prayers with me."

"Well." Carol wondered what to do now. She wasn't about to pray. "Why don't you pray this time by yourself."

"Okay." Julia sat up in her bed, folded her chubby hands together, and closed her eyes. "God bless Mommy and Daddy and everyone in the whole world. And God bless Carol. Amen."

"Okay, now to sleep with you." Carol pulled the covers up around Julia. "Good night."

Before she could leave, Julia grabbed her neck, planted a kiss on her cheek and said, "I love you. Jesus does, too."

"I love you too, Julia." She gave her a kiss on her soft cheek. Carol could feel tears forming as she left the room. Julia had such a simple idea of love. Sometimes she did wish she could become a child again and have a mother and father like Amanda and Steve. *Don't be foolish, Carol. Be happy with the life you have.* She went into the living room and turned on the television.

Chapter Twenty

"I can't believe we're finally here." Carol sat by the window in a jet plane headed for Paris, France. She could hardly sit still. Her fingers moved from her face, to her lap, to her mouth, to the book on her lap, to the arms on her chair, to her face.

"Is this the first time you've been on a plane?" asked the girl next to her. Her name was Chelsie, and she would be her partner on the trip.

"Is it that obvious?"

"Well, I wasn't sure if you were just excited or nervous." Chelsie set down her *Mademoiselle* fashion magazine. She was a cute blond who obviously did not fit in with the country bumpkins of Deerfield, Vermont. She had moved to Deerfield from Connecticut halfway through her senior year. Most of her classmates classified her as a Flat-Lander snob, and at first Carol felt uncomfortable and dowdy next to her. But they soon found camaraderie because they shared the role of misfit among their peers.

"Actually, I'm both. I feel like I'm in a dream. Still, do people get sick easily on planes?" Carol pulled out the plastic-coated bag from the side compartment. "I mean, they wouldn't give you these if you didn't need them."

Chelsie laughed. "I've never seen anyone use one of those on a plane, but I guess there must be some people who get sick or they wouldn't have them. I suppose cleaning up puke at 6,000 feet wouldn't be much fun."

"So, how many times have you flown?" Carol put the bag away.

"Oh, I don't know. I've flown to Florida to see my Grandparents almost every year I can remember. I've also been to California and the Caribbean. This is my first trip to Europe."

"I'm glad we at least have one thing in common." Carol paused for a moment, opening the travel book on her lap. "So, Chelsie, what are you looking forward to the most?"

"Paris! Meeting cute French boys. Eating, eating, and eating. And buying *chic* French clothes." Chelsie nudged Carol. "Wait until we go shopping together. I'll help you pick out the coolest clothes, then we'll go out on the town and see how many guys try to pick us up."

Carol turned away and peered out the window. "I don't know about the guy thing, Chelsie. You know I'm taken."

"Oh, Carol, you need to learn to live a little. It's not like you're going to cheat on Todd by flirting a little here and there. Every girl needs to play the field just to build her esteem, just to be reminded that she's still attractive and desirable."

"We'll see. I already feel guilty about leaving Todd behind."

"Pooh." Chelsie shook her head. "I can see you're going to be a challenge. But that's okay. Just stick with me. We're going to have a great time, girl."

"Stewardesses, prepare for take-off," the pilot announced. The stewardesses stood in front of the plane and instructed the passengers on emergency procedures. Carol paid close attention. The thought of being stuck on a life boat in the middle of the Atlantic flashed through her mind. They had a lot of ocean to cover. She noticed Chelsie was reading her magazine again, acting like she was sitting at home relaxing on her bed. A loud roar rushed through the cabin, and soon the plane jerked forward. Carol gripped the arms of her chair, waiting, waiting. It seemed like a year before they made it to the runway and the plane was released to fly. The inertia pushed her into her seat as the plane picked up speed. It went faster and faster, just like her heart-beat, until it moved away from the ground, and they were airborne, the massive 747 magically rising up in the sky.

Carol exhaled with relief. She hadn't realized she was holding her breath. Once she adjusted to the fact that they were in the air, excitement replaced the nervousness. "This is fun," said Carol out loud, her eyes riveted to the window. She watched as trees, houses, and cars grew smaller and smaller. First they were like a miniature village, the size a child could play with, but soon, as they went higher and higher, the landscape became patches of greens, grays, and blues, covered here and there by the puffy clouds which were below the plane. As a child, she would sit on the grass and pretend the clouds were magic pillows. She would lie on them, and they would take her wherever she wanted to go: through the woods, over the ocean, to exotic places with camels or kangaroos or belly dancers dressed in colorful costumes. It was so obvious now that clouds were nothing but water vapor as the plane cut through them like a ghost passing through a wall.

Soon they were over the ocean, a monotonous blue stretch that seemed like a sky on the ground. The sun was setting behind them, deepening the color of the water. Carol sighed, stretched her legs, and prepared for a long night.

"Chelsie, do you think you'll sleep tonight?"

"Sure. I brought a sleeping mask."

"I doubt I will. I'm too excited."

***

"Wake up sleepy head." Chelsie shook Carol's bed. "We're in Paris, *le Ile-de-France*."

"Let me sleep just a couple more minutes," Carol rolled over. She had only dozed off for a few minutes during the all-night plane ride. That and the five hour time difference gave her a good dose of jet lag.

"Come on Carol. You'll wake up once out in the fresh, Parisian air."

"Fine, I'm getting up." Carol slid her feet over the side of the bed and rubbed her eyes. The clock on the table read 6:00 PM. She inspected their Parisian room, modest yet still very stylish. On one wall, thin white curtains covered a French door that lead to a small, black, wrought-iron balcony. Filtered sun-light shone through the curtains onto a tightly knitted, gold carpet with swirl patterns. On the adjacent wall stood a full-length mirror, a sink, and a bidet, which Carol at first thought a toilet. She hadn't quite figured out how to use it yet. On the next wall stood Chelsie's twin bed and an armoire. All the furnishings had an antique quality, finished in dark walnut with massive, clawed legs and carvings. Heavily framed, Impressionistic paintings of The Seine River and a sunny garden completed the décor. Unlike hotels in the United States, they did not have a television or their own bathroom. Actually, in France, bathrooms or *sal-de-bains* were separate rooms from the toilet. *Sal-de-bains*, kept immaculate, had showers, sinks, and sometimes a bidet, but *les toilettes* were closets with only a toilet, which were usually dirty and stinky. To make it even more confusing, *de toilette* translated as toiletries or sometimes as toilet water, a cologne used after washing. If Carol wanted to shower, she had to go down the hall and share it with the rest of the guests.

Chelsie had already dressed in a pink, Gunne-Sax dress with black embroidery lining the waist, shoulders and cuffs. Her blond curls bounced out of a black beret, which showed off the dangling, pink crystal earrings and matching necklace. Her black boots completed the *tres chic* outfit.

"Chelsie, you look like a Parisian already. Man, how can I compete with that wonderful dress? I know you didn't buy that around Deerfield."

"You've got that right, girlfriend. I bought this in Boston over Christmas break. What better place for a peasant dress than Paris. I think it accentuates my boobs, don't you?" Chelsie stuck out her chest and strutted around the room.

Carol didn't know what to say. Chelsie had so much confidence, and she was ready to take on the streets of Paris with boldness. She, on the other hand, felt like costume jewelry next to diamonds.

"You look perfect, Chelsie. The French men will be lining up to take you away."

Chelsie laughed and finished with her lipstick. Carol opened her suitcase and started pulling out possible outfits. "Chelsie, what do you think of this?" She held up her jean skirt.

"Hmm," said Chelsie with a frown. "What else do you have?" She rummaged through Carol's bag, and pulled out a gauzy, white blouse. Then she went to her side of the room and took a blue and white, peasant-type skirt from the closet.

"Now, these would go perfect together. Do you have any boots?"

"As a matter of fact, I do. Todd bought them for me in Burlington when he still went to school." Carol unzipped the back of a garment bag and took out a pair of brown, leather boots.

Chelsie took them from her hand. "These will work great. You have some style after all. The most important thing to remember is that we don't want to look like Americans, who are usually obvious because they wear blue jeans and sweat shirts. You and I will blend in with the crowd, that is, until we open our mouths."

"That will give me away for sure. I read and write French well, but I've never been good at speaking it." Carol took her brush out of her purse and started working on her tangled hair.

"You'll get the hang of it, before the week is out." Chelsie paused, watching Carol struggle with her hair. "So, did Todd graduate from the UVM?"

"Yes, just last year. He has a teaching degree, but still hasn't found a teaching position yet."

"Well, I'm going to the UVM this fall. I heard you were accepted there, with great scholarships to boot."

"You're right. I did get accepted at University of Vermont, as well as several other schools. The UVM is my first choice because with financial aid, my tuition would be covered. Still, I probably won't start this fall."

"Oh, Carol, why not? With all those scholarships?" asked Chelsie with an incredulous expression.

"Well, you see, Todd wants more time to find a teaching position in Burlington. If he does, we can move there and live together while I go to school. The registration fee is due at the end of the month, and unless Todd finds a job before then, I don't think I'll be able to do it this year. Besides, taking a year off will give us time to save money, and maybe we can afford to buy a house by then."

"Carol, I'm sorry, but that plain sucks. I think you should take your scholarships and go. You shouldn't give up your life just for Todd."

Carol's face went hot, like it had been slapped. Chelsie had no idea what she was talking about. She was still a little girl compared to Carol, her main concerns about clothes and makeup and hair. She'd never had a serious relationship with a man, so she could not understand. Angry as Chelsie's comment had made her, she didn't want to ruin her new friendship. She took a deep breath and swallowed hard before answering.

"Chelsie, I'm sure you didn't mean to hurt me, but I don't think you understand how important Todd is to me. We plan to spend the rest of our lives together. My relationship with him is more important than anything else. It has to come first. That's what real love is all about."

"Hey, man, I'm sorry." Chelsie touched her arm softly. "I didn't mean to hurt your feelings. It just seems such a shame to waste all that scholarship money."

"I'm sure I can get the same scholarships for the next year."

"Maybe so." Chelsie rose up from Carol's bed and took out her box of jewelry. "So, are you and Todd engaged then?"

"Well, not officially. But we've both said we want to live together for the rest of our lives. Todd believes traditional marriage is unnecessary. It's the individual love and commitment of the couple that's important."

"I'd still want a diamond ring. Say, I have the perfect earring and necklace for your outfit. Come see."

Relieved that Chelsie had changed the subject, Carol went over to look at the jewelry. The pearl white and silver earrings and silver necklace were an ideal match for her outfit.

"Chelsie, I love them. Are you sure you don't mind if I wear them? They aren't too expensive are they?"

"Oh, no. It's just costume jewelry. I'd never bring expensive stuff on an informal trip like this. It's too dangerous. Some thug would probably steal them right off my neck."

"You've been so kind to me, thank you."

"Well, you won't be thankful to have me for a roommate if you don't get going. I'm getting hungry for authentic French cuisine. *Vous allez!*"

"Yes, Madame DeFarge."

Cheslie gave her a playful punch. "I'm going to see how Mrs. Meeks is doing in the room next door so you can have some privacy to get dressed. I'll be back shortly, so don't dawdle."

Carol obeyed and gathered her outfit as Chelsie left the room.

***

"I feel like I've been zapped backwards in time," said Carol. She and Chelsie lagged behind the rest of the group. They were walking down a cobblestone alley to a Parisian restaurant Amanda Meeks had chosen.

"It's pretty cool, isn't it?" Chelsie lifted her arms and twirled around. "Watch out Paris, here we come."

Carol giggled. She raised her eyes to the six storey buildings on both sides of the narrow passage, rows of centuries-old stone facades with French doors and wrought-iron balconies. Dusk was descending, and Carol could see movement behind the lighted windows. It had been a warm May day, so the girls were comfortable without coats. A brief shower left the cobblestones wet and shiny and smelling of sun-warmed rocks splashed with a sudden rain. This mixed with the delicious aroma of Parisians cooking dinner.

"You know, I expect to see a musketeer jump out from behind one of the buildings with his sword. Or a monk run by us on his way to evening prayer."

"I'll take the musketeer."

"Chelsie, did you read Dickens' *The Tale of Two Cities*?"

"Sounds familiar. What was it about?"

"It's one of my favorites. It's about the French Revolution. There's a scene in the beginning where a keg of wine falls off a wagon into the cobblestone streets. All the poor peasants stop what they are doing and run to drink some of the wine."

"Hmm. I'm trying to remember it."

"It started out with 'It was the best of times and the worst of times.' Dickens wanted to show the desperation of the oppressed French people with the wine scene. It foreshadowed the blood that would later flow through the streets when the commoners rose up against the French aristocracy."

"It think I remember it now. This guy who's in love with the main girl character looks just like her husband and dies for him at the end. Hey, is that why you called me Madame Defarge earlier? Wasn't she in that book?"

164

"Yes, she was the evil wife of Jacque, the leader of the underground movement. She would put the name of people she wanted dead in her knitting so their heads would get chopped off by the guillotine. She knitted Lucy's husband's name, and later Lucy's."

"Oh, Carol. This is morbid." Chelsie hugged herself.

"I'm sorry. It's just being here reminds me so much of the book. It's like I can live it out in my mind."

"I'm sure you'll get a chance to see a real guillotine before we leave."

"Well, I don't know if I want that part to be too clear. It's a little spooky."

"Hey, let's change the subject. What do you want for dinner?"

Carol didn't answer. Though it was still dusk, a sinister shadow overtook her from behind with its cold fingers. She could not move or speak, her feet glued to the stones, her body convulsing in chills. She let out a weak scream.

Chelsie turned around. "Carol, what's the matter?"

Carol stared at her friend, eyes opened wide, speechless.

"Are you okay? You look like you've seen a ghost!"

She stood there, fists clenched, teeth chattering, tears escaping.

"Carol, what the heck is wrong with you!" Chelsie scanned the alley to see if she could find the object of Carol's terror. "I don't see anything. Carol, talk to me." Chelsie put her arm around her. "You're as cold as ice."

"I don't know. I thought I saw or felt someone, something behind me."

"I think your imagination got the best of you, Carol. There's nothing here. We've got to hurry. The rest of the group is way ahead, and we'll lose them."

"I don't know if I can move."

"Come on, I'll help you." Chelsie took her hand and pulled her along. "You'll feel better once you get into a warm place and get some warm food in your stomach."

Carol walked stiffly. Chelsie had to prod her keep her moving. "What am I going to do with you, girl? It's a good thing I'm here to take care of you."

"Chelsie, wait." Carol stopped. "I want to tell you something. I have this weird feeling that this has happened before. Déjà vu or something."

"Don't be silly. You've never been to Paris before."

"I know it sounds crazy, but the feeling is so real. It felt like the person or whatever was behind me was someone who knows me, who I know. It doesn't make sense, but it's so strong I can hardly stand up."

Chelsie turned, met Carol's eyes, and shivered. "You're not kidding, are you? Now you're giving me the creeps. Let's get out of here."

Chelsie pulled Carol's arm and forced her to run. Though her heart pounded and she still struggled with dizziness, her legs managed to work. They finally caught up with the group.

"Hey, Chelsie, please don't tell anyone what happened, okay? I'm embarrassed enough."

"No problem. It'll be our secret. You never know, there may have been some thug hiding in the alley for all I know. We are in Paris, you know. The city does have its fair share of degenerates."

"That's why I have my money hidden in my belt."

"Well, I have all mine hidden in my bra."

"That sounds like you, Chelsie."

"You know it."

A few minutes later, they emerged from the alley to a main street. Carol felt better, but the strange feeling still swirled around within, her thoughts playing ping pong, bouncing back and forth from logic to emotion. *You just let your imagination take over. There was nothing there. There's no such thing as ghosts or evil sprits.*

But I know what I felt was as real as the stones beneath my feet. There had to be something behind me.

Carol, you've got to stop with this foolishness. It's going to ruin your evening.

Why would it feel familiar? Where have I felt that before?

Just stop thinking about it.

It's like my old nightmares come to life. That's it! It felt just like the stalker in my dreams!

See, Carol, then you know it's all in your head. Dreams are part of your subconscious. You caused the experience with your overly sensitive imagination and past traumatic experience. It probably all began after watching that scary movie about a demon years ago. Now put it out of your head and have some fun.

Listening to "common sense," Carol followed Chelsie, Amanda Meeks, two other chaperones, and eighteen students to the front of La Saveur de Paris, a restaurant on the bottom floor of what appeared to be a hotel much more expensive than their own. A *concierge* dressed in a tuxedo was instructing his bell-hops in fast French. Unlike the alley, people crowded the sidewalks, speaking so fast that Carol could not understand a word. Customers waited inside and outside the restaurant.

The most tantalizing, delicious aroma hit her as they walked through the tall, stain glassed, double doors into the most elegant restaurant she had ever seen. As the murmurs of the crowd's unfamiliar words surrounded her, Carol felt so tiny and out of place. She turned to Chelsie.

"J'ai faim," said Chelsie in French with a smile.

"Moi aussie," Carol squeaked out, surprised that she remembered the words.

"Carol, Chelsie, I thought we'd lost you." Amanda Meeks made her way to the front.

"I'm sorry, Mrs. Meeks. We had to run to catch up to you."

"Carol, are you all right?" Amanda's eyes met Carol's, concern in her expression. "You look a bit pale."

"I'm fine." Carol averted her eyes. "Just jet lag, I'm sure."

"Well, let's see if some fine French cuisine helps. We have a room reserved in the back."

The girls followed Amanda further into the restaurant. *La Garcon* led them to a separate room through a massive arched door etched in carvings on the top and down the sides, with glass windows on each end, covered in pastel green curtains. Their tables were set in front of a wall with a floor to ceiling, glass-covered bookcase filled with antique books. A huge, crystal chandelier provided indirect lighting, creating a romantic ambiance.

As the waiter pulled out a chair for her next to Amanda, she noticed the tables were double clothed, a gold table cloth on the bottom and a bright white one on the top. Their place settings consisted of a white, cloth napkin, two forks on the left, two knives and two spoons on the right, and a large wine glass. Carol replayed the etiquette training Amanda had given her. *The outside fork for salad, the inside for dinner. The duller knife for butter, the sharper for meat. The rounder spoon for soup, the other for dessert. It's okay to put your elbows on the table as long as you are eating. The napkin goes on the lap.*

"*Il est parfait*," said Chelsie. "*Magnificent!*"

"It sure is. I feel like I'm in a movie, Cinderella at her first ball." Carol put her napkin in her lap. "The smell is so delicious. It reminds me of my Grandmother's at Thanksgiving. She was French Canadian and made the best turkey soup."

"*La Saveur de Paris*, The Flavor of Paris. What a great name for a restaurant. And I love the décor. Look at this carpet. The gold and green and chocolate and rose swirling things match the wallpaper and the colors in the ceiling." Chelsie looked at the huge bookcase. "And look at all these old books."

"I love all the dark woodwork, in the ceiling, in the wainscoting. And look at that shade. I've never seen anything like it. So feminine with all those curves. I bet there's nothing that comes even close to this anywhere in the whole state of Vermont."

"That's because our country is so new. We're in old country here. The only thing missing are the balls gowns. We should be dressed to the hilt in sleek ball gowns."

"De filles, que aimez-vous passé cammadne ce soir? » Mrs. Meeks asked the girls in French.

"I have to translate the menu first," said Carol, opening her menu. "What are *truffles*?"

"They're mushrooms," said Amanda. "And *foie gras* is goose liver."

"Okay, that's what I'm having. Raviole de foi gras avec des truffles." Chelsie set down and look around the table.

"Goose liver? No, merci. Chelsie, you're not afraid of anything. Is *canard* duck?"

"Oui," said Amanda. "That's what I'm having. *Canard a L'Orange*, duck in orange sauce."

"I think I'll stick to the *poulet roti*, roast chicken."

"Mrs. Meeks, could you help me translate now?" Jeff Nickerson tapped Amanda on the shoulder. "I don't want to get stuck with snails or squid."

Carol was so overwhelmed she hadn't even noticed who was at the table with them. She soon realized, however, that Jeff was smiling at Chelsie.

"Ahh, Jeff, you need to learn to live a little. Escargot is supposed to be delicious." Chelsie returned his smile.

"Have you ever had it before?"

"No, but I will before I leave France, you can be certain of that."

"I bet you will, too. Well, I think I'll stick to the *boeuf de rotis avec des pommes de terre d'ami.*"

"Typical male. Roast beef and French fries. Stick with the familiar." Chelsie sat up in her chair and crossed her legs.

"We'll see whose typical, Mademoiselle Chelsie." Jeff brushed a dark lock from his face. "Mrs. Meeks, do we get to order wine?"

"You can have table wine only, which is highly diluted with water. But you do get to choose a soup and a dessert."

"But there's no drinking age in France."

"Jeff, you know you aren't going to get away with that. Now, pick out a soup."

"That's easy. I've always wanted to try authentic French onion soup."

"*J'aussie*, me too," said Chelsie.

"I would have guessed squid soup for you." Jeff laughed.

"I'm going to have *Crème de Broccolie*." Carol pointed to the item on the menu. And for dessert, *tart au chocolat*."

"Etes-vous preta commander Madame?" The waiter addressed Amanda Meeks.

"Oui, Monsieur."

***

"I still can't get over how delicious dinner was. I can still taste the sauce that was on my roast chicken, rich in garlic, onions, and some kind of flavorful herb. The soup was so creamy and tasty. And the dessert—it was to die for, so rich and chocolaty. I know I'm going to gain weight." Carol patted her stomach. She and Chelsie were resting on a bench in a Parisian mall.

"You should have tried the goose liver. It was out of this world good. So were the truffles. It's amazing that the French can make such ugly foods so appetizing and yummy."

"What do you think happened to Jeff and his friend, Adam?"

"I don't know, but he was cramping my style."

"Chelsie, you're so mean sometimes. Jeff's a nice guy, and he likes you. Deliberately going into a lingerie shop just to brush him off, now that's tricky. I bet he's still waiting for you to come out."

"Oh, I'll appease him later. But Carol, how can we flirt with French men if Jeff and Adam are following us everywhere? For one thing, they give us away as Americans." Chelsie perused the walkway.

"Can you believe their malls are still open at 10:00 at night? It's so much more alive around here. It makes Vermont look like the Hicksville of all time."

"It *is* the Hicksville of all time. Hey, Carol, don't be too obvious, but we have a couple of admirers watching us from that bench over there." Chelsie slanted her eyes to the left.

A few feet down, two young men sat at an identical bench to theirs, and, sure enough, they were looking in their direction and grinning. Both wore dress

169

slacks and sport coats; both had dark hair, dark eyes, broad shoulders, and nice smiles. Carol had to admit they were handsome. She wondered if they were brothers, they looked so much alike.

"Chelsie, just what kind of devilish plan do you have in mind? We're in a strange country where we don't even speak the language."

"Don't worry, we're in a public place. And the rest of our party is close by. I can always get Jeff back here if I need him." Chelsie stood up, smoothed the wrinkles in her dress, stretched, and pretended to inspect the contents of her bag. She deliberately did not look at the young men as she did this.

"Okay, Carol, here's the plan. You get up casually, and we walk by them and go into that candy shop."

Carol wavered. On the one hand, she knew it was a bad idea to flirt with strange men. On the other hand, she wanted to see the reaction they would have when they walked by.

"Okay, but don't get too carried away with this." Carol stood up, tucked in her blouse, and picked up her bags. She followed as Chelsie sauntered past the men in a perfect model pose, her head held high, her blond hair flowing on her shoulders.

Carol saw the men give them a good look over as they passed by. They went into the candy shop and inspected rows of enticing chocolates. From the corner of her eye, Carol could see the men walk into the store. Perspiration was forming under her arms, and she picked at her thumb. She knew Chelsie saw them come in, yet she behaved as calm and cool as ever.

It seemed like they were looking at candy forever as the men pretended to be shopping at the same time they did. The shop owner approached them. "Este-ce que je puis vous aider?"

Carol turned to Chelsie. Her French was better than hers.

"J'aurai cele, s'l vous plait. » Chelsie pointed to a dark chocolate with nuts.

"Non, merci," Carol mumbled. She noticed the men were now standing behind them. She could smell their cologne.

"Ainsi, vous de filles aimez le chocolat, oui? » one of the men asked.

Chelsie turned to him and smiled. "Oui."

"Je connais un endroit avec du chocolat bien meilleur que ceci., » said the man. The only words Carol understood was chocolate, but she did notice the shopkeeper, an older woman with her hair pinned back under a scarf, give the man a nasty expression. If Chelsie didn't understand, she gave no indication.

"Merci, mais nous devor aller." She took the change from the shopkeeper and brushed by the man, slightly touching his coat. Carol went around the other side to avoid them.

"Mademoiselle, attente. D'ou etes-vous?"

Chelsie's steps were brisk and quick, and Carol had to work hard to keep up with her. They turned a corner and went on an escalator.

"Chelsie, what did the guy say to you? I know he said something about us liking chocolates, then you turned around and said *yes*, flashing that smile of yours. But I'm lost after that."

"He told me he knew a better place to shop for chocolate. I told him I had to go, and he asked me to stop."

"You got him all excited, then dropped him like a hot potato. You're a big tease. Do you think we lost them?"

"I think so. They aren't on the escalator."

"Let's look from the top." The second floor overlooked the bottom one.

"Oh no, there they are. They're headed for the escalator. Let's get out of here." Chelsie grabbed her hand.

"Did they see us up here?"

"I don't know. I'm going to find and elevator and go back to the bottom floor, back to the lingerie store. Maybe we can find Jeff and Adam. If that doesn't work, we can go to our meeting point and wait for Mrs. Meeks."

They went a short ways, found an elevator, and rushed into it.

"This is so much fun!" said Chelsie as the doors closed.

"You think so? I don't know. I'm kind of scared."

"We have nothing to worry about, Carol. We're just two pretty girls that got the attention of two handsome men. We're mysterious and intriguing, and they want to know more about us. The chances are pretty low that they're rapists or murderers."

"Still, Chelsie, we shouldn't be taking chances."

The elevator door opened, and they made their way back to the lingerie shop. Jeff and Adam weren't there.

"Okay, Mrs. Meeks said to meet at the Boulangerie. Let's head there."

Carol took the lead this time, as Chelsie had slowed her pace. It was if she wanted the men to find them again. As the neared the Boulangerie, Carol saw Jeff and Adam sitting on a bench. They stood up.

"Where've you girls been?" Jeff, who was at least six feet tall, towered over Chelsie, his arms folded. "We waited for you forever outside the lingerie store."

"I'm sorry, Jeff. We lost track of time in there. Please forgive us."

"Boy, are we glad to see you." Carol slumped onto the bench.

"Why?" asked Adam.

Chelsie gave Carol an expression that said, "What are you doing? Keep quiet!"

"Oh, because we felt bad that we lost you, that's all." Just as Carol gave a sigh of relief, she noticed the Parisian men who had been following them approach.

"Mademoiselle, pour quoi courez-vous loin? Vous avez oublie votre chocolat. » He handed Chelsie the chocolate she had purchased at the candy shop.

"Je suis desole. Merci." Chelsie took the bag.

The man noticed Jeff and Adam eyeing him, looked at them briefly, then turned to Chelsie.

"You girls American?"

"Oui." Chelsie put her bag of chocolate in a larger bag.

"Ah, touristes." he turned to his friend, and they laughed together.

"You girls not look American. You *tres chic, belle fleurs.*"

Chelsie blushed. The man's companion smiled at Carol. She understood the complement.

So did Jeff. "Chelsie, I think it's time we got going."

"Merci, monsieur. Mon nom est Chelsie. Quel est votre nom?"

"James Louis Bernard. A pleasure to meet you." He extended his hand.

"You speak English well." Chelsie shook his hand. He held it longer than normal.

"You speak good French. This is my brother, Jon."

"Bonsoir." Jon also shook her hand.

Chelsie turned around. "And this is Carol, Jeff and Adam."

Jon came up to Carol. "Bonsoir, Mademoiselle Carol. Ce's un plairsir de vous rencontrer."

"Bonsoir."

"Bonsoir." Jeff and Adam greeted the Parisian men.

"How long you in Paris?" asked James.

"A few days."

"If you like, we show you around, yes?"

Jeff came up next to Chelsie. "Thanks, but we're here with our high school. Chelsie has to stay with the group."

"High school?"

"Ecole Secondaire." Jeff translated.

James looked at Chelsie. "How old you are?"

"Dix-huit. I graduate this year."

"Me and Jon, we go university. You like it."

"Chelsie, we really need to go."

"I give you my number. You call if want to see university, oui?" James pulled out a piece of paper and a pen from his pocket and jotted down a phone number. He handed it to Chelsie.

"Merci." Chelsie took the number. Jeff folded his arms and tapped his foot.

"Nice to meet you, James. Chelsie, let's go."

"We don't want to get into trouble," said Adam to Carol.

James met Jeff's eyes, then focused on Chelsie. "Nice to meet you, Chelsie." He took her hand in his and kissed the top. "Hope to see you again. Bonne nuit."

"Bon nuit, James." Chelsie pulled her hand away slowly.

"Bon nuit, Carol," said Jon. The men nodded to Jeff and Adam, then walked away.

As soon as they were out of sight, Jeff turned to Chelsie. "Chelsie, what the heck was that all about? Do you want to get us all in trouble? I can't believe you took that guy's phone number."

"Just because I took it doesn't mean I'm going to call him."

"Well, you know what Mrs. Meeks would say about that."

"Oh, come on, Jeff. Like how could I get away to spend time with him anyway? I'm just having fun. I don't want to see him again."

"Well, one of these days your kind of fun's going to get you in big trouble. You led that guy on, sure as day, and if we weren't here to protect you, God knows what he would have done. Don't you have any idea what guys like him are thinking about?"

Chelsie looked up at Jeff, eyes flashing, sly grin on her face. "I know exactly what they're thinking."

Jeff turned away to hide his blush. He sat down on the bench, crossed his arms and legs, stared straight ahead and said nothing more. Chelsie gathered her belongings, sat down next to him, and took out her compact to adjust her make-up. No one spoke for a few minutes.

"What time is it?" Carol broke the silence.

"It's almost eleven. The rest of our group should be here soon," said Adam.

"Good. I'm suddenly beat."

"Me, too."

***

Running and searching, searching and running, down dark alleys, through men and women who moved like statues, unable to see her or hear her pleas for help. She had to find her. The young girl was lost in Paris, and something terrible was about to happen.

She was in a park. Children played, mothers sat in the sun sharing news, fathers wrestled with their sons, artists painted on easels on the large, green expanse.

"Avez-vous vu une jeune, americaine fille?"

The mother ignored her, as if she were invisible, turning to her little girl and speaking to her in rapid French.

"Madame, svp, j'ai besoin de votre aide !"

The little girl giggled, and the mother stooped down and scooped her into her arms.

They don't see me. She sprinted through the park into another alleyway. The passage was elongated and narrow, the buildings tall on either side, blocking much of the light. At the very end, a long distance off, a man held a girl, threatening her with a knife that flashed even in the duskiness. She leaped forward, throwing all her energy into her legs, dashing with all her might toward the images.

"Stop! Leave her alone!"

Even as she willed her legs to reach the lost girl, she could see herself propelling like an actor in a movie turned to slow motion. As she approached the end of the corridor, the girl's face became clear, bewildered, helpless, terrified. Yet the girl did not fight her attacker. He had the knife in one hand and stroked her hair with the other like a cat licks the fur of a mouse it is toying with. His face remained shadowed, even as she almost came close enough to touch him. She reached out, but they remained a few inches from her grasp. The man plunged the knife into the girl, and her body slumped to the ground. Then he turned to her and laughed: a hideous, evil cackle that echoed into the alley, surrounding her like a thick fog. She stood paralyzed, unable to help the girl. He faced her and grinned. He had the most beautiful and dreadful face she had ever seen. His seductive eyes bored into her, at first

174

attractive, then turning into two red balls. She closed her eyes and cried out. "Jesus, Jesus, please help me!"

It took several minutes before Amanda remembered where she was. She had just experienced one of the worst nightmares of her life. Fearing the red balls were still above her, the evil presence still in the room, she kept her eyes closed and prayed. Her prayers helped her gain the courage to open her eyes and check on the three girls in her room. They slept peacefully, unaware of the horror she had just endured. She needed to pray more, but did not want to wake the girls. The clock read 3:00. She moved her stiff limbs over the edge of the bed and shivered. Careful to be quiet, she tiptoed to the coat closet, took out her coat, gently opened the door, and padded down the hall to the bathroom. She fell on her knees on the cold, tile floor and prayed. "Lord, I don't know what evil is after Carol, but please, please protect her…"

***

"It's a perfect day in May. The sun is shining warm and bright, the birds are singing, the flowers are smiling, everything in the world is right. Hey, that rhymes." Carol looked over at Chelsie and Jeff. From the expression on Jeff's face, Chelsie's transgressions from the previous night had been forgiven. He walked about as close to her as he could without actually touching her. Chelsie did not seem to object.

"This park is like a breath of fresh air after the Louvre. I mean, I like art as much as anyone, but after five hours of walking through room after room of paintings, it's nice to be out in the air." Chelsie twirled around in her flowing turquoise skirt and white sandals, brushing against Jeff.

"I have to agree. Nothing can compete with God's own works of art." Jeff smiled at Chelsie. "But I'm glad I can say I've seen the Mona Lisa with her mysterious smile."

"It is amazing how Leonardo Davinci made her so life-like," said Carol. "And I loved all of Monet's impressionistic paintings, so vivid in color, re-creating flowers and trees and water on a day just like this one. Look at the little kids over there sailing their miniature sailboats." In the distance, families surrounded a man-made pond with a fountain in the middle. Vendors rented colorful sailboats, but many of the local children launched their own. The tiny boats bobbed in the gentle waves, glinting cheerfully in the afternoon sun.

"Les Jardin des Tuileries is the perfect place for kids and poets and lovers. Look at all the artists with their easels." Chelsie pointed to a large expanse of lawn that bordered the walkway to the Louvre. Local artists had set up individual shops in various spots. Many displayed oil paintings, fine-line drawings, and watercolors for sale while they worked on a new piece. Several portrait artists were sketching tourists for money.

"Chelsie, I just had a brilliant idea. Let's get our portraits done so we can remember this day forever. It'll be my treat."

"Jeff, that's a great idea. But I can help pay for my own. I brought plenty of spending money."

"Let's go see how much it costs." Jeff took Chelsie's hand and started leading her toward the artists.

"Wait, what about you, Carol? Do you want to have your portrait done?"

"Um, no, I'm okay. I'll just sit on that bench over there and watch you." Carol didn't want to admit that she could not afford it. She had spent a large amount of money on the dress she was wearing. She bought it at the mall the previous night, before their adventure with the Parisian men.

"All right, it shouldn't take too long. Are you sure you'll be okay by yourself?"

"I'm fine. Now go and stop worrying about me." Carol shooed them away with her hand.

"I'll see you in a little bit, then." Chelisie walked off with Jeff. Carol strolled to a bench nearby and sat down. She took off her white sweater and admired the way her new blue and white peasant dress draped over her legs. It had tiny bluebells interwoven with white lace, a white, low-cut bodice, and puffy, short sleeves. The sun felt wonderful on her bare skin, and she knew she looked good sitting there. Her only irritation was her feet. After walking for hours in the museum in her brown boots, she had developed calluses on both her feet. She took off her boots and let them breathe.

Life stirred all around her, yet she was not a part of it, as if plunked down in the center of a movie. Tourists tromped toward the Louvre, talking to their companions, pointing at maps. Children splashed and giggled with their sailboats in the shallow pool while mothers conversed, their voices like babbling birds, the words unintelligible yet a hypnotic song lulling her to sleep. Young men played Frisbee, their shirts tossed to the ground in the heat. Lovers sat or lay together on blankets. Pink, blue, white, and purple pansies dazzled from their flower beds, blossoming apple trees gave off a sweet smell as they swayed in a balmy breeze. Carol place her bags and purse on the bench, put her feet up, and lay her head on her bags. The sounds, the colors, the odors all mingled together and became like a beautiful dream as her eyes became heavy. They drifted away as she sank into a place of warmth, comfort, and contentment. She was like Dorothy in the field of poppies, unable to resist the intoxication.

"Mademoiselle, Etes-vous bien?"

Someone was speaking to her. Startled, Carol sat up. The blood rushed to her head, and she could hardly make out the person talking to her.

"Excuse me. Excusez moi." Carol rubbed her eyes.

"You speak English. Sorry to startle you, Mademoiselle. You look like a painting sleeping there."

Carol could now see that a young Parisian was speaking to her. From his white t-shirt covered in paint and his beret, she guessed he was one of the artists.

Carol tried to stand up, but her head swam and her stomach lurched. "I'm sorry, but I think falling asleep in the sun has made me dizzy."

"Let me help you. Here, drink this." The man handed her a bottle.

"What is it?"

"You call it mineral water. Don't worry, it's never been opened." He pulled out a bottle opener and flipped off the top. "It's only water."

Grateful, Carol took it. "Merci, Monsieur." After drinking the carbonated water, she sighed and looked at her benefactor.

He was very handsome, with curly brown hair peaking out from his cap and a well-groomed moustache and goatee. She could not make out his eyes, as he was looking out into the park, not at her.

"A magnificent day, would you not say?"

"Yes. You speak English very well."

"I went to school in Chicago for a while."

"Well, thank you for the water. I'd better go find my party." Carol put on her boots, gathered her belongings and prepared to leave.

"Wait, don't leave yet." The Parisian artist touched her arm, sending electrical impulses throughout her body. A tiny voice deep in the recesses of her brain warned her to go, but the excitement of something she had not experienced for a long time kept her from moving.

"If you don't mind, I'd like to draw you, free of charge of course. You are a beautiful woman. Please, my supplies are just over there on the lawn."

The man walked in front of Carol, and she followed. What harm would it be to get a portrait of herself? She would have spent the money to do it if she could afford it. They were out in the open, and she could see Jeff and Chelsie sitting by the pool together.

"Here, sit in this chair, jolie fille." The young man sat behind his easel and took out a fresh piece of paper and drawing pencils.

"I want you to look at that maple tree in front of you, and try not to move. Oui?"

"Oui." Carol set her eyes on a branch of a large maple tree. Immediately, she had an itch on her nose. She resisted for a moment, but the itch intensified. She gave it a quick scratch, then put her hands back in her lap. The artist didn't seem to notice.

She kept herself as much like a statue as possible for what seemed like an hour but was only a few minutes, scratching and moving only when she could no longer resist. The sound of charcoal pencil traveling across the surface of the paper was the only noise from the Parisian artist. From time to time, the man would rub the charcoal and blow on it. It would catch the wind and tickle her nose, but she somehow avoided sneezing.

"Voila! Je suis fini."

Carol jumped up from her chair. "Can I see it?"

"Certainly." The artist turned his easel around so she could see.

"Wow! It's like looking into a black and white mirror. Except I look even better than real life."

"No, mon cheri. This is how you really look. Perfect."

"Merci beaucoup." The man turned and looked at Carol straight on for the first time. Something about his eyes was so familiar. He had the same flashing brown eyes, the same knowing expression, the same weakening effect. His breath even smelled of peppermint. But how could *he* be here in Paris. *It's your imagination,* she told herself. *Shake it off.*

"Mademoiselle, I would like to paint you. Could you come to my studio?"

"No, merci. I must go now." Carol turned her eyes from him. She had to resist his charm. If there was any chance it was him, she would not let him dupe her again.

"But Carol, I have never had a chance to show you the truth about me."

He used her name! It couldn't be! As he reached out to touch her again, heat rushed through her veins, from her toes, to her fingertips, to her ears.

"How do you know my name? I never told you."

His eyes penetrated, bore into her like superman with his x-ray vision." Carol, you know who I am."

"No I don't. You've never even told me your name."

"Then come with me now, and I will explain everything. Please, Carol, it will make sense to you once you give me a chance."

Why did she not turn away? Why did her feet stay frozen to the ground? No one had ever made her feel so weak, so vulnerable, or so excited. His eyes stayed locked to hers, luring her like a magician with a snake.

"Come with me, Carol." He took her hand in his.

***

"Chelsie, Jeff, have you seen Carol?" Amanda Meeks marched up to the couple. They were sitting at the edge of the pool, dipping their feet in the water.

"Hi, Mrs. Meeks. Carol should be over there on the bench." Jeff pointed, then turned and looked at Chelsie. There was an old man sitting on the bench.

"Well, that doesn't look like Carol to me. When was the last time you saw her?" Jeff and Chelsie turned to each other. "Well." Chelsie spoke first. "I guess it's been a while. We lost track of time. She was there last time we looked."

"Chelsie, you know the rule was that you stick together always. So, what were you doing when you last saw her?"

"Mrs. Meeks, we're really sorry. Chelsie and I went to get our portraits done. Carol said she would stay at the bench and wait for us. When we got done, she was still on the bench, but she was sleeping so peacefully, we left her there. Then we came down here to talk. We thought she would see us when she woke up and come join us. I don't know where she went."

"Great, this is just great!" The dreadful panic she had experienced with the nightmare returned.

"Okay, we've got to find Carol. I want you to look for her to the right. I'll go tell the rest of the group to wait for me right here while I search to the left. Meet me back here in fifteen minutes. Do you have your watch?"

Jeff lifted his wrist. "Yes. We'll be back in fifteen minutes. I'm really sorry, Mrs. Meeks."

"We'll discuss this later." Amanda headed back to her group of students and chaperones who were waiting on the lane. After quick instructions, she started down the row of artists. *Dear Lord, this is just like the dream I had. Please, Lord, you have to help me find Carol.* Amanda stopped and asked each of the artists if they had seen her, but none had. At the end of the row, she found an easel, two chairs, and art supplies that had been abandoned. There was something very odd about the scene, so Amanda looked around for anything that might be Carol's. She was about to move on when she noticed something on the grass. It was a white sweater; Carol's sweater. She had been there. Amanda picked it up.

"Carol!" she called. "Carol, it's Amanda. Where are you?" She quickly headed back on the path, further into the park. As she turned a corner, she noticed a man and a woman ambling in the distance, their backs to her. She recognized the blue and white dress. It was Carol.

"Carol, stop! Come back here!" She ran to catch up to them. She finally reached them and grabbed Carol's shoulder.

"What are you doing?"

Carol turned around. She had the expression of a perplexed child, like she didn't understand what was happening. She would have expected guilt or rebellion, but not the confusion on her face.

"Amanda."

"You had me so worried." Even though she was furious with her, Amanda took Carol into her arms. "Who is that man you're with?" She turned to confront him. The man wasn't there.

"Where did he go?"

"Oh, no!" Carol cried. They searched for him, ran ahead on the path, then back to the drawing of Carol, still on the easel. He had disappeared.

***

"Amanda, I'm so sorry about all this. I don't know what came over me." Carol sniffled and wiped her eyes on her sweater. Tears kept pouring down her face. "You've got to believe me, I never intended to let this happen."

"Why don't you sit down." Amanda led her to a vacant chair at the sight that the mysterious artist abandoned. Then she dug into her purse, found some tissues, and handed them to her. She was furious at Carol for taking off with a strange man, yet instinct told her if she were too harsh, she would lose her trust. *God, help me know what to say. Help me hold back my anger.*

"Please, Amanda, don't tell anyone what I've done. Please. I'm so embarrassed." Carol stared at her with puffy, red eyes and that fearful, lost expression.

Her heart softened. "I'm not sure yet what I'm going to do. Let's talk about it a while first."

"If Todd were to find out, he would be furious! I don't want to lose him. I do love him. I don't want to cheat on him." Carol put her face in her hands and sobbed.

"I believe you, Carol. But what possessed you to do such a thing?" The question only made her cry louder. Amanda handed her another tissue. "Why don't you blow your nose?"

180

"I can't believe I'm so stupid! I told myself it wouldn't happen this time. Yet he did it to me again."

"He did it to you again?" Amanda let the words sink in. Could Carol possibly know the strange, Parisian artist? It didn't make any sense. A frigid chill passed over her, even though she sat in direct sunlight. Something was very wrong with the situation. She folded her arms and rubbed them, then took a deep breath, speaking very gently.

"Carol, did I hear you correctly? You've met this man before?"

Carol sat up, and an expression of horror passed over her face. She directed her attention away from Amanda, toward the path, and did not answer.

Amanda touched her shoulder. "It's okay to tell me. You can trust me. What has this man done to you?"

Carol pulled away. "I can't talk about it. Don't ask me anything else."

Lord Jesus, now what do I do? Amanda studied the lost, petrified young woman before her. Someone needed to help her, to reach her, to bring her to a place of healing, but how? She had just set up a stone wall to protect herself from her. Yet if she didn't confide in someone, whatever malice that was behind that man would destroy her. *Wait, pray, and love*, the Lord spoke to her heart. She touched Carol's shoulder.

"Okay, Carol, I won't pressure you, and no one else needs to know what happened here today. I just want you to know that I'm here for you when you are ready to talk about it. Or, if you can't tell me, please tell someone. I don't know who that man is, but I do know he's up to no good. The fact that he ran off proves it. He's hiding something, that's for certain."

Carol turned and their eyes met. "Thank you, Amanda. I know you care about me. I wish I could tell you, but I just can't."

"I understand, but you really can tell me. I wouldn't think any less of you. I love you Carol."

"You wouldn't believe me. No one would believe me."

"I already believe you." Amanda deliberately made eye contact.

"Thanks. I'll think about it." Carol turned, wiped her eyes, and found her possessions. The conversation was over for now.

Amanda looked at her watch. "Oh my goodness, I forgot I told Jeff and Chelsie I would meet them back in fifteen minutes. The whole group is waiting for us. We've got to go!"

As they were about to leave, Amanda remembered the portrait the strange man had drawn of Carol. She went over to the easel.

"We'd better take this with us. It will give some validity to your story. We'll just tell them you went to have your portrait done and lost tract of time. That part is the truth."

Amanda took off the drawing, rolled it up, and handed it to Carol. Carol stepped back, afraid to touch it.

"I'll carry it for now. We'd better go."

They ran up the lane to rejoin their party.

Chapter Twenty-One

As the deer panteth for the water, so my soul longeth after thee.
You alone are my heart's desire, and I long to worship you.
You alone are my strength, my shield.
To you alone does my spirit yield.
You alone are my heart's desire, and I long to worship you.

Margaret watched Pastor Wilcock sing with passion, his eyes closed, his hand strumming his guitar with skill. He was accompanied by two female vocalists, a piano, a bass guitar, drums, and a flute. The harmonized words filled the room with a beautiful sound, as the musicians raised their voices in devotion. They believed the words they sang. Next to her, Jim lifted his hands and closed his eyes. When he said, "To you alone does my spirit yield," she knew that was his heart's desire. Yet here she was signing with them, not being honest with the words that came out of her mouth. She was a fake.

How could she worship a God who had abandoned her? Once, so long ago, she had loved Jesus. She could see in her mind the little girl who touched the baby Jesus in the nativity displayed in their living room. "Mommy, is this the same Jesus that's on the cross at church?" she had asked her Mother.

"Yes, dear, he loved us so much that he came into the world as a baby and then, as a man, he died for our sins."

She didn't understand exactly what her mother said at the time, but had accepted his love blindly. She saw herself in a pure, white dress, kneeling before the priest, accepting her first communion. She had dedicated her life to serve Christ that day, to be a devoted Catholic. She loved him then, because she believed he loved her. Then she flashed ahead to her wedding day, again clothed in white. She had obeyed God's commandments, remained pure for her husband, and made a commitment before God to love, honor, and cherish him until death. She kept her part of the bargain, but God didn't keep his. She saw the face of the woman who now lived with Richard. An ex-nun of all things.

How could she yield herself to a God who let such a horrible thing happen to her?

She attended church because it made Jim happy. Actually, her whole family loved the church. Liz had made new friends in the youth group, and Marie and Jeanne raved about their Sunday School teacher. Sure, the people in the church had never condemned her for living with Jim, but she knew they believed the Bible. One day, they would tell her she was living in sin. The pastor and his wife had no idea what real life was all about, how mean and cruel the world could be. How could they? They had the perfect little family with two angelic children. They were always so cheerful and positive about everything. Let them try living in her shoes for a while.

She looked around the room. It seemed she was the only one who didn't accept the words of the song. No, she didn't belong here.

Worship time ended, and the children left for their classes. Pastor Wilcock put away his guitar and began to speak. "Turn in your Bibles to Matthew 6:14-15. I will read it. 'For if you forgive men when they sin against you, your heavenly Father will also forgive you. But if you do not forgive men theirs sins, your Father will not forgive your sins.' Put a marker in your Bible and turn also to Romans 3:23. It says, '…for all have sinned and fall short of the glory of God.' We're going to refer to these two scriptures today, but before I begin, I want to tell you two stories. The first is from the Bible, the second is from our generation."

Margaret listened as the pastor read in Acts about the disciple Paul and how he persecuted and ordered the death of many early Christians when he was known as Saul of Tarsus. "One day, while on the road to Damascus, Jesus appeared to him and asked him why he was persecuting him. After Jesus spoke to him, Saul was blinded. Saul went to Damascus and waited, as the Lord had told him to, and he repented of his great sin."

"Jesus then spoke to a man named Ananias and told him he must go to a certain house and pray for Saul of Tarsus. When Ananias heard that name, he could not believe it. He knew this very man had killed many of his fellow brothers and sisters in Christ, and could even order that he be killed. Yet he obeyed the Lord and went to pray for a man who was his enemy. Saul's vision was restored, and he immediately went out, was baptized, and began to preach. Can you imagine how hard it would have been to pray for the man who was responsible for murder? Yet, Ananias forgave his enemy and accepted him as a brother."

"Now let me tell you the story about a little boy. This little boy's father died when he was only five years old. His mother remarried a few years later, to the meanest, cruelest man. This boy's stepfather would beat him if he made too much noise, then lock him in the closet for hours. The boy's mother knew her husband mistreated her son, but she never interfered. At the age of sixteen, the boy ran away from home and lived with an Aunt and Uncle in New Hampshire. There, he was loved and cared for. There, he learned the love of Jesus. Then one day, when the boy was in college, the Lord told him to go back and visit his mother and step-father. Oh, how the boy fought with God. 'Lord, you have no idea how it hurt when he would beat me,' he cried. And the Lord replied, 'I was beaten beyond recognition.' 'But I endured long hours of agony and despair and loneliness when no one loved me.' He replied, 'I was shunned, despised, and spit on by the very people I came to save.' 'But my mother, how she betrayed me and rejected me.' And the Lord replied, 'even my father in heaven rejected me so that I could bear your sins.' 'Lord, it hurt so bad, I thought I'd die.' And the Lord replied, 'My son, I did die.'"

"Jesus led the young man to the two scriptures you have marked in your Bibles. Then he showed him that his hatred of his mother and step-father was as much a sin as the hatred and abuse they had poured out on him. All of us have fallen short of the glory of God, all of us deserve the punishment of death, yet Jesus took it for us. If this man could receive the freedom that came from receiving forgiveness from God, so did his estranged family deserve the same love and forgiveness."

"'But I can't do it!'" the young man protested. 'You don't have to do it by yourself. I will be there to help you.' So the boy returned home and forgave his mother and step-father. At first, nothing seemed to change. His step-father continued to dish out cruelty, and his mother did nothing to stop him. But as he continued to pray, over time, his mother received Christ and was set free from years of physical and emotional abuse."

"So, I ask you today, are you harboring anger and hatred toward anyone? Perhaps you are even angry with God? Do you feel like he has forsaken you? That young man felt the same way. I should know. That young man was me."

Margaret felt as if she had been hit by a tidal wave. She felt terrible that she had judged the pastor and thought he would not be able to understand her pain. It was as if Pastor Wilcock had read her mind and was speaking to her alone.

"If your anger and un-forgiveness has kept you from accepting the love and grace of Jesus, this moment is for you. Perhaps you have been hurt deeply by another human being and have blamed God for it. God created us with free will. It was not God who chose to hurt you. Perhaps you don't blame God, but still can't find a way in your heart to forgive the person who hurt you. Or perhaps you are ashamed of what you have done to others and can't forgive yourself. The commandment to forgive includes forgiving yourself, for Jesus said, 'Love your neighbor as yourself.' To say that God can't forgive you is to say that you are above God."

"John 3:16 & 17 says, 'For God so loved the world that he gave his one and only Son, that whoever believes in him shall not perish but have eternal life. For God did not send his Son into the world to condemn the world, but to save the world through him.'" He came into the world for you, for me, for my mother, and for my step-father, even for murderers like Paul. If you have not made the decision to accept his free love and forgiveness, or if you have walked away from him, now is the time to receive him. If he is speaking to you, come to the front.'"

Margaret thought her heart would swell and break. She realized now that God had not broken his promises to her, rather she had broken her promise to him. Richard had become her god, and when he failed her, she blamed it on God instead of seeing that both she and Richard were sinners who needed Jesus. She did not know how she could forgive Richard, yet before her stood a man who had lived through even worse circumstances and now dedicated his life to serving others. If he could do it, surely God could help her. She took a deep breath, stood up, and walked to the front of the church. As Pastor Wilcock prayed for her, tears flowed like cleansing water down her face. Several women from the church surrounded her, offered her tissues, and joined in the pastor's prayers. Never had she experienced such love and acceptance. Then she felt one more hand on her shoulder. She looked back and saw Jim's face, also full of tears. He said to her, "Margaret, did you know that whenever a soul is saved, the angels rejoice in heaven? There are a host of angels rejoicing over you right now."

***

Carol stared out the window without seeing a thing. She could feel the wheels of the bus speeding down the highway, could hear voices swirling around her, knew Amanda sat next to her reading a book, knew Chelsie and

Jeff were chatting behind her. Yet, all if it remained far in the background of the noise running through her mind.

Did she really want to go home? Her time in France, in spite of the incident with *him*, had been the best experience of her life. She had become part of her French family, had visited so many exciting places, and was now Chelsie's best friend. She and Chelsie had roamed the streets of Paris, shared wonderful French pastries, tried on stylish French clothes, braved the halls of a French school with its Spartan cafeteria and disgusting bathrooms, become lost together at the zoo in Lyon, and laughed with their French sisters at misunderstood communication. Then there was Amanda. She treated her like an adult, even when she did not deserve it. She listened to her complain about constipation and cry about her stupidity. Amanda never pressured her to talk about *him*. She never brought it up again. Carol felt like she really belonged.

If only she could go to the University of Vermont with Chelsie in the fall. They would have so much fun. They could explore, go shopping, study together, and spy out cute boys. Oh, there she went again, having bad thoughts about other men. She knew it wasn't fair to Todd. She knew he loved her, and it was wrong to think of such things. But their life had become so stale. They had no fun together anymore. Should she tell Todd they needed to have more fun? Maybe there was a way to make their life more exciting.

But then he would feel she didn't love him anymore. Did she still love him? She had to still love him, after all he had done for her. If Todd had not helped her, she would have never done so well in school. He taught her so many things: how to speak correctly, how to write well, how to research, how to be a woman. He was always available when she needed someone. He had taken care of her now for almost three years. In a few weeks, she would be out of high school and seventeen. She wished she were already eighteen like Chelsie, then she would be a legal adult.

Stop feeling sorry for yourself. You should be happy with what you have. How many women her age had someone they knew would love them for the rest of their lives? She should appreciate the fact that Todd wanted her when he was so much older and could pick from lots of girls his own age. No, she had to go home and be happy and loving. Somehow, she had to keep her rotten thoughts a secret and be a good, devoted lover for him.

"Carol, you're so quiet. Is everything okay?" Amanda set her book on her lap.

"Sure, I'm fine. I'm just thinking, that's all."

"You had a great time on this trip, didn't you?"

"It was the best time of my life."

"Carol, you have a lot more responsibilities to go home to than most girls your age. Is that hard for you?"

Carol turned to Amanda, amazed at her insight. She always seemed to know what she was thinking about. "I guess, but I should appreciate what I have."

"That's true."

Amanda paused a moment and cleared her throat. "I hope you aren't offended by what I have to say, but I need to say something to you. I'm going to say it because I really care about you, and I'm worried about the pressures you've put on yourself. You are such a smart, talented young woman with much to offer the world. You're young and have your entire life left to live. I guess this is what I want to say. Don't be in such a hurry, Carol. You're awfully young to be tied down in a permanent relationship. Are you sure you really want to spend the rest of your life with Todd?"

"What do you mean, of course I do!" Carol picked at a pimple on her chin and looked out the window. If Amanda doubted her devotion to Todd, would he be able to see through her, too? Hot tears started to form, but she had to hold them back. Amanda could not see her doubt any more. She had to be faithful to Todd. She had to keep loving him. She didn't want to be like her mother, sleeping around with many different guys.

"Amanda, you don't have to worry about me. I love Todd. He's the right man for me. What happened in Paris was crazy and stupid, but it's over and will never happen again."

"Okay, Carol. I hope I haven't hurt our friendship."

"No." Carol touched her shoulder. "I want us to be friends. You've been so good to me. I can understand why you would think I might not love Todd because of what I did. But you've got to trust me now."

"All right, I'll trust you. But, please remember I'm here for you any time, any place. I don't care if it's in the middle of the night, you can call me any time." Amanda squeezed her hand.

"Thanks." Carol stared out the window again. It took everything in her to stop the tears.

***

188

Todd looked at his watch for the fifth time. The bus was five minutes late. He wished he could go stand with the crowd of parents and family members that waited at the school, but that would be too risky. He told Carol he would be in the car in the parking lot. If she were older, he could be first in line and run up to kiss her when she stepped off the bus. He'd been waiting fourteen days to kiss her again. It felt like a year.

He took a sip from the spiked drink in the seat next to him. He needed something to steady his nerves. So much had happened while Carol was gone, and he had so much to tell her. He put his hand in his pocket and fingered the box inside. It was going to be hard to keep it a secret until later that night. He had it all planned out. Her would take her to a nice restaurant, then home for chocolate cake, already waiting with a dozen roses, then give her the ring and show her the contract. After she accepted it, they would make passionate love all night. He would share the rest of the good news the next morning.

He heard the familiar diesel noise of the bus pulling up the drive into the high school. From his vantage point, he could not see them unload, but he could hear them. After a while, he saw families get into their cars in the parking lot above, then drive away. What was taking her so long? She was probably saying goodbye to Mrs. Meeks and all the other students. Didn't she remember he was waiting for her?

He looked at his watch another three times before seeing Carol make her way slowly toward him. She looked great in her tight fitting blue jeans and what must be a new white, peasant style shirt. But she wasn't even smiling or looking in his direction. Maybe she did that because she didn't want anyone to know he was in the car waiting for her. As she neared the car, she pulled her keys out of her handbag and opened the trunk. She was playing it cool. He stayed in the car and waited for her, thumping his thumbs on the steering wheel. After she shut the trunk, he watched her look around before opening the passenger door.

"Baby, baby, I missed you so much." Todd pulled Carol toward him, smashing his mouth on hers.

She let him kiss her for a minute, then pulled away. "I missed you, too."

He pulled her back, trying to re-engage the kiss and grabbing at her, but she stiffened. "I'm exhausted, Todd. I have jet lag really bad. I'm sorry I'm not more lively, but I feel horrible."

"Oh, okay. Why don't you get a cat nap on the way home cause I have plans for tonight." Todd squeezed Carol's knee, then started the car. Carol rolled the seat back and closed her eyes.

It wasn't the home coming he had imagined. She didn't seem at all excited to see him. She had sent two post cards while away. Both had said little, except that she was having a great time and had made a new friend named Chelsie. He had no idea what she had been doing the last two weeks. He'd been fretting about it the entire time, wondering if she had met some other guy. How long did he have to wait to find out what she'd been doing? He'd let her sleep until they arrived home, but then he wanted to know every detail of her trip.

***

Carol watched Todd push his yellow Volkswagen to the limit as they raced down the freeway. She hoped he was not angry with her anymore. They almost had a fight because Todd was irritated by her fatigue and lack of enthusiasm about being home. He kept asking her questions about her trip and groping at her. She didn't mean to, but she put off his affections. She assured him it was just jet-lag, that she'd feel better after a little rest. She felt horrible that she didn't miss him as much as he missed her, especially when he had cleaned the house and bought her a dozen roses.

Things had gone better at dinner. Todd took her to an expensive restaurant in Brattleboro, Foster's Seafood and Steak House, and she had Chicken Cordon Bleu. It was not nearly as delicious as the food in France, but it was better than cooking, and she knew it was an extravagant sacrifice for Todd. He shared his wine with her, so she had relaxed. At the end of the meal, he smiled, held her hand, and told her he had a surprise.

Now, as long as Todd stayed in a good mood, she actually wanted to spend time with him. She did miss him after all. She reached over and put her hand on his knee.

"Are you excited about your surprise?" Todd set his hand on top of hers.

"Yes. But I also wanted to tell you how much I missed you."

"Then, how about a kiss?"

Carol leaned over and kissed him on the lips. He put his arm around her and held her there. She lay her head on his lap and let him caress her. By the time they made it to the apartment, she was ready to accept him. As Todd closed the door, he kissed her long and hard, then broke away.

"Before we go any further, I have to show you the surprise." He reached into his pocket, pulled out a small white box and handed it to her. "Go ahead, open it."

Carol took of the lid. Inside shone a sparkling, emerald ring.

"It's fourteen carat gold and a real emerald. Not costume jewelry," said Todd. "I've been saving up for it for months."

"It's beautiful." Carol set the ring on her right index finger.

"Wait, not on that finger." He took the ring off her right hand. "Come, let's sit on the couch. I have something else to show you."

Carol sat down on the couch while Todd took a pile of papers from the desk. Then he cuddled up next to her. He took off his glasses, placed the papers and ring on the coffee table, took both her hands in his, and stared at her with his big, grey eyes.

"Before I give you this, my dearest Carol, I want you to know that I love you and want to spend the rest of my life with you. This ring is a token of my commitment to you. If you accept it, you are agreeing to spend your life with me and me alone, that you accept my commitment to you and will also commit yourself to me."

Carol flushed, her heart beat faster, and her throat tightened. "Todd, are you proposing?"

"Well, in a way. Here, I want you to read this." He picked up the papers and handed them to her.

The title on the first page read, "Commitment Contract between Todd Anthony Barrett and Carol Lynn Weiderman." As Carol scanned the lengthy, typed document, she realized Todd had drafted his own kind of marriage contract.

"You don't have to read it all right now. It basically says that we both agree to love and respect one another all our natural days. We can go over it in more detail tomorrow. I just want to know if you will accept this ring as a symbol of our commitment." Todd picked up the ring.

"Todd, why don't we just get married? What's the difference between this contract you wrote and a marriage contract?"

"Not much, except that we don't need to be under the authority of this capitalistic regime. The state shouldn't tell us how to commit our lives to one another. With our own contact, we can personalize it to fit our needs, not the needs that society dictates."

"Oh." Carol was torn between the excitement that Todd was sort of proposing to her and the confusion about the contract. When she had dreamed about this day, it had been so much simpler. Maybe it would have been better if Todd had showed her the contract later. It sort of spoiled the mood.

"Don't worry about the contract right now." Todd took it out of her hands. "The important thing to remember that I am pledging my love for you." He touched her cheek with his fingers. "Carol, I love you and am willing to give my life up for you. Will you accept this ring?"

"Yes, of course." Carol set her hand out in front of him. Todd placed the emerald ring on her left index finger, then gave her a fierce hug.

As Todd kissed her neck, Carol examined the ring on her finger. "Why did you buy me an emerald instead of a diamond?"

"To match your eyes." Todd pushed her gently down on the couch.

Later in bed, as she started to fall asleep in Todd's arms, Carol played with the ring on her finger. It was final now. She would be Todd's forever, until death. What would their future together look like? She would go to college, they would both become famous writers, and Todd would rise to the top in the political arena. He would make great changes to improve their country. Eventually, they would have enough money to buy their dream home in the country. Maybe she could even hire someone to help her with the cooking and cleaning. But what about children? Todd said he never wanted children, and she agreed with him at the time. Yet it seemed strange to imagine a future without children.

"Todd, are you asleep."

"Hmm. I was. What is it?"

"Do you think you'll ever want kids?"

"Kids! What made you think of that? We've talked about it before. The world's already overpopulated." Todd rolled over on his back.

"I know, but one or two more can't make that much difference. Do you think you might change your mind later down the line, years from now, when we accomplish everything else we want to do?"

"No, never! I told you before, I plan to get a vasectomy as soon as I can find a doctor willing to do it. There are too many children in this world who have no one there to take care of them. If you want to help kids, you can volunteer at Head Start or something."

"But it's not the same."

"I thought you agreed with me about the children issue. What made you change your mind?"

"I don't know. I guess I never thought that far into the future before."

"Carol, I know it's been drilled into you that all women need to have babies in order to be fulfilled. But trust me. There are so many more opportunities out there for fulfillment. You'll have a full life. I promise."

"I guess." Carol rolled over and curled into the fetal position. Deep within, a great sadness engulfed her. The emptiness rose up and spilled over, down her cheeks and onto the pillow.

"Carol, you're okay, aren't you?" Todd touched her shoulder.

"I'm fine," she lied.

"Good, cause I'm dead tired. Good night."

"Good night, Todd." Within minutes, Todd's heavy breathing was the only sound in the room. Yet inside her mind, Carol heard the anguished cry of a rejected child.

Chapter Twenty-Two

Margaret pulled into the driveway of Carol's apartment and turned off the car. She'd been waiting for this moment for days. She hadn't seen Carol since she came home from France, and so much had happened. She played with the diamond on her ring finger, wondering about the best way to share the news. A new joy had sprung into her life. Just like the trees and flowers and plants had blossomed, so had she come alive after being dead for so long. Today was a day where anything could happen. Perhaps God could even restore her lost relationship with her daughter. The sun and the Son shined with hope.

She watched Carol, dressed in jean shorts, climb down the steps with an overnight bag. Her hair was still wet, and she appeared pale in the bright light. Carol gave her a weak smile as she opened the passenger door of her old Ford station wagon.

"Good morning, Carol? How are you feeling?"

"Hi, Mom. I'm okay. I don't know if I really want to go through with this, though. I've never stayed at the hospital before."

"I can understand. Hospitals aren't exactly resorts. But the doctor said this procedure is really quite easy, and you'll only have to be there for a day." Margaret rattled out of the drive and headed toward the freeway.

"I'm sure I'll be fine." Carol leaned back in the seat and closed her eyes.

Margaret drove in silence for a few moments. She didn't know if Carol was falling asleep, so she waited. How long did she have to wait? She was going to burst if she didn't say something soon. She couldn't stand it anymore.

"Carol, are you asleep?"

"No, Mom. I'm just resting."

"Good, cause I want to tell you some good news."

"Oh? What? Are you and Jim going to get married?"

"Carol, you stole my thunder. How did you know!"

"I didn't, but you've been playing with your engagement ring ever since I got into the car."

"How did you know that when your eyes have been closed?"

194

"I can hear it." Carol looked at her mother's finger.

"I'm happy for you, Mom. I like Jim. He'll make a great husband."

"Thank you, Carol. It means a lot to me that you like him. He'll be your step-father in a few weeks."

"Mom, I like Jim, but not as a father." Carol turned toward the window. Margaret felt the tension rise up between them. This is exactly what she didn't want to happen.

"I understand, Carol. You're on your own and don't need another father. You and Jim can just be friends."

"I'm glad you understand, Mom."

"We've set the date for the week after you graduate from high school. It'll be a simple ceremony. Mostly family and a few close friends."

"Where are you going to have it?"

"At our new church."

"Oh, I didn't know you were going to church. Where is it?"

"It's the same church Amanda and Steve attend. Pastor Wilcock is going to perform the ceremony."

"Really? So Amanda and Steve will be there?"

"Of course."

Margaret noticed Carol chewing on her thumbs. She had the feeling that Carol didn't like the fact the she and Jim were friends with Amanda. She also noticed Carol was wearing an emerald ring. Now she was torn between asking her about the ring or sharing the rest of her news. She'd rehearsed how to do this every day since she had made her life-changing decision.

Her younger children had all taken it quite well. Liz confessed that she had already made the decision in youth group to accept Christ. She had hugged her long and hard. Marie and Jean had joined Liz in the hug. They cried when Jim told them he was moving out, but after he explained about the wedding and their marriage, they accepted it. Her oldest, Maurine, had said very little when she told her over the phone. Jessica said, "I figured that would happen sooner or later," and went about her business as usual. She knew Carol would probably be the most negative because Todd was so anti-Christian.

"Carol, this marriage means the world to me, but something even better than marrying Jim has happened."

"Oh?" Carol stopped her picking and turned her attention toward her. "What is it? I have to admit, you sure did look happy when you picked me up this morning."

"When I was at church two Sundays ago, I re-dedicated my life to God. Jim also made a decision to live honor God in all his actions, so he moved into his own apartment until we get married."

"What! Mom, why on earth did you do that? How did they suck you in? Did you do it because of Jim?"

Margaret took a deep breath and said a short prayer. *Lord, help me stay calm and give me your words.* She wiped her sweaty palms on her slacks before speaking.

"No, I didn't do it because of Jim. I made the decision because I realized that Jesus loved me and gave his life up for me."

"Oh, good grief. I can't believe you'd fall for that crap." Her daughter put her feet up on the dash board and folded her arms. It was not going the way Margaret had rehearsed.

"Carol, I can't expect you to understand my decision, but you can at least respect me enough to not judge me for it. I know you don't believe in God, but I do. He's as real as the trees and the sky and the birds, and he's saved my life."

"And what's this garbage about Jim moving out? Is that suppose to make the fact that you've been living together all this time okay? Are Todd and I going to hell because we live together?"

"No, it's not like that at all. The people at the church never told us what to do. But God says in the Bible that he created marriage as the best and only way to have a family. We want to honor God in every part of our lives."

"The Bible's an outdated book. It doesn't apply to today. Heaven and hell are just something people in power made up to keep their subjects in line."

"I don't agree. Jesus isn't like that at all. He's full of love, compassion, and forgiveness, and he doesn't want to see anyone in hell. He loved me so much that he gave up his life on the cross, died, so that I could be forgiven for all the mistakes I've made."

"If you want to believe a fairy tale, go ahead. It's your life. But I don't need some God to be my crutch. Just don't try to push it on me."

Margaret squeezed the steering wheel. Carol's sharp words cut like a knife. She remembered Jim's warning that Carol may be hostile, that persecution came with the territory of becoming a Christian. Jim told her not to take it personally, but how could she not?

"Amanda is a Christian and you like her just fine. Why can't you treat your own mother with the same respect you treat her? What you said a moment ago was not very nice."

"I'm sorry. I probably shouldn't be so mean. Amanda never pushes her faith on me. As long as you do the same, I'm sure it'll be fine. But you're my mother, so I just assumed you'd want to tell me all about it."

"It would be nice to share, but I won't if it makes you like this."

"I'm sorry, Mom. I know I'm not being very nice. I'm just in a bad mood is all." Carol was twirling her ring again.

"Okay, let's just start over. Why are you in such a bad mood?"

"Cause I have my own news."

"Oh. Does it have something to do with your ring?"

"Well, I do have news about the ring, but that's not why I'm in a bad mood. There's been a lot of changes happening with Todd and me."

"Oh, like what?"

"Well, Todd and I are going to be moving at the end of June."

It felt like someone punched her in the stomach. She didn't want to hear what Carol had to say next. Even though sun shone through the window, it felt like a dark cloud come over their car, and goose bumps erupted on her arms.

"Where are you moving?"

"We're moving in with Dad at his new place in Wilton, New Hampshire."

"What!" For a moment, the road in front of Margaret blurred. This could not be happening. Why would Todd and Carol move in with Richard? She had planned to talk to Carol about going to college in the fall and was going to offer to help her with the cost. If they went to live with Richard, she would be out of her grasp completely. She'd been so hopeful that things were improving between them. Now it was as if someone had taken a bowling ball and smashed all the progress they had made, all her hopes of reconciliation, her plans to draw closer to Carol during the summer.

"Wha…why are you going to do that?"

"Todd went to visit Dad while I was in France, and they hit it off. Todd loves him. They share the same vision, and he wants to help Dad with his work. Todd hasn't been able to find a teaching job since he graduated. Now he doesn't know if teaching is what he even wants to do. He's thinking he's more cut out to be a political activist."

"But Carol, what about you? How are you going to go to school if you move away?"

"Todd and I talked it through. He promised that I could go to UVM next year. We're going to save up the money, and I'll re-apply for the scholarships. Working in the real world for a year will be good for me. I'll be better prepared for college."

"But you could go now! Jim and I are willing to help. You have enough scholarships and financial aid to make it work. Carol, please reconsider your decision. You're so smart and talented. I hate to see you waste a year."

"How is spending a year getting to know my Dad a waste?" Carol folded her arms again and pouted.

"It has nothing to do with your Dad. It's just that most young people who don't go to college right away never go back."

"Well, you have a lot of faith in me, don't you?"

"That's enough, Carol. You know that's not true. You can't fault me for wanting to see my little girl fulfill her dream of college. Gee, I'm your mother. I'm going to miss you."

Carol's body became a little less rigid. "I'm sorry. I know this must come as a shock. But Mom, I am going to go to college. I promise I will. It just won't be right away."

"I hope so. You have so much going for you."

They drove in silence for a few minutes, Carol picking at her fingers, Margaret rubbing her arms and trying to hide the tears that rolled down her cheeks. She wished Jim had come with her. She needed to break down and let out all the grief and disappointment. But she had to be the strong one again, like always. She recalled the long days and nights when her children were very young. She thought then that nothing could be as difficult as the sleepless nights, wrecked house, and diaper changings. Yet at least then she could pick up her babies and keep them safe in her home. Now she was helpless to do anything. Carol sat next to her, but she may as well be a thousand miles away. She had slipped out of her grip when Todd stole her away three years before, and every attempt to get her back had failed.

"So, do you want to know about my ring?" Carol broke the silence.

"Yes, I do."

"Todd gave it to me. It's a commitment ring."

"A commitment ring? What's that?"

"We've both signed a Commitment Contract to love and stay with one another the rest of our lives."

"Oh. And where did you get the contract?"

"Todd wrote it."

Figures. Todd was such a weasel. "Is it like an engagement ring, then?"

"Sort of. More like a wedding ring."

"Oh." Margaret thought she might vomit. This was just too much for one day. She was glad that they had reached the exit for the hospital. She needed to find a bathroom.

***

Margaret sat on Carol's bed, careful to stay away from the I.V. line in her daughter's arm. She had become her child again in these last minutes before being wheeled into the operating room.

"I'll be right outside waiting until you're back safe in your room."

"Thanks Mom. I'm scared. What if I don't wake up?"

"Hon, this is an easy operation. You have nothing to worry about. You'll be sleeping before you can even count to ten. You won't feel a thing."

"Are you sure?"

"I'm positive. I've done it before."

"I'm sorry I'm such a baby."

Margaret took her daughter's hand into her own. "Everyone is scared when they go through something like this. It's perfectly natural. You're no more a baby than I was when I went through it."

"It's time to go," said an orderly.

Carol squeezed Margaret's fingers as they started to pull her away. She held Carol's hand and walked with the orderly to the elevator, down to the second floor, to the double doors of the operating room. Just before the contact was broken between them, Margaret moved close to her daughter's frightened face and kissed her forehead. "I love you, Carol. I'll be out here praying for you." Carol's lips curved up a little as she was whisked through the doors.

Margaret was glad she had maintained her composure after the horrible drive into the hospital. It had to be God who helped her through, helped her keep her mouth closed, her tears locked within, her stomach from spilling over. Now the grief was back with a bang. If only she could take her home after the operation, away from that conniving Todd. He did whatever he pleased with Carol. He cared only about himself. As long as she was available to him for his pleasure, he could care less if Carol threw her life away. Heat poured through her blood vessels, tension formed in her fists, and she wanted to punch something. If moving in with Richard wasn't enough of a blow, what was this foolishness about a commitment contract and an emerald ring? The guy was too chicken to be legally commit himself in marriage, but he knew Carol would feel just as bound to him with a stupid ring and her signature on a piece of paper.

199

She was so glad Todd wasn't with Carol right now because she would let him know what she thought of his schemes.

Thankfully, the waiting room was empty, so Margaret paced back and forth. Wasn't there anything she could do about the situation? Maybe she could talk to Richard and ask him to encourage Carol to go to school. No, she knew he was probably elated at the idea of having Carol live with him. Why else would he accept Todd into his home? Every time she talked to him, they fought. No, she would leave Richard out of it.

Maybe she should talk to Pastor Wilcock about it. He's had a lot of experience with wayward youth. Or maybe Amanda. Yes, Amanda told her on Sunday that she and Carol had become closer on their trip to France. She would talk to Amanda later that night.

She sat down, picked up a *Lady's Home Journal*, and thumbed through the recipe section. The image of the emerald ring on Carol's finger blocked the pictures on the page. She was only a child. What kind of future would she have bound to that man? *Oh, Lord, I can't bear it. I can't watch my baby destroy her life.* Margaret put her head in her hands as the hours of despair and grief boiled over.

I've got to talk to someone. I've got to talk to Jim. She reached for her purse and found the number to Jim's work. She walked to the nurse's station.

"Is there a pay phone close by?"

"There's one in the cafeteria. Take the elevator to the first floor and turn left."

"Thanks."

Margaret rushed to the elevator and made her way to the first floor. She found the phone. She knew Jim would be busy, but he was a supervisor, so they should let him talk to her. She hoped he would not be angry. She just needed to share with him what was happening. She inserted a dime in the phone and dialed the number.

"Hello, Thompson's Tool Works. How may I direct your call?"

"I need to speak to Jim Carlson please."

"One moment."

Margaret waited a few minutes before she heard his deep voice on the other end of the phone.

"Jim, I'm so sorry to bother you at work. I just really needed to talk to you."

"It's okay, Margaret. Is there something wrong with your wayward girl?"

"Carol's fine. I mean, physically that is. Oh Jim, so much has happened. Carol's leaving town with Todd to live with Richard. And that tricky Todd talked her into signing some stupid commitment contract and wearing a ring she considers a wedding ring!"

"Whoa, Hon. Slow it down at notch."

"Todd and Carol are moving to Wilton with Richard after our wedding. And Todd bought Carol this emerald ring and gave her a commitment contract to sign that's suppose to be a substitute for a marriage contract. Can you believe it?"

"That Todd's a piece of work."

"That's too polite."

"Yup. Hey, Hon, I wish I could talk. I've got to finish this job. I'll come up right after work."

"I understand. I'm sorry to interrupt."

"Hey, enough of that sorry stuff. How else can a guy get a break unless his wife calls? Now, are you going to be okay for a few more hours?"

"I hope so. Carol will be in surgery for about another hour. Then she'll be in recovery."

"Listen, let me pray for you real quick. Jesus, you know how Margaret loves her daughter. You know how hard is for her to understand. She needs your comfort. Help her know you love her child as much as she does. You're watching over her every step. You'll never leave or give up on either of them. Bring your peace. In Jesus name, Amen."

"Amen." She sighed. "Thanks Jim. I feel better. I love you."

"I love you, too. See you tonight. Bye."

"Bye."

Margaret hung up the phone and returned to the second floor to wait for Carol.

***

Margaret sat by Carol's bed watching her drift in and out of consciousness. She had opened her eyes for a moment and seemed to see Margaret next to her, but she was unsure whether she recognized her. Now she could see rapid eye movement under her eye lids. Margaret picked up her magazine to take up the time.

A few moments later, Carol jerked in her sleep. Margaret set her magazine down and watched. From the expression on Carol's face, she was having a bad dream. She moaned and thrashed. In a quick motion, she sat up and opened her eyes.

"No, leave me alone! I won't go with you! You're a trickster. I know that now." Carol thrust out her arms, almost breaking the attachment to her I.V. "Go away!"

Margaret held her hands back. "Carol, wake up. It's only a nightmare. I'm here for you." Carol ignored her and stared straight ahead as if talking to someone in front of her.

"I don't want to go with you. Leave me alone."

"Carol, it's me, Mom. You're not going anywhere."

"I thought you liked me. You came to our door. You said I was pretty. You said you'd come back. You lied."

Carol's eyes were big, focused on someone or something invisible to Margaret. She was talking to someone in her dream. She must be in a semi-conscious state.

"Carol, wake up!"

"You came to my house when I was home alone. You tricked me. You pretended to like me. You know my name. What is yours?"

"Carol, who are you talking to?" Margaret now wondered if she was dreaming or re-living something that actually happened.

"No, you left without telling your name! You just disappeared! You always disappear! You disappeared at school. I looked for you for days. Todd was so jealous. You showed up in Paris. You left again without telling your name. Get away!"

Carol started thrashing her hands around.

"Carol, stop! You're just dreaming!" Margaret tried to calm her, but she could not see or hear her. All she could see or hear was the person inside her mind.

"No, you don't love me! Go away!" Carol stopped for a moment, and her expression changed from anger to fear. She let out a scream that sent the nurse running.

"What's going on here?" An older nurse with salt and pepper hair rushed in and checked Carol's monitors. After her shrill scream, Carol had collapsed onto the bed. She lay still now.

"I don't know. I think she's having a nightmare, but she acted half awake."

"She seems okay now." The nurse adjusted her arm so the I.V. would drip better.

"What happened to her? What caused this?" asked Margaret.

"I've seen it before. She was probably having a night terror. It's more common with children, but some patients react to the anesthesia in strange ways. A night terror is kind of like sleep walking. The person looks like they're awake, but they're still locked in their dream. It's really hard to help them because they can't see you. They can only see the people in their dream."

"Will it happen again?"

"I doubt it." The nurse marked a note on the chart. "She should be coming around any time now."

"What should I do if it happens again?"

"Ring the bell. I'll come right away. But I doubt it will happen again." The nurse finished her note and left. Margaret slumped into the chair. She had a nagging sensation that Carol was re-living a traumatic experience. If this were the case, someone had visited their house. Who could it be? It couldn't be Todd because she used his name. She said the person in the dream didn't tell her his name. And she said she saw him in France. It was all too strange, and Margaret wondered if she were stuck in some horror film. The thought that it might be true sent a freezing chill up her spine. She looked at her watch. She still had two hours to wait for Jim. She rose from the chair and looked out the window. The sun shone gloriously, oblivious to her pain. Something evil had come after her daughter. She knew it. She wanted to destroy it. *God, if you live in me like you say you do, how I need you right now. Please show me what to do. And protect my little girl.*

***

Amanda had almost forgotten Carol was having surgery. At school on Monday, she promised to visit her. She remembered just after lunch and had to call Steve to let him know he would have to watch Julie. Margaret had missed her call, so her visit would be a surprise. Margaret was probably struggling with the news Carol had shared with her that week. Hearing about Carol and Todd moving in with her dad and the ring he gave her would be enough to tear any mother apart. Margaret would need her friendship tonight as much as Carol needed it.

"Excuse me, can you tell me which direction room 304-A is in?"

"Straight down the hall to the right." The nurse at the desk pointed.

"Thank you."

When Amanda entered the room, she knew instantly that Margaret was upset. Her eyes were puffy from crying, and she saw panic in her expression

203

as she watched Carol sleeping in the hospital bed. She didn't notice Amanda until she spoke.

"Margaret, how's everything going?"

Margaret turned toward her, then stood up in a rush. "Amanda, I'm so glad to see you!"

"You look wiped out." Amanda gave her a hug.

"It's been a horrible day. Do you think it would be okay if we go someplace to talk? They gave Carol another pill because she's been having night terrors. She's been sleeping calmly for the last half hour."

"Sure, I think it'll be okay. Let's see if we can fine a quiet place to talk. Do they have a chapel in the hospital?"

"I'm sure they do. Let's go ask."

Amanda found where the chapel was located, and she and Margaret took the elevator to the first floor. Fortunately, no one was inside. As soon as they were alone, Margaret let it all spill out.

"It's hard enough to hear about them leaving to go live with Richard and that ridiculous contract. But when I saw Carol have that night terror, it entered the realm of unbelievable. I'm scared to death that some strange man might be after my child."

A cold chill swept over Amanda as she recalled the experience in France. "Tell me about it."

"Well, Carol was talking in her sleep. She was talking to a man she said had come to our house while Carol was home alone. He knew her name, but he didn't tell her his. Then she said she saw him again at school. Then she said she saw him again in France."

"Oh, dear Lord. Forgive me!" Amanda swallowed and looked down at her lap. "I knew I should have told you about it."

"Tell me about what? What happened?"

"I should have told you sooner. Carol insisted I keep it a secret, but now I wonder if I should have gone to the police."

Margaret clutched Amanda's shoulder. "Tell me what happened!"

"First, I had a horrible nightmare that a murderer was after Carol in the park. Then the next day, when it was time to return to the hotel, Jeff and Chelsie didn't know where Carol was. So I went looking for her. I found her taking off with an artist. I pulled Carol away, but when I turned around, he was gone. Just disappeared. He even left all his art supplies and easel behind."

"Did you see him at all?"

"Only the back of his head."

"Did he threaten Carol with a knife or a gun?"

"No, that was the strange thing. Carol was going with him willingly. That's why she didn't want me to tell anyone. She was so ashamed."

"Oh, Amanda!" Margaret put her hands to her face. "What are we going to do?"

"I don't know. I can't go to the police now. Where back in the U.S. And, unless Carol's willing to tell the police about her other encounters, there's not much we can do."

"Then we need to convince Carol to tell the police."

"Margaret, wait. Something inside me says to be cautious about this. I'm afraid we might lose Carol if we confront her."

"But, Amanda, there's someone out there trying to hurt her! We can't just ignore it!"

"No, but remember that she went with the man willingly. At this point, there's nothing to charge him with. Besides, she is deathly afraid of Todd finding out about him. I'm afraid if we push Carol to tell us more, she'll refuse to talk to us again."

"Are you sure? It seems wrong to just stand by and do nothing." Margaret pulled on her hair.

Amanda turned to Margaret. "There *is* something we can do. God warned me about the incident in the park in Paris. He protected Carol then. He can protect her now. Let's pray and ask the Lord for wisdom."

"Are you sure that's all we can do?" Tears were welling up in Margaret's eyes again.

"I think it's best for now." Amanda paused. "Margaret, as horrible as it was to watch Carol have that night terror, I believe God let it happen so the truth would be revealed. Now that we both are aware of it, we can pray."

"I guess." Margaret sighed and looked at the floor. "You know, it's all my fault, all of this. Just before Carol met Todd, I let her get away with treating me with disrespect. I remember the day like it was yesterday. She insisted on staying home from school and called me a horrible name. I knew I should have stood my ground, but I didn't. Instead, I ran out the door. I was too ashamed of myself. That's when everything went down hill. If I'd only protected her, never let her date Todd, never let her stay home alone. The only time she was alone in the house was when everyone else was at school. I bet that's when the man showed up at our house."

Amanda shook her head. "You don't know that for sure. Besides, punishing yourself for the past isn't going to do anything to help Carol now. The past is over, you've been forgiven. Let's concentrate on today."

Margaret put her head in her hands. "I know, but it's just so hard. I made so many mistakes. I was weak. I wasn't there to protect her."

Amanda put her arm around her. "Please don't beat yourself up. You've got to let it go. Why don't we pray."

"If you don't mind, can we wait until Jim gets here to pray for Carol? He should be here in an hour or so. I want to go back and check on Carol. She might be having another night terror."

"Can I at least pray for you real quick?"

"All right. I am quite a wreck. My mind's like cottage cheese."

"Dear Lord, help Margaret trust you right now. Give her your peace. Help her to forget the past and forgive herself. Help her know how much you love her. In Jesus' name, Amen."

"Thanks, I feel better." Margaret dried her eyes with the tissue.

"One more thing. Before we go check on Carol, I want you to know that I am committed to praying for Carol every day. You're not alone in this." She gave her a hug.

"Thanks, Amanda. You're a true friend."

***

Later that night, while Todd visited with Carol upstairs, Jim, Margaret, and Amanda gathered together in the chapel and cried out to their Lord and Savior for a lost child. After they finished, Jim spoke.

"Todd may be a slug, be we need to pray for him. Jesus loves him, too.

"But Jim, how can I?" Margaret clenched her fists

Jim unclenched her fists and put her hand in his. "I know you can't do it. But Jesus can. He lives in you. Jesus died for Todd just like he died for us. There's this verse in Ephesians. It says we shouldn't fight against people, but against the devil."

"I know that verse," said Amanda. It's Ephesians 6:12. It says, 'For our struggles are not against flesh and blood, but against the rulers, against the authorities, against powers of this dark world and against the spiritual forces of evil in the heavenly realms.'"

"I don't get it," said Margaret.

"Our fight isn't against Todd. It's against Satan and his demons who are out to get Todd and Carol."

"Jim's right." Amanda agreed. "The only difference between Todd and us is that we've received God's free gift of grace and forgiveness."

Margaret still didn't fully understand, but she said nothing as Jim prayed to the Lord for the man who had taken her baby away from her.

Part Four

New Face, Same Dirty Rat

A Year Later

Hebrews 4:12: *For the word of God is living and active. Sharper than any double-edged sword, it penetrates even to dividing soul and spirit, joints and marrow; it judges the thoughts and attitudes of the heart.*

Chapter Twenty-Three

Carol went to the window, lifted the corner of the shade, and peeked out. Yes! It was a nice, sunny morning. She'd been looking forward to this day for months.

"Hey, the light's too bright." Todd grumbled from the mattress on the floor. "I don't have to get up yet."

"Sorry," Carol whispered. She tiptoed around the room, gathered her clothes, and slipped out the door. She could hear the high pitched voices of children below, already arriving at Denise's day care. She noticed her dad's throaty laugh as he greeted them. She had agreed to rise early this morning and work for a little bit before beginning her trip to Burlington, Vermont. Chelsie invited her to come up and stay in the place she shared with several other college students, and she couldn't wait to see her again. Everything was coming together for the fall. She was going to prove to her mother taking a year off before college had not stopped her from following through with her plans.

She stepped into the large, upstairs bathroom. Her father's house was old, so she had to wash her hair in a huge, porcelain tub with claw legs. She missed showers. For one thing, there was no way to warm up the cold room before taking her clothes off. For another, it was hard to rinse her hair under the faucet. But it was better than being dirty.

She ran the water in the tub and let if fill up while she used the toilet. It was hard to believe she and Todd had been living with her father almost a year. At first, she felt awkward about sleeping with Todd in her father's house. Then she realized he wasn't married to Denise, so what difference did it make? He never brought up the subject, so she never talked about either of their relationships. She never even told him about the ring or the commitment contract. Instead, they had many long conversations about politics and social reform.

She liked living with him well enough, but hated the work. Her jobs were to help Denise with the day care and fill out hundreds of refund forms every week. At first, she felt guilty about sending in requests for refunds when no one had purchased the products. It was her dad's grand scheme to steal money from the rich corporations and give to the poor. Dad also managed the books for a local grocery store. When he sent the coupons in for redemption, he always added extra to the pile. She would help him cut coupons out of the paper or magazines, and recently he had turned over the responsibility of redeeming the coupons to her. It was illegal. She read the warnings on the back of the forms. Her Dad told her it was okay because the money went into a defense fund to aid the poor, as well as run their day care, which offered a large discount to the underprivileged. Still, sometimes she wondered if the police would come in and arrest her.

Carol lathered her hair, then used a cup to rinse it out. The water felt warm running down her head onto her face, but when she finished, the cold air always gave her a chill. She wrung out her hair, then wrapped a towel around it. She had to finish sending in a pile of coupons before leaving and wanted to hurry and get it done.

She walked downstairs into the kitchen. Her Dad was busy ringing up fake receipts from a cash register in the dining room that served as his office. It smelled like coffee. Though she didn't drink the stuff, she loved the smell of a fresh brew. Her Dad drank at least four cups every morning, so there was always coffee in the pot.

He turned to greet her. "Good morning, Carol."

"Good morning, Dad. I suppose those receipts are for me?"

"Yup. This is the last one." He finished punching in a number, tore off the receipt, circled an amount, and added it to a pile. Then he took the pile and rolled his chair to another table and set it next to a bag. "It's all set."

"Thanks Dad. I'll get to it as soon as I get my juice and eat a bowl of cereal."

Her Dad rolled his chair on wheels to a spot on the table with a typewriter and started to type. His hands moved with dexterity as he punched the keys. He had on his usual dungarees and plaid, button-up shirt. His hair was a big black and gray bush on top of his head.

Robby, a four-year old boy, came rushing in from the large living room. "I gotta peee!"

"Hi Robby."

"Carol!" Robby came over and gave her a big hug. "We're watching Sesame Street. Are you going to watch it with me?"

"Not today, Robby. I'm going on a trip."

"Oh, can I come?"

"No." Carol saw him wiggling. "You'd better get to the bathroom."

"Yeah! I gotta pee!" Robby disappeared into the bathroom.

Carol opened the refrigerator, found the orange juice behind two gallons of milk, and poured herself a glass. Missy, one of Denise's three cats, came and rubbed her head against her legs. She pet her while thinking of the weekend ahead. She didn't have to work for three whole days, and she and Chelsie were going to have a great time together.

An hour later, Todd stumbled into the dining area. Carol was just fishing her last entry on the coupon report.

"So, when are you leaving?" He set a cup of coffee on the table and pulled out a chair. His hair was tussled on top of his head, and he was wearing a t-shirt and shorts.

"As soon as I finish this."

"Are you sure you don't want me to come with you?"

"No, I'll be fine. My Dad needs you to finish the research on non-profit grants for him. Besides, you'll be bored with all the girl stuff Chelsie and I am going to do."

"Carol, Todd doesn't have to finish that research yet." Her Dad took a sip from his cup and looked at Todd.

"Really, I'll be fine. I know you want to finish that research. You've been talking about it all week."

"But I want to be with you, too. I want to help you pick out a place."

He touched her hand. She wanted to pull it away, but resisted the urge. They had been through this at least a hundred times. She wanted to go by herself, to see her friend. He was so clingy. And her Dad. He thought Todd was so smart and enlightened. Sometimes it seemed Todd was the son he never had. Sometimes she thought he liked Todd more than he liked her.

"Todd, I'm all set to go. I have my bags packed and already in the car. I'm going to be back on Sunday. You don't need to worry about me." She turned away from him and handed the finished report to her father.

"I finished this. Do you want to look it over before I mail it?"

Her dad stroked his thick, black beard streaked with gray. "No, I trust your work. Do you have the map I made for you?"

"Yes. It's in the car with the rest of my stuff."

"Do you have all the paperwork you need to turn in for Fall quarter? And the check?" Todd stood up.

"Yes, I double checked everything."

"Okay, then I guess you're ready." Her Dad sighed and returned to his work. He never stopped working, from 5:00 in the morning to 11:00 at night.

"Great. I'll use the bathroom, then I'm off." She walked past Todd and headed upstairs. He followed her. She went into the bathroom and closed the door. He came right in on her.

"I want to talk to you before you leave."

"What is it now? Are you going to try to convince me to stay home or wait for you to come with me again?"

Todd swore. "You can be such a cold fish at times, do you know that?"

"I'm sorry. But you make me feel like I'm cheating on you just because I want to spend the weekend with a friend." She pulled up her pants, flushed the toilet, and pushed by Todd to the sink to wash her hands.

"It's not that at all. I just want to spend time with you. Is that such a crime?" He reached out and touched her hair.

"I can understand that. But you're making me not want to spend time with you when you suffocate me like this."

"Fine. Go!" Todd pushed her away and stormed out the door.

Carol thought about going after him, but decided against it. He'd just drag it out even longer. She combed her hair, tromped downstairs, grabbed her purse, waved a quick goodbye to her busy Dad and a sulking Todd, and ran out to the car. The sun had warmed the inside of the Volkswagen, and it felt good. She knew she should probably have apologized to Todd and feel bad about leaving him, but instead her heart leaped with glee. Today she was free and on her way to fulfill her life-long dream of going to college, and no one was going to ruin it for her. She started the car, turned the radio on full blast, and was on her way.

***

Chelsie and Carol lay on the bed eating ding-dongs. Chelsie had her own room with a double bed and even her own television. She shared a large, nineteenth century house with several other college students. The house was three stories tall, and each floor had its own communal kitchen and bathroom. It wasn't a frat house, however, and Carol was glad of that. The only thing she remembered about frat houses is that was where Todd usually went to buy marijuana.

"Chelsie, I haven't had this much fun since France. I promise I'll pay you back. I just love my new outfit!"

"You look pretty sexy in it, if I do say so. I can't wait till you come up here and room with me this fall." Chelsie popped the rest of her ding-dong into her mouth.

"I'm just so glad Todd is letting me come here by myself in the Fall. When he decided he wanted to stay in Wilton with my Dad, I thought I'd never get to come here. It'll mean I'll have to go home every weekend, but it's only a two hour drive. Still, I wish Todd would move here with me."

"I'm kind of glad he's not." Chelsie threw her wrapper on the floor.

"Chelsie, how can you say that?"

"Because if he were living up here with you, I'd never get to spend any time with my friend."

"Chelsie, you sound like you're jealous." She hit her on the arm playfully.

"No, it's just every time we get together and Todd's around, he hogs you."

"But you have plenty of friends. And what about Jeff? The two of you have become quite an item. Should I be jealous of Jeff when we all go out tonight?"

"No. I'm just kidding, Carol. It's just that my other friends aren't you. Not even Jeff. I can tell you anything."

Carol felt warm and comfortable and loved. "Thanks, Chelsie. That means a lot to me." She gave her a hug.

"So, let's get ourselves all dolled up for dinner tonight. I have a great night club I want to take you to." Chelsie rolled off the bed and took a shopping bag off the dresser.

"But Chelsie, I'm not going to be eighteen for two more weeks."

"Shoot. I forgot about that. Well, we can come back here and play records downstairs." She took out a shiny, silver shirt. "Just look at my new shirt sparkle. I can't wait to show it off tonight. Jeff's going to love it."

"Still, it'd be more fun if I were already eighteen." Carol took out her new pair of jeans and a tank top.

"Oh, poo! We can have just as much fun by ourselves. Have you seen *Saturday Night Fever* yet? John Travolta is such a hunk!"

"No. I haven't."

"Well, that's what we're doing tomorrow night. I'm taking you to see that movie." Chelsie took off her shorts and pulled on a leather mini-skirt. "Say, Carol, just what are you doing for your eighteenth birthday?"

"Oh, I don't know. Probably nothing, if Todd has his way."

"Well, that just won't do. Jeff and I are both going home for vacation in two weeks. We'll be in Deerfield. The drinking age is eighteen in Vermont, and we can all go out on the town to celebrate your birthday."

"Oh, Chelsie, that would be great! I can't wait to tell Todd. We'll have a great time!"

"And, now that I'm thinking about it, consider that outfit as an early birthday present."

Carol pulled out the last item from the bag, a pair of sandals with two inch heels. "Chelsie, do you really mean it?"

"My best friend deserves nothing less. Now why don't you put on your new outfit, and I'll do your hair."

"You're the best!" She picked up her petite friend and twirled her around.

"Girl, you're squishing my boobs." Chelsie laughed.

***

Carol wiggled away from the arm draped over her, careful not to wake her friend. She'd been trying to go back to sleep for at least a half hour, but it didn't work. Since living with her father, she had been unable to stay in bed past nine o'clock. She knew Chelsie would probably sleep until noon, especially after all the alcohol she had consumed the night before.

They'd had a great night, in spite of the fact that she was too young to go to the discothèque. Jeff had brought his friend Adam with him to dinner, and they all had a great time. Jeff and Adam bought a couple of six packs of beer and some wine coolers for the girls. They played loud music in the basement until 2:00 AM. After a couple of wine coolers, Carol let Adam dance with her. Uninhibited, she let her body twist and twirl to the music. She had never felt so free. She had no idea the effect it had on Adam until he made a pass at her. She was so intoxicated, she let him kiss her. Then she realized what had happened and pushed him away. Adam just thought she was teasing him, and after they danced some more, he pulled her onto his lap. She pulled away and fell onto the floor. Chelsie proved her friendship again and came to her rescue. Even though she and Jeff had been busy making out, she left his side and helped Carol up off the floor. She suggested they all play a game of pool. The idea appealed to both guys, and she was able later to escape Adam before he asked for a good-night kiss. Today, she would tell him she was engaged to Todd and show him her ring.

Carol put on a pair of shorts and a sweater, then tiptoed over to Chelsie's bookcase to look for something to read. As she went over titles, one caught her attention: *Till We Have Faces* by C.S. Lewis. She recognized the author from somewhere, but she couldn't remember from where. She read the back of the book. "C.S. Lewis reworks the classical myth of Cupid and Psyche into an enduring piece of contemporary fiction." Intrigued, she took the book, snatched a box of doughnuts from the dresser, and snuck out the door.

She sat reading the book and eating doughnuts in the quiet nook next to the kitchen. She used another chair to prop her feet, then leaned back. It appeared that no one was up early on a Saturday morning in this house.

She was already well into the second chapter, intrigued with Orual and her motherly love for her sister Psyche, when someone come into the kitchen. He was obviously another college student, a young man with long, blond hair.

"Hi," he mumbled starting the coffee pot.

"Good morning." She glanced at him for a moment, then dived back into her book. Out of the corner of her eye, she could see him stand and watch the coffee percolate into a glass container. A few minutes later, he poured himself a cup of coffee, loaded it with cream and sugar, and sat down at the table next to her.

"I've never seen you around here before."

Carol lifted her head from the book. "I'm just visiting. I'm a friend of Chelsie's."

"Oh. Well, I'm John. Please to meet you." He extended his hand.

"I'm Carol." She put her legs on the ground and shook his hand. He had a nice, firm grip.

"So, what are you reading?"

"*Till We Have Faces*," said Carol, showing him the cover of the book.

"I think I had to read that for an English class. It's a pretty cool book, if I remember."

"I just started reading it, but I like it so far."

"So, do you go to the UVM?" John took a sip of his coffee.

"No, but I plan to go this Fall."

Carol noticed John had nice arms, a good tan, warm brown eyes, and the face of a model. If someone wanted to find a boyfriend, college was the perfect place. "Oh, so are you still in high school?"

"No, I graduated last year. I took a year off to work first."

"I admire you already."

"Why, thanks. I have to admit, though, I'm looking forward to quitting my job." Carol noticed John was staring at her. Nervous, she returned to reading her book.

John moved toward her. "Why did you look down? I was getting a kick out of looking at your eyes. I saw at least three colors in them. Blue, brown, and yellow. From a distance, they look green, but up close, they have all those colors."

Carol didn't know what to say.

"Hey, don't get freaked out. I scared people off sometimes because I just say what comes to my mind. And I have to tell you that you have an aura around you, a glow of some kind. I bet you're a real spiritual person."

John was definitely weird all right. "Actually, I'm not a spiritual person at all. I don't believe in God."

"Who said anything about God? Do you mind if I have one your doughnuts?"

"Sure, go ahead."

John took a doughnut from the box and bit into it. He swallowed, and continued. "When I say spiritual, I mean you probably think a lot about life and why people behave the way they do. I bet you're sensitive and can tell what people are thinking. Real in tune with them, if you know what I mean."

"Well, maybe I am spiritual as you say. I've always been fascinated with sociology and psychology. It amazes me that we only use such a small portion of our brains. I've often wondered what we could do with the rest of our brain if we found a way to connect with it."

"Exactly. We're on the same wave-length now." John set down his doughnut and leaned toward her. "I think I can trust you enough to share something with you, Carol. You see, I have a special gift, but most people just think I'm crazy. I can see into the fifth dimension, into the spirit world."

Now would be a good time to leave, Carol thought. But she was curious about this strange man.

"What are you talking about when you say the spirit world? Are you talking about ghosts or something?"

"That's part of it. There's an entire world out there we can't see. Most of us won't see it until after we die, but I can see it now. There are good forces and bad forces at work all around us. The souls of people never die. There are souls floating around you right now that lived a thousand years ago. Some are loving, caring souls. Others are purely evil and are out to hurt you. I've found a way to communicate with them."

"This is giving me the creeps." Carol closed her book and started to get up.

"Hey, I'm sorry. I'm going too fast. Don't leave yet." He touched her arm. "Let me prove what I've said." He focused his eyes on hers. She felt a familiar excitement rise within with the feel of his hand on her skin.

"How can you prove there are spirits hanging all around us?" Carol pulled her arm away. "Are you tripping on something?"

"Ask me a question about yourself and see if I can answer it. For example, ask me how many brothers and sisters you have."

"Okay, how many brothers and sisters do I have?"

"No brothers. Five sisters. And your parents are divorced."

Carol flushed. "How did you know that? You must know Chelsie and she told you about me."

"No, she didn't. Ask me something else." He finished the doughnut while he waited.

"Okay, where do I come from?"

"Deerfield, Vermont. Your mother's name is Margaret, you father's name is Richard, and your lover's name is Todd."

Carol stared at him in amazement. He knew all about her. This had to be a joke.

"Okay, that's enough. Jeff and Chelsie put you up to this, didn't they?"

"No, they didn't. I'm telling you, I have special powers. I can see into your soul." He leaned over and put his face close to hers. "I know one more thing about you, Carol. Your lover boy, Todd. You don't really love him, do you?"

Carol sat staring into his eyes, flustered and aghast with his last statement. "The joke's gone far enough, John. I'm going to get to the bottom of this."

She took her book and stomped out of the kitchen, back to Chelsie's room. She shook her awake. "Okay, Chelsie, whose idea was it to play this joke on me?"

"What?" Chelsie sat up. "What are you talking about?"

"This crazy John guy and his special abilities. You really pulled a good one."

"Carol, I don't know what you're talking about."

"Oh, come on Chelsie. Get out of bed. I'll show you." Carol pulled on her arm.

219

"Okay, just give me a minute."

Carol dragged Chelsie into the kitchen, but when she arrived, it was empty.

"Now he's conveniently gone. Okay, tell me the truth. Who is this John guy?"

"I don't know anyone named John who lives here. What's he look like?"

"He has long blond hair, tall, muscular, a real looker."

"I don't know anyone who fits his description that lives in the house. The only blond guy here is someone named Carl. He has short blond hair and is overweight."

"Come on Chelsie, tell me the truth."

"I am." Chelsie sat down.

"Then who was he?" A thought flashed into her mind, and she felt weak. No, it didn't look anything like *him*.

She ran back to Chelsie's room, dug through her purse, and pulled out a now tattered photograph. No, the picture she held was not him. Except, wait. She examined his eyes. Yes, the eyes were very similar. Could John have been *him*?

What kind of games was this guy playing with her? At least now she had a name. She put the picture back into her purse before Chelsie saw it.

Chelsie came back into the room and sat on the bed. "I'm sorry, Carol. I wish I knew who that guy was."

"Well, will you help me? I'm going to find him. He couldn't have gone far. I'm going to knock on every door in this building."

"Okay, Carol. Let me get dressed, and I'll come with you."

***

"I just can't believe it. It's so eerie. We've checked everyplace in this house, even the basement, and that guy is nowhere." Chelsie slumped into the chair by her desk.

Carol fell onto the bed, curled up in the fetal position, and hugged a pillow. She was sure now that it had to be *him*. Whoever this man was, he was slippery and unpredictable. She had no idea what he wanted to do with her, except maybe scare her to death and make her life miserable. And the way he was able to disguise himself. This time, she had not caught onto him until he took off. How did he know where she was all the time? He had to be watching her. He knew all about her family and all about Todd. Was he watching her right now? Maybe she should call the police. Carol pulled the covers over herself.

The strange thing was that she was always so attracted to him. And he seemed very attracted to her. He pretended to like her, to come onto her. If he really wanted to hurt her, he could have done it any one of the times she had seen him. They had been alone whenever he showed up. Why did he treat her so nicely if he wanted to harm her? If he wanted to kill her, he would have done it by now. It made her feel better to know he probably didn't want to kill her. So, he was stalking her. There had to be a reason he didn't just come out and tell her who he was. This time he had introduced himself as "John." Maybe he wanted to tell her more about himself but was afraid. Maybe he was a fugitive, running from the law. That had to be it! It made sense. Maybe he wanted her to help him, but he didn't know how to ask. Then why had he picked her of all people? Did he know her from somewhere? Was he a distant relative with a dark secret? The way he told her that she didn't love Todd. Was that his way of saying he wanted her to leave Todd for him?

"Carol, do you think we should call the police about this?" Chelsie asked.

Carol rolled over to face her. "I don't think it will do any good. He didn't really do anything wrong."

"Yes he did. He broke into this house."

"We don't know that for sure. One of these guys could have invited him in when they were stoned. Remember, some of the guys in the rooms didn't bother to get up and talk to us."

"Oh, I didn't think of that. We do get a few weird people that come in and out of this place. But still, won't you feel better if we at least let the police know?" Chelsie left the desk and sat on the bed next to her.

"I don't know. I still think someone may have put him up to it as a joke. Maybe Adam or Jeff did it. We haven't talked to them yet."

"They wouldn't *do* that. Besides, I know all their friends. I would remember someone like that if I'd met him."

Carol was tempted to share the whole story with Chelsie. But if she did, Chelsie would want to call the police for sure. Then there was always a chance that someone else may find out. If it ever got back to Todd, that would be a disaster. No, John had to remain her secret.

"I'm okay, Chelsie. Don't worry about it. He's gone now, so I doubt there's anything else we can do."

Chelsie stared at her, her expression doubtful. "I don't know, Carol. I still don't get how he knew all about you. It gives me the creeps."

"Yeah, I know. But he never laid a hand on me, Chelsie. I don't think he's the violent type. He was probably just high on drugs. Maybe drugs can give people psychic powers or something."

"Don't be ridiculous! Maybe that guy put you under a spell."

"No, I'm sure I'll never see him again. Let's just forget about the whole thing. I'm tired. I didn't get much sleep last night. Do you mind if I take a nap?"

"Sure, go ahead. I'll take my shower. But lock the door while I'm gone. I'll take my key."

"Okay." Carol looked at her friend. "Hey, Chelsie, thanks for being here for me. You're the greatest."

"That's what best friends are for." Chelsie gathered her clothes and bag of toiletries and headed out the door.

"Now, lock this behind me."

"I will." Carol got up and locked the door, retrieved the book she had been reading from the floor, and crawled under the covers. She read for a few moments, then fell asleep.

***

She was running again, through the woods, in the dead of night. He laughed behind her, and when she turned around, the cold glint of a blade flashed. He was covered in a black robe. Adrenaline spurred her on, into a field, toward a house in the distance. If only she could make it to the house, it would be safe. She focused on a lonely, lit window, willing herself forward. A sharp pain tore through her side. He was getting closer. Soon he breathed on the back of her neck. He grabbed her shirt. She turned around and shrieked, but the knife didn't plunge into her. Instead, she saw his face, so handsome, his eyes, so warm and inviting. "Carol, it's only me," he whispered. She stopped fighting and melted into his arms.

Carol awoke with a snap. It was still dark outside, and Chelsie slept peacefully beside her. Her dream had never turned out like that before. What did it mean? Would John save her from the horrible, robed figure who had invaded her dreams all these years? She closed her eyes and visualized his face, his perfect features, his penetrating eyes. She let the thoughts of him intoxicate and arouse, let her imagination come up with an answer to all her questions. He came for her, explained the reasons for his mysterious behavior, and asked her to come with him. She left her world behind and took his hand, surrendered...

***

All through the worship service, Amanda had been distracted. She needed to speak to Jim and Margaret, but wondered how to present her concerns without causing them to panic. It had been a difficult year for Margaret, still a new Christian, still struggling to accept that sometimes it takes years to see how God works in situations. Margaret's oldest daughter, Maurine, married a man older than Margaret. Jessica had become pregnant, married the baby's father, and lived in a run-down trailer without running water. Carol still lived with Margaret's first husband, Richard, and she had little contact with her. She watched Margaret sing with enthusiasm in her powerful voice, holding onto Jim's hand. Her marriage to Jim was her anchor and her joy. He helped Margaret grow through her many trials.

She felt Steve next to her, grateful for her own marriage. He agreed that she needed to talk to them. He had listened to her, held her in the night as she struggled over it. Even though he couldn't understand, he knew God used her in uncommon ways.

The song was over. Now was the time to make her move.

"Jim, Margaret, can I have a word with you?"

"Sure," said Jim. "What's up?"

"Can we talk in private? I'm sure Pastor Wilcock wouldn't mind if we used his office."

"Okay," Margaret picked up her purse. "But first let me check on the kids. I'm sure Liz will keep an eye on them."

A few minutes later, Amanda, Jim and Margaret sat in the pastor's small office. Amanda wondered whether she should have taken the big leather chair at the desk. She felt like a high school principal. Margaret had a worried expression and was fidgeting with the strap on her purse.

"What I'm going to tell you may sound a little strange, but I believe we need to pray for Carol more than ever."

"Why?" Margaret leaned forward. "Have you heard from her?"

"No. I haven't spoken to her since Christmas. She hasn't replied to my letters. I'm not sure exactly what's going on, but I do believe the Lord is speaking to me."

"We trust you, Amanda. We're all friends here," said Jim. "Tell us what's been going on."

"Well, remember I told you about the nightmare I had in France and how it came true the next day? I've been having dreams about Carol. I think that strange man might be after her again."

"Oh no!" Margaret clutched Jim's hand. "What did you dream?"

"The dreams are not as clear as the one in France. I see Carol with this man. He looks totally different from the artist in Paris. Carol isn't afraid of him. In fact, she seems enthralled with him. In one dream, they're dancing together. The man grins at me over Carol's shoulder, a sinister grin that says, 'I've got her now.' In another dream, he's driving away with her. As he pulls away, I see the same creepy grin. All around me, I hear this horrible laughter. I wake up petrified.

"Amanda, that's terrible! Oh, Jim, what are we going to do? How can we warn her?"

"Let's not panic, Hon." He turned toward Amanda. "Thanks for telling us your dream. I think you had that dream so that we could pray for Carol. It's just like when Margaret heard her dream in the hospital. I'm coming back to that verse, the one that says our struggle is not against flesh and blood but against rulers and authorities in high places. It's the same thing we've been praying all year, against evil forces."

"I've been wondering all week if I should tell her. My relationship with Carol hasn't been the same since she moved to New Hampshire. I'm afraid she'll think I'm totally whacko. Yet, if I don't warn her and something happens, I don't know if I can live with myself."

"Well, it might be a good idea to tell her. There's another verse that comes to my mind. God hasn't given us a spirit of fear, but of love, power, and a sound mind." Jim stood up. "Let's just get to praying."

They formed a circle and sought the Lord. As they progressed in the prayer, Jim's words became a war-cry. "Lord Jesus, protect Carol from the evil one. Surround her with warrior angels. We bind Satan from destroying her life. Oh Jesus, show us how to fight for her."

When all three finished praying, Amanda was certain about what she must do.

"I'm going to call Carol and tell her the truth about my dream. She may reject it, but at least I will have tried."

"Thank you, Amanda." Margaret hugged her friend.

***

"Todd, I already made plans with Chelsie and Jeff for my birthday. I don't understand why you're being so difficult. It's not like I turn eighteen every day."

"I'm not being difficult!" Todd sat at the desk in their room taking notes. He threw down his pen and stood to face Carol.

224

"I've told you before, your Dad is working with Paul Berkett on an important bill in the state senate that will provide medical assistance to low-income families. Paul Berkett is a well-know lawyer and political activist. He's going to be here this weekend, and Richard needs the research I'm doing on similar programs in other states."

"So, what you're telling me is that my Dad and this Paul guy are more important than me." Carol turned away and sat on the bed. She wasn't going to give in to him this time. She told Chelsie she was coming, and Todd wasn't going to spoil her plans.

"No, that's not true, and you know it. I had plans with your Dad to take you out to dinner Saturday, on your birthday."

"I don't want to just go to dinner. I'm turning eighteen, and I can go out on the town legally for the first time in my life. You know that's what I've wanted to do for months!"

"Yes, and I planned to take you to Vermont. But this came up. After you turn eighteen, we'll have plenty of opportunities to go out."

"Sure. Like I can believe that. My Dad has you trained to be just like him. When do you ever see him go out?"

"Carol, sometimes you can be so childish!" Todd sat back at his desk. "There are more important issues in this world than going out drinking. I thought you understood the importance of what your Dad is doing."

"Good grief! You pull the same line on me every time, and I always fall for it. Well, this time I'm not going to think of everyone else but myself. This time I'm going to have fun on my birthday. You can stay here and do your political stuff, but I'm going to stay with Chelsie whether you go with me or not!" Carol stood up and threw a book across the room.

"Carol, don't be so irrational! You're having a temper tantrum. Let's talk this out like mature adults." Todd went over to her and tried to touch her arm. Carol pulled away.

"Forget it! I'm going, and that's final."

Todd grabbed her arm and squeezed it hard. "Sit down right now and discuss this with me calmly."

Carol looked at him straight in the eyes, and for the first time in her life, she was determined not to back down. He had hurt her, not a lot, but enough to show that he was in charge. She actually hated him at this moment. He even looked ugly to her, his hair having grown out as long as hers and his sideburns reaching down to his chin. She realized he used his age and maturity to make her feel like a little child whenever she did not agree with him. When that didn't work, he would grab her like a naughty kid who needed a spanking. Well, she had enough of it. Todd wasn't going to push her around any more.

"You get your hands off me or I'll scream, Todd Barrett!"

Todd held her stare. Time seem to stand still as Carol wondered what he would do next. Like a beaten dog that had made her mind up to stand up to her master, Carol refused to lower her eyes. Finally, she felt his hand relax around her arm, and she knew she had won.

"We'll talk about this later, after you come to your senses." Todd dropped her arm, retreated to his desk and opened a book.

"Don't count on it, Todd. I'm leaving tomorrow morning." She snatched her purse and left the room, slamming the door. She stormed down the stairs and outside into the street. Todd was going to find out she had become a new woman in Burlington. If he wanted a relationship with her, he'd have to start showing her some respect.

Chapter Twenty-Four

Amanda slammed down the phone. "At this rate, I'll never get through."

"Still no answer?" Steve put his hand on her shoulder.

"This time, it's been busy all day. Its either busy or no one answers. I'm trying to obey the Lord, but it's not working." Amanda went into the kitchen and started making their lunch.

"Don't give up, sweetheart. Have you thought about sending a letter?"

"Yeah, but that will take time. I wanted to let her know right away." She took some bread out of the bread box.

"Why don't you write the letter just in case you can't get through? Then just keep on the calling." Steve opened the refrigerator.

"I suppose I could do that. Do you mind making lunch so I can do it right now? I won't be able to sleep until I at least try to communicate with Carol."

"Sure." Steve took the bread from her hand. "Go write your letter."

***

"I'm eighteen. A real, legal adult. I can do whatever I want!" Carol talked to the image in the mirror as she applied another layer of mascara. Tonight, if she were carded at the night club, she didn't have to worry about being kicked out.

The sting of her last words with Todd were far behind her. Chelsie and her family had prepared a dinner party with a store-bought cake decorated with pink and purple roses and her name on it. She felt a little guilty that her family wasn't there, but she called her mom and told her she would be over the next day. Margaret was surprised, as Carol forgot to tell her she was coming to town.

Her dad gave her Green Giant toy vegetables for her birthday. They were like stuffed animals but were vegetables: Mr. Corn, Green bean, and Tomato. He received them for free. He said he would take her out to eat when she returned home. Todd did not give her his present. He was too angry that she

227

was going without him. Oh well, he had better get accustomed to the new woman.

Chelsie knocked on the bathroom door. "Hey, aren't ready yet? You've been in there a long time. I'm the one who's supposed to spend all day in the bathroom primping."

"I'll be right out. You look good," she to her reflection. Before leaving the bathroom, Carol took off her ring.

"You do look good," Chelsie repeated as she walked out the door. She was wearing her sparkly, disco shirt and short shorts. Carol wore a tight-fitting, white sundress Todd had bought her last summer. The whiteness of the cotton material made her completion appear darker. She hoped the night would stay warm because she didn't bring anything to wrap around herself if it became cold.

"Jeff's waiting for us in the car," said Chelsie.

"Just let me stuff my driver's license and some money in this little white purse." Carol put her ring in a zippered compartment in her hand bag, then transferred a few items to the small bag she was taking with her. She followed Chelsie out the door.

The day had been hot and muggy, so the warm, night air blowing through the open window was refreshing. Carlie Simon's *You're So Vain* was on the radio, and she sang the song and thought about Todd. Vain was a word to describe him. He thought he was so smart, and she was supposed to worship his great wisdom and intelligence. Tonight, he could not reach her. *I'm going to have a good time.*

Carol just knew something new and exciting was going to happen. As Jeff and Chelsie chatted in the front seat, she searched the sides of the road, believing John would appear. She'd been hoping for it since her trip to Burlington. If he knew everything about her and was watching her, he would know that today was her eighteenth birthday.

Jeff parked his Mustang in the back of the Village Inn where the door to the night club was located. Several cars arrived at the same time, but none of the occupants were men with long, blond hair. The loud music reached the parking lot, and Carol recognized the song *One of These Nights* by the Eagles.

"They just have a D.J. right now, but later there should be a band from New York playing live. I heard them last year, and they're pretty good." Jeff locked his car.

"I don't need a band to get in a dancing mood." Chelsie took Jeff's hand and wiggled around him. "You *are* going to dance the night away with me, aren't you?"

"Like I have any choice. If I don't dance with you, you'll probably dance with every guy in the place." Jeff grinned.

"Oh, why would you think I'd do that to you?" Chelsie gave him a coy look, then lay her head against his chest.

"Oh, I don't know. Maybe it has something to do with your incredible sex appeal."

"Come on, you love birds. Let's go find a seat." Carol nudged Chelsie with her elbow.

They paid the huge man at the door a cover charge of $3.00. Carol was disappointed he did not ask for her identification. He didn't check Jeff or Chelsie's either. Did they all look older than eighteen?

Inside, smoke swirled in the red, blue, and yellow light that moved around the room. It came from a large, rotating, silver ball hanging over the dance floor. Tables with oil candles filled up one side of the room, and on the other side a long bar took up the entire wall. The bar chairs were full, mostly with men. A mixed crowd sat at the tables, though with more women than men.

"Let's get the last table next to the dance floor." Chelsie pulled on Jeff's arm.

They sat down, and a waitress came and asked them what they wanted to drink. She ordered a Tom Collins, a sweet drink that disguised the taste of the liquor. Chelsie order a Margarita, and Jeff had a beer. Carol scanned the room for John as inconspicuously as possible. None of them came close to his appearance. She hoped he hadn't changed his disguise again.

Sta'yin Alive by the Bee Gees started to play. Carol tapped her feet and swayed to the music in her chair. She wished someone would ask her to dance.

"I love this song," Cheslie yelled over the music. "Come on, Jeff, dance with me."

"There's no one on the dance floor. They're all waiting for the band."

"I don't care." Cheslie pouted when she realized Jeff wouldn't budge. Then she turned to Carol. "Hey, Carol, let's go dance together. We don't need a man to have fun."

"What?"

Chelsie stood up and blared into her ear. "Come dance with me."

"Okay." The two girls stepped onto the dance floor alone. Within a few minutes, more couples and single women joined them. They danced to the next song, then sat down when *Ain't no Mountain High Enough* by Diana Ross started to play.

"Come on, Jeff." Chelsie stood over him. He took her hand, and they slow danced together.

A young man named Ryan she knew from high school sat down at their table.

"Hey, do you remember me? We went to school together."

"Sure, in Biology and English. You always asked for help on your homework."

"Yea," he laughed. "You were always so quiet in high school. I never realized how cute you were."

"Thanks." Carol blushed. Being a good student in high school must be a hindrance to getting asked out on a date.

"Hey, Carol, will you dance with me?"

"Sure."

Carol danced with Ryan and his friend. Then there was a break before the live band came on stage. Ryan and his friend invited themselves to their table.

Carol asked Chelsie to go to the bathroom with her. "Chelsie, how can I get rid of those guys?"

"You don't like them?"

"Not really. I know Ryan was popular in school, a real jock that had his share of girls to pick from. But he's too conceited for me, and stupid."

"I know what you mean." Chelsie was reapplying her lipstick. "But you could just dance with him tonight to have a good time, then drop him at the end of the night. You don't want to get serious with anyone because of Todd, right?"

"Oh, I don't know. Things aren't that great with us right now."

Chelsie looked at Carol's left hand. "I noticed you took off your ring." She paused. "Hey, Carol, I've never told you this before because you're my best friend and I didn't want to hurt you. But I think leaving Todd would be the best thing you could do. He's more like your father, and you've never had a chance to enjoy your youth."

"Do you really think so? Then how come I feel like a scum bag leaving him?"

"Because he's had control of your life for four years." Chelsie touched Carol's shoulder. "Don't get me wrong. I believe in faithfulness and marriage. I'd never cheat on Jeff. But you were just a kid when Todd came into your life. You never had a chance to find out for yourself what love was all about. I think coming here today is your first step toward freedom."

"You think so?" Carol studied her reflection in the mirror. She was only eighteen, but sometimes she felt so much older. What Chelsie said was true. She had spent her entire high school years being a lover and a type of wife to Todd, meeting all of *his* needs, doing what *he* thought best. She had even given up going to college so he could move in with her Dad. And when he didn't get his way, he always made her feel like it was her fault. No, she didn't need to feel bad about it any more.

"You're right, Chelsie. I'm eighteen now, and no one, not even Todd, can tell me what to do. I'm going to do things my way from now on."

"I'm glad to hear it. So, how do we get rid of Ryan?"

"I was hoping you had an idea."

"Well, as soon as the band starts playing, you and I will dance together so Ryan and his friend don't have a chance to ask you. Then we can hang around the dance floor instead of going back to our seats. Jeff will get the picture and join me, and hopefully someone else will ask you to dance."

"If Ryan doesn't get it by then, he's more stupid than I thought." Carol ran a comb through her brown curls. "Okay, it's a plan. Let's go get another drink."

"We'll get our drinks from the bar so Ryan doesn't offer to pay for it."

"Good thinking."

Chelsie's plan worked. By the third song the band played, someone else did ask her to dance. Carol was still disappointed John had not shown up, but she was impressed by her new dance partner. This man was older, confident, and incredibly handsome. He knew how to dance, not just move his body around. Carol did her best to keep up with his steps, and she must have done a good job, because he asked her to dance again.

They danced together through an entire set of songs. The band was skilled at playing the hits. They rocked to *American Woman*, *Band on the Run*, and *Hotel California*. When they sang *Bridge Over Troubled Water*, he took her hands in his and slow danced with her. Carol never danced like that before. He used calculated steps and moved her around the floor. But he was so smooth, she seemed to float in his arms. His hands were strong, tan, muscular, not like Todd's pale, weak hands. His white, cotton shirt, unbuttoned at the top, matched her white dress, and she knew people were watching them dance. She felt like Cinderella at the ball.

When the band took a break, her dancing partner sat with them.

"How's it going? I'm Troy Palinski."

"I'm Carol. This is Jeff and Chelsie."

"Please to meet you." They shook hands all around, then Troy sat next to Carol.

"You're a great dancer. Has anyone ever told you that?"

"No." Carol smiled to hide the blush. "I think you're the great dancer. I just followed as best I could."

"Well, you fooled me. Say, what are you drinking? I'll get you a fresh one."

"Oh, are you sure? I still have some left."

"No problem." Troy flagged down a waitress and ordered more drinks, including a rum and coke for himself. He took a package of cigarettes out of his pocket, put one in his mouth, and lit it.

"I'm sorry, do you smoke?"

"No. But it's okay."

Troy looked at Chelsie and Jeff. "None of you smoke. Well, I'm trying to quit anyway." He crushed the cigarette in the ashtray. "So, tell me about yourself, Carol."

"I'm a college student. I'm going to the University of Vermont."

"That's in Burlington isn't it? It's been a few years since I've been here."

"Oh, where are you from?" Chelsie sipped her drink.

"From outside of Seattle, Washington. That's Washington State."

"Wow, you're a long way from home. That's clear across the country, on the Pacific Coast, isn't it?" Carol played with her straw.

"That it is. But I grew up around here. I'm back visiting family."

"So, how did you end up in Seattle? Did you go to school out there?" Jeff joined the conversation.

"No, I had a business opportunity. Fell in love with the place and never left." He turned to Carol. "The place I live is nice and modern. The mountains out there are so large, the trees so tall. Mount Rainier is the highest mountain in the continental U.S. I have a view of the Cascade Mountains from my house."

"I heard it rains a lot in Seattle," Jeff said.

"It can in the winter. But we don't get the darn cold you guys get. It hardly ever snows and stays green all winter. And the summers are dry and sunny.

Once you get used to the city lifestyle, it's hard to come back to a place like this."

"I don't know. I like Vermont, and I used to live in the city," Chelsie said. "Of course, I have to go to the city from time to time to buy my clothes, but the people here are real friendly."

"I always thought Vermonters didn't like outsiders. At least that's the way my family acted." Troy took a good gulp from his drink. Carol noticed his lips were nice and full, his moustache trim and attractive around them. His eyes were a hazel color and wide-set, and he kept directing them at her, even when Jeff and Chelsie talked to him. His face was so handsome, his sandy hair so soft looking, he reminded her of a deer. Yet he was rugged at the same time.

"Not all of us are like that." Jeff put his arm around Chelsie. "My family's lived in Deerfield all my life, and we've always been accepting of outsiders."

"Well, I'm glad you've at least accepted me." Chelsie cuddled next to him.

"Who could resist a beautiful girl like you?" He kissed her hair.

"So, are you two college students, too?"

"We all are going to the UVM. We went to high school together."

"I guess I'm the old guy here." Troy laughed. "I haven't been to school in a while." He turned toward the dance floor. "Looks like the band should start up any minute. Carol, how'd you like to be my dance partner the rest of the night?"

"I'd love it. Maybe you can teach me some new moves."

He reached over and put his hand over hers. "My pleasure." An enjoyable sensation spread in a rush of heat. It felt like her heart was beating in her finger tips. She was certain this man was not John disguised because his eyes were a different color and shape, but he made her feel the same way John did whenever he showed up. If only Troy didn't live so far away.

Carol danced with Troy the rest of the night. The band showed off at the end with *Stairway to Heaven*, so Troy held her close through it. She felt his body pressed against hers, and the excitement surpassed anything she had ever experienced with Todd. Troy kissed her neck, stroked her back and played with her hair. Then he moved his face in front of hers and their lips met. The noise, the smoke, the music all disappeared as a powerful connection ignited between them. She went limp in his arms. She didn't even think twice when he took her hand and lead her outside when the song was over. Once outside the door, he gathered her into his arms and kissed her with more passion.

LAURIE PALMER

"I want you, Carol," he whispered into her ear. "What're you doing the rest of the night?"

"I have to go home with Chelsie."

He kissed her again. "Are you sure? I'm on fire."

"I don't really know you, Troy."

"Oh." He pulled back. "What're you doing tomorrow? Can I take you out?"

"Yes, I'd love to."

"Carol, there you are." Chelsie and Jeff came walking toward them. "You know my curfew is 1:00. I have ten minutes to get home."

"I'll be with you in just a minute."

"Okay, Jeff and I will be waiting in the car."

"Why don't you give me your phone number." Troy pulled out a pen and a matchbook from his pocket. Carol took it and wrote down Chelsie's phone number.

"I'm supposed to meet my family for a birthday party around lunch, but I should be free by four or five." Carol handed him the matchbook.

"Great. I'll call you after four." He touched her face, and they were in each others arms again. "Man, I wish you didn't have to go."

"Me too." They kissed one last time, then Carol broke away and headed for Jeff's Mustang.

"I can't wait until tomorrow," he called after her.

She waved goodbye and opened the back door of the car.

***

Carol put her suitcase in the back of the car and slammed the hatchback. Chelsie stood watching, barefoot on the driveway in front of her house.

"Carol, are you sure you don't want me to come along? I could give you a ride back to your mother's house. That way, you won't have to take a bus."

"No, but thanks anyway. Troy is going to pick me up at the bus station late tonight. Besides, I already have the ticket."

"Are you sure you can stand up to Todd? It's going to be quite a shock for him. There's no telling what his reaction will be."

"My dad and Denise will be there if it gets out of hand. I'm going to make it as quick as possible. I'll take a taxi to the bus station. Mom gave me some extra money, so I'll be okay."

"I feel sorry for your dad. He's going to be stuck with a crazy man. But I'm really glad you're leaving him. I'm happy for you."

"Thanks, Chelsie. You've helped me a lot to see it. If I hadn't come up here this weekend, I wouldn't have realized that I never loved Todd. After being with Troy, I see how Todd took advantage me. I didn't know any better at fourteen. Now I know how a man should treat a woman."

"I take it you're talking about Troy."

"Oh, Chelsie, I'm so in love with him!"

Chelsie put her fingers through her tangled hair. "I just hope he doesn't hurt you, Carol. He lives so far away, and you still don't know much about him. How's it going to work?"

"I'm not going to think about that right now. All I want to think about is seeing him again tonight. He loves me, I know he does. If he just wanted a one night stand, he wouldn't have offered to pick me up at the bus station."

"I hope so, for your sake." Chelsie leaned over and picked a weed from the side of the driveway.

"Well, I'd better get going. I'll call you and let you know how it goes."

"You'd better." Chelsie hugged her friend.

Carol popped into the car and drove away.

To keep from thinking about what lay ahead, Carol relived the past two days with Troy. She could not recall a time when she had been so happy. Her intimate experience with Todd was like comparing a flashlight to the powerful rays of the sun. Just being next to Troy excited her, and when he touched her, when he kissed her, when he...it was fireworks on the fourth of July. She couldn't get enough, be with him enough. Thoughts of him made it so much easier to get out of her dad's house. The idea of Todd ever touching her again disgusted her.

Troy was a real man. He didn't push himself on her, and when she talked about her dreams and goals, he listened and told her she was smart beyond her age. He wasn't intellectual like Todd, nor did he have a college education, but he had good common sense and knew how to have fun. It sounded like he had done well for himself in Washington State. He lived in his own house, had an expensive sports car, and worked on exotic race cars. "You should see the engine of a Jaguar XJ12. It has twelve cylinders. Everything has to be done just right or the owners will jump down your throat. Man, the stress can really get to you. But you feel proud when the engine roars to life and accelerates from zero to sixty in only seven seconds."

He was such a gentleman. He picked her up in a newer Buick borrowed from a friend and opened the door for her. They went to a carnival in Rutland,

and he went on the roller coaster with her. At the shooting range, he won a huge, stuffed bear and gave it to her. They ate lunch at the fairgrounds, then he took her for a long ride and they talked about everything. He was honest with her, and she was honest with him.

"Carol, I want to be open with you. I've been married before. Her name was Diane. We've been divorced ten years."

"Oh, that's okay. Do you have kids?"

"No, we never had kids. Diane was totally into her career. She started out as a secretary and worked her way up the ladder. She's in advertising. Always could draw real good. Once she started selling her ideas to the big wigs, things between us went down hill fast. I wanted to start a family. She wanted to make a name for herself. I wasn't good enough for her anymore. Then we both had affairs, and that was the end of it."

"I'm so sorry, Troy. Did you really love her?"

"I did at the time, but I'm long over it. I should have known from the beginning a down-home boy like me wouldn't fit with high-brow girls like her."

Troy paused and looked over at Carol. "Hey, don't get me wrong. I think it's great that you want to go to college and stuff. But your family's like mine. Just common folks. You're not a snob."

"No, you can say that again. I think everyone should be accepted for who they are. A college degree doesn't make you any smarter than anyone else. I should know. I've been living with the biggest snob of all time."

"Oh, really? You're only eighteen. You've already been living with someone?"

Carol picked her fingers. "I guess it's my turn to be honest with you."

When Carol finished telling Troy all about Todd, she could not believe his reaction.

"Hey, Carol, don't feel bad. If you want to know the truth, that boyfriend of yours was a statutory rapist." He swore. "If someone had done that to my daughter at fourteen, I would have chained his "you-know-whats" to a tree."

Carol felt a little embarrassed and didn't know what to say. She didn't know if it were fair to blame it all on Todd. Troy must have sensed her awkwardness, because he took her hand. His touch was enough to make her forget about Todd.

"I didn't hurt your feelings, did I?"

"Hey, it's okay. Let's not talk about Todd. Tell me more about Seattle. It sounds so pretty there."

Troy drove her to a small town called Westminster West where he grew up on a farm. He took her to the end of a dirt road, and they hiked through the woods. Troy helped her over fallen logs and down steep banks. They followed a stone wall, and Troy shared childhood memories. "My friend and me shot our first animals in these woods. We were about ten. Good old Mike was so anxious to shoot something he kept firing on anything that moved. So, he sees this small critter moving in the brush and shoots at it. A skunk comes running out, flips up his tail, and sprays poor Mike right in his shoes and pants. Man, did it stink! Well, we didn't have much to show that day." Carol loved watching Troy laugh, his eyes sparkling with mischief. He started tickling her to keep her laughing. She ran away, and he chased her down to a stream. They sat down on a rock together. The water sang a love song as it gushed over the rocks, the sun reached through the trees to warm their backs, and Troy smiled at her with his deer-like eyes. He put his hand on her cheek, and she felt like she was going to explode. They started kissing, but Troy stopped before going further.

"We don't have to do this if you're not ready."

"It's okay. I want to."

The blare of a horn broke through her daydream. She had swerved over into the other lane for a moment. *Stay focused, Carol, or you're going to get yourself killed.* She had at least forty-five minutes left before reaching Wilton. If only she could call Todd, it would be so much easier. But then she wouldn't be able to get her belongings out of the house or give him back his car. She had nothing of hers left at her mom's house.

***

Carol could not believe her good luck. When she arrived at her dad's house, Todd was gone. That meant she would have to only talk to her dad and maybe Denise.

She walked through the door, trying to appear casual, leaving her suitcase in the front yard. She held a box of garbage bags behind her back. More good luck. Her dad was on the phone. She waved and rushed up the stairs.

With frenzy, eager to finish before Todd returned, Carol threw all her belongings into the garbage bags: clothes, shoes, toiletries, jewelry, her favorite records. All the furniture and most of her books would have to stay behind. She hurried to the window from time to time to see if Todd had come back. Her hands shook, her stomach hurt, but she had to keep moving.

Carol called information, wrote down the number of a taxi service, and requested a taxi. She left a note she had drafted the night before on the dresser.

She was just starting to take the bags down the back stairs when her dad came into the hallway.

"What's going on here?"

"Dad, I'm really sorry, but I'm moving back home."

"What the…?"

"I'm leaving Todd, today, right now."

"Are you crazy?" He ran his fingers through his thick hair. "You can't just take off like this!"

"I'm really sorry, but I can't stay with Todd anymore. I don't love him."

"Come on Carol, let's sit down and talk this out. What's the big hurry?"

"I want to get this done before Todd gets back." Carol went back into the room and took out another bag. Richard followed.

"Aren't you at least going to wait for him to get home? That's the least you can do."

"Not if I can help it. It will be better for all of us. Todd will just make a big scene. He'll try to get me to stay."

Richard stepped in front of her. "Carol, you may be eighteen, but you're still my daughter. I want you to sit and wait for Todd to get back."

"Dad, please. Just let me do this my way. I know it's unfair to leave him here with you, but I know Todd better than you. He'll get violent."

"Can you blame him?" Richard swore. "Just what happened to make you change your mind so fast?"

"I've been thinking about this for a few weeks now. When I was in Burlington, I realized Todd was holding me back, that he had complete control over my life. Well, I'm sick of him controlling everything. I'm in charge of my own life now."

Carol argued with her Dad for several more minutes. Finally, she said, "It's no use Dad. I'm really sorry, but I have to leave."

Her dad sighed, shook his head, turned away and stomped down the stairs. She carried her bags to the street and waited for the taxi. Every time a car came down the road, she feared it would be Todd. Sweat from the physical work and the stress trickled down her face, and she wiped it with her shirt. What was taking that taxi so long?

Her dad came out the door, a bottle of ale in one hand, a letter in the other. "Here, this came for you."

"Oh." Carol saw that it was from Amanda. She stuffed it in her purse. Her dad gave her a nasty look and guzzled down his bottle of ale. He reminded her of an angry bully sitting in a bar, looking for a fight. And she was his target.

He swore at her again. "I can't believe how stupid you are. It's pretty darn selfish of you to just leave here with this mess you've made."

Carol squeezed her eyes shut to keep the tears from falling. What right did he have to judge her this way? He's the one who left her mom with her and her sisters. Besides, Todd was a great help to his "political movement." Todd was the one who wanted to move here in the first place. She wanted so much to stand up to her dad, but was too afraid. Especially the way he looked at her. She kept her eyes on the ground and waited for him to leave.

"Fine. Be this way. I open my home, and all you can think about is yourself. If you go now, don't plan on coming back." Richard opened the garbage can, threw the bottle inside, breaking the glass, then whacked the lid back on with his powerful arm. Then he turned and went into the house, slamming the door.

It seemed forever before a yellow taxi pulled into their driveway. The fat, greasy-haired driver didn't seem too pleased with the three trash bags and suitcase he had to load into the car. He gave her a quick look-over, rolled his eyes, then threw them in the trunk. She hoped they didn't break. She got into the passenger side and waited.

"Let me guess, you want to go to the bus station." The driver shut the door and started the engine.

"Yes, please." Carol turned toward the window and chewed on her thumb. She was so relieved that Todd had still not returned. They pulled away, down the only street in town. They passed her dad's noisy Toyota put-putting up the hill in the opposite direction. Todd kept his attention focused on the road and did not even see her. Whew! Carol took a deep breath and waited for her heartbeat to return to normal. She had missed him by less than a minute.

***

Carol sat back in her seat and let the tension ebb away. She'd made it. She was safe on the bus, headed toward Deerfield, her bags stowed in the compartment below, Todd far away from her. She wished she could take a shower before meeting Troy. She was hot and wet and sticky and hungry.

She rummaged around in her purse, looking for a package of gum. She noticed the letter her Dad had given her and took it out. A tinge of guilt came over her as she remembered Amanda. She hadn't been much of a friend to her lately. Amanda had written several letters she never answered. She'd have to go visit her when things settled down. Amanda didn't like Todd, so she should be happy that she left him.

She tore the top of the envelope and pulled out two sheets of lined paper.

Dear Carol,

I hope this letter finds you well. I've tried to call your father's home several times, but the phone is either busy or no one answers. I hope this gets to you sooner than later.

This is a hard letter to write, but I know in my heart I must share this. Remember how I had the dream in France just before the strange artist tried to lead you away? I've had another dream. I believe it's a warning, just like the first one. Whether you believe in God or not, please at least consider that my first dream stopped you from leaving with a stranger in the middle of a foreign city.

Here it goes. I saw you with a man, but he didn't look the same as the man in Paris. In this dream, you weren't afraid of him. You were dancing together. I didn't have a clear picture of him except his face. When you could see him, it was handsome, but when you couldn't see him, it was ugly. The man pretended to like you, but when you weren't looking, I saw his face become evil and his grin malicious. He wanted to lure you away for some bad purpose. In the second part of the dream, he was driving you away somewhere. He turned and glared at me from the window with that horrible grin. Then he started laughing. It was a sinister laughter that echoed. It was saying, "Ha, ha, I've got her now."

Carol, I hope this doesn't hurt our friendship. I would not tell you this if I were not fearful you might be in danger. I could not rest until I told you. Please be careful what you do in the next few days or weeks.

I'd love to see you again. I'm here anytime you need anything. I'll even drive to Wilton if you need me.

Love,
Amanda

Amanda's letter worked like air conditioning. Carol hugged herself as fear replaced her earlier excitement. She read the letter again and shook her head. Amanda's dream just couldn't be true! The only man she'd danced with was Troy, and he was the first man she'd ever truly loved. There was no way the dream could be about him. But what did it mean? Amanda had dreamt about John in Paris. She couldn't deny that fact. She knew Amanda well enough that she would not send the letter unless she felt strongly about it. But it just couldn't be a warning about Troy.

The date on the letter was almost two weeks ago. She'd have to thank her Dad for being so prompt about it. Amanda had tried to call her before writing the letter, so that meant she must have had the dream before Carol went to Burlington. Her first dream warned her about John. So, this dream also had to be a warning about John, not Troy. But what about the dancing part? John never tried to dance with her.

She did dance with Adam, but Carol felt absolutely no connection with him. No, the dream couldn't be about Adam. Or Ryan, for the same reason. The only one that made any sense was John. He just showed up again, out of the blue. To think she had daydreamed about him. Wait! That's it! Her last dream about John started out as a nightmare. John must be the same person who was trying to kill her in that dream. Now she was shaking. Was he the same one she'd been dreaming about for years? Oh, if that were true, how creepy it all was. To think she'd almost left with him more than once. No, Amanda's dream had to be about John.

Still, what about the dancing? Maybe John was there the same night she met Troy. Maybe she would have danced with him if she hadn't met Troy. That had to be it. No, the dream wasn't about Troy. Troy was the one who saved her from John. She couldn't prove it, but it made the most sense.

Still, she didn't know Troy very well. But he was so nice her, such a gentleman, not at all like the man in Amanda's dream. And he was honest. He even told her about his old girlfriend back home named Debbie. John never even told her his name until their last encounter. Troy did take her for long drive, but nothing bad happened to her. He never forced her to sleep with him. It had been her decision.

Carol put the letter back in her purse. No, the warning was about John, and if she ever saw him again, she'd run away as fast as possible. Suddenly, she was afraid John might be out there somewhere waiting for her. She turned and looked at all the people on the bus with her. None had any resemblance to John. Still, she wished she were already back in Deerfield, back with Troy.

The rumble of thunder startled her more than it should. Outside the window, she could see they were heading right into a storm. Within seconds, a harsh wind whipped the trees, sending leaves flying through the air. Then the rain pounded the windows, as lightening flashed, followed by more thunder. Carol usually enjoyed thunder storms, but tonight it only made her think about John. He could be anywhere. She wished her coat wasn't in her suitcase, underneath the bus. She put her legs up in the seat and curled her body to try to bring warmth, but she would always remember her ride to Deerfield as long and cold.

Chapter Twenty-Five

"Jim, are you sure I should go on this retreat? Carol's back home now, and I want to take advantage of every minute with her." Margaret moved the hangers in her closet, but took nothing out.

"Yup. You've been planning this for months. Besides, that girl is hardly ever here. Spent the last two weeks with a stranger from Seattle. Never even brought him around." Jim took a pair of slacks from a hanger. "Take these. You look good in them."

Margaret put the pants in her suitcase. "I know Carol hasn't been here much. That's why I think I should stay. I want a chance to get to know her again, especially now that guy has gone back to Seattle."

"Margaret, you need this retreat. You're going."

"But Jim, I keep thinking about Amanda's dream. What if something happens while I'm gone?"

"You can't live in fear. I'll be here. And God's not going anywhere. You're going."

How could Margaret fight her husband's determined blue eyes. "All right, I'll go."

Jim pulled out a long, silky negligee. "I guess you won't be needing this."

"Oh, Jim."

"You could try it on now. See if it still fits."

Margaret took it from him, as he hugged her. "I've got to finish packing. I'm leaving in an hour." She put the negligee away and took out a top to match the pants.

***

Margaret waited. She let all the rest of the group receive prayer before going forward.

"Did you want me to pray for you?" Gail Summers asked.

"Yes, but I have some questions first."

"No problem. Ask away."

"Are you sure you have time?"

"Of course. If I weren't talking to you, I'd be out there eating snacks that I don't need." Gail laughed and sat down next to Margaret. Gail was probably in her late forties and slightly overweight, but her face radiated youth and vitality. The instant one saw her dark blue eyes, they knew something was different about her. They emitted life, hope and compassion, even behind glasses.

"Your name is Margaret, isn't it?"

"Yes. Thanks for remembering. Anyway, I'm not sure I understand the end of your talk tonight. I still don't see how we can *be* perfect when we are still being *made* perfect. From what you've taught us this weekend, we can't be perfect. That's why perfectionism never works. So how can Jesus see us as perfect?"

"Let's look up Hebrews 10:13-14." Gail opened her Bible and turned to the reference. "Here, why don't you read it to me."

Margaret took the Bible and read, "Since that time he waits for his enemies to be made his footstool, because by one sacrifice he has made perfect forever those who are being made holy."

"What does it say we are?" Gail asked.

"It says we are perfect forever. But how can we be perfect if we are in the process of being made holy?"

"That's the glory of Christ's love. When he looks at you, Margaret, he sees the perfected Margaret, the Margaret who will rule and rein with him in his kingdom. Because you have accepted his sacrifice, you are completely cleansed of all imperfection and unrighteousness, completely holy to him. There's nothing more you need to do to receive his love and acceptance."

"But how can that be? If we think we're already perfect, won't we never strive to be better Christians? Won't we just take advantage of Jesus and never change?"

"Not if we understand where our perfection comes from. It's not within us. Let's read the rest of the verse. It says we are being made holy. If we're being made holy, then we aren't living in our perfected role yet, are we?"

"No. This is confusing." Margaret put the Bible down.

"I know. Maybe if I share a story it'll help." Gail sat back in her chair. "I shared a little about my divorce and my son's reaction to it. He turned his back on God and everything I taught him. He started experimenting with drugs, and after messing with LSD, he was never the same again. He's living on the streets of Boston, doing who knows what to support his habit. I'd just spent thousands of dollars on rehabilitation, and he came home for a while, then left again. I was so frustrated. I'd done everything in my power to help my son, and I'd failed. Thoughts of suicide plagued me daily."

Margaret could connect with Gail's story. It made her think of Maurine and her troubles with drugs.

"Anyway, I'd been a Christian all my life, was raised in the church, married a Christian man, taught my children all about God, but I never really understood how much Jesus loved me. I'd spent my life being a good Christian, doing all the right things, but not knowing Jesus. When it all fell apart, I figured I'd failed God. I was so ashamed, I didn't feel welcome in my church anymore. I was afraid everyone would point at me and condemn me for all my mistakes. I wasn't a good enough wife or mother, so how could I be a good Christian? I decided the world would be better off without me."

Margaret looked at Gail. A few minutes before, she saw her as a professional speaker who had blazed through life making an impact. Now she saw her as someone who suffered pain and grief, just like her, who experienced times of total despair, just like her.

"I never thought about Christians struggling with these things. I figured only non-Christians had troubles like that," Margaret said.

Gail smiled. "The only difference between a Christian and a non-Christian is that we are saved by grace. We face the same problems, the same temptations. It's only through Jesus we can be any different. And that's what I didn't understand. That Jesus didn't see me as a failure. He saw me as a cleansed, born-again daughter, arrayed in a white robe, perfect in his sight."

"It's still hard to accept." Margaret played with the tassel on her Bible cover.

"It took everything in my life falling apart for me to see it, to give control over to the Lord. A good friend of mine counseled me and set me straight. She told me I had no business telling Jesus I was worthless when he saw me as valuable. She told me I was full of pride. I was stunned. How could looking down on myself be pride? Because I was setting myself above my creator, telling him I was nothing when he loved me and sacrificed his life for me. I was throwing his gift, a gift that cost him everything, back in his face."

"Wow. I've never seen it like that before."

Gail paused and took a sip from a cup of water. "My friend told me it's just as much a sin to judge yourself as it is to judge someone else. That's why accepting who you are in Christ, as perfect in his eyes regardless of where you are in the process, is fundamental to growing in him. If you forget, you find yourself back in the same hopeless spot of relying on yourself. Then you end up doing exactly what you don't want to do, just like Paul described in Romans 7. It's a vicious cycle of guilt. And your all-time enemy, the devil, will have his demons ready to convince you you're worthless. When you think you're worthless, you are worthless."

"I'm beginning to get it." Margaret sat up in her chair. "I won't grow in Christ, or become more holy, until I see that I am already perfect in Christ. If I don't see myself that way, I just end up wasting my time putting myself down, beating myself up."

"That's right, Margaret." Gail grinned, her blue eyes joyful.

"So, is that what stopped you from being suicidal?"

"Well, it took time to put it into practice. My friend and others prayed for me, helped me every step of the way. But that was my first breakthrough."

Margaret thought of Amanda and how much she had helped her in the last year. Even with her friend's help and that of the church, she kept falling short. "But what do you do when you keep screwing up, falling back into the same bad habits? It's hard not to get angry at yourself all the time."

"You confess your sins and Jesus will forgive you. Then you throw them away never to be brought up again, just like he does. Remember, he's focused on the perfected Margaret, not the one who makes mistakes. One of my favorite verses is Lamentations 3:23, 'Because of the Lord's great love, we are not consumed, for his compassions never fail. They are new every morning, great is your faithfulness.' Every day, you have a chance to begin fresh, to start over."

"So you don't think believing that Jesus sees you as perfect makes you a lazy Christian?"

"No, it does the opposite. His love frees you up so you can hear his voice. The more you rely on him instead of yourself, the more effective you become. It's all about relationship. It's all about Jesus."

"I like that. It's all about Jesus." Margaret paused and looked at her lap.

"Did you have something else you want to talk about?"

"I know that Jesus forgives our sins, but how do you cope when the consequences of your sins come back to bite you over and over?"

Gail crossed her legs and put her elbows on her knees. "Like how?"

"My kids. The oldest three have chosen destructive lifestyles because of my divorce."

"Wait a minute, Margaret. Listen to what you just said. My children have chosen. Is this something you did?"

"No, but they probably wouldn't have done it if Richard hadn't left us."

"Again, whose choice was it to leave? Richard's?"

"Still, I also made bad choices after the divorce."

Gail took another sip of water. "Okay, you do need to own up to your own failures. Ask your children to forgive you for your mistakes. Repent and don't return to those negative things. It's true that we must live with consequences to our actions." Gail leaned closer to Margaret.

"But be careful to separate *your* choices from your ex-husband's and your children's. Just like my own son, I didn't make him take drugs or run away. He did that. He knew right from wrong. Sure, I made mistakes. But I never abused him. Even if I had, he's an adult now and makes his own choices. I've seen strong, mighty Christians come from the most horrific life-styles."

Margaret could feel emotion rising and was afraid she would soon cry. "I still can't help wondering if I'd been a better mother, my children would've turned out differently."

Gail touched Margaret's shoulder. "Margaret, the past is over. All you have is the future. You can't control what others do. All you can control is what you do, and trust me, if you start living your life knowing you're precious to your Lord and Savior, you'll begin to have victory. You'll begin to see God work in your life. It all starts with you—and Jesus."

Tears spilled onto her cheeks. "Do you really think so?"

"I know it with everything in me." Gail found a tissue box and gave her a tissue. "It looks like you've been wounded. Why don't you tell me about it. The Lord wants you to put aside the scars of the past and start fresh."

"Okay." Margaret told her all about her ugly divorce and Maurine, Jessica and Carol. When she was finished, Gail prayed for her. She left the room feeling like someone had just removed a pile of bricks from her back.

***

"Carol, the phone's for you. It's Todd again."

"Tell him I'm not here." Carol was sprawled on her bed in a pair of shorts and the same t-shirt she wore to bed the night before. She was trying to finish a poem she was writing for Troy. She wanted to find something that rhymed with 'rainbow.'

"Carol, I refuse to put him off again. You go answer the phone or I'll tell him the truth." Liz looked down at Carol, her hands on her hips. She had grown into a lovely young woman with dark eyes, dark complexion, and thick, silky dark hair. But she didn't have a boyfriend yet. She'd become involved in her mother's church. Certainly, she had to be her mother's favorite. Not only that, she sounded more like her mom than her sister.

"Come on, Liz. Tell him I call back in an hour."

"I *will not*. I'm sick of talking to him. You've totally devastated him, and you don't even have the courtesy to answer his calls. He said you left without even talking to him."

"I'm surprised at you, Liz. You never liked Todd. You know he's a jerk. Why the sympathy all of a sudden?"

Liz folded her arms. "Because he's a human being and deserves to be treated like one, no matter what he's done."

"Good grief. Fine. I'll go talk to him." She turned her attention to the phone in her room, which used to be Jessica's room. She'd heard the phone ring moments before, guessed it was Todd, but had not made a move to answer it. It was three hours earlier in Seattle, and Troy didn't usually call until after 9:00, when he came home from work. She sighed and picked up the phone. Liz, satisfied that Carol had indeed answered, left the room.

"Hello Todd."

"Hi, Carol. How are you?"

"I'm fine. Sorry I haven't taken your calls. I've been busy."

"Have you read any of the letters I sent?"

"Um, not yet."

"Will you please read them."

"Sure. I've been out looking for a job." She lied.

"Carol, I don't want to start a fight with you, but it hurt the way you just left the without warning. Please have the common courtesy to read my letters. I never had a chance to speak to you in person. The least you can do is read what I have to say."

"Todd, I'm *sorry*! I just figured it would be easier that way." Carol sat up in the bed and thought of a way to end their conversation.

"We spent four years together, four years! You'd think I'd deserve more than a stupid good-bye note."

"Todd, I *said* I'm *sorry!* What else can I say? I don't love you anymore."

Todd said nothing for a moment. Carol thought about hanging up, but that would be too cruel. She knew he was crying.

"I don't believe it Carol. Love just doesn't die in one weekend. We have a contract, an agreement. Doesn't that mean anything to you?"

"Oh, that reminds me. Do you want me to send the ring back?"

"What?" Todd swore. "I could care less about the stupid ring. It's what the ring stood for that's important."

"Todd, I'm sorry. I don't know what else to say. This conversation's going nowhere. I think it'd be best if I hang up now."

"No! Carol, please don't hang up. Just tell me you'll at least read my letters."

"Okay, I'll read your letters."

"Tonight."

"Okay, tonight. Can I go now?" Carol was doodling on the pad of paper.

"Wait. You left several of your belongings here. I was going to drive them up there this weekend."

"Oh, you don't have to do that. I'll come get them myself sometime."

"No, I insist. I need closure. It's only fair to me to be able to see you face to face one last time."

"I don't know if I'll be home. I might go with Chelsie to the UVM."

"Carol, please stop being so selfish! After all the time we spent together, you can at *least* let me say goodbye in person. Even if you don't love me or ever talk to me again, I want to at least have a chance to see you one last time. Don't I at least deserve that?"

"I suppose. Okay, Todd. You can come this weekend. I'll let my mom know."

"Thanks, Carol. It means a lot to me."

"I've got to go. Dinner's ready. I'll see you this weekend."

"All right. But remember, you said you'd read my letters."

"I *will*. Goodbye Todd." She hung up before he had a chance to stay anything else. She put the receiver back on the phone and looked at a pile of letters on the night-stand, all five of them bulging. She opened the first one and began to read the six pages. It was full of one apology after another. He apologized for not going with her on her birthday and not being more fun. He apologized for spending so much time studying, for being too clinging, for not giving her a birthday present before she left. He even apologized for moving to Wilton and not going to the UVM with her after she graduated. He admitted to being selfish. Carol had never seen Todd apologize with real emotion before, and it moved her. For the first time since her birthday, she actually felt sorry about her behavior. Maybe she should have waited and talked to him in person, or at least taken his calls sooner. Still, there was no way she could ever go back to him. Not now, not after being with Troy.

Carol put the letter on the stack and did not open the rest. It was 6:00. Dinner would be ready soon, and she should go help her mother. It would make the time go faster. Todd said he'd call her around 9:00-9:30 her time. She couldn't wait. She had so much to tell him.

***

Carol finished her poem, then glanced at the clock. It was 9:35. He should be calling any second. She doodled on the note pad, picked at her fingers, tried to read, then turned to the clock again. It was 9:45. He probably was stuck in traffic. She got off the bed and looked out the window. It had rained all day. She wondered what the weather was like in Seattle. Last night, Troy said it had been sunny all week. She imagined being at his house, the sun still shining through the windows, his cat sleeping on his bed. His bed. She wondered what color sheets and bedspread he had. Would they be a masculine color like brown or green? Or maybe they were silk. That would feel nice against her skin. Of course, no matter what they looked like, she would be happy just to share them with him.

The ring startled her. She picked up the phone.

"Hello," she said in a cheerful voice.

"Hi, Babe. It's me. Sorry I'm a little late in calling."

"That's okay. I miss you."

"I miss you, too. Hey, I told Debbie about you today."

"You did."

"Yeah. She wanted to see me. Asked me why I hadn't returned her calls. She wasn't too happy about it, when I told her I couldn't see her anymore."

"Oh, Troy, I'm so glad. Not that I don't feel sorry for her, but, you know."

"I know. I told her I can't stop thinking about you. Our relationship was more for convenience anyway."

"So what's our relationship about?"

"The best sex I've ever had." Troy laughed into the phone.

"Is that all?"

"No, Babe. You know it's a lot more. You know I love you."

"I love you, too." Carol hugged her pillow. Oh, how she wanted to be with him at that moment, to see him say it with his eyes.

"So, what's the plan? Did you find anything out?"

"Yes, I did." Carol pulled a folder from underneath her bed. "I haven't bought it yet, but I went to the bank and took out some money. Todd and I have a joint account, so I still had access to it."

"So, when do you think you'll do it?"

"Tomorrow, on my way to Chelsie's."

"Have you told anyone yet?"

Carol turned toward the door, as if someone might come in. "No. I haven't got that far yet."

"Okay. Just let me know the details."

"So, did you get my letter?"

"Yes. I got it today, but I haven't read it yet."

"I hope you don't think my poems are silly."

"Oh, Carol, not at all. You're the first girl to write me poems since grade school."

"Oh, and who wrote you poetry in grade school?"

"Sally Thompson. She was my first crush."

"Man, Troy, girls have been after you forever."

"Yeah, but not one of them's been you."

"Oh, Troy."

They talked for about an hour. Each time they were about to hang up, one of them would think of something else to say, to linger the moment a little longer. She'd never wanted to be with someone as much as she wanted to be with Troy, and she knew it would be hard to sleep without him. Only one thing made her hesitate about what she was going to do. She told her mom, Jim, and Chelsie she'd start college in the fall. Now she wasn't sure how to do both. Maybe she could talk Troy into moving to Burlington with her. If that didn't work, she'd just have to find a school in the Seattle area. Troy was a mature man. He'd help her find a way. It would work out; it had to work out. They loved each other.

Tomorrow, she would buy the ticket. In a few days, she would be in his arms again.

***

Margaret was humming while she made Jim's lunch.

"You're in a good mood this morning." Jim kissed her on the back of the neck.

"You were right. That retreat was good for me."

"Knew it would be." Jim took a sip of coffee from his special mug and glanced out the kitchen window. The sun was just rising. "Looks like the making of a fine day."

"Did you notice the chickadees using the bird feeder you put up?"

"Yup. I saw them fighting over it. Garden's doing great, too. We'll have plenty of zucchinis this year."

"Great. Just what I need. A thousand zucchinis to cook."

"You can make me that special zucchini bread." Jim tickled her.

"Careful. I'm using a knife to slice a tomato."

Jim laughed and sat down to eat his oatmeal.

"So, you get to be a slacker while I work. Must be nice to sit around all day, soaking up the sun, watching soap operas."

"Jim, you know I don't watch soap operas." She threw a paper towel at him. "Besides I have plenty to keep me busy just taking care of this house."

"Sure." Jim spooned more oatmeal into his mouth. "So, you going to talk to that girl of yours today?"

"Yes. I figured it's about time to apologize for the mistakes I made in the past. Pray it'll go well. She's been real moody since Troy left. Spends most of her day in her room." Margaret put Jim's sandwich into his lunch box.

"Love sick. I don't like it. She needs to get out of the house. Maybe we can go someplace this weekend."

"Todd's supposed to come by on Saturday."

"Great. Another love sick kid. I hope Carol'll be decent to him."

"Here's your lunch." Margaret set the lunch box on the table.

"Thanks, sweetheart." Jim got up. "Where's my hug?" Margaret rested her head on Jim's pale blue supervisor uniform.

"I'd better get going." Jim squeezed her and gave her a kiss. "By the way, that dream of Amanda's been on my mind. Been praying a lot about it."

Margaret watched a chickadee outside the window put a seed in its beak, then fly away. "Carol's never mentioned the letter or called Amanda about it. I was worried when she was going out with Troy. I feel better now that he's in Seattle."

"I don't know. Let's just not stop praying." Jim gave her one last squeeze. "See you tonight."

Margaret wasn't going to let thoughts about Amanda's dream keep her from enjoying the day. Since returning from the retreat, she started each morning by reading part of the Bible and praying. She reminded herself that she could only work on Margaret and do her best to extend the love of Jesus to those around her. It had been effective on everyone but Carol. She prayed, "Dear Lord, help me today to know what to say to Carol. Break down the barriers between us. Help me forgive her if she doesn't respond to my apologies. Help me give you time to work in her heart. Thank you for bringing her home for the summer so we can re-establish our relationship. And Lord, please protect Carol from the man in the dream. Let her heed Amanda's warning. I pray all this in Jesus name. Amen."

As soon as she finished praying, Marie and Jean came out in their nightgowns and snuggled on the couch with her. She cherished the few moments of affection, until they woke up enough to want breakfast. She wished she could spend every morning like this with them. She and Jim had been discussing whether they could afford for her to quit her job and stay home full time until her youngest girls graduated from high school.

Margaret went into the kitchen. "So, how does French toast sound for breakfast?"

***

"Carol, there's still some French toast batter left. Would you like me to make you some?"

Margaret watched her daughter pour a glass of orange juice. This was the first time all week Carol had been up before 11:00. Liz had taken the girls to swim at a neighbor's house, so it was the perfect opportunity to talk to her.

"Sure, Mom. That'd be nice."

Margaret started the stove and put a piece of bread in the egg mixture. "So, what are you up to today? I see you're already dressed, like you're going someplace."

"I'm going to Chelsie's." Carol popped a vitamin in her mouth and gulped some orange juice.

"Oh. So, I suppose you want to borrow the car?"

"If you don't mind. I should be home by dinner."

Margaret put two pieces of bread on the skillet. "Um, Carol, I wondered if we could sit and have a chat before you leave."

253

Carol turned to her mother. "Why?"

"Oh, don't worry. I just haven't had much time to talk to you, that's all. I thought it'd be nice to spend some time together."

"Oh. Well, I have a few minutes, but not much. I told Chelsie I'd be over before eleven. It's already after ten."

"I guess if that's all the time you have, it'll have to do."

"I'm sorry, Mom. You should have talked to me about it last night."

"I understand. It's okay." Margaret waited until the French toast was finished before speaking again. Carol was reading the newspaper Jim left on the table.

She set the plate of French toast next to Carol with a bottle of maple syrup and sat down. "So, I take it you miss Troy."

Carol looked up. "Yeah, I do. But I'll be all right." She set the newspaper down. "Is that what you want to talk to me about? Troy?"

"No, not unless you want to. I just wondered if you are doing okay, that's all."

"Well, I'd rather not talk about that right now."

"Sure, fine. That's not what I wanted to talk about anyway." Margaret took a deep breath and rubbed the palms of her hands on her pants.

"So, what is it, mom?" Carol leaned back in her chair.

"Well, I don't think I've ever sat down with you and talked about what happened after your dad left us. I know some of the things I did then made you unhappy. I just wanted to say I'm sorry if I hurt you or made you feel unloved during that time."

Their eyes locked for a second, then Carol turned away and touched a pimple on her cheek. "I don't know what to say. That was a long time ago."

"I know. But I think it's time we got it out in the open. Did I hurt you back then?"

"Well, yeah. But I'm over it now. You don't need to bring up it." Carol squeezed the red mark on her face.

"I just want you to know, my behavior was less than acceptable. I shouldn't have brought guys into the house the way I did. I think it bothered you the most out of all the children."

"Why do you say that?" Carol's voice rose an octave.

Margaret picked at a dirty spot on the table. "Maybe I'm wrong, but you were pretty angry about it just before you left home."

"Well, it was pretty disgusting the way you brought those married guys home. I couldn't stand Mac."

"Mac was pretty bad, I have to admit. That's why I wanted to apologize to you, Carol. I know it hurt you."

"It didn't hurt me. I just thought you were gross."

"I can understand that, now." She paused. "What I want to know is will you forgive me for the way I hurt you?"

"Sure, Mom. I forgive you." Carol answered without looking at her. She was picking at her hang-nail.

Margaret got up from her chair and hugged her daughter from the back. "I hope so. I love you, Carol."

"I love you, too," Carol said in a whisper.

Margaret kissed the top of her head.

"I need to go brush my teeth and get ready to leave." Carol stood up, breaking the embrace.

"Well, you have a good day with Chelsie."

Margaret watched her daughter leave the room. She couldn't see her face. She hugged her body and closed her eyes. Talking to Carol was like walking on tiny pieces of glass. It was impossible to know when the almost invisible fragments would pierce your skin. *Don't cry, Margaret. You did your best. What she does with it is up to her.* Still, a few tears escaped. She picked up Carol's plate and the maple syrup and brought them over to the sink.

***

Carol parked her mother's old, blue station wagon on the street and shut off the engine. She glanced across the road at the Tom's Travel Agency sign. Inviting pictures of palm trees, white sand, and turquoise beaches were tacked on the windows. The address matched the one on her directions. She had deliberately driven to the closet agency outside of Deerfield. If she had used the one in town, someone would have seen her go into the office or the owner would have told someone else and it could get back to her family. Jim worked just down the road. No, she didn't want anyone to know what she was doing.

She hesitated. Her palms sweat, her heart raced, her gut galloped. Was she really going to leave Vermont and fly across the country? Part of her could hardly contain the excitement of being with Troy again. He was all she thought about, day and night. Another part of her thought about Chelsie and their plans to room together at college. She'd waited four years to reach this point. She had already given Chelsie's landlord money to hold her room. She'd already signed up for her classes. She had spent the last year daydreaming about the University of Vermont campus with its view of Lake Champlain, its green expanses of lawn, its landscaped paths adorned with flowers, its nostalgic brick buildings. She would write papers and her professor would rave at her insight and skill. She would be asked to join the Honor's Society. She would publish her poetry and begin her first novel. It would be a dream come true, except Troy would not be there.

She could see Troy's face and his tan, muscular body, perfect like a Greek sculpture. If she opened the door and went into the travel agency, it would be only a matter of hours before she could sleep in his arms, taste his lips. He was waiting for her. She told him she was going to do it. She had to keep her word. Seattle was a big city. There had to be universities as nice if not better than the UVM. All she had to do was find out about transferring her scholarships and financial aid to the new school. Her high school transcript was exceptional. Even if she lost some of her scholarships, it shouldn't be hard to find new ones. Besides, she graduated a year ahead of her class. That meant she would be the same age as the students coming in, even though she'd been out of school a year. No, it would be okay. Troy had to come first. She loved him.

Carol opened the door, crossed the street, and entered the travel agency. Only one, large desk filled the front of the small office. A middle-aged woman was talking on the phone. She smiled and signaled with her finger that she'd be just a minute. Carol sat in one of the chairs in front of the desk. She took out her wallet. The money was right were she left it. Her hands were shaking.

"Hello, I'm Kathy Holt. How may I help you today?"

"Hi. I'm Carol. I called you earlier in the week about a plane ticket to Seattle, Washington. I'd like to go ahead and buy that ticket."

"Oh, yes. I remember now." Kathy rummaged through some papers and pulled out a hand-written note. "I quoted you $325.00. Flight 208 leaves from Hartford Connecticut at 11:45 in the morning, connects with flight 4107 in Chicago, and arrives in Seattle at 8:25 PM. That is if you leave on Saturday. Is that still what you want?"

"Yes. That'll be fine. Is the price the same?"

"I locked it in for you."

"Great. I'll take it."

A few minutes later, the transaction was complete. When she got into the car, she took the tickets out of the United Airlines jacket and read them again.

She had really done it. She was going to fly away, leave everything behind, run to her lover. It was like being in a movie, playing a role, like someone else was really doing this. But the tickets were real and they were hot in her sweaty hands. She put them away. Chelsie was waiting for her. She dreaded the next few hours. She knew Chelsie would be hurt, that she would not understand. She would cry and try to talk her out of it. But in the long run, as her best friend, Carol knew she would relent. She was the only person she trusted to keep her secret.

***

It had been the longest day of her life. Carol had stayed up late packing the large suitcase she had snuck into the house on Thursday night. She had to wait for everyone to go to bed, then she had to dig it out from underneath two tires and a tarp in the garage. She hated all this sneaking around, but she needed to leave before Todd came the next day. She knew if he had any idea what was happening, he'd be in his car in an instant, desperate to stop her.

At dinner, Margaret wouldn't stop talking about her going to college. She asked if the family could drive up to the UVM. with her so she could show them her room. She smiled as best she could, said it sounded like a great idea, but couldn't finish her dinner. All day, her stomach had been upset. The only good thing about it was when she told her mom and sisters she was too sick to do anything, it wasn't a lie. She spent most of the day in her room, trying to read, packing more when everyone was outside. She felt like a criminal planning her escape from prison. But the crime wasn't what put her here. It was the leaving that was the crime.

Now came the tricky part. Chelsie was supposed to drop by before 8:00 to pick her up. She told her mom she was going to a movie and would be home late. The problem was, she had to have all her stuff outside before Chelsie arrived. It was already 7:30. Everyone was upstairs watching television except Liz, who had been talking to a friend on the phone in her room for twenty minutes already. Her room was right next to hers, and her door was wide open. She had been waiting for Liz to finish her phone call and go upstairs. Now she wondered if there was a way to get her off the phone.

Carol tiptoed and peaked into Liz's room. She was sprawled on her bed, looking at the ceiling as she talked. She didn't see her, but she knew if she made noise, Liz would see her. She had to find a way to close her door. She had an idea.

She walked out again, this time making plenty of noise, went to Liz's room, and started to close the door.

Liz put the receiver down for a second. "Carol, what are you doing?"

"I'm sorry, Liz. But I have a horrible head-ache and your talking's bothering me."

"Good grief. I'm not loud at all."

"You keep laughing. Come on, let me close your door."

"Fine. Whatever, Carol. But I think you're crazy."

Carol closed the door, walked back to her room as normally as possible, and pulled her suitcase out from underneath the bed. She grabbed her other bag, and with slow, soft steps, tiptoed down the hall, into the family room, to the sliding glass door. She unlatched it and edged it open. It made a noise, and she stopped to listen for Liz. The muffled sound of Liz's voice came from her room. She pushed the suitcases through the opening and stepped outside. After a quick scan to make sure no one could see her, she put the suitcases on the side of the garage and covered them with a tarp Jim had left out near the woodpile.

Carol took long, quiet steps back into the house, closed the glass door, and made it back to her room without being noticed. Whew! Her shirt was soaked with perspiration, but she had outwitted her sister. Now she only had to wait and few minutes for Chelsie to arrive and it would be over.

Carol made her bed and set out an envelope on the dresser. She draped her purse strap over her shoulder and watched the clock. As soon as she heard a car, she shut off her light, closed the door, and forced herself to walk up the stairs calmly. She took a deep breath as the reached the top.

"Mom, Jim, I'm leaving now. I'll be back late, so don't wait up."

Her mom came out of the living room. "Are you sure you feel up to it? You looked flushed and sweaty." She touched her forehead. "Well, no fever, but you feel clammy. Is your stomach still upset?"

"It's a little better. I promised Chelsie I'd go to this movie with her. She's waiting out in the car."

"Okay, Carol." Her mom gave her a hug. "Just take care of yourself."

"Goodbye Mom. Goodbye Jim, and Jean and Marie."

"See ya," said Jim. His blue eyes locked with hers for a moment, and she was afraid he knew something was up. But he turned back to the television.

Carol turned around, walk down the stairs, out the front door, to Chelsie who waited in her car. That final good-bye would burn in her memory forever.

"I already put your bags in the trunk."

"Thanks, Chelsie. You're the best friend a girl could ask for."

"I don't know. I wonder if a better friend would kick your butt for doing this to her."

"I'm sorry. But I love Troy."

"I know. It's okay." Chelsie touched her friend's shoulder. "Are you sure you're all right? You look sick."

"My stomach's tied in knots, but its nerves. I'll feel better once we make it to the bus station."

"Well, I guess it's time." Chelsie put her car in drive.

Carol took one last look at the house. Was this really happening? It was like she had killed someone and was running away before being caught. She swallowed hard and held onto her stomach. She should have told her mom and Jim and her sisters that she loved them.

***

Jim sat with his wife drinking his second cup of coffee of the morning and reading his Bible. She had bills and papers spread out on the kitchen table and was in the middle of writing a check to the power company when the phone rang.

"Jim, can you answer that for me?"

"Sure." Jim put his Bible down and answered the phone.

"It's Todd. He wants to ask Carol a question before coming over."

"What time is it? I haven't seen Carol up yet today."

"It's almost 11:00. I think we'd better wake her up."

"I guess we'd better." Margaret pushed back her chair. "Tell Todd to wait a minute."

Jim watched Margaret dash down the stairs. "She'll be here in a second," he told Todd, then set the receiver down. He could hear Margaret speak to Carol through the door more than once. Something was wrong. A thought came to his mind, and he hoped he was wrong. Then he heard his wife cry out, "Oh no! Oh, Lord, No! Oh, *Carol!*" She had done it. The stupid, selfish girl had done it.

He ran to Carol's room. Margaret was in a heap on the floor, a letter clutched to her chest, tears spilling onto the paper. He dropped to the floor beside her, gently took the letter from her hand, and read the first few sentences. Yup. Just as he thought. She flew the coop, took off for Seattle.

"Oh, Margaret. I'm so sorry."

He rocked her in his arms. A few moments later, Liz came into the room.

"Mom, Jim, what's going on? What's Carol done now? Todd's still on the phone waiting. What should I do?"

"Carol left," said Jim. "Without the decency of telling her own mother."

"I guessed that's what happened. What do I do about Todd? I don't want to tell him."

"I'll do it." Jim gently released his wife and picked up the phone on the night stand.

"Todd, it's Jim."

"Where's Carol?"

"I hate to have to tell you this. She's gone."

Todd's voice cracked on the other end of the phone. "No! She can't be! Where?"

"She's gone to Seattle."

Jim heard Todd swear, and the phone went dead.

***

Jim had let Margaret spend the entire day in her room. Liz, Marie, and Jeanne had kept quiet, respecting their mother's grief. It was an unspoken understanding that now was not the time to ask about Carol or place any demands on their mother. He did his best to make jokes and pretend everything was normal, and Liz stepped right into the motherly role, doing her best to be strong for her mother and sisters. He respected that girl.

It was now 9:00 PM, and the girls were watching television. He could hear *The Brady Bunch* song on the television. He'd been reading his Bible, praying to God to help him know what to say. He had several scriptures marked. He needed to talk to Margaret, but how long should he wait? How long should he let her hide in her room?

He closed the Bible, put it under his arm, and went down the hall into their bedroom. Margaret's dinner was untouched, in the same place he had left it two hours before. She was propped up on a pillow, starting straight ahead, her face puffy from hours of crying. A box off Kleenex lay next to her, and crumpled tissues littered the bed and the floor. He picked up the tissues, threw them in the wastebasket, and sat down on the bed, his Bible still under his arm.

"Margaret, its time we talked."

She stared straight ahead. "I don't want to. There's nothing to talk about. She's gone, and there's nothing I can do."

"Hog wash. You're wrong. You're falling right into the devil's trap."

Margaret's eyes came alive. "Don't talk to me about the devil! He's got my little girl! You know Amanda's dream's came true. The dream warned us an evil man would take Carol away, and now it's happened! Why did God even warn us if he knew it would happen anyway? What's the use of praying when it all turns to garbage in the end?"

"It may look like the devil's won, but he hasn't. If you think he wins, he wins."

"He has won!" Margaret sat up in the bed, her fists clenched. "I've tried everything to get her back, and what good has it done? She was all set to go to college, now that's down the drain. She got away from Todd for what? So she could end up with another looser, this on the other side of the country? She's gone! Out of our reach! Thrown her life away! How can you say he hasn't won?"

"She may be out of our reach, but she's not out of God's reach."

Margaret shook her head and threw a pillow onto the floor. "It's no use. Everything just turns out like garbage. My whole life's nothing but one pile of garbage after another." She turned toward the wall and wailed.

"Margaret, stop crying, for goodness sake. I'm going to read you something, and you're going to listen."

She turned toward him, pulled a fresh tissue from the box, and blew her nose. "Fine, read me the scripture." She crossed her arms over her chest.

"It's in Deuteronomy thirty, starting in verse nineteen. 'This day I call heaven and earth as witnesses against you that I have set before you life and death, blessings and curses. Now choose life so that you and your children may live and that you may love the Lord your God, listen to his voice, and hold fast to him. For the Lord is your life, and he will give you many years in the land he swore to give your fathers, Abraham, Isaac and Jacob.'"

"I did choose life, I did choose to serve God, Carol chose death. Why? I can't take it anymore, Jim." Margaret threw her tissue toward the wastebasket.

"Look at me, Margaret. Yes, for now, Carol chose death. But what are you going to do? Are you going to lay down and let Satan ruin your life, too? Or are you going to stand for God and fight for your children?"

"How can I fight for my children? Carol didn't even have the decency to tell me she was leaving. She wants nothing to do with me."

"You can fight for her by choosing to live. You can't control what she does, but you *can* control what you do. It says, 'choose life so that you *and* your children may live.' It doesn't say wait for your children to choose life. You have to do it first."

"So, I choose life. How does that help Carol?"

"Because when you choose life, you can hear God's voice. You can pray for her."

"But I have been praying."

"So we keep praying." Jim paused and took his wife's hand. "I think God's shown me something about Amanda's dreams and that strange guy who shows up, then disappears. I want to show you. But first, get up out of that bed and eat some food."

Jim pulled back the covers and helped his wife stand up.

***

Chelsie held Jeff's hand and pretended to watch the movie. She knew Carol was on a plane, soaring thousands of miles away, and would soon be landing on the other side of the continent. When she had dropped her at the bus station, she looked so small and frail dragging her huge suitcase and everything she owned into the building. Would she ever see her again? Had she done the right thing? Should she have tried harder to stop her? Should she have told her mother?

Carol said she might be back by fall, but Chelsie knew it wouldn't happen. The phrase, "Love is blind" was a perfect description of Carol. Here she was, throwing her life away for someone she met in a bar, someone who was years older than her, when all her life she had dreamed about going to college. She remembered the night Carol met Troy. She was so happy and had made the decision to give up on Todd. Carol thanked her that night for helping her see the truth. But had she only helped her leave one jerk for another? Should she have been so flippant about it?

Chelsie wiped her eyes. Since the first time they talked on the plane to France, she had thought of Carol as the sister she never had. She did her best to bring so joy into Carol's desolate life. College was not going to be the same without her. She was going to miss her best friend.

***

Richard took another ale out of the refrigerator and went outside. Though still warm, the night air took away some of the suffocation of the hot, muggy cloud that hung over the house. It infiltrated all the nooks and crannies of not

262

only the building, but his skin. The sweat just kept pouring out, soaking his clothes, sticking to his face and beard. He felt like a sponge laden with water, saturated, heavy and leaking everywhere.

He took a sip of ale, then put the cold bottle against his forehead. Only a few short weeks ago, Carol had taken a taxi and left her boyfriend, not giving one thought to what it did those left behind. He was the one who had to tell Todd Carol had gone home. He had to watch him get drunk, cry, and lie around all day, then cry some more. Todd had just started to work again and now that crazy girl pulled another fast one! Now she was on her way to Seattle. He swore again. How could anyone be so selfish? Now he was stuck with a sobbing, sniveling, weak kid who couldn't stand to live without his daughter. *Thanks a lot Carol. Now I have a nut case to live with.* He swore, gulped some more ale, and paced on the front lawn.

What the heck was he going to do with this mess of a kid? All day long, Todd interrupted his work, either sat looking pathetic like he was going to cry again or pacing back and forth, mumbling to himself. He was good for nothing. He was way behind on his refunds. First he lost Carol, now Todd was worthless. Denise helped as best she could, but she had to run the daycare. The case he'd be working on with Paul Berkett was set to go to court next Tuesday. Todd had agreed to type the depositions. Now he'd have to stay up all weekend just to get it done.

And how was he going to get rid of this kid? He could only subsidize him for so long. If he didn't pull his weight, he'd have to kick him out. Man, when he had kids, he never thought he'd have to take care of their boyfriends.

He finished his ale, then went inside for another one. He'd better get started on the pile of papers on the table. Todd was coming down the stairs. *Great, I hope I don't have to listen to him whine for another hour.* He went to the other end of the room so Todd wouldn't see him.

Todd took something from the refrigerator and went out the kitchen door. He heard the squeal of tires as Todd roared out of driveway. Good. Now he could get some work done.

***

Amanda tossed and turned in her bed while her husband slept beside her. The call from Margaret had been a shock. Was the man from Seattle the sinister beast in her dream? Oh, dear Lord, how she prayed he wasn't. The thought that it might be had her spinning on a merry-go-round of "what if's."

What if she had tried harder to get through on the phone? What if she had gone to see Carol in person and shared the dream? What if she had taken more time to see Carol after the guy from Seattle left? What if she had prayed harder? What if… What if's were useless. It was too late now.

When she closed her eyes, she could see his face, his evil grin, his deadly laugh. This had to stop. Amanda knew that if she allowed this entity, whatever it was, to ruin her night, she would be letting the devil win. She needed to stop agonizing over the past and go forward into the future. Carol was gone. That was a fact. She made the decision to leave. All Amanda could do now was make a commitment to pray for her. Jesus loved Carol. If he didn't, he would not have given her a dream to warn her.

The Bible says, in Jesus' name, his people have power over Satan and his demons. Amanda sat up in her bead and declared out loud, "You think you've won, but you haven't. You will never win. Jesus triumphed over you on the cross. In Jesus' name, you are defeated. Now get out of here." When Amanda closed her eyes again, the image and laughter were gone. She spent several minutes praying for Carol before drifting off to sleep.

***

Todd poured himself another drink and picked at the ground with a stick. He was parked on a gravel road out in the woods. The thick, wet air smelled of skunk, but he could care less. The sound of crickets singing made him mad. Even they had more to live for than him.

He smashed the stick hard on a rock and broke it Then he threw the half in his hand into the woods and took a good gulp of his vodka and orange juice. He wanted to drink until he passed out. Maybe he wouldn't wake up. That would be better than the real-life nightmare he was living.

So the reason Carol left was another guy, a guy from Seattle, Washington. Todd swore to keep himself from crying again. Short of a few days here and there, he had spent more than four years with her. He brought her up from an ignorant child into a beautiful woman. And what thanks did he get? A broken promise.

He remembered the first night they made love. She had been so young, yet so enticing, so innocent, yet so provocative. She was all his. Or had she been, even then? He also recalled when they had stayed at the dorms at the UVM. She saw someone she knew, another man. She said he meant nothing to her, but he knew she searched around the campus for him. No, she had always kept back part of herself, a secret place he couldn't reach. Still, he'd take her back in an instant if she just came to her senses. He'd do anything to kiss her soft lips, to touch her supple body. He couldn't live without her. Why didn't she even let him say goodbye? If he could just see her one more time, maybe he could talk some sense into her.

But what were the chances of that now? She was more than 3,000 miles away, and he had no idea where to find her. It was no use, hopeless. It was over. He had to accept it. But he couldn't. It was worse than death. Death would be an escape.

Todd finished the drink and threw the empty glass into the woods. The sound of the shattering fragments reflected what was happening in his heart. She had broken it into a million pieces that could never be glued together again. He staggered back to his car and revved the engine. No, life was useless now. Death would be release. He put his foot to the pedal and pushed all the way to the floor.

***

Jim put his arm around his wife. "You feel better now?"

"Yes. Thanks, Hon, for being so patient with me."

"No problem. You ready to talk?"

"I think so."

"Good." Jim picked up his Bible from the coffee table. "You think Troy is the evil man in Amanda's dream, don't you?"

"Yes. It makes sense. Don't you think so?"

"Nope." Jim opened his Bile to a place he'd marked.

"But the dancing, the part about taking her away, it all fits." Margaret flipped the belt to her bathrobe around as she spoke. "Nothing else makes sense."

"I think the dream was a warning for Carol. But the man in the dream isn't Troy."

"How can you say that?"

"I'll read you some verses." He moved the Bible so they could both read. "First one's in II Corinthians 11:14. It says, 'And no wonder, for Satan himself masquerades as an angel of light.' The second's in I Peter 5:8-9.'" Jim turned to the marked page. "This one says, 'Be self-controlled and alert. Your enemy the devil prowls around like a roaring lion looking for someone to devour. Resist him, standing firm in the faith, because you know that your brothers throughout the world are undergoing the same kind of sufferings.'"

Margaret frowned. "What are you trying to say? Were Amanda's dreams about Satan?"

"I think so. Every time I pray about Carol, I come back to the same verse. It's the one in Ephesians that says our fight isn't against flesh and blood. When I was praying today, God gave it to me clear. The fight's not with Troy or Todd or any person. Satan just uses people as pawns."

"So, you think Satan used Todd and Troy to ruin Carol's life?"

"Yup, he sure did. And he did it by pretending to be an angel of light. Carol wanted someone to love her. Satan used these men to trick her into believing she got it. He used them like a lure, like bait on a hook. He used them to open a door so he could come in and take her out."

"Oh, if only I could have seen that years ago. Maybe I could have stopped it."

"Don't go there again. Stick to now."

Margaret twisted her robe belt into a knot. Jim let her take some time to think. So, what you're saying is Satan used Todd to seduce my daughter, then he used Troy the same way. But what about the guy who showed up at our house years ago? Then again at the UVM and Paris? What was he? Amanda saw someone who wanted to kill Carol in her dream when she was in Paris. Then she saw a real man leading her away. Was he also a person used by Satan?"

"A person or something else. Haven't figured him out yet. But it doesn't matter. We know how to pray now. That's what's important."

"I don't know." Margaret pulled her knees to her chest and hugged her legs. "Todd and Troy still seem like predators to me. I have a hard time not seeing them as the lions who want to devour my little girl."

"Listen." Jim put his hand on her knee. "What use is it to hate Troy and Todd? Doesn't it just add fuel to the fire? Satan wants to destroy everyone. That includes you. All he's got to do is keep you full of hate and anger, and he wins."

"But how can they be so selfish to prey on a young girl? I think Troy is a lot older than Carol, from what it sounds like. And Todd went after her when she was only thirteen. Can't they see how wrong it is?"

"They don't know any better. They're love sick, just like Carol. They're just looking in the wrong place, that's all. We weren't any better when we first met. Remember, I was a married man."

Margaret lay her head down. "Man, you know how to set me straight. You're right, Jim. How could I forget my own sin? I was sleeping with a horrible man when Carol met Todd."

"Easy to do, isn't it? That's why I keep coming back to that scripture. We've got to keep it clear who we're fighting."

Margaret lifted her head. "God forgive me. I've been so judgmental. What should I do?"

"First, remember what I just said about who we're fighting. Next, pray— every day."

"Okay, let's pray for Carol right now."

Jim put his hand on Margaret's leg. "Not just Carol. Todd and Troy, too. Todd's hurting real bad right about now."

"You're right, Jim. Carol's been pretty mean to Todd lately."

"I've got one more scripture. It's in I Corinthians 13."

"I know that chapter. It's the love chapter."

"Yup. Let's start in verse four. 'Love is patient, love is kind. It does not envy, it does not boast, it is not proud. It is not rude, it is not self-seeking, it is not easily angered, it keeps no record of wrongs. Love does not delight in evil but rejoices with the truth. It always hopes, always perseveres. Love never fails.'"

Jim stopped and looked into his wife's eyes. "We pray with this kind of love. We've got to think the best for the people we pray for. We've got to be patient, not angry all the time, and not bring up what they've done wrong. We've got to always hope for the best, believe Jesus' love won't ever fail. No matter what happens, no matter how hard it gets. It's the only thing that lasts in the end. His faith, his hope, his love. And the greatest is love."

Jim wiped the tears from Margaret's eyes with his fingers. "Jesus' love for Carol's not going to stop. No matter how far away she is or how stupid she acts. He's going to do everything in his power to get her away from Satan and to himself."

"I believe it."

Margaret took his hand and they prayed.

***

"Please fasten your seat belts, put your tray tables away, and return your seat to the upright position," a flight attendant spoke over the speaker. "We should be landing in Seattle in twenty minutes. Temperature is 60 degrees, skies clear. It's a nice night out there."

Carol sat up in her seat, straightened her wrinkled clothes as best she could, and found a piece of gum to freshen her breath. It had been a long, exhausting journey, but she had been too excited to sleep. This was it—the start of her new life with Troy.

Above, below, and around her was a flurry of activity she could not see. It happened in a realm invisible to her eye. Next to her stood The Seducer, cocky, confident in his success, laughing with his sinister cackle. He was already planning his first deed of destruction to his assignment below. One side of his face appeared handsome, even enlightened. The other side displayed the truth: his skin full of soars, maggots eating away at his flesh, his eyes vacant of life, his mouth trickling with the blood of his victims. What he didn't notice was a group of angels sent to keep a watchful eye on him, to make certain he stayed within the boundaries of the Creator of the Universe. He was watching her, they were watching him, and above all, Jesus watched over everything. He joined the prayers of his saints that came up from the earth and shed tears with them. But he also rejoiced for the joy that was set before Him. He knew the end of the story.

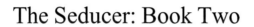

The Seducer: Book Two

Chapter One

Carol pulled back the curtain on the sliding glass door and let the sun flood the room. It was the same sun she knew growing up in New England, yet it seemed so much bigger here in the West, stronger, brighter. She'd been with Troy a week today, yet it still felt like someone had taken her in the middle of the night and transported her into a new world. People said it always rained in Seattle, but not one drop of moisture had touched the parched lawn of Troy's back yard the entire week.

Troy. She loved him so much, yet life with him in this town of Redmond, Washington did not turn out to be with the rich and famous. Troy didn't own his house; he rented it. As a matter of fact, the lease was up at the end of the month, and they'd had to find a new place. It was far from new either, nor large, with three small bedrooms and a bath all on one floor. As she reached down to scratch the swelling red bumps that dotted her ankles, she looked forward to a house without fleas. The thick, green, shag carpet was full of them. She cleaned and vacuumed the house as best she could, but only an exterminator would kill the vicious, invisible enemy. Funny thing, they only seemed to bite her, not Troy. Still, she loved his Siamese cat, Sammy. The feline was so smart she could open cupboard doors.

Her daydreams about life with Troy shattered the moment Troy picked her up at the airport. Instead of the shiny, red sports car she imagined, he came in a dented, brown Chevy with a noisy muffler. The sports car sat in the garage with a tarp over it. It had been totaled in a car accident three years before, and Troy never used the insurance settlement to repair it. It soon became apparent that his fancy job was also a thing of the past. Troy worked as a front desk helper for Ditch Witch, which made machines that dug ditches. He lost his job as a mechanic for Edmond's Exotic Cars around the same time he had the accident. Troy didn't come right out and say it, but she guessed it had something to do with driving while intoxicated. She also learned his real age. He was thirty-eight.

Still, she loved him, and thoughts of their nights together made her forget the rest. All he had to do was smile and gaze at her with those big, hazel eyes that would became greener when he talked love to her.

She opened the door and let in the cool, morning air. It had an exotic smell, like a breeze on the beach, promising leisure and love. Her entire day lay before her, scheduled. She would spend the morning soaking up the sun and reading, then start a special dinner for Troy. The recipe for Chicken Cordon Blue was marked in the cookbook, along with a chocolate cheesecake, and all the ingredients were stacked together in the refrigerator. Troy raved about her cooking. She had even found two candlesticks and candles so she could create a romantic ambiance.

Everything went just as she planned, and now all she had to do was wait for Troy. Carol walked to the front room and glanced into the hot street. Three little girls splashed and giggled in a small pool across the road while their mother sat in a lawn chair watching. Two towering evergreens rose high above the family, the deep, forest green striking against the cobalt sky, dwarfing the single story home. It still awed her the way the trees were so tall, and the mountains of Washington made the peaks of Vermont look like foothills.

Troy's house was situated at the end of a cul-de-sac, so traffic was rare. Carol would know when Troy's noisy jalopy came up the road. It was now 4:45, and the chicken she had slaved over, pounding the chicken breasts between wax paper until her hands were sore, would be ready in forty-five minutes. Troy should be home at any moment. Every day so far, he had made it by 4:30. His boss probably needed him to stay a little late. Watching the road wouldn't make him come home. She turned on the old television and messed with the antenna so she could watch a Beverly Hillbilly's re-run.

Four forty-five turned into five, then five-thirty, then six. Still no Troy. Her special dinner was drying out in the oven. The table, adorned with matching plates, lit candles, and two yellow roses she picked from the rose bush in the front of the house, sat poster-card perfect, waiting to ignite romance and love. Carol blew out the candles and paced. Where could he be? She had no way to call him, no way to find out where he was. She had called Ditch Witch five minutes ago, and the answering machine announced they were closed. So, Troy wasn't at work. Maybe he stopped for a beer with a friend. That morning, he told her he would see her at 4:30, so it didn't make sense. Unless he lied.

He wouldn't lie, would he? Maybe he did. He had masked the truth about how much money he made. Still, she knew he loved her. He told her that no woman had made him so happy. He had kissed her goodbye that morning and told her he couldn't wait to see her again, that he missed her already. She could still feel the kiss. She rubbed her fingers on her lips, then curled up on the coach. *Troy, please come home. Please let me know what's going on.*

Six ticked away to seven, which inched its way to eight, then nine, then nine thirty. Carol hated the tick, tick of the clock in the living room, the standard white and black type they had in school. Every tick tortured her, telling her again that Troy should have been home hours ago. She threw a pillow at it, and it crashed to the ground. The ticking still went on, now from the floor.

The table was bare. The white tablecloth and candles were in a heap on the floor, the yellow roses thrown on the lawn outside where dusk was just turning to night. The enticing aroma of chicken, ham and cheese was replaced by the rotting food of dishes stacked in the sink. The only light in the house came from the muffled television, which Carol couldn't stand watching anymore. She wanted to do something, anything, but listen to that taunting clock. Yet, she came back to the same place again and again, by the floor next to the terrible timepiece, unable to concentrate on anything else.

At 10:05, the phone rang. Carol jumped and ran into the kitchen.

"Hello," she said, out of breath.

"Hi, Babe. It's Troy."

"Where are you? I've been waiting all night for you."

"Sorry, Babe. I went out with the guys. Lost my job today."

"What?"

Troy swore. "Yea, those jerks laid me off."

Carol slid onto the kitchen floor. "Oh, no! That's terrible. When will you be home?"

"Not too long. Sorry I didn't call sooner. I'm really messed up about it."

"Troy, I made dinner for you. I can still warm it up. Can't you come home now?" Carol could hear someone calling his name.

"I'll be home soon. I've gotta go."

"Troy, wait."

"Bye, Babe. See ya soon."

"Troy…" He already hung up.

Carol dropped the phone and let it hang. Had she heard him right? He said he lost his job. What would they do now? How would they find a new house without an income? What had she gotten herself into? Maybe she should just pack up and go home.

But no one made her feel like he did. All those years with Todd she had never felt as special as she did with Troy. Going back to Vermont meant facing Todd, her mother, her friends. They would all point their fingers and tell her how stupid she had been to go off with a complete stranger. Still, how could she start college now if Troy didn't have a job? Did that mean she should look for one? She realized there was no way he would help her pay for school. He had about $1,300 in his checking account, and $1,000 would have to go toward renting a house.

Sammy sauntered up next to her and brushed her arm with her warm fur. She picked her up, carried her to the bed, and lay down next to her. Sammy immediately conveyed her loyalty by jumping off the bed. She had no one to comfort her. Carol squeezed the pillow as she watched the red numbers of the alarm clock march into the night in slow motion.

Printed in the United States
86734LV00003B/199/A

9 781424 186631